SILVERSWORD

SILVERSWORD

Phyllis A. Whitney

Doubleday & Company, Inc.
Garden City, New York

SILVERSWORD

1

All the way out to Pacific Heights in a cab I dreaded the coming meeting with my grandmother. I'd wanted for a long time to free myself of dependence upon Grandmother Elizabeth Kirby. I had managed to pull myself out of a marriage that was failing, and had begun to make my own life in my small San Francisco apartment. I didn't want to hear any more of what I knew would be critical advice.

From the first, Grandmother Elizabeth had sponsored Scott Sherman as the perfect husband for me. I was in love and willing enough, until I discovered that I was really in love with an imaginary ideal. Now my grandmother was totally incapable of accepting our divorce. Since Scott worked for her, I had another reason to be reluctant about obeying her summons.

Nevertheless, Grandmother Elizabeth's cool, cultured voice on the phone gave me no chance to refuse, or even postpone. Ever since my parents' death in Hawaii, she had regarded me as her possession—all that remained of the son she still idolized. As a child I couldn't escape her, and if I were honest, perhaps my marriage had been a means of running away from her direct control. I was certainly not going to run back, and today I would make that clear.

In a few minutes we would reach the hotel, and I must face her in that strange place that was her special creation, and in which I had lived since I was six. It didn't matter that Grandfather James had inherited the Prince Albert Hotel before Elizabeth married him. She'd made it her own from the moment she could get her hands on it. "Elegant, exclusive"—these were words she valued, and she had old Nob Hill money and wealthy friends to back them up.

Guests were apt to be a special clientele who avoided downtown showiness, and preferred the aristocratic quiet of the Prince Albert. Certainly Elizabeth Kirby had a drive that would never allow her to accept the idle life of a rich woman, and the hotel offered a splendid outlet for her ability to manage and direct.

Since the building dated back before the earthquake and fire of 1906, and was located well beyond Van Ness Avenue, where dynamite had stopped the fire, the architecture belonged to an old and distinctive San Francisco era. Its bay windows looked out at the water, and its high ceilings were carved with plaster rosettes from which crystal chandeliers still hung.

I can remember my sense of awe and dismay when I first came to live with Grandmother Elizabeth. In up-country Maui, where I was born, there had been nothing like the venerable Prince Albert. Nor had my Grandma Joanna Docket been anything like my father's mother, Elizabeth. In fact, I was told at once never to say "grandma." The word was "grandmother," and that was what Elizabeth wished to be called.

When my parents died I had been told as little as possible. Because of something never explained, I knew only that three frightened horses had fallen down a steep place on a trail, and my father had been killed outright. My mother was so badly injured that she had died some weeks later. Her sister, my Aunt Marla, had been hurt at the same time, and was found unconscious. Grandmother Elizabeth would never talk to me about any of this, though she'd been on Maui at the time. She had brought her son's body from the island for burial in California, and had taken me home with her.

I suppose this had seemed the best solution, though the wrench was painful and bewildering for me. After being cherished by my father and my beautiful mother, as well as by Grandma Joanna and Aunt Marla, I was taken from my lovely island and plunged into life with a woman who had been taught that demonstrations of affection were in bad taste; a woman, perhaps, who had never loved anyone except her son Keith, my father.

There are some wounds dealt to a child that, if left untended, never heal. It seemed as though these last twenty-six years since I'd come to the mainland had been years of restlessness and futile searching. I knew very well that this had to stop. I knew I must make something more sensible and satisfying of my life. But how?

The cab pulled up to the door of the hotel, and I paid the driver and got out. Even now, when I stepped into the Prince Albert's regal aura of dark, polished woodwork, handsome parquet floors, and ruby-red rugs, I could feel a sense of awe ready to take over. *Watch it, Caroline,* I told myself, bracing against the old intimidation these rooms had once held for me.

The lobby where guests checked in was small, with a black-and-white marble floor. I crossed it quickly, hoping that Scott, who managed the hotel for my grandmother, would not be around. If she had planned a meeting between us I would leave at once.

I nodded to the clerk at the desk and went into what Grandmother Elizabeth had always called the drawing room. There I stood for a moment looking around. These furnishings had not come from antique stores, but from my grandmother's home when she moved here from Nob Hill to take over the hotel and rescue it from becoming nondescript. Red damask draperies still hung at tall windows, and walnut paneling gave the room a dignified gloom.

As a child, I had grown to have a certain respectful affection for this room, if anything so beautifully grand and austere could inspire more than reverence. A wave of nostalgia swept me back to another room —a room in Grandma Joanna's house on Maui. That had been a room filled with treasures, where I'd felt comfortable and happy, and where I was allowed to touch anything I liked—a bright, cheerful room, in contrast to this dignified and somber atmosphere.

Grandmother Elizabeth's private sitting room—she had never called it an office—lay just beyond, and today the door was closed. That meant I would have to knock, and I postponed the moment when I must raise my knuckles to that forbidding panel.

It was all too easy to fall back into childish fears, and I mustn't allow this to happen. I wanted nothing from this grandmother who had given me a home, but never shown me love. By this time I could recognize that it hadn't been entirely fair to blame her for not being like Grandma Joanna. Circumstances had damaged her, and there'd been nothing left but duty toward her son's child, who came from an alien place of which she disapproved.

Still remembering, I moved about the room. The black walnut sofa with its matching chairs had undoubtedly had its original red velvet replaced several times, since Grandmother Elizabeth would never tolerate shabbiness. I stopped before the banjo clock that had come from the East in the last century, and never quite kept time. It had fascinated me as a child, and so had the Queen Anne desk. I sat down for a moment, recalling the painful efforts I'd made in the beginning when I'd tried to write letters to Grandma Joanna, who never answered. That is, I'd used this desk until I was banished from a room that was intended for guests, whom I must never disturb.

I still recalled with the old stab of hurt the way I'd ended every one of those futile letters: *I want to come home to Manaolana, Grandma.* The island was still in my blood, as it always would be. And so was the ranch house that had been given the Hawaiian word for hope and confidence, though Grandmother Elizabeth had always put down such optimistic virtues. The memory of my mother had grown hazy, since Grandmother Elizabeth would never talk about her, and had quietly removed any pictures of her that might grieve me. At least, that was the excuse she gave for their disappearance.

Yet I could still remember my mother as a lovely, magical creature who wore scented blossoms in her hair and held me gently in cool, loving arms. She had never called me Caroline, or even Caro, the way others did, but sometimes Carolinny, and often just Linny. This I remembered clearly. Just as I remembered her beautiful, melodious name, Noelle. Sometimes as a child here in San Francisco, I'd spoken it aloud to myself over and over, trying to bring her back. Her hair had been pale gold and very long. I was dark like my father, and I wore my hair short, curling in below my ears. I couldn't remember the color of her eyes. Mine were a rather dark gray—almost charcoal gray. Scott had been an artist of sorts, though only as a hobby, and he'd attempted to paint me—but he could never get my eyes right, and he gave up trying.

In the beginning, whenever I asked Grandmother Elizabeth about my mother, she had put me off with unkind words. "Noelle was weak, fragile—a vapid sort of woman. I won't have you grow up to be like her." Since I didn't want to hear such things, I stopped asking, and lived with an emptiness and longing that never quite went away.

It was different when it came to my father, Keith Kirby. His memory had been kept vigorously alive, both for Grandmother Elizabeth and for me. There were albums of pictures—up to the time of his marriage, though none taken in Hawaii; none when I was small. Grandmother Elizabeth told me endless stories about him, and since I'd loved my father dearly and missed him so much, listening to her talk about him kept him alive for me over the years. I'd grown up loving and admiring him as I could never love and admire anyone else. Probably no real man could ever match the dashing romantic figure she'd built up for both of us to believe in. Certainly not Scott Sherman, even though he'd swept me off my feet in the beginning, and seemed to be all that I would ever want in a man.

Sitting here at the desk where I'd written letters to Grandma Joanna, I thought about her. I could remember her far more easily than I could my mother, and I had never understood her abandonment. I knew how much she'd loved me—not gently like my mother, but always fiercely, demanding more of me, teaching me, telling me I *could* do what I feared, and rewarding me with vigorous hugs. She never smelled of tropical blossoms like my mother, but more often of horses and sweat and sunshine.

Two strong grandmothers were more than enough for any child, heaven knows, but at least they were strong in different ways. Grandmother Elizabeth's strength required that others lean on her, listen to her, depend on her, obey her. Grandma Joanna had wanted me to be strong for myself, and she had done her best to instill something of her own courage and determination in that small child who was the daughter of her daughter, Noelle. I was still trying, without any notable success, to be what she'd wanted for me.

One thing would remain with me always—the sadness of that last day at the ranch house on the mountain, when Grandma Joanna had taken me on her lap and held me tightly—loving, but never smothering, wanting to send me away strong, even though her own pain must have been very great at the time.

There was nothing soft about Grandma Joanna—she had ridden horses all her life, and her thighs were hard and muscular. Just touching her I'd felt a sort of power that was always there for me—as though I could draw it into my own being and possess it myself. I'd had need of it in the time before Grandmother Elizabeth brought me to her home in the States. During those days so much that seemed frightening was going on around me that I couldn't understand, and which no one explained. I knew that something awful had occurred up on the mountain. A horse had needed to be shot, and people were hurt. One day I'd found Grandma Joanna crying, and that frightened me most of all—because she never cried. Aunt Marla had been in the hospital too, badly hurt, and I never got to see any of them again.

On the last day Grandma Joanna had held me and talked to me for a long time. "This will be hard for you, Caro honey," she warned. "But right now it's better to go with your Grandmother Elizabeth. I love you and I'd like you to stay, but that would be for my sake, not yours. You're very young, but you're already a special person. *You* are Caroline Kirby. You will stand up to life and earn the right to be happy. Even though everything here is *pau* for you, there are exciting times ahead and a good life. Because *you* will make it that."

Pau! The Hawaiian word still crept into my speech at times when something was finished, done. I'd clung to her then and cried, and she'd cried too, because she never held back feelings of love. In a strange way these new tears comforted me and made me stronger, when the other tears she'd shed only frightened me. I'd known her better than I did my mother or father, and she meant all that was safe to me, all that I loved and felt happy with—horses, the beautiful trees and flowers, and of course the mountain. Always the great mountain that flung its shadow across our days. *The House of the Sun,* Hawaiians called it. In its way it had ruled our lives, at times benign, but sometimes without mercy when the old gods were offended. Always there'd been a heart of mystery for me about the crater where flames had once burned, though Pele, the goddess of fire, had long ago left for an active volcano on the island of Hawaii, which was often called the Big Island, to avoid confusion with the name of the state. It was in the crater on Maui that the riding accident had occurred.

"You'll write to me, of course," Grandma Joanna said that day when she held me. "You're already good at your letters. And I will write to you. I'll be here when you need me."

But she hadn't been. Not one of my letters had ever been answered, and by now I didn't know whether she was dead or alive. Grandmother Elizabeth had said I must forget her; forget about Maui and Hawaii, and my dead mother. I had never forgotten. The last thing I'd said to Grandma Joanna had been that I would come back. But there had seemed to be no one to go back to—no one who wanted me. San Francisco, for all its wonders, could never make up to me for what I had lost, but I'd always felt I couldn't return to beauty that would break my heart, when those I'd loved were gone. Now perhaps that would change.

At thirty-two I still didn't know what I wanted to do with my life, but I had to get on with it—whatever that life was going to be.

Right now, I could put off the confrontation no longer, and I went to the door of my grandmother's sitting room. I knew very well why she wanted to see me, but there was nothing she could do to change the facts of my life, and my resolve to stand against her stiffened as I knocked.

"Come in." Her voice had never aged with the years. It was clear and strong, and every word was carefully formed, since slurring would have been abhorrent to Elizabeth Kirby. She had always worn her pride as an armor.

I stepped into her sitting room, where the colors were muted green and gold, and a fire burned on the hearth to warm this late September afternoon. She stood up to greet me, an elegant figure in her navy blue jacquard silk frock, with a heavy cameo framed in silver on a silver chain about her neck. Her upswept hair was nearly white, and, as always, every lock was in place, and a jade-studded comb my father had once brought her from Honolulu helped to restrain its heavy coils.

At least she came to greet me, though her kiss on my cheek was formal—she didn't like kissing and touching. Sometimes I'd wondered how my grandfather, dead now for twenty years, had ever come close enough to her to conceive a son. Unfortunately, she had loved that son far more than she'd seemed to love James, my grandfather. He and I had been friends, but he was even more afraid of her than I was, and sometimes I'd felt older than he would ever be.

"Sit down, Caroline," she said, gesturing toward a Chippendale chair drawn near the fire.

This room too I remembered from my early years. Especially since one end of it had been turned into a shrine to my father. Here I had always been welcome to study the pictures on the wall, the framed letters, the racing trophies he'd won in school. Even though this wasn't the father I remembered from Maui, it had been the closest I could come to him, and these memories were what Grandmother Elizabeth encouraged, until I almost believed they were really mine.

She had drawn a chair for herself close to the fire, sitting opposite me. "You know why I want to talk to you?"

"Yes." I met her look. "And it's too late. My divorce was made final two months ago."

The tightening of her straight lips betrayed disapproval. "I know that."

"I've taken back my own name," I told her. "I don't want to be Mrs. Scott Sherman anymore. You should be pleased to know that I'm still a Kirby."

"I am not pleased. I am shocked that you have so little sense of loyalty and commitment that you weren't willing to give your marriage more effort."

"There were five years of effort." They had been years of hurt that I would never let her see.

Her slender hands, graced by apple jade and black Hawaiian coral —again my father's gifts—clasped each other tightly. "Your grandfather and I were married for thirty years. If he had lived we would still be married. He wasn't always what I hoped a husband would be, but at least I was brought up to the idea of devoted loyalty and making a marriage work."

"I'm sorry," I said. "I have to be myself."

"That's something you've always been determined about—without much to show for it. A little more giving flexibility would be more becoming."

I knew who had been giving and flexible in her marriage.

"I was flexible long enough about Scott's love affairs."

"But men always have love affairs. Women must accept that."

I doubted that Grandfather James would ever have dared to look at another woman.

"I understand why you were so fond of Scott," I said. "And why you always supported him—he reminded you of my father." She stared at me, and I added dryly, "Perhaps that's why I fell in love with him—because he seemed so much like that ideal you built up for me." I waved a hand toward the end of the room. "Perhaps that's why I was happy with Scott in the beginning, and why I couldn't forgive him when I found out how really different he was from my father."

Such talk made her thoroughly uncomfortable, as I expected it to, and I felt a little mean. She was well read, well educated at finishing schools, but she still believed there were matters that should not be discussed openly in polite society. It was a matter of good taste, as she'd often reminded me.

But I didn't want to talk about Scott. There were older hurts, older questions, that had never been answered, and this was my opportunity to probe into the past that she had always refused to discuss with me.

"Sometimes," I said, "I think that the reason why I've never settled down to anything is because of all those unfinished, unexplained happenings back in Hawaii. Perhaps I need to return and find out what Maui holds for me."

Her betrayal of inner emotion startled me. "No! You must never go back—I forbid it!"

She'd forgotten that she could no longer "forbid" or make decisions for me, and she was immediately uncomfortable with her own outburst. Any open discussion or revelation of emotion was something she shied away from, and her control was in place again when she went on.

"Scott is going to join us in a few moments. He asked me to arrange this meeting without letting you know ahead of time. When he comes in, I'll leave you two together."

This was the last thing I wanted, and I stood up quickly. "I have nothing to say to Scott and I'll leave right now."

She sat back, watching me calmly, and I knew it was already too late. Her hand had touched a bell nearby, and when I looked around Scott Sherman stood in the doorway. Grandmother Elizabeth slipped quietly past him out the door, closing it behind her, and I was trapped.

I stiffened as I stood looking at him across the room. Like my father, Scott was dark, with eyes that were deeply blue. He wasn't as tall and he was a bit more slender than Keith Kirby had been, but he had the same winning charm that could break any woman's heart. I knew all about that from my grandmother, who had always been charmed by her son. The awful part was that it could still reach me. I knew everything about him. I knew how crisp his hair would feel to my fingers where it grew back from his forehead. I knew how he looked with the shadow of a beard in the early morning, and the way the sleepy look in his eyes could quicken to something else. I knew how gentle he could be, how disarmingly tender—when undoubtedly he gave such tenderness easily to other women who attracted him.

"Hello, Caro," he said. "Don't be angry with your grandmother. I had to see you."

He was coming toward me across the gold rug and I stood my ground stiffly.

"It's over," I said. "There isn't anything left for us. I have nothing to say to you."

He was so close that I could catch a whiff of his spicy cologne. "I don't think you ever wanted to leave me, Caro. I know you were hurt, and I'm sorry. But we still love each other, and if you'd give me another chance we could work things out. Don't you remember all the plans we made, all the happy times we had together?"

I remembered everything, and hated the remembering.

"Caro . . ." I heard the break in his voice. A calculated break that had so often twisted my heart in the past. Now I could resist—I had to resist.

"If you won't leave, I will," I said.

For a moment he hesitated, but he must have sensed my resolve. "All right, Caroline—if this is the way you want it. But I don't give up easily."

No, he didn't, I thought, and one of the things he hated to give up was the chance of my someday inheriting a great deal of money from

Grandmother Elizabeth. He'd even admitted this to me one time when he'd wanted to put down my own personal worth and make me all the more unsure of myself. No more!

I held quite still as he touched me lightly, caressingly, his fingers stroking along my cheek, leaving an electric trail. Then he walked out of the room and I looked after him, hating the old response he could rouse in me. This was a man I never wanted to have touch me again. I *must* get away!

When he'd gone, Grandmother Elizabeth came back into the room and sat down. She'd seen Scott's face, and she shook her head in disapproval.

"You are a foolish young woman, Caroline. I suspect that there are too many unsettled ghosts in your life."

"Not ghosts," I said. "Just unanswered questions. That's why it's time for me to go back to Maui. I wonder if Grandma Joanna and Aunt Marla are still alive."

She stared at me fixedly for a moment, while I waited for her further disapproval. For once, she completely surprised me.

"I've changed my mind. It may not be wise, but perhaps you do need to go back and take care of those ghosts. Joanna Docket, at least, is still there. I've heard from her recently."

I dropped into a chair. *"You've heard from her?"*

"Yes. For the first time in years." She gestured, and jade on her hand flashed green in the firelight. "There's a letter lying on that table. Get it, please."

I reached for the envelope, which had been opened, but when I would have handed it to her, she shook her head. "No—read it yourself."

I noted the recent postmark from Maui, and that the letter was addressed to Grandmother Elizabeth. At the top of the single gray sheet was printed the name MANAOLANA. The signature was that of Joanna Docket.

"Read it aloud," Grandmother Elizabeth commanded.

I steadied the sheet by resting it on my knee, and did as she ordered.

"Dear Elizabeth:

"It's time for me to see my granddaughter again. I have learned that her marriage is failing, so she may need a change of scene. Even though she has never answered my letters, she may

still remember the mountain and Manaolana. Send her to me for
a little while. I need her here,

> "Yours,
> "Joanna Docket."

I choked over the words and blinked back my tears. Manaolana—
that lovely name Joanna Docket had given the ranch house. A word
that meant all those hopeful qualities of spirit of which *she* was made.

"What does she mean—that I never answered her letters?" I demanded. "What letters?"

Grandmother Elizabeth shrugged. "Oh, they kept coming for a
while. Letters from your Aunt Marla too. I thought it best to keep
them from you. Just as I never mailed your letters to her. It was far
better, as you must agree now, to help you to make a clean break.
Otherwise you'd have pined and moped, instead of settling into your
life here as you did reasonably well."

I couldn't speak. Shock held me silent. She saw my face and looked
faintly surprised. "Why, Caroline, you aren't going to mind at this
late date, are you?"

Somehow I found my voice. "How dared you! By what right could
you do such a thing to a small child? How could you be so heartless?"

I stood up and walked to the door. I never wanted to see her again,
and I had to get away before I burst into furious tears. All my life I'd
nursed this pain that I'd tried to sublimate in restless ways. All need-
less—all for nothing. My longing for Grandma Joanna might have
lessened gradually if there had been letters between us for a while.
As it was, there had been only a deep, sharp wound that had never
stopped aching.

"Sit down, Caroline," Grandmother Elizabeth said.

The habits of childhood years die hard. This was my Grandmother
Elizabeth at her most commanding. I came back into the room and
sat down.

"I've been worried about you for a long time," she said, surprising
me again. "I knew you weren't doing your best when it came to your
marriage or your life. These silly jobs you hold—they never amount
to anything, and you're always changing to find something new.
Someday you will be a very rich woman. Someday you will own this
hotel. I think the time has come for you to work at the management
with me. So take your little vacation in Hawaii and answer those
questions that trouble you. Then come home and start a new life. It

may even be that you'll eventually get back with Scott again. I don't think *he* wanted this divorce."

My anger died. I knew how useless it was. She would never understand. Even her relenting about my return to Maui didn't really show understanding. Her very concern was for the wrong aspects of my life. She was simply woven of different cloth, belonging to a different time, and she didn't realize in the least how atrociously she'd behaved.

"I'll think about what you suggest," I said. I would think about it for all of three minutes, but it was senseless to tell her now that her hotel was not for me. "I'll write to Grandma Joanna right away," I added.

A water glass stood on a small table beside her chair, and she moved her hand, knocking it over. Grandmother Elizabeth was never clumsy. On the way to the door I looked around, and was alarmed by what I saw. The hint of rouge on her papery skin stood out against her pallor, and both hands were gripping the arms of her chair.

I went back to her quickly.

With an effort she relaxed her hands and folded them in the lap of her silk jacquard skirt. "There's something I've never talked about, never been willing to discuss with anyone. Perhaps because if I brought it into the open I couldn't live with it. Yet it's been there, trying to destroy me for all these years. Now it must be your burden to carry. There's no one else I can pass it on to."

I couldn't imagine what she was talking about. I sat down again and waited.

"Caroline, I've always believed that your father's death was no accident. Someone hated him. Someone wanted him dead. I don't know whether your Grandmother Joanna ever suspected this, but if you go back you must face the possibility that a terrible crime was committed. You are Keith's daughter and you owe him something. You must search for the truth."

Her words opened a possibility so terrible that I couldn't accept or believe. Some of my shock crept into my voice.

"If this is so, why didn't you—" I began.

She answered before I finished, in a tone bereft of all feeling, cold as stone dropping on stone. "Because I was afraid. Because I was a coward. I couldn't face up to what was possible. Perhaps I could have prevented what happened—and that was too awful to live with. Besides, I had you to think of. I had to get us both away as quickly as I could. It would have done no good to stay—there was never any proof. The police were satisfied that it was an accident. But something in me always knew better. I tried to make it up to Keith—" She waved a hand toward the end of the room where all the record of my father's early life hung on the wall and stood around on tables. "I had to make you understand and love him—I did that for you both! But I didn't want you ever to go back, so I broke the bonds that might have held you."

Staring at her, I saw for the first time that her eyes had sunken with age, and the lids had begun to droop. I had no idea whether there was any truth in her words, or whether she had built up some awful fantasy over the years—just as she might have built up a fantasy of what my father had been like. Only lately, since the breakup with Scott, had I begun to question her ideal of Keith Kirby, and recognize that it was only my loving memory of my father that was true. A small child's memory. If I returned to Maui now, it wouldn't be to do as my grandmother asked, but I would try to find out what he had really been like as a man. So I could get to know him as I never had.

"Promise me!" she cried. "Promise that you'll try."

It was the first time I'd ever pitied her. I kissed her crumpled cheek lightly. "I can't promise. But I'm glad to be armed with what you've told me. Of course, any trail would be too cold to follow."

"Be very careful, Caroline. There were those who hated your father."

This was melodramatic and very unlike her.

"I'll let you know when I leave for Maui," I told her, and this time I made my escape.

Elizabeth Kirby had so little in her life besides a hotel. Grandma Joanna had made money raising horses, and she'd inherited pineapple money besides. But she had been rich in so many other ways, whereas Elizabeth, when it came to loving and caring, had lived at a poverty level. She'd lived as well with a secret that had been eating at her for all these years—though the facts might not even be as she thought them.

I caught a taxi back to the small apartment I'd taken when I left Scott, and as the distance increased between me and the Prince Albert, a strange sense of freedom and hope began to rise in me.

The moment I was inside I went to an old camphorwood chest in my bedroom—a chest that had come with me from Maui. I opened it and took out my scrapbook. Grandmother Elizabeth had never discovered this book because I'd been very clever at hiding it from her in a series of ingenious places. In its pages I had lovingly pasted every picture, every article I came across that told me anything about Hawaii. There was a stunning photograph of Iolani Palace in Honolulu, and of course pictures of Diamond Head, which had been easy to come by. Scenes of Maui had been harder to find, but there was one whole page from a newspaper, worn from much handling by me. It was about the mountain, Haleakala. I could still roll those syllables on my tongue: *Hah-lay-ah-kah-lah.* They'd been fun to say as a child, and I spoke them aloud now to confirm my decision.

I was going back, as I'd always said I would. I would see my Grandma Joanna again, and perhaps my Aunt Marla, whom I hadn't thought about in years. She had been hurt in the same accident in the crater of Haleakala as the one that had killed my father, and so injured my mother that she had died weeks later. I refused to let the dreadful suspicion Grandmother Elizabeth had planted in my mind take hold. She was quite capable of believing what might not be true at all. She had done that about Scott and our marriage. But I didn't need to believe. And when I saw her, Grandma Joanna would undoubtedly clear the air. Not only would I be able to find my father again—the real father of my early years—but I would learn about my beautiful mother too, so she could become a stronger memory for me.

I made up my mind suddenly.

I wouldn't wait to write. I would find out Joanna Docket's telephone number and call Maui as soon as the time there made it possible.

It was Grandma Joanna who answered the phone, and we could hardly talk for the tears that choked both her voice and mine. I told her about never receiving her letters, and how they'd never mailed mine to her.

She moaned, *"Auwe!"* several times—that expressive Hawaiian wail that I remembered very well. I told her about my divorce and said that Grandmother Elizabeth had shown me her recent letter. "I want to come home," I said. "I want to come home to Manaolana and you!"

"I want you to come, Caro honey," she told me, and the old affectionate name poured soothing comfort around me. With Grandma Joanna I'd be able to figure out my life. I'd been unsettled and searching for too long a time, without knowing where to look for answers. Or even what the questions were. Now they were ready to pour out of me.

"I'll make flight reservations and let you know," I said. "I suppose I'll need transportation up the mountain to Makawao." That was the nearest town to the ranch, and the name came readily to my lips.

"I may not be able to meet your plane, Caro," she went on. "Your mother—"

"That's the main thing I want to know about," I broke in. "I need to know what happened that awful day in the crater. I need to know more about her death in the hospital."

It was her turn to interrupt, and now there was something strange in her voice. She spoke slowly and deliberately. "Caro honey, your mother didn't die. Whoever told you that? Noelle is very much alive."

I couldn't speak. A wilder anger than any I'd ever known filled me against Elizabeth Kirby. How *could* she have lied to me like this?

"I—I didn't know," I faltered. "My Grandmother Elizabeth told me—"

"I'd like to wring Lizzie's neck," Joanna said. To call Elizabeth Kirby "Lizzie" was almost as bad as sticking a knife in her back.

We talked a little more before we hung up. Then I lay down on my bed to stare at the ceiling, and after a time a slow joy rose up in me to wipe out present rage and past anguish. I was going *home.* I would be with Grandma Joanna again, and somehow my mother had been given back to me miraculously. My beautiful, fragile mother, who had always smelled so delicious, and who had held me so lovingly and sweetly all those years ago. She'd loved to laugh too—I could remember that now. I'd had a mother all along! Was there to be a happy ending at last?

But there are very few happy endings. Just to know that she was alive wasn't enough. There were still too many questions. Why hadn't she come after me, no matter what the obstacles? There had been something in Joanna's voice, something unexplained. I wondered suddenly if Grandmother Elizabeth had really believed that my mother was dead. Had she been hoodwinked herself? If that were true, why would she have been told such a lie?

I had no answers now—but they would come.

At least I would escape from Scott Sherman. Today's meeting had shown me that I might still be vulnerable. In San Francisco he would always be too close.

For now I would simply look ahead. I was going home to Maui.

2

The women flight attendants on the plane wore *muumuu*—those long, graceful garments that had evolved from the Mother Hubbards that had been requested of the first missionaries by the queens and high chiefeses of Hawaii. They used the word *"mahalo"* for "thank you" frequently, and I recognized it with pleasure. Though the word seemed clipped on American lips—the vowels not as musically soft as I remembered.

As a child I had known quite a few Hawaiian words, and perhaps they would come back to me. It was a language of emotion, of spirit, so that even the simple *"mahalo"* meant more than our English phrase. A sense of warm gratitude and affection was implied, and now the word reached out to me as a Maui-born stranger coming home.

I settled in my seat for the nearly six-hour flight from San Francisco and closed my eyes so that I could let my thoughts drift. Fortunately, there was no one in the next seat, so I didn't need to talk.

When I'd called to let Grandma Joanna know my arrival time and flight number, she told me that Tom O'Neill had agreed to meet my plane and drive me up the mountain. "Agreed," she said, which seemed strange.

"Do you remember Tom?" she'd asked.

I remembered vaguely a vigorous, red-haired man who had worked for her. He had been an Irish *paniolo*—a cowboy who had worked with the horses in the old days.

"He manages what's left of the ranch for me now," she told me. "And he still has red hair. So you'll recognize him. He gave you your first ride on a horse, sitting in front of him in the saddle. I depend on

Tom around here. Though I don't raise as many horses anymore. But I have to warn you that he doesn't approve of your coming."

There was no time on the phone to ask why, so I let that go. It didn't matter anyway. All that mattered was that my Grandma Joanna wanted me and I was on my way. All the questions could wait. I tried to shut out completely the grim suspicion Grandmother Elizabeth had planted in my mind about my father.

Before I left I called to tell her my plans. She sounded subdued, even a little anxious, and there was no point in being angry with her. I promised to write, and we said goodbye stiffly. She didn't mention either my father or my mother.

There were pleasanter things to think about. My childhood, for one. The Kirbys had not lived on Grandma Joanna's ranch. My father and mother had bought a large house a mile or so down the road. It was an awesome house built years before in the Italianate style with tile and marble, huge high-ceilinged rooms, and a winding staircase at one side of the entry hall. I remembered the stairs because of all the times I'd watched my mother drift down them in her long dresses, always with a flower in her pinned-up blond hair, and bubbling laughter on her lips.

Now, with my eyes closed, I heard, not the sounds of the plane, but the musical notes of her laughter. Did she still laugh like that? What had the sudden and apparently simultaneous loss of her husband and daughter done to her all those years ago? I remembered the teasing little jokes that I'd loved her for, and the way she'd teased my father too. Though not always. I seemed to remember that there had been little laughter during our last months on Maui before the accident happened. Even as a small child I'd sensed that something was wrong.

My memories of my Aunt Marla were hazy, but affectionate. She'd have been about nineteen or twenty then, younger than my mother. She'd seemed fond of me, and sometimes she'd read me stories. Mostly I remembered her eyes—large and very bright and quick-moving, as though there was so much to see in the world that she could never take all of it in fast enough. Grandma Joanna hadn't mentioned her on the phone, so perhaps by this time she had married and lived elsewhere.

Lunch on the plane was standard fare, but with a few Hawaiian touches—macadamia nuts and tiny orchids on our trays. I watched clouds and ocean drift by beneath a wing. We flew ahead in space, but backwards in time. It was earlier in Hawaii than in San Francisco.

The movie didn't interest me, so I read a little, and slept a lot, having lain awake so long last night in anticipation.

When I opened my eyes the cabin was stirring and we were coming in to land. Green islands floated on rippled blue water, but I had no way of identifying what I saw. Then one island grew in size until I knew it was Maui, even though the mountains were diminished from the air. Eagerness quickened in me. There was still the long drive up Haleakala before I would be with Grandma Joanna and my mother, but at least I was here. Once more I wondered why Tom O'Neill didn't want me to come—I'd probably find out when he met me. No one on Maui was real for me yet, except my grandmother. Not even my mother, who was only a hazy, troubling memory. What color *were* her eyes?

With the other passengers I gathered my handbags and light coat, filed down the aisle, exchanging alohas with the attendants, and hurried off to Baggage Claim.

Tom O'Neill was waiting for me, and I had no trouble recognizing him. He was probably in his mid-fifties now, his skin tanned to a leathery brown from all those outdoor years with horses, and his eyes a faded blue. His hair was certainly as red as I remembered, and only a little grizzled at the temples. He wore work jeans and a short-sleeved green shirt that hung outside his pants.

When I walked over to him he dropped a pink plumeria lei over my head, though he skipped the customary kiss on either cheek. "From your grandmother," he said. Its fragrance enveloped me—the fragrance of plumeria *was* Hawaii!—and I felt the special welcome these islands held for me. Tom O'Neill had little to say, but he made an odd remark as he waited for my bags.

"You don't look like *her*," he said, and I knew he didn't mean Grandma Joanna.

"My mother?"

"It's your hair, maybe. Dark. And her eyes aren't as dark a gray. You're taller too."

It was a strange, coolly delivered inventory, as though he added me up in some way that carried a hint of accusation—as though I had no business not resembling my mother. I held back any questions in the face of his disapproval.

When we'd caught my bags off the carousel, he led the way outdoors into bright sunshine. It was October now, but my San Francisco clothes were immediately too warm, even though the sun of late afternoon was dropping down the sky toward West Maui. At once the breeze caught at me, blowing my hair back, whipping my skirt—a familiar wind that carried an island scent of sea and flowers. These were the trade winds that blew so much of the year in Hawaii and kept the climate moderate.

Tom strode ahead with my bags, not looking back as he led the way to the jeep that was to take us up the mountain. When we'd stored my luggage, he opened the door for me.

"Your gramma said I could bring her car, but I like this better." It wasn't an apology.

"This is fine," I said, and pulled myself up into the front seat.

Away from Kahului Airport, we turned onto Haleakala Highway, and started up those slopes that began in some places at sea level. I looked for the mountain the moment we left the airport, and my heart lifted at the sight of it rising steeply ahead, high above us, blue-shadowed now, with afternoon clouds filling the unseen crater, spilling fluffy white cotton over its rim.

This I remembered. The mountain spoke to me as it had done when I was small, touching my spirit and my imagination—always a place of mystery and magic. I knew that it held a tremendous power —*House of the Sun!* Hawaiians called it that because there was a moment at dawn when, from certain places on Maui, the sun seemed to rise from the very crater—born every day in the heart of the mountain. There were legends about the demigod Maui—how he had trapped the sun in his net and slowed its course because it was traveling too fast to dry his mother's tapa.

Haleakala, with its more than ten thousand feet, dominated all of East Maui, casting its great shadow across one sea in the morning and another in the afternoon. Off to my right as we drove, were the mountains of West Maui beyond the flat isthmus where the airport was located. I had pored over maps when I knew I was to return, and the strange human shape of the island of Maui was clearly in my mind. It had been likened to the head and upper body of a woman. The head showed clearly in profile, the isthmus formed the neck, and all of East Maui the larger body. Once Maui had been two islands, but volcanic eruptions had sent lava down the slopes to fill in the channel between to form the plain that connected the two sections.

Today there were no more eruptions. The mountain had lain dormant for more than two hundred years. One referred to the "crater" of Haleakala. The word "volcano" was used for the active mountains on the Big Island of Hawaii. Beyond the lower, more jagged mountains of West Maui lay the "Gold Coast," with its hotels, beaches,

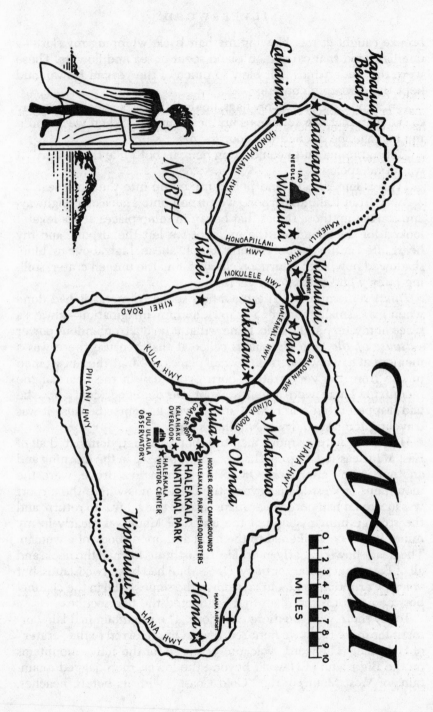

surfing—all major attractions for the tourist. This side, I hoped, would be like the old Maui, not too much changed since my childhood.

Cars on the other side of the road were coming down, some of them from the summit, and I knew the road up near the top was a mass of switchback turns that slowed all travel. I had never been inside the crater, though I'd listened to all the stories about it as a child, and had longed for the time when I would be old enough to be taken down into what had once been Pele's home. My mother had loved the crater. She'd said it was full of spirits and sorcery because it was the home of the old gods—something my father had called nonsense, but my mother was born on Maui and had grown up listening to her mother—Joanna.

"How is my mother?" I asked out of my thoughts.

Tom glanced at me, and then looked back at the road ahead. "Just about the same," he said curtly.

I wanted to ask, *the same as what?* but I didn't dare. I recognized dangerous ground, and knew I'd better stay clear until I saw my grandmother. Yet I wanted to talk because of all the questions swelling inside me—there was so much I wanted to know and was impatient to learn.

"At least tell me about my grandmother," I said. "You can talk about her."

He caught the reproach and ignored it. "Sure. What do you want to know?"

"Is she well? What does she do with her life these days?"

"She's as healthy as they come, except for one knee she hurt in a fall off a horse last year. And a good thing she's strong, with all the loads she's had to carry."

Again there seemed a hint of accusation, as though I might be one of her burdens. I moved to a safer topic.

"She said she still raises horses, and that you manage the ranch for her."

"It's not like it used to be. She breeds a few, and keeps some studs. Sometimes we rent our horses for parties going into the crater."

"Grandma Joanna told me on the phone that you gave me my first ride on a horse."

"Look," he said, "I'm not much on chitchat. I'm not sure why you've come here now, but I hope you won't add to Joanna's problems. She can handle what she has to handle, but she doesn't deserve any more. She told me you'd been divorced. So now you'll probably throw all your troubles on her!"

He was making me angry. "That's not why I'm here. She warned me you didn't want me to come. Will you tell me why—aside from the troubles I don't mean to throw on her. I'm trying hard to handle my own."

"You've stayed away too long. You won't be what she expects."

"How could I be? From six to thirty-two is a big jump. She'll expect that. You might hold off judging me until you know me better."

"Okay, I can wait." He sounded as though he wouldn't change his mind, and I didn't need to convince him of anything.

"What about Aunt Marla? Has she married?"

"No—though she should have. She still collects local kids at the library in Makawao and tells them stories of Hawaii. She's even put some of her stories into books for kids. Though, mostly, she looks after your mother."

I caught him up on that. "Why does my mother need looking after?"

At once he was evasive again. "You'll find out." He grinned a bit cynically, as though I wouldn't like what I found out. "What do you do for a living these days?"

There was no use pressing him, no use being annoyed. "Right now I don't have a job. Which is why I could come to Maui."

"What do you do when you do have a job?"

That was a question I always found hard to answer. "I've worked at a lot of things. Sometimes I do research for writers. And I worked for a couple of years helping teachers of handicapped children. I've tried real estate, and I've been a salesclerk. I don't seem to have any special talents."

"Kind of drifting around like your father? He sure wasn't much of a rancher."

I didn't want to discuss my father with Tom O'Neill, and I tried a counterattack. "What about you? Do you have a family?"

"I have more sense than to get married," he said shortly, and gave his attention to driving, shutting me out.

There was no way to be friends with Tom O'Neill, and that was all right with me. I didn't know what was bothering him, and I didn't much care. The scent of the lei around my neck had grown too sweet and heavy. I was sure that plumeria—frangipani—wasn't the flower my mother had liked to wear.

"We're getting there," he said after miles of silence in which I watched the sparsely populated hill country slip by, with the road always rising, though we were still far below the switchbacks that led to the summit. Eventually we turned off the highway to Makawao and drove through that little ranching town, where the business section boasted false fronts, and looked like a street in America's old West. Except for the banana plants and other tropical foliage.

A country road lined with flowering hedges led up the mountain, and now I glimpsed larger houses set back among trees, some with ornamented gateposts and long private driveways leading to their seclusion. Always there were flowers, along the road and in the gardens.

"Will we pass Ahinahina?" I asked.

"Where your parents lived?"

"Yes. It means silversword, doesn't it—that plant that grows in lava soil in the crater?"

He nodded. "You remember quite a lot, don't you? That's the house now—back behind those monkeypod trees. It's used by an art society these days."

I could see only a high red tile roof. Perhaps I would visit the house while I was here—just to explore a few more memories.

Stone gateposts marked the entrance to Manaolana, and we followed the narrow drive back through trees and vegetation that grew wild until a final clearing made way for house and lawn.

Tom stopped the jeep and got out. "I'll bring in your bags. Go on ahead—your gramma's waiting for you."

I climbed a few stone steps that led to the lawn from the side drive, and passed the great camphor tree that I'd loved to swing from as a child. Across the wide spread of grass was the house I'd so loved as a little girl—low and very wide, with sloping roofs that overhung the deep porch that fronted it. Though here, of course, the porch would be called a lanai—which meant an open living space. Comfortable rattan chairs were set about, and plants grew abundantly in large and small pots. All this seemed familiar as I took it in at a glance, though it also looked much smaller than I had remembered.

It was the woman who held my full attention. Grandma Joanna stood in the wide doorway, and she looked almost the way I remembered—a little chunky, with broad shoulders and tanned hands that could handle any horse. Her face was round and brown from the sun, and the strange thing that sometimes happened to older women had taken place—a sort of melting of the features, so that former strong lines were lost in more recent, looser creases. Only her straight beak of a nose held its own, unchanged. Most of all, I remembered her eyes, still a pale gray-green that was almost the color of silversword leaves. Above them, her hair was no longer brown, but thick and gray —carelessly cut as always, and short so it wouldn't get in her way. She probably chopped it off herself. Now she wore a long, pale blue *muumuu* with a white lace yoke at the top. A concealing garment, which nevertheless lent a certain grace, even to my sturdy grandmother.

For a moment she stood looking at me, questioning. She must now rid herself of the memory of a small child who had crawled so often onto her knees, and replace that picture with someone new and strange.

The deep lanai was only a step or two up from the lawn, and I walked across it hesitantly, suddenly unsure of my welcome. Then she opened her arms, and I ran into them as the child had done so many times. She hugged me hard, and I felt her strength flowing through me, just as I remembered. There was still power in Joanna Docket. But there was need now, as well—perhaps even a hunger that I could respond to as I hugged her back.

"Caro!" she said. "I can't really believe it yet—that you're here. I've needed you."

Tom waited on the lanai with my bags, and she stepped out of the doorway. "Thanks for bringing her, Tom. Will you take Caro's things upstairs, please? I've put her in the room where she used to stay when she visited overnight. Do you want to go up right away, Caro honey?"

No one else had ever called me "honey." My father had given me funny nicknames that constantly changed, and my mother had called me Linny. Grandmother Elizabeth never called me anything but Caroline.

"Not right away," I said. "I'm too excited over seeing all this again. May I just look around downstairs for a few minutes?"

"Of course. We'll be having dinner in an hour or so. Marla isn't home yet. She's gone to Wailuku with a friend."

"What about my mother?" I asked.

Grandma Joanna hesitated, and her warmth toward me seemed to diminish just a fraction. "Sometimes she prefers to eat by herself in the kitchen, since strangers make her uneasy." She broke off apologetically. "Not that you're a stranger, Caro, but this may be difficult for you both. It's been so long . . . you'll need to prepare yourself for change. Now I have something cooking and I'd better see to it." She was clearly anxious to get away, to postpone any talk of my mother.

"Have you told her I was coming?" I asked, uneasy lest for some reason she hadn't.

We'd stepped into the long living room that ran the width of the house, except for a room or two at the far end. Grandma Joanna turned in the direction of the kitchen. "We need to talk soon," she said, evading my question. "Just wander around inside, if you like, and I'll be with you in a minute."

From the first I'd known that something was wrong about my mother. Something difficult for my grandmother to reveal. Was it possible that my mother had believed I was dead? I wanted to run after Grandma Joanna, and ask her to tell me the worst right away, just to lessen my anxiety. But she was gone quickly, and I knew I mustn't follow.

I began to picture some terrible disfigurement of my mother's face, or crippling of her body that had destroyed her beauty, made her want to hide from strangers. But *I* wouldn't care. I was ready to pour out a child's love to her again—a love that had had nowhere to go for so long.

Tom came downstairs and I thanked him for meeting me. He nodded curtly and went off toward a side door, his indifference clear. For a few minutes I stood looking around the lamplit room, its pools of light shining on polished wood, on bookcases lining an inner wall, catching the reflection of brass hearth fixtures, and the jewel colors of a cloisonné box. Teakwood chairs stood at the far end of the room, and I remembered how my small fingers had loved to explore the open fretwork of their carving.

It was all very much as I remembered—and yet different. To a six-year-old the room had seemed enormous—a room filled with treasures to be endlessly explored. I'd been allowed to touch all I liked, and I'd been very careful. I had made the room my own special delight as it fed my imagination. Quite unlike Grandmother Elizabeth's hotel drawing room, where I must never touch anything.

This room had the same warm ambience that I'd reveled in as a child. I'd loved it not only for the books that I hadn't been ready to read, though I'd paged through them eagerly for their pictures, but because so many exotic treasures had been collected here. Some came from the Hawaiian Islands, and others from faraway places. The grandfather I'd never known had been a naval officer, and Grandma Joanna had sometimes traveled abroad with him. He had died much too young at Pearl Harbor.

Now I noticed two lovely Hitchcock paintings that struck a chord of memory. One was of dawn on Haleakala, with clouds filling the crater, and peaks piercing through. The other I'd been especially fond of because it showed a rainbow over Manaolana, arching down through the trees—just as I'd seen it—with mountain slopes toward Olinda rising behind. Hitchcock's Maui paintings of another time must be treasured today.

Along the front of the house were tall windows framed by draperies in a green and brown Hawaiian print of ti leaves. In their center a French door opened onto the lanai, and I walked to it and stood looking outside. The brightness in the sky was fading—the sun ready to disappear in a little while behind the distant West Maui mountains. I thought of a place I might still visit before it grew dark. There'd been a rose garden that my mother had loved, and I wondered if it was still there. It would take only a moment to find out.

I went outdoors and crossed the drive to a path that wound into a tangle of rioting growth. The way that I recalled was still there. Once, all this had been kept clear of vines and shrubbery. Nevertheless, a narrow path remained. Sleepy birds were twittering—there was always the sound of birds in Hawaii—and I could catch the scent of roses as I pressed through. The rose was Maui's flower, and on special occasions my mother had loved to wear roses in her hair, or in leis around her neck. Though this still wasn't the flower scent I connected with her. I wished I could remember.

A turn in the path brought me to a cleared space of grass, where a white trellis stood, though its wood was rotting, and paint had peeled away. Rose bushes grew all around, wild and untamed. Perhaps I'd known that I would find her here—that lovely, magical lady of my childhood. *Noelle.* I stopped at the edge of the clearing and tried to prepare myself for whatever shocking change I might find in her now. The light was dimming in quick tropical twilight, and I couldn't see her in clear detail.

She sat on a bench of black lava rock, her long white dress filled with remaining light in the shadowy ruin of a garden. Her head was turned away from me, and a rose had been tucked into hair that seemed as fair as I remembered, though it was boyishly short now, and trimmed above her ears. She heard me and turned, and as I came closer there seemed no awful change—no disfigurement of any sort in face or body. In fact, she seemed not to have aged or changed at all, and perhaps that was what frightened me most.

"Hello?" She spoke softly, questioning. "You're our visitor, aren't you? Mother said someone was coming. Welcome to Maui."

She still hadn't been told who I was, I thought in dismay. Why on earth hadn't Grandma Joanna prepared her?

Before I could speak, she stood up, her long dress flowing gracefully as she moved. I wanted to rush toward her, to fling my arms around her and recover this mother whom I'd lost so long ago, and so cruelly. I didn't dare. Though she smiled at me, her look was a little vague, and I suspected that she hadn't really focused on me. Of course, she couldn't have been expected to recognize me, or have the faintest idea of who I was. This wasn't the meeting I'd dreamed of, and I hated my own hesitancy.

She moved past me, anxious now. "Have you seen Linny anywhere? My little girl? I seem to have lost her. She's only six and she shouldn't be outdoors alone at this hour. I wonder if she's gone inside?"

I felt as though someone had struck me in the midriff with a clenched fist. All the breath went out of me, and for a moment I couldn't speak. She ran anxiously along the path toward the house and I pulled myself together and followed.

At the edge of the lanai she seemed to remember me, and turned to wait, courteously. "Won't you come inside? I'm sorry, I don't know your name."

Grandma Joanna spoke from the doorway. "This is Caroline, dear."

Noelle stood in the light from the front door, and she seemed almost as young as I remembered her—as if something had arrested her, frozen her in time long past, so that she would never age.

She smiled at me again. "Caroline? That's my little daughter's name—though of course I always call her Linny. Mother, have you seen her? Did she come inside?"

"I think she's gone to bed," Grandma Joanna said, and gave me a warning look. "Noelle, will you join us for dinner tonight, since we have company? David will be here too, and you like David."

"That will be fun. I'll just go up to tuck Linny in, and then I'll come down."

Grandma Joanna put out a gentle hand to stop her. "I've already done that—and kissed her good night. So stay with us now, Noelle."

"All right." She continued to smile a bit vaguely and drifted ahead of us into the living room, where she sat down in an armchair at some distance from the fire that had been lighted against a cooling evening. When she picked up a bit of sewing from a basket, I saw that she was hemming a small blue dress.

I leaned upon the back of a chair and closed my eyes, feeling completely disoriented—lost. Empty.

Grandma Joanna put an arm around me. "Steady now. This wasn't something I could tell you over the phone, or announce the moment you arrived. I'd hoped we'd have some time together to talk before Noelle came inside. Come and sit down by the fire. She'll stop searching for a while, though the moment something reminds her, she'll start again. Don't worry—she's not listening to us. She's off in her own world and she's not unhappy, Caro."

"Won't she believe in *me*?"

"I've wondered about that. But she doesn't know that time has passed. She's stopped her private clock, and she's way back there in the years—a young wife with a small daughter, and a husband who has always just gone out. She's never understood that Keith died at the time when she was hurt. She doesn't look for him, or seem aware that he never returns. Perhaps she's better off this way."

I shook my head, clearing my thoughts, trying to find a way to relate to the new picture of my mother.

"I'm sorry you found out like this," Grandma Joanna went on, "though you'd have been shocked and hurt however you learned the truth. It was best for Elizabeth to take you away. I thought at the time that you might return when your mother improved. But that never happened. And when my letters were never answered, and Elizabeth didn't write, it seemed wiser to let you go. Perhaps better for you."

"I wish you hadn't," I said. "So much that was unfinished has been left floating around in my life."

She sighed deeply. "I loved you very much, Caro, and I missed you. But in the beginning Marla was injured, your mother had chosen her own escape, and your father was gone. Our life here was confused and unhappy. It would have been wrong for a child."

"Was it the shock of my father's death that caused this in my mother?"

"Caro, we don't know."

"You'll tell me about it—about my father's death? Grandmother Elizabeth would never talk about it, even though I understood she was here at the time."

"Yes, we'll talk, but not right away. Of course you must know as much as we can tell you."

I felt faintly relieved. No matter how much I wanted to thrust Grandmother Elizabeth's terrible suspicion from my mind, it

lingered, waiting for any nuance of feeling I might pick up to corrob-
orate or deny. Grandma Joanna's manner was not that of a woman
who had helped to conceal a murder.

Nevertheless, she looked weary and sad, and I recognized the
burden she must have carried all these years. There seemed a double
loss for me, since the vital, energetic grandmother of my early years
only emerged now and then. Much of the time this was a woman I
didn't know. But I wanted to know her. I wanted to catch up on all
those years that I'd missed here on Maui.

I leaned nearer to the fire's warmth, still chilled and shaken.
Grandma Joanna sat nearby, while my mother worked serenely some
distance away down the long room, her needle moving. She paid no
attention to either of us.

"I don't want to wait," I said. "Please tell me now what happened
that day in the crater. What made her like this?"

"I don't suppose we'll ever know. Tom O'Neill and I had gone on
ahead to make camp, and when the others didn't join us, we rode
back. Your father was dead from terrible head wounds caused by his
fall. His horse had run away. Marla lay on the ground unconscious.
Her mare, Pilikia, had kicked her. That horse always lived up to her
name—Trouble. Tom had to shoot her because she'd broken a leg in
two places. At first Noelle seemed unhurt. Tom found her sitting a
little way off from the other two at the base of a cinder cone."

Grandma Joanna's voice broke for an instant, and then she steadied herself and went on.

"A silversword plant grew beside her, and Noelle was plucking its
leaves one by one, and tearing them into bits. Caro, honey, she was
completely off in her own strange world. If she knows what happened, she's never been able to tell me anything about it."

Her words made me see the horror and I couldn't speak.

Again she continued. "Tom gave what little first aid he could manage to Marla, and then rode for help from Park headquarters. I stayed
with my daughters until a helicopter came to lift us out. Noelle
seemed unhurt physically, but she had no memory of what had happened, and she's stayed fixed in that point of time ever since. Like a
butterfly in amber. She recalls her life only up to the accident in the
crater. Of course you were still here, but it didn't seem wise to take
you to the hospital to visit Marla or Noelle. We thought it best at that
time for Elizabeth to take you home with her when she flew her son's
body to San Francisco. The idea, as I've told you, was that you would
return when your mother was better."

"And that never happened," I said softly.

"No. And she's been looking for her—her little girl—ever since. All these years!"

My hands felt numb with cold and I held them out to the fire. The room wasn't cold—it was me.

"Marla was the only one to recover," Grandma Joanna said. "She had a severe wound on her head and she was unconscious for nearly twenty-four hours. Though she recovered completely, she had no memory of what happened to any of them. No one ever knew what frightened the horses. They were all good riders, and the horses were used to the crater. They should never have fallen down that steep place, even though it was a treacherous spot. So that's it, Caroline, and we won't talk about it again."

I sat up and stared at her. "Why not? I'm sure there will be questions I'll want to ask, once I've absorbed all this."

"I haven't discussed it in years, and I shan't again. Just remember that we can only be happy during your visit if we leave all that tragedy in the past, and make what we can of the present. The subject is *kapu* around here."

This I wouldn't accept. I couldn't even begin to accept the way my mother was. But the word *"kapu"* stopped me. It was the old word from the days of the chiefs, and it meant forbidden. As a little girl I'd thought it a scary word, heavy with a threat I didn't understand. In those "old" days before Hawaii was opened to the world by Captain Cook—really only two hundred years or so ago—*kapu* had been the terrible law that ruled common people. There were arbitrary rules on every hand, set by the chiefs and the *kahuna*, the priests, who were all-powerful. Men and women couldn't eat together; pork was not to be eaten by women; privilege was for the ruling *alii* class—the royalty. The laws went on and on, and many of them discriminated against women. To break one of the laws of *kapu* was to invite instant punishment. It was a woman, the mother of the young king Liholiho, who, with others, had advised her son to end all this. So the *kapu* laws were abolished before the missionaries came.

I simply wouldn't accept my grandmother's *"kapu."* She might be used to my mother's state and accustomed to this dreadful status quo. *I* was not, and I meant to do anything I could to break through the mists that surrounded my mother. How my father had died was far less important to me than my mother's life.

Grandma Joanna was watching me, and perhaps she sensed inner rebellion and didn't want an open confrontation, for she stood up, ending our talk.

"It's nearly dinnertime. Suppose you run up to your room, Caro, and settle in a bit, while I have a look in the kitchen."

I glanced at Noelle, rapt in her sewing, paying no attention to anything else, and followed my grandmother into the long hallway that ran parallel with the front of the house, dividing the main floor into two rows of rooms. The stairway rose steeply nearby, and I followed it up to rooms tucked under the eaves.

We'd called this the "attic" when I was little, though it was rather grand for that. I'd always loved the way the ceilings slanted up here, and that one of these rooms had been mine whenever I stayed overnight at Manaolana. I knew my way, and the open door invited me.

The room was comfortably familiar. A wide four-poster bed of koa wood was big enough for several little girls, and I'd loved to bounce around on it. The quilt was new from my day and its colors were the red on yellow that one saw often in Hawaii. The dark frame of the dressing-table mirror had been carved by some fanciful hand, and I remembered searching out strange little faces and queer animals in the wood.

On the wall hung a framed color photograph that I recognized—a statue of King Kamehameha the Great. At the foot of the statue were several Hawaiian women in long black dresses, with leis of yellow ilima flowers around their necks. Yellow was the color of royalty. The king wore the helmet of the chiefs, with its distinctive forward curve, and his outstretched arms were heavy with leis of pink and white plumeria that hung in great ropes almost to the ground. The women, of course, were descendants of the *alii*, and this must be the celebration of the king's birthday that I'd read about, and which was still remembered by Hawaiians. I had always been fascinated by Hawaiian history, which was like that of no other Polynesian island.

I sat for too long staring at the picture, letting it hypnotize me so that I could postpone thinking about the problem of my mother. It wasn't possible to deal with that now anyway, and I must hurry and get ready for dinner, get ready for whatever else awaited me downstairs.

The adjoining bathroom was one I remembered. I'd needed to stand on a stool to reach the pedestaled marble basin. And I'd had to be lifted into the huge tub that stood on lion's feet. Small cakes of English soap with the scent of lavender carried me back to those happy years when this house had been my favorite place to visit.

Everything I did now was in a desperate effort to keep from being submerged in despair. I had to swim against the current—lest my mother be lost forever.

I dressed carefully and deliberately—putting on my armor! My cream silk dress was patterned with tiny brown buds, and I clasped long amber beads about my neck—a gift from my father long ago. I must try to find him again too. When I'd changed to cream leather sandals, I went slowly downstairs, ready to face whatever must still be faced in this house.

"You look exactly right," Grandma Joanna approved. She'd never cared much about how she looked, but she wanted the women around her to be pretty and neat. "And you're nicely on time. I've just heard the car arrive. That will be Marla and David returning from Wailuku. Do you remember David Reed, Caro? You must remember David."

3

My mother sat quietly with her sewing and didn't look up when I came in. I couldn't shut away my pain completely, since each new sight of her was a stab.

"Of course I remember David," I told my grandmother.

I hadn't thought of him in years, though when I'd been six and he twelve, he'd been my hero. I remembered him as a headstrong, exciting boy who could ride a horse as well as any *paniolo,* and who had developed, even at that young age, a passion for everything to do with the Islands. He'd told me wonderful stories of the old chiefs, and of Kamehameha the Great, who had made himself the first king. They'd been pretty bloody stories sometimes, but I'd listened eagerly, even while I shivered in all the right places. There had been a real Hawaiian princess way back on David's family tree, and that had made him seem all the more a romantic figure in my eyes.

"David used to visit here at Manaolana sometimes, didn't he?" I said.

"Yes—I'm his godmother. Helena Reed, his mother, is still my good friend. His parents live in Hana, and David's son Peter lives with them now. His wife died a few years ago—she was a psychotherapist. For a while David worked for the Park Service, but now he freelances as a photographer and shares a cabin on the Olinda Road with a ranger friend, Koma Olivero, who is part Hawaiian. Koma's father came from Manila. There are a lot of Filipinos and Japanese on Maui, and we still use those racial labels, even though we're all really Hawaiian Islanders. And we say *haole* for white person, *kamaaina* for native-born, and *malihini* for stranger. I suppose you are all three."

She seemed to be talking nervously—almost chattering—uneasy with me now, unlike the assured grandmother I remembered.

I watched as David and Marla came in from the lanai, and I looked at him first, seeking an old friend. He met my eyes gravely, but with a question in his that I didn't understand—almost a challenge. I remembered his dark brown eyes as being filled with light—the light of the sun. And I remembered the inner excitement that had always seemed to drive him. Quenched now? Life had touched him too with a heavy hand. He'd grown tall in maturity, and he was good-looking in a rugged sort of way, with black hair that still fell over one temple. The boy's mouth that I remembered had firmed above a strong cleft chin. He would not, I thought, be a man to cross, and somehow I found myself missing the young friend who had seemed so remarkable when I was small. I'd tried to write to David a few times too, but gave up when he never answered. Those letters had probably gone the way of all the others that would have tied me to Maui.

I would never have recognized Marla as the aunt I remembered. At nineteen she'd been sturdily built like my grandmother, never as beautiful as Noelle, but quite pretty, and able to hold her own in a spirited way that would never take second place to an older sister. Now she had grown much heavier, and she looked impressively handsome in her long, graceful *muumuu* that concealed curves that had become opulent. Her face was round and smooth-skinned, her eyes dark and lively, searching, measuring, questioning, as they'd always done. Her hair, as dark as Joanna's had been, was worn cut short and straight, to hang in points on her cheeks, her forehead fringed with long, even bangs.

The moment she saw me, she came toward me and drew me into her ample embrace, though I was taller than she was now. Then she held me away, her bright dark eyes searching my face.

"So this is Caroline grown up. You don't look a bit like your mother." She glanced toward where Noelle still sat with her sewing, and then gave me another hug. "I remember you as a curious little girl who always got into everything. Of course, you're someone else now—just as we've all turned into different people. Just your eyes look the same—though, well, they look a little haunted now."

Her open inventory, however warmly given, embarrassed me, and David must have sensed this, for he crossed the room with the quick flash of a smile that I remembered, and hugged me as he'd done when I was little.

"Don't mind Marla," he told me. "She collects characters for her books, and you're not likely to escape. As for haunting—that seems natural enough in this house. Don't you think so, Joanna?"

Once my grandmother would have risen to the challenge in his words. Now she shrugged and changed the subject.

"Of course you'll stay to dinner, David? Noelle's going to join us too."

"Maybe that's not a good idea," Marla said. "It could be upsetting —with *her* here." She glanced at me. "I'll just take Noelle out in the kitchen and we'll have our supper there."

Marla had turned into a woman who took charge—something she'd never have dared to try with her mother in the old days.

Grandma Joanna, however, could still speak with authority. "The kitchen is where we're all going to eat tonight. This is Susy Ohara's day off and I'm the cook. So we'll keep this simple. I think the stew's nearly ready."

I remembered from the past that my grandmother had never wanted many house servants around. Those she employed became friends and partners, both indoors and out, but they were few. She'd enjoyed cooking, and made herself at home in the kitchen with whoever was working there.

Marla gave in with good grace and went to where her sister was sitting. She took the sewing from Noelle's hands and put it aside.

"We're going to dinner now, dear. David's here and so is—" She threw her mother a questioning look and Grandma Joanna spoke quickly.

"I've told Noelle that Caroline is visiting us."

My mother looked at me brightly, accepting. "Yes—she has the same name as my Linny."

I steeled myself to show nothing. I couldn't endure this visit if I was to be torn by every casual word. Nor did I want to accept the compassion I sensed in others.

I went to Noelle and slipped my hand through the crook of her arm. "May I sit by you? I'd like to get better acquainted."

Noelle glanced at her mother uncertainly, and seemed reassured by her nod. "It's all right, if you want to, Caroline," she agreed.

But even as we walked down the room together, I knew she was hardly there, and I wondered what sort of dream world she lived in. What went on behind that smooth forehead? At least she didn't seem unhappy, except when she remembered that she couldn't find her child.

Only in Marla did I sense unspoken disapproval, and I was aware of the way she watched me. Lest I make some misstep with Noelle?

The big kitchen had been redone since my day, and now there was a terra-cotta tile floor, cabinets of eucalyptus wood on each side of double steel sinks. In the center of the room was a huge round table made from the trunk of a koa tree. I admired the table and hand-made chairs, and Grandma Joanna nodded agreement.

"They're treasures. Tom O'Neill made them for me. I've told him that anytime he wants to stop being a *paniolo* he can start a shop in Lahaina for his beautiful furniture. Mainland people would be crazy about it, and so would Islanders."

Tom O'Neill came into the room in time to hear her, and he grinned. "I'm happy where I am for now." He looked at Noelle, and then at me, and again I sensed the disapproval I didn't understand. He had changed to clean chinos, and his red hair was slicked back with water, but to me he seemed no more prepossessing than ever.

Joanna ladled generous servings of savory fish stew from the pot on the stove, and Tom helped her to set big green bowls before us. The stew was aromatic with herbs, and pink shrimp floated on the surface.

Sitting next to Noelle, as I'd planned, with Marla on her other side, watching over her sister, I found myself longing to make my mother aware of me—at least as a friend. Only if she learned to like me could I talk to her, probe into these mists that floated around her shrouding reality.

Around the curve of the table, David sat next to Marla, and his look still seemed to question me. Sooner or later I wanted to talk to him too, and see if I could find my old friend again.

When green salads and crusty loaves of whole-grain bread had been placed on the table, Grandma Joanna sat down and reached out her hands on either side, clasping David's and Tom's. Noelle sat with her hands in her lap, staring into her own space. Marla and I looked at each other, and then I followed suit as Marla reached for one of Noelle's hands, and I took the other. It was the first time I had touched her, and her fingers curled trustingly in mine, as though she were younger than I. Tom held my hand on the other side, though I suspected that he didn't want to. For a moment we all sat in a simple human joining, and even Tom relaxed a little.

"It's good to be together," Grandma Joanna said. "And good to have Caroline with us again."

Then the chain broke apart, and we gave our attention to the hearty food on the table.

Grandma Joanna talked to Tom about the horses, and I thought of a question I wanted to ask.

"I remember the word *paniolo* for cowboy, but I've been laughed at back home for talking about cowboys in Hawaii. Didn't we have them here before the American West did?"

"Tell her, Tom," Grandma Joanna said.

"That's right. Hawaiians started to raise cattle here in the last century—before 1830. In the beginning they didn't know how to go about it. So they brought in *vaqueros* from Mexico, and Hawaiians learned to rope and tie a steer, and to ride straight-legged. They learned how to manage cattle drives down the mountain to the boats, and they called themselves *paniolos* because that word resembled *Espagnol.*"

"It's all a lot tamer now," Grandma Joanna said. "Raising horses is easier. Of course you ride, Caro?"

"I've done a little city riding," I told her.

Noelle looked up from concentration on her food. *"Caro?* Do they call you that too, Caroline?" she asked, wide-eyed.

"Sometimes," I said gently, and then ventured further. "There used to be someone who called me Linny when I was a little girl."

She rejected that at once. "Oh, no! That's what I call my little girl. I don't think anyone else would use that name."

Grandma Joanna broke in quickly, asking for bread to be passed, and Noelle slipped away again into her own space.

"Don't do that," my grandmother warned me. "You mustn't remind her, or we'll have trouble. I shouldn't have made that slip with your name in front of her. Never mind—you can't know all the danger points yet. Tell me how Elizabeth Kirby is these days?"

"She's a strong woman, and she goes right on running her hotel."

"Yes, I suspect she would. I'm afraid she didn't approve of us very much when she was here. She was a white glove sort of person. Keith wanted to take her up to the crater, but she distrusted Haleakala, so she wouldn't go."

"Why?" David asked. "Did she think it was going to erupt?"

"We assured her that it wouldn't," Grandma Joanna said. "The last spurt of lava was easily two hundred years ago, and it didn't come from the top of the mountain. A side vent opened in the direction of Makena. The mountain's safely dormant these days, and we don't have earthquakes, even when the live volcanoes over on the Big

Island stir themselves. We've all seen that show from the summit here, and it's pretty awe-inspiring."

"I was able to get some good shots of the last Kilauea eruption," David said. "She blows her top every once in a while. I'll show you the pictures sometime, if you like, Caroline. Oh, by the way—I'm going over to Ahinahina tomorrow morning to take some photographs for the art society brochure. Would you like to come along? Since you used to live there."

"I'd love to," I said.

Beside me Noelle stirred. "Ahinahina—silversword."

She looked so troubled that Marla put an arm about her. "That's just the name of a house, Noelle. But you probably don't remember the house."

"Of course I remember." She nodded at Marla with assurance. "I haven't been there for a long time."

I wanted to suggest that she come with us, but my grandmother was already shaking her head at me, and Tom spoke a low warning in my ear.

"Let her alone, Caroline."

Marla said strangely, "That's right, Caroline. Don't stir sleeping serpents."

What did she mean—that my mother slept safely in some sort of Garden of Eden, and mustn't be awakened to outside dangers? But I couldn't ask now, with Noelle listening.

"I don't remember the house as well as I do Manaolana," I told David. "Just bits and pieces of it. Though I'm sure memories will come back when I see it again."

"Will you use the pictures for your book, David?" Marla asked.

"Maybe some of them, since that house is still a showplace. But the brochure is my first job right now."

"Is Koma still planning to do the text?" Again the question came from Marla.

"I hope so. He's pretty busy with his Park job—"

"And all that activist stuff," Marla put in.

David let that pass. "Marla, have you shown Caroline *your* books?"

"There hasn't been time. I'll show her the ones you've done the photos for." She spoke with more eagerness—this was something that clearly interested her.

"Tell me about your books," I said.

"I write them for children—about Hawaii. Mostly they retell the old legends, though I want young people to know about the monarchy too. David has done the photographs—really good!—for the last two."

Noelle spoke gently, "Your paintings are so beautiful, Marla. Will you use them for your book?"

Unexpectedly, it was Tom who answered Noelle. He'd had nothing to say until now, and I wasn't sure he'd even been listening.

"Marla doesn't want to paint anymore. You remember that. You're the one who paints beautiful pictures."

Noelle only shook her head vaguely and slipped away again. She seemed to move in and out of a web of forgetfulness she wove about herself, so that one could never be quite sure what she paid attention to, or understood.

"I'd like to see some of your photographs, David," I said into a silence that became suddenly uncomfortable.

"There are several around the house," Grandma Joanna told me. "That stunning sunrise picture of the crater over the mantel in the living room is one David took up there a few years ago."

"There's a photograph in my room upstairs," I recalled. "Of a statue of Kamehameha the Great, with leis hanging from his arms clear to the ground. Did you take that, David?"

"Yes, for the anniversary of the king's birthday."

Marla's enthusiasm returned. "There's a wonderful resurgence of interest in the past all through Hawaii. For a while people seemed not to care very much."

"A lot of that history was pretty brutal and ugly," Tom O'Neill put in. "Some of what they're doing now could get ugly too. We can't go back to the way things were before Cook came in and everything started to change. Besides, I don't think today's *kamaaina* would want to go back—not most of them."

"Koma does," David said. "He gets pretty fervent at times."

"Oh, sure!" Tom sounded scornful. "That whole Kahoolawe affair —crazy!"

"I don't know about that," Grandma Joanna said. "The protests have had some effect. If I'd been Koma's age, I'd probably have gone along to try to stop the bombing."

"Bombing?" I was lost.

"The Island of Death," Noelle sounded suddenly excited, and Marla put a gentle hand on her arm, quieting her.

"It wasn't really called that," David said, "except in a novel that chose to be fanciful. But a jealous goddess was supposed to have put a curse on the island. There's no water, and in modern times few have lived there. Goats ate it barren, and the U.S. Navy leased the island for practice bombing. It's the bombing that a lot of Hawaiians resented."

"What happened?" I asked. "I mean, what did Koma do?"

"A few years ago he and several other boys took a boat out, and then swam over to the island by night and camped near where the Navy was target practicing. There have been other invasions of what the military regards as its property."

Noelle looked around the room, suddenly tense. "Did you hear that, Mother?"

"It's only the wind, dear."

"No—it's Linny! She's crying. I can hear her. I must find her right away—she needs me!" Noelle jumped up from the table and ran from the room.

"I'll take care of her." Marla rose more slowly and went after her sister, undisturbed—perhaps used to this, as I wasn't.

How could I ever accept what had happened? To find my mother alive after all these years, yet lost to me, seemed unbearable.

Grandma Joanna saw my face and stood up. "Help me clear the table, Caroline. We're having papaya for dessert."

She was accustomed to Noelle's reactions, and her matter-of-fact words steadied me. I carried dishes down the big room, and when we stood together at the steel sink, my grandmother spoke to me softly.

"Perhaps she's better off this way—not remembering. Try not to mind so deeply, Caro honey."

How could I not mind? "Why do you protect her all the time and keep her the way she is?"

Joanna Docket could freeze into a woman who seemed made of stone—lava rock perhaps! A woman whom no amount of battering could change, and her gentle affection for me vanished.

"You don't know what you're talking about, Caroline. Perhaps you had better make this a short visit, so that *you* don't upset her too much."

She put plates of sliced papaya in my hands, and I carried them automatically to the table, where David and Tom were talking. By then I hardly knew what I was doing. I'd not only found and lost my mother, but apparently I'd lost my grandmother too. I could never go back to being the child who had loved her so dearly and found comfort in all she had to give me. She was old now, and a stranger. It was at this moment that I stopped calling her "Grandma." That was a child's word. From now on she would be Joanna to me. I still wanted to know her better as she was now, but the relationship must be different for us both—more equal—if it could ever be found and developed. She already seemed to be urging me to go home.

I went back for more plates of papaya and lemon wedges, and she looked at me sadly, as though she sensed a change that separated us still more.

"Perhaps I was wrong, Caroline. We couldn't either of us turn out as we dreamed. You're remembering a younger grandmother—a woman who wasn't as tired as I've become. And I'm recalling a small granddaughter who is as lost to me as Noelle's Linny is to her. Perhaps we could find a newer, richer relationship, if only there were time. But I know now that you mustn't stay. For your sake, as well as Noelle's. We must do nothing to send her more deeply into her withdrawal from reality."

I wanted to cry for all those lost people who had lived twenty-six years ago, and were gone now, even though some were still alive. But my eyes were dry and I felt mostly hollow. I could find no words to answer her—neither to reject nor to accept. Yet—how could she be so sure she was right?

She stared at me with eyes that were still the silvery green I remembered. "It's no use, is it, Caroline?"

I wanted to protest that this didn't have to be true. Yet I knew it was true—because Noelle stood between us now. And I was no longer on my grandmother's side.

"Whatever you're thinking, don't try," Joanna said.

I carried the rest of the papaya to the table just as Marla brought her sister back into the room. There were traces of tears on Noelle's cheeks, but she was smiling again. An empty smile that broke my heart. Joanna was older and wiser than I was—I allowed her that. But perhaps somewhere over the years she had learned to take her older daughter's condition too much for granted. If I moved slowly, gently, and with love, surely a change would come. Only now there wouldn't be time.

What had happened had set a restraint upon us all, and we talked very little as we finished our dessert. At least, in a small way, I could enjoy the yellow-orange fruit on my plate. Taste was like smell— never really forgotten, once experienced. Yet almost impossible to describe when it came to subtleties of fragrance and a feeling on the tongue.

I spoke to Joanna deliberately. "When I was little, my *mother*"—I emphasized the word, stealing a look at Noelle, who seemed not to hear—"used to wear flowers in her hair. I can almost remember the scent, and I know they weren't roses." I turned to the ageless woman beside me. "Did *you* ever wear some other flower in your hair?"

She gave me the smile that meant so little. "I like to wear *awapuhi* —ginger blossoms. It's easy to find yellow ginger because it grows wild all over the island. I love the perfume of ginger."

"Of course," I said, "—ginger blossoms. I'd forgotten."

"You must make our visitor a ginger lei, Noelle," Joanna said quickly. "Caroline would like that."

"Please," I said to Noelle. "I'd like to watch you make a lei."

She nodded absently, picking up a lemon wedge to squeeze over her papaya slice. Almost visibly she escaped into her misty world— mists that could come over her as quickly as clouds could cover the crater of Haleakala.

When Tom had finished his coffee, he excused himself. "I've got to get back to the stable. Lihilihi is expecting her foal and I want to see her through."

He included us all in his casual "good night" as he left.

Joanna looked after him affectionately. "I don't know what I'd do without Tom."

"Sometimes he scares me," Marla said. "It's always surprised me that you trust him so completely, Mother. What do you think of Tom O'Neill, Caroline?"

I hesitated. "I can't give you a fair answer. I know he doesn't want me here. He seems ready to judge me in some way, without giving himself time to find out anything about me."

David Reed was watching me. "Perhaps Tom wonders why you never came back to Hawaii—why you never wrote to your grand-mother when you were old enough to write proper letters. Or to your aunt or your mother."

So he was judging me too, and just as unfairly.

"I did write," I told him. "I even wrote to you."

David looked startled, but Joanna was shaking her head. "I don't think that's the reason for Tom's hostility. I've told him you never received our letters, Caroline, and that yours were never mailed."

"I'm sorry," David said to me. "I didn't know. Just the same, you might have tried to get in touch after you grew up."

"When I thought my mother was dead? When I thought my grand-mother didn't care anything about me?"

David was looking at me in a different way—perhaps pitying me, and I didn't want that either.

When Marla got up to put dishes into the washer, and Noelle went dutifully to help her, Joanna waved me out of the kitchen, still not pleased with me.

David drew me onto the lanai, where an overhead light touched the ferns and other plants to soft green.

"Come outdoors and see the sky," he said.

4

I went outside with David and when we reached the lawn he stopped me. "Do you remember how close the stars can seem on Haleakala?"

Gazing up at the luminous sky, I remembered not only how the night had looked—I also remembered a small girl who had stood beside her father watching the heavens in delight. There'd been nights when he'd pointed out Polaris, the North Star, and Orion and the Pleiades. If only *he* could have brought me here again—that long-ago loving father whom I still remembered.

The same feeling of wonder he had evoked came back to me as we moved away from the lights of the house, and the night spoke with voices I recognized. The birds were quiet except for a few that woke up at night, but there were insect sounds and wind in the trees. There was also something I'd called "the voice of the mountain." Which wasn't a voice at all, but only a vast silence—something so enormous, reaching clear to the sky, that it had seemed to speak to the small girl I'd been.

A three-quarter moon shed its radiance on clouds that patched the mountain, and the glittering constellations added their own radiance to a luminous night. All this was familiar, and filled with whispering memories as wind stirred the branches of the camphor tree. High on the slopes a few lights shone, but those of houses nearby were hidden, so that only black treetops stood against the night blue overhead. Though the wind felt strong on my face, it was not biting, and it murmured like rushing water, carrying a scent that mingled all those Hawaiian flowers the sun had warmed during the day with those that bloomed only at night, like the cereus that grew over a stone wall and shone white in the darkness. A sweetness heavy with nostalgia for all I had lost so long ago.

I tried to put something of the wonder I felt into words. "It's strange how clearly so much comes back to me—the island, the ocean, and always the mountain. Though my feelings are different now—perhaps even stronger because of all I've missed. And because of my mother. If only there weren't so many gaps—so many things I can't remember at all."

David didn't move into this world of the senses with me, as he might have done when we were children. Instead he asked a practical question.

"How long are you going to stay here, Caroline?"

The enchantment and mystery around us fell away.

"My grandmother doesn't want me to stay. I'm not sure I want to anyway. It hurts too much to watch my mother and see the way she is now. I'll stay long enough to find out if I can help her. Which may not be very long."

"Not if you expect failure," David said. "And of course there is a risk."

I looked at him quickly, but I couldn't read his face in this soft, unfocused light. "What do you mean? What risk?"

He didn't answer, and we walked on across the side lawn. Over near the camphor tree we were approaching I heard something rustle and caught a movement in its spangled shadow. But when I looked closely everything was still. Some small animal probably. We stopped a little way off from the tree and David put his hand on my arm.

"I'm sorry I've been hard on you, Caroline. Because I love Joanna as though she were my own grandmother, I've blamed you for some of her unhappiness. I know how much she grieved when your other grandmother took you away and she never heard from you again. Perhaps she wanted you here because she was always more lonely than she'd admit. She'd lost Noelle too, and Marla—well, Marla is Marla, and not the most lovable person in the world. Though I must say she's been very good to her sister."

I shook my head. "I don't know—tonight there seemed so much antagonism between us. Perhaps we've changed too much to ever come together again. What she wants and I want are at opposite poles."

"Give her time. A grandchild can be pretty important. My own parents couldn't be more loving to my son."

"I don't know very much about you anymore," I said. "I'm sorry about your wife. Joanna told me a little while ago."

"I'm getting used to it—though I expect one never does entirely. Kate died three years ago. We had one child. Peter's eight now, and he stays with my parents in Hana. That's a good place for him to grow up since it's mostly unspoiled, and I can see him often. I understand you've gone through a divorce recently. That can be a sort of dying too."

This "dying" was too recent and I couldn't talk about it yet. I stretched my arms to the sky and breathed deeply before I let them drop. "The peace here is heavenly. The rest of the world seems far away."

"We'd like to keep it that way. On Maui we're trying to protect what we have left before it's all lost. The way Waikiki on Oahu has been lost."

"You mean because they're developing West Maui—all those luxury condominiums and hotels?"

"It's no simple matter. We're pretty ambivalent. We need visitors and the money they bring, God knows. But this makes living expensive for the ordinary Islander. Most of the jobs easily available are tourist-serving jobs. Our young people can be anything they want these days—lawyers, doctors, scientists. Not just guitar players and hula dancers. Or workers in sugarcane and pineapple fields, the way it used to be. But there's never enough money for the education they need, and sometimes they're not motivated to care. We need the tourists, but we can resent them too. Mainland people can come in with all the same hang-ups they had at home, and the same prejudices. And they start making the same mistakes here that they made at home. So I'm glad there are a few fighting organizations coming to life now to take a stand."

"This up-country part of the island seems almost the way I remember it. There's still open country around here."

"Even Hana's in danger of changing if too much money comes in from outside and too many rich *malihini* start grabbing. Hana's always been hard to get to, so it's been able to stay isolated. But now, with helicopters and planes, people can move in. The Park has managed to preserve more than twenty-eight thousand acres from development—land that can stay wild, the way it always was. But there are some who feel the Park system's taken too much land for its own purpose. There's always a difficult balance between what people need and what the land needs."

I liked David's concern and involvement.

He went on soberly.

"There's a strange aspect to the Navy's bombing of Kahoolawe—the island we talked about at dinner. That very bombing has kept the island off-limits for so many years that the artifacts over there have been preserved. They haven't been looted as they were in other places. Bombs were never dropped on the whole island and the Navy claims they've just moved the surface dust around a little in their target practice. But sometimes bombs fall where they're not supposed to, and it's all too close to our island. Koma Olivero, who shares a small house with me, has been working with an organization dedicated to stop the bombing. I help when I can."

We'd reached the shadow of the big camphor tree, and David returned to a more personal present. "How long *do* you think you'll stay, Caroline?"

"How can I tell, when Joanna doesn't want me to stay?"

"Maybe she needs you more than she's ready to admit."

"Noelle is the only one who needs me. Everyone else is trying to shield her and keep her the way she is."

"What if you make her worse?"

"Worse than being nothing?" I cried. "A minute ago you sounded as though I shouldn't expect failure. But now you're warning me."

"If you try to change her, you've got to believe that it's possible. But at the same time you need to face the risk of causing still more regression. You may have to choose."

"I wish Joanna could have warned me! It's all happened so fast."

"You know what the people at Manaolana remind me of?"

"Tell me."

"When I was a kid growing up in Hana, a Japanese friend brought me a box of water flowers. A tiny box with bits of pressed paper in it. When I sprinkled them in a bowl of water they opened into beautiful shapes and colors that floated for a long time."

"I remember," I said. "My father gave me some of those too, when I was little. What made you think of water flowers in connection with Manaolana?"

"Because everyone here—Marla, Joanna, Noelle, maybe even Tom O'Neill—are all like that now. Pressed into tight little packages that are still set in the past. I wonder if you are their bowl of water, Caro? Maybe that's what they're afraid of. Because if you are, no one may be able to stop what you'll make happen. And what if they aren't all beautiful flowers when they uncurl? What if there are dragons—monsters?"

I didn't much like the picture he was presenting, and I remembered how tantalizing he had been sometimes as a young boy, teasing me with questions I couldn't answer.

"Then why would my grandmother ask me to come?"

"She's capable of dreaming. And of making a mistake."

"Do you think I shouldn't have come?"

"I haven't decided yet. Anyway—what does it matter, since you're here? And if you're that bowl of water, maybe all the secrets will open up, in spite of anything you or they can do to hide them."

"What secrets?"

"*I* wouldn't know. But what if it's better if they stay hidden?"

He reached up to pluck a leaf from the camphor tree and rolled it in his fingers, releasing a nose-tingling scent—a delaying action while he made up his mind before going on.

"What if they were set—pressed—into this pattern when the accident happened up in the crater all those years ago? If it really was an accident."

"Why do you say that?" I asked quickly.

"I can't give you a reason. Maybe when we're young our senses are more open to nuances than they become later. I was twelve or so when it happened, and I was visiting Manaolana. Even before I knew what had happened, I could feel something awful in the air—something threatening. Joanna came as close to falling apart as I've ever seen her. I don't think she ever recovered from the change in your mother. In fact, no one was the same afterwards. I'd used to love visiting my godmother, riding the horses, talking with Tom. But after that they all made me uneasy, and Noelle scared me. So for a while I didn't come back."

I had been here too, with whisperings going on around me that I couldn't understand. It had been terrifying to be shut away from my parents, when nobody would explain. That was the first time I ever saw my grandmother cry. I had come upon her sitting in the dark on the lanai of the empty ranch house one evening. When she saw me she took me on her lap and held me close, and in a little while her tears stopped. Perhaps because she had to keep me from knowing all of what made her cry.

"No one told me right away that my father was dead," I said to David. "Not until we were on the plane for home did Grandmother

Elizabeth tell me that my parents had been killed in a riding accident. She let me believe my mother had died too!"

"Sometimes I think children have more sense than grownups."
David sounded angry. "That was a rough time, but I think you'd have
done better with more of the truth. You were such an eager little girl.
I used to enjoy that. It gave me a chance to show off how much I
knew. And you were smart enough so that I was flattered at the way
you soaked everything up and wanted more."

"If only I could have understood . . ."

"I was nearly in my teens and I couldn't understand. Of course,
they packed me off to Hana fast, and I doubt if my parents knew
much more than was picked up in the papers. But, Caroline—all of
this is so long ago. Can't you just let it go and think about what
matters now?"

"It's long ago for all of you, but for me it's almost as if it had just
happened. Especially when it comes to my mother."

I looked off at the high black silhouette of the mountain, where a
portion of its summit rose above the clouds, the night sky lighter
behind it.

"I've never forgotten the mountain," I said. "Sometimes I've
dreamed about it as though there were magic there."

"The crater's still a holy place to many Hawaiians. They believe
that those who don't respect its power can come to harm. Though
they can be a bit afraid of it too. Some of us never go up there without
some little offering to Pele wrapped in ti leaves." He laughed a bit
sheepishly. "Oh, well, no need to get mystical. Maybe Marla's been
telling me too many of the old legends that she puts into her books."

"You told me a lot of those legends yourself, David. You always
liked the gory ones. And you made me believe them all."

"You can remember that? I think you wanted to grasp at everything there was to know."

I'd lost most of that in growing up, I thought. Or perhaps I hadn't
found anything lately that I'd wanted to reach for. Now there was
Noelle, and something was stirring in me—possibly a sense of purpose, in spite of all the warnings.

"What do *you* think happened up there, David?"

"I've told you—I don't know. In the old days they might have
brought in a *kahuna*. There are still priests around for those who
want them. At least Joanna might have. She has strong feelings for
the past and old Hawaiian ways. But of course your father came from

the States, and he wasn't into any of that. Respect for the crater, I mean. Maybe he was even the one who offended the mountain."

He was only half joking, and I shivered. "Stop it! Are you still trying to scare me? I'm not a little kid anymore."

"No, you're not," he said, and there was a questioning rise in his voice. "Our ages seem to have caught up—almost."

I went on quickly. "Surely the accident was investigated thoroughly at the time?"

"As much as it could be. Which doesn't mean that all the facts came out. So what about it, Caro? Are you going to open everything up and hurt them all over again? Is it worth it to do that? Or even safe?"

There seemed a challenge in his words, and I tried to see his face in the moonlight. All I could catch was a dark shining in his eyes, and for the first time since I'd met him today, I sensed again an old, almost dangerous excitement in him that I remembered. It troubled me, since I didn't know what drove him now.

"Look," I said, "don't push me into anything. I can't accept your whimsy about pressed flowers."

He laughed. "I'm not worried—you'll push yourself. But those flowers illustrate something, don't they?"

"I don't care about that. It's my mother who matters to me."

"It might take a lot of nerve and determination to stir everything up. I suspect you'll be blocked at every step."

"Why? What are they hiding?"

"They like the status quo. It's what they're used to—especially Noelle. You might make everything worse for them. Worse for you too."

I still sensed that hint of suppressed excitement in him that I didn't understand. He seemed to push me with one hand and pull me back with the other. Testing me, perhaps?

"I just don't know . . ." I turned from him and started toward the house.

He stopped me a few feet from the tree. "Caro, I'm sorry. You've had too much thrown at you for one day. I can understand now why you didn't come before, but you're from the mainland, so you don't know how different things are in Hawaii. In some ways being an American here is a veneer. For a while being Western was very popular, but now the pendulum is swinging. *You* can't know what's going on underneath. Maybe something that's part of a new Hawaii, and not altogether American. Something Hawaiian first."

Right now I didn't care about that. A certain single-mindedness was growing in me.

"I'll tell you something," I said. "My Grandmother Elizabeth believes that my father was murdered."

David was quiet for a moment. Then he said, "I've always had the feeling that might be so myself. The atmosphere at Manaolana was too strange for the accident theory."

His words chilled me. I'd hoped for contradiction, dismissal. He accepted the idea too readily, and that was all the more frightening. But it was my mother I must concern myself with—not some awful deed that belonged to the past. My concern about the crater and what had happened there had only to do with my mother. There was nothing more I could say—or wanted to say.

Near the camphor tree something moved again, and I listened intently. "There's someone over there."

David had heard the sound too, and he ran back to the tree and into the bushes beyond. But whoever had been there was already crashing away into the darkness, and the night was quiet again, except for buzzing insects.

David rejoined me. "Whoever it was is gone. Let's go back inside."

I sensed excitement in him again. It was as though part of him wanted whatever danger might exist to come into the open where he could deal with it. Another part held him back and wasn't so sure. "Danger," of course, was too strong a word to use in this peaceful Hawaiian night. Probably the explanation was simple and casual—of no consequence. My mind took a contrary turn. "Peace" wasn't exactly the right word to associate with Hawaii's turbulent past.

I let it all go and when we were halfway across the side lawn and on neutral ground where no one could hear us, I asked a more ordinary question.

"David, do you know why Tom O'Neill seems so set against my being here? I can't see him as a pressed flower."

"Why not? He was part of it all. Sometimes I've wondered if he was protecting someone and knows a lot more than he's ever told. Noelle always seemed like the enchanted princess in the tower to me in those young days. I'd have loved to rescue her. Perhaps I still would."

If that was so, then I might have an ally.

We were close to the house now, and he put a hand on my arm, so that we halted, still in the open. Someone stepped out from the shadows of the dimly lighted lanai and came toward us. It couldn't have been whoever had hidden behind the camphor tree, since that person had run off in the opposite direction. This man was dark and slim, and David recognized him.

"Hi, Koma. What's up?"

"I've been waiting for you. You were talking over there, so I didn't want to bust in."

"Caro, this is my friend, Koma Olivero. Caroline Kirby, Koma."

"I know. Hello, Caroline." He used my name easily, and his voice carried the musical lilt that I associated with Hawaiian voices. A cliché, perhaps, but there was a natural melody in the Hawaiian-born who wasn't *haole*.

We went onto the lanai together, and I could see him more clearly. His skin was a warm brown, his face wide at the cheekbones, with a generous mouth, unsmiling now. Reflected light shone in eyes that were almost black, and his hair was dark and thick and unruly, blown by the wind.

"So you're Keith Kirby's daughter," he added, and the words sounded almost like an accusation.

"Did you know my father?" I asked.

"He couldn't have," David said. "He wasn't here then."

Koma spoke directly to David, and I felt as though I'd been dismissed. He might not have known my father, but I had the strong feeling that he didn't like whatever he'd heard about him.

"There's a meeting being called tonight, and I'm on my way. Maybe you should come, Dave. But first we need to talk."

David said, "I'll see you in the morning, Caroline, when we go to Ahinahina."

I told them both good night and went into the house.

The long living room was empty, the fire on the lava-rock hearth dying. I picked up a magazine and sat down, paging through it idly. If I went straight up to my room I'd only start too many thoughts stirring around in my head, and night thoughts were apt to be anything but cheerful or hopeful. Scott was always there, waiting to move in, much as I wanted to push him away. San Francisco had an unexpected pull for me too. At least I'd been on familiar ground there—and not in the tossing seas that troubled Manaolana.

Even a fireplace reminded me of sitting before the hearth in our first little house across the bay, holding hands and planning our wonderful future. I'd believed that I was as important to Scott as he was to me, and in the beginning we'd had lovely times together. Charm was something Scott had in overabundance, and he'd loved to please—providing it wasn't too much trouble. But charm without sensitivity eventually wore thin. It was quite possible to love and despise at the same time.

When we were married, Grandmother Elizabeth had given us a handsome sum that I didn't want to accept. Scott thought it better to take it, rather than hurt her feelings. He'd welcomed gifts from her on other occasions, once to pay for a trip he took with his latest love. And of course he had been eager to accept the job Grandmother Elizabeth offered him at the Prince Albert—even though I'd opposed it. We'd needed more than anything to be clear of obligations to her.

There! I was doing just what I'd feared. Thoughts of Scott always wound up unhappily. Better to think of my father, though that could be painful too. Once I'd sat on his knee before this very fireplace, and he'd built wonderful images for me in the flaming logs. Maui was full of memories of him, and of my mother the way she'd been. Only now, David's words, with all their unsettling possibilities, were there at the back of my mind to torment me with questions I wasn't ready to face.

No one came to join me in the room and distract me from my own thoughts, so the house began to seem too quiet. I tossed the magazine aside and climbed the steep white stairs to the upper floor. The door of my room stood open, and a band of light from the hall showed me Marla Docket curled up in the dark on the window seat.

"Is that you, Caroline?" she called. "I've been waiting for you. We need to talk."

Those were the same words Koma had spoken to David, and somehow they had an ominous ring.

I touched the light switch and lamps came on in the room. This rather secretive meeting made me feel all the more uneasy.

5

Marla had changed to pajamas and a blue-patterned Japanese yukata. She looked plump and comfortable and good-natured on the window seat. The casement was open, and the night a lustrous ebony behind her. From outdoors a breeze ruffled the straight brown bangs across her forehead, and the neatly cut points of hair moved against her cheeks when she turned her head, giving rather an exotic effect. Calculated? I wondered.

For the first time since I'd arrived, I wondered what Marla's life had been like. Had she ever been in love? Why hadn't she married? When I was little, she'd been good to me, and with her liking for children she should have had babies of her own.

"My room's up here too," she said conversationally, as I pulled a chair near the window. "So we have this floor to ourselves. Mother's knee makes it difficult for her to climb stairs these days, and of course she wants Noelle near her, so their rooms are down below. Nobody can hear us up here. We can say anything we like."

This sounded like an invitation, but I hadn't anything I needed to open up with my Aunt Marla.

"Secrets?" I asked, remembering the word David had used.

Her smile had an impish quality that I recognized from the past. There had sometimes been an appealing sense of mischief about Marla, which was probably why children liked her.

"If you want to call it that," she said. "There's something I'd like you to do, Caroline, if you ever get up to the crater. Something you can make right. Maybe I'm even a little superstitious about this."

"I don't suppose I'll go up there, but what is it you want me to do?"

She didn't answer directly, but waved a hand toward the bed. "I brought you one of my books. It's over there."

I went to pick up the thin volume that lay on the spread. The jacket was bamboo green and lava black—with a striking splash of crimson. For fire, of course. I read the title: *The Legend of Pele.*

"Thank you," I said. "I'll enjoy reading it."

Marla had a habit of tilting her head at times, as though she listened to something far away that no one else could hear. I had no idea what she heard now as she went on dreamily.

"You remember that Pele's home was once in the crater of Haleakala? She made it a place of great fires and poured lava down its sides."

"Yes, you used to tell me stories about Pele," I said.

She looked pleased. "I'm glad you remember. Of course, it was the sea goddess who drove Pele away. She sent a water dragon to destroy her rival. But Pele's spirit never died, and it flew away to make its home on the Big Island, where she could stir up more volcanoes. So now Haleakala is dead and cold."

"But Pele comes back sometimes, doesn't she?" I said. "To look over her old home?"

"Right! And she can appear in all sorts of guises—a wrinkled hag, or a young girl. Even as a child. I think I've seen her up there myself a couple of times."

If anyone could, I thought, it would be Marla, who had always been able to stretch her imagination in any direction she pleased.

I leafed through the book. "Did David Reed do the photographs for this?"

"Yes, he appreciates the old legends as much as I do. And he can do imaginative things with his camera. There's one picture in there of the crater that looks like Pele emerging out of the mist. He's helped me with my research too. We were down at the Historical Museum in Wailuku today getting something for my next book."

I paused in my page turning to study a stunning color photograph of Kilauea's fires—Pele's present home. "David's very good, isn't he?"

"He's one of the best. Of course, I wish Noelle could illustrate my books with her drawings and paintings. But though she still paints lovely watercolors, she can't be counted on to concentrate and fill assignments."

"I can remember pictures she painted for me," I said.

Marla sighed. "I know how hard this must be for you, Caroline. It may help a little if you can remember that she really is happy most of the time now. Just think of the pain she has missed."

"Without pain she isn't alive. And she still looks for her child."

"But never for long, since she's easily distracted. She's like a child herself."

I wondered if I dared open the subject of the crater incident with Marla, but I didn't know her well enough yet, and this wasn't the time.

"Do you try out your stories by reading them to children, the way you used to read to me?"

"I read them to Noelle now," she said quietly.

I put the book down. "Is there any hope for her, Marla?"

She shook her head sadly. "We don't think so. There are moments when she's almost back to what's real—and then she escapes just in time."

"What do you mean—just in time?"

Marla left the window seat and stretched her body beneath the yukata—the stretch of a plump cat. "You know, of course, that she's been like this ever since the accident in the crater. Sometimes I think she knows what happened there and has run away from it. She wasn't as badly hurt as I was. So maybe it's better for her not to remember. Better not to stir up sleeping serpents, Caroline."

"You've said that before. What are you talking about? What serpents?"

"It doesn't matter, so long as they stay asleep. But Noelle isn't what I came to talk to you about." She sat down again and waved a hand. "Go over to those shelves across the room—the ones with books and ornaments. I don't want to touch what's there."

I went to the row of shelves. "What am I supposed to look for?"

"There's a piece of lava rock on the middle shelf that your father brought down from the crater."

I picked up the gray-black rock and found it surprisingly light, almost like pumice. Its sides were rounded and pocked, as though it had been tumbled along with other rocks that hadn't become part of a solid, molten mass.

"That rock should go back to the mountain," Marla said. "Will you take it there?"

"Why should it go back?"

"Because Pele's anger is to be respected. Everyone knows that trouble comes to the person who steals a rock from Pele. Of course, your father laughed at the legend, the way he laughed at everything.

He had to dare Pele by bringing that rock down on an earlier trip—
just to prove that nothing would happen. He wasn't from Maui or
he'd have known better. We've all paid for what he did—Keith with
his life. Maybe the bad luck will go on and on if the rock isn't carried
back to where it came from."

"If you really believe this, why haven't you returned it yourself?"

"It needs to be someone of the same blood. So you're the only one
now who can appease Pele and ask her forgiveness for what your
father did."

There was something eerie about the way Marla's voice dropped to
a whisper as she spoke, and I knew that she was deadly serious. Not
liking the rock in my hand, I set it down quickly.

She went on, her low voice weaving its spell. "Remember where
you are, Caroline. This is *Maui*. There are mysteries here that men
have never touched—good and evil. I don't want to deny any of the
old powers. Protect us, Caroline—please. You were born here. You
are Keith's daughter."

But I had grown up in the modern world of the mainland, and I
hadn't learned to listen to the voices Marla seemed to hear. She saw
doubt in my face, even though I didn't put it into words.

"It really did happen, didn't it?" she challenged. "There was damage to all of us—and it's still going on. In Noelle. Even in my mother
and in me. Perhaps in Tom O'Neill too, since he's never had what he
wanted from life."

"What do you think Tom has wanted that he doesn't have?" I
asked.

She looked a little sly. "Of course you were too young to know what
was going on—in fact, it was before you were born. What Tom never
stopped wanting was Noelle. He was in love with her when we were
all very young. Though of course after Keith appeared, Tom didn't
stand a chance. He's never married, and after the accident Noelle
was lost to him in other ways. But Tom doesn't matter anymore—he
belongs to the past. What interests me a lot more is the present, as I
know it interests you. I was sitting here by the window when you and
David came up to the house. Koma was waiting, and he and David
went off together. What are they cooking up now?"

"If you heard them, Marla, then you know as much as I do. Koma
wanted to talk to David, so I came inside."

"Yes, I gathered that. And they're still out there, since I haven't
heard their cars leave. Koma brings trouble. He cares too much about
the old ways and I hate to see David get involved."

"But you were just talking about the old ways as though you believe in them, Marla."

"I was talking about the *old gods.* Koma wants to throw the *haoles* out and go back to the land for the people. That would mean fishing and raising taro and living in houses with grass roofs! There are some who can still do that, but I don't think it's for Koma. He just likes to stir things up because of the anger that's always eating at him. I suppose what happened to his mother still sticks in his craw, so he doesn't like white skins. Do you remember Ailina?"

The name seemed vaguely familiar. "I seem to remember someone singing . . ."

"She's the one. But you wouldn't know about the rest, of course, and maybe that's just as well."

With that tantalizing remark, Marla walked toward the door.

"If Koma doesn't like white skins," I said, "how does he happen to share a house with David?"

"David's different. He can get into other people's skins. He's on Koma's side in a lot of ways. They became friends when they worked together as park rangers."

As she stepped into the hall, Marla paused, listening. Then she said, "Come along with me. Maybe something's going on that we should know about."

She turned to the right down the long hall, and I followed her, curious now, and at the same time uneasy. The main stairs by which I'd come up were on the left of my bedroom door, but there were other, narrower stairs at the far end of the house. Marla hurried toward them and leaned upon the guardrail at the top.

Voices came up to me—Tom's and my grandmother's. I didn't want to listen, and I started to turn away.

Marla's smile was derisive. "I suppose your Grandmother Elizabeth taught you to behave properly and never eavesdrop! But you'd better forget that, since they're talking about you—right now."

When Tom O'Neill spoke my name, nothing could have budged me.

"Caroline's bad luck, Joanna," he was saying. "You don't want her to get too close to Noelle, do you?"

"Noelle carries her own protection." Joanna spoke sadly.

"Better be smart before it's too late. Caroline Kirby isn't that little Caro you remember anymore. No more than she's Noelle's Linny. Let her stay a few days and then send her home."

"I suppose that's what I must do. Yet sometimes I almost hope . . ."

"What you hope isn't possible, and it might even be dangerous—for Noelle. She's better off the way things are."

Joanna spoke with more of her old spirit. "That's only a notion you've cooked up, Tom. Maybe the truth would be easier for all of us to face. Easier than the way we've lived."

"What truth?" He answered her uncertainty with impatience. "Whose truth? Do you really know? I gave you what I found in the crater, and you didn't turn it over to the police. I didn't think you would. You didn't want any real questions to start about what happened up there. You wouldn't want that."

"I *should* have given it to the police! I shouldn't have let myself become frightened. But with Noelle the way she was—I waited. And then it was too late."

"Let her stay that way, Joanna. You know it's best."

"Sometimes I don't know anything. Maybe that's why I was so happy when Caro telephoned me from San Francisco. Perhaps she's the one person who could be good for Noelle. Isn't that possible?"

I could hear Tom in the room below, not answering her, though his very movements sounded angry.

"Go home, Tom," she told him. "I'm tired and I don't want to talk about this anymore tonight. There's a lot I need to think about."

"Don't do anything foolish you'll be sorry for," he said. "Just get rid of Caroline as quickly as you can."

I heard him go off along the lower hall, and turned toward my room, feeling a little sick. Marla came with me.

"Are you all right, Caroline?"

"Not really. I feel as though I'd stepped into quicksand—as though I might sink any minute. What did they mean?"

"You won't sink! You've got a lot of your Grandma Joanna's gumption. It was there when you were little, and it's been showing in spurts ever since you arrived. Just don't do anything silly and impulsive. For Noelle's sake."

I steadied myself. "Marla, do you understand what they were talking about—Joanna and Tom?"

"Maybe I don't want to understand. I was unconscious that day, and a piece of my memory never came back. It's gone in a different way from what happened to Noelle. Do you see this scar?" She pushed her bangs back from one temple and I saw the triangular white mark. "That's where Pilikia's hoof struck me. Though there was no lasting damage. I came through fine in the end. But I think they're right, Caroline. Your best bet is to get away from all this as soon as you can. Don't try to learn anything more than you can handle. It won't help Noelle, anyway. When you're gone, we can go back to living in our safe fantasy, where nothing more can touch us."

"Like the truth about my father's murder?" I asked.

The mischief that often lurked in her eyes was gone, and the smile lines were only wrinkles. "Don't ever think such a thing! Let it alone! It's much too late for all this talk about truth. Tom's right about that. I'll see you in the morning. We're up early at Manaolana. Good night, Caroline."

She went into her room and closed the door firmly. I thought of David's words about pressed flowers. Were some of them starting to open? I remembered those of my childhood—once open they could never close again.

Weariness took over as I got ready for bed, yet I felt stirred up at the same time. For a few moments I stood at the open window where cool air washed away the warmth of the day. October was a pleasant month on Maui—not really hot, and here on the mountain it was always cool at night. The quiet seemed intense at first, until I began to listen to the small sounds—insects, a horse stamping in his stall, the barking of a dog. Car sounds were few, so I heard the nearby engine start. Then a car drove away, followed by another. So Koma and David had finished their talking and had finally left. I was no longer interested. Too much else had intruded.

When I turned off the lights and got into the wide four-poster bed, it was only to lie awake thinking, as I was afraid I would do. I didn't dare puzzle over Marla's visit to my room, or about the conversation I'd overheard between Joanna and Tom. In that direction lay the quicksands I dared not step into. Yet I hated to think of Scott, as I so often did before I fell asleep.

If I could just let him go entirely, but my memories were so mixed. In the beginning he'd been fun to be with. He'd brought a lighter, more playful note into my life, and it wasn't until after we'd been married for months that I began to see what a put-down of others most of his funny stories were. At first I'd been impressed because he had so much talent as an artist. But it was quickly evident that he wasn't going to work at his painting or do anything with it.

He was in total agreement with Grandmother Elizabeth in so many ways, and of course that pleased her, though sometimes it seemed to put me on the outside against them both. They shared the same degree of narrow intolerance for so many things that I liked and enjoyed. Intolerance for people, mostly.

What a shock Hawaii must have been for my grandmother. Never mind that a great many different races lived in San Francisco—there she was able to mix only with her own kind and ignore whatever lay outside. In Hawaii she must have found that altogether too many mixes of people lived together, more or less accepting one another. Of course, it had been my adventurous father who had brought her to Maui for a visit after he'd been married to my mother for several years, and I had been born. He had fallen in love with the island, just as he'd fallen in love with Noelle. He'd often talked to me lightly about both his loves, and I'd felt safe because my mother and father loved each other and loved me.

My thoughts were not helping me to sleep. Noelle could be the key to everything. How could I let her stay frozen and lost, no matter what happened? I must do *something*—I must make a plan. Not much time was left to me, and tomorrow I must begin. Suddenly I knew the first thing I would attempt.

In the morning I would go with David Reed to the house where my mother and father and I had once lived so happily. At least, Ahinahina had seemed a happy place to me then. Not as exciting, of course, as my Grandma Joanna's house, where something was always happening. But there must have been happy times there for Noelle that she would remember better than I. So tomorrow we must take her with us. Perhaps we could give her an experience that would prompt some chain of memory that would start her on the road back. Her mind had moments of lucidity so that I sensed a consciousness in her, however long buried. Even my own presence might stir some hidden memory to life.

Now at last I could relax a little and begin to feel drowsy. Pictures began to form in my mind and run along of their own accord on an unwinding reel. I was content to let my thoughts wander while I watched what appeared on the screen of my memory.

Strangely, the pictures didn't concern Scott or my father, or even Joanna as she used to be. Though Noelle was there. The time that came back to me was a long-ago day spent with my mother and a young David, whom I still knew so much better than the man he had become.

The excursion had begun easily. My mother had been a great fiction reader, so she sometimes drove down to Wailuku to the main library of Maui. David had been visiting Manaolana at the time, so on this occasion my mother invited David to come with us.

"I'm going to Wailuku early in the morning," she told him. "If you like, I'll drive you up Iao Valley and you can take Linny into the gorge. She's never seen the Needle. Then I'll go back to town and when I'm through at the library I'll pick you up at the Japanese Gardens. We can take a picnic lunch and it will be fun."

My mother always made whatever we did seem fun. David liked the idea, and I was enthusiastic. A whole adventure in the company of my hero! What more could a little girl ask?

It was easy to remember the way my mother had been, because I'd found her not all that much different. Except that there was no gaiety in her now. Old memories that I'd shut away were pouring back.

I'd loved the drive down the mountain, with the sea coming closer, and the marvelous view of West Maui across the isthmus. The West Maui mountains had always seemed more mysterious to me than Haleakala, which lived on my horizon every day. Haleakala's drama lay beyond her summit, where I'd never been. The West Maui mountains didn't rise to our mountain's more than ten thousand feet, but their jagged peaks always looked dramatic and inviting.

We drove across the flat plain where nothing much had grown until two sons of missionaries, who were pioneers in the sugar industry, brought water clear from wet country near Hana, and the isthmus came to life with sugarcane fields. Wailuku was just across the plain on West Maui, beyond the larger, commercial city of Kahului. Visitors were always confused by the *k*'s in Hawaiian place names, but I'd loved to click them on my tongue when I was little.

Even as a little girl, I knew what Wailuku meant. Stories of old Hawaii were my fairy tales, my giants and dragons, except that some of them were true.

A great battle had been fought in Iao Valley and the narrow gorge that ran up to the Needle. There Kamehameha the Great had defeated the chief who opposed him on Maui. David had told me that the king had the advantage of guns given him by foreigners, so it hadn't been a fair fight against spears and shields. The gorge had run crimson with blood from the awful slaughter that gave the town its name. Wailuku meant "river of blood."

But all that was distant history on that lovely autumn day when my mother left us to climb the black gorge on foot, while she drove back to town for her books.

Perhaps I'd loved David so much as a little girl because while he

was always kind, he never made fun of me, he expected me to live up
to whatever physical demand he might put upon me. That my legs
were so much shorter than his didn't matter. He would wait for me,
and he would slow his own stride. He would even lift me over some
rocky place that I found it hard to climb, but he would never carry
me, as my father was so quick to do. And with David, I never com-
plained. I *had* to keep up. His excitement about whatever he
planned was catching, and I could be excited too.

We followed the easy trail that climbed the gorge toward the
Needle, and he told me of times when, along with other boys, he'd
clambered over the great boulders down in the stream. That would
be much too rough going for me. Partway up, we stopped at a place
where we could watch the "river" that had once run with blood—
now tumbling peacefully toward the sea, its voice filled with ripples
and gurgles of musical sound. The sun, risen high enough by this
time, made the water sparkle with light as it leapt over black rocks.
David, already interested in camera effects, pointed out the contrast
between white water and the dark, shadowed recesses of rock. He
made everything interesting and alive for me. Not even Grandma
Joanna was as exciting to be with as David. Part of it was that he liked
to make things *happen.*

But the gorge hadn't been all black rocks and water. The mountains came steeply down on either side, lush and green, narrowing to
the valley. Candlenut trees grew so thickly in some places that they
made a glorious soft cover that was a lighter green than the mountains, hiding the water. Kukui trees, Hawaiians called them. In fact,
they looked so soft and feathery that I told David I'd like to jump
right off the trail and be caught in all that bouncy green. He'd said I'd
better not try—I'd go crashing right through to the rocks in the
stream below.

That was the day he promised to bring me a kukui nut lei—but he
never did. Not after what happened in the crater just a little while
later.

I remembered something else he had told me about the history of
the gorge.

"Once not even fighting armies could have lived down here, Caro.
This was all volcano fire. Lava built up the Needle and through
millions of years it wore down to the way it looks now. From here it
seems green and soft because of all the tree ferns clinging to its sides.
But it's lava rock underneath. We've come at the right time—later in
the day there'll be clouds hiding the top."

The things David had told me, taught me, still seemed to echo through my mind as I relived that day.

The Needle was a spectacular formation. A curve in the road below made it suddenly visible, where it thrust twelve hundred feet straight up above the valley floor, cutting into a blue Hawaiian sky.

We'd climbed a hill where we could best view it, and everything around us seemed as quiet as if we'd been in a church, with only the birds singing choir. I could still see the shining look in David's eyes. For once I'd asked no questions, and because of his own vivid imaginings I could picture—not the warriors fighting Kamehameha's army —but the roaring flames of the volcano all this had once been part of. When I reached my hand to touch the black rock of an outcropping, I was surprised to find it cold. On the way down it had been comforting to hold on to David's large, sure hand.

Now I lay in my bed of koa wood at Manaolana and marveled that all of that wonderful day had somehow been preserved in my consciousness, so that it could surface in pictures that were almost intact. Of course, there were gaps that I could never fill. About the rest of the day, I remembered only vaguely that we'd gone to the Heritage Gardens to see the Japanese pavilion with its green tiles and red columns. We'd followed walks among plantings, and crossed an arched bridge over a pond. My mother had driven up to meet us there, but I remembered nothing else of our picnic, or of the trip home.

It was enough. This would be my "peaceful place" to return to in my mind when I needed it. A small girl who was long gone, and a boy of twelve who didn't exist anymore, could still occupy that lovely gorge below the Needle and bring me comfort. I went to sleep feeling my fingers once more in David's strong, protecting clasp.

It's strange the way vivid dreams, or vivid relivings of the past, can affect one afterwards. Joanna had invited David to come for breakfast, and when he walked into the kitchen, I found myself looking at him with a new self-consciousness that was almost embarrassment. I wondered if he had ever relived our trip to the Needle. But of course he couldn't have. He probably had no idea of all he'd meant to a small girl that day, or of how deeply I'd loved him with a child's yearning, innocent affection.

Marla was already at the big table when I came in, and she smiled at me, and then quickly gave me another look. I think she recognized that I'd gone into some new place in my mind. Joanna caught the change in me too, and her eyes seemed thoughtful as they rested on me.

Once or twice as we ate, David glanced my way, questioningly, and I realized that I'd been staring at him, trying to find *my* David in this grown man who was a stranger to me.

I wrenched my thoughts from pleasant memories and gave myself determinedly to the disturbing present. Noelle was *now*, and when she drifted into the kitchen, greeting us all vaguely, and with no memory of having met me yesterday, I tried to face the immensity of the challenge I'd set myself. How could I possibly reach my mother in the short time before Joanna would send me away?

At least Tom wasn't with us this morning. He had breakfasted earlier, and Joanna had been up in time to serve him, since Susy Ohara wouldn't come in until later. In the past, Joanna had been accustomed to cooking for the ranch hands some of the time. Only because she liked to. In those days there'd been a lot more help. Tom would probably disapprove of my taking Noelle with us to Ahinahina, and he might have opposed me openly, swaying Joanna.

"Do you remember our family parties?" Joanna asked, sitting down beside me with her coffee. "A lot of us are more or less related up here on the mountain. The Baldwins and other families went into raising sugar, pineapple, and ranching, and some of them built homes up here. But there are enough of the older family members left who are curious about you, Caro, and dying to meet you. I'm holding them off."

"Why shouldn't I meet some of them while I'm here?" I asked.

Joanna looked at David, who had been listening with interest. "You tell her for me," she directed.

As he spoke I again found myself trying to find the boy I remembered in his man's face, with its dark look that still seemed exciting. For a moment last night he had been touched with that quality that I'd loved as a child, but which now made me uneasy.

"By this time people call it the Legend of the Crater," he said. "There are a lot of different versions about what happened. It shocked the whole area. Especially when nobody could give a clear account of what happened and your father suffered two wounds. There was still more buzzing because of your mother's state, and when your San Francisco grandmother took you away. Sympathetic buzzing, since everyone was concerned about Joanna. Over the years it all died down. But now that you've returned, you can't help being a center of interest. That's just what Joanna doesn't want to see revived." He looked at my grandmother. "Is that the story?"

"Yes. That's about the way it is, Caroline," Joanna said. "We don't want the whole thing dredged up again."

Across the table Noelle was buttering toast, and paying no attention. Her own protective shield seemed to close about her so that little meaning touched her. Sometimes it took an effort to gain her attention. This was exactly what I had to break through. Every instinct told me that it was better for her to be hurt, to feel pain again, because only then could she adjust to living in the present. Now she was in a limbo where nothing existed except in the most trivial way. Morning was a time for courage, a time for action.

I spoke to her deliberately, touching her hand. "Noelle, David is taking me to Ahinahina this morning. Do you remember? That's the house where you used to live a long time ago. Would you like to come with us?"

Marla made a sound of protest, but Noelle was already responding.

"Ahinahina," she repeated softly. "Do you know what that means in Hawaiian? It means *very gray.*"

"That's why it's the name given the silversword," I said. "It was a beautiful name to give our house."

Joanna noticed the pronoun and looked unhappy, but Noelle didn't hear it because another word had caught her attention.

"Yes, I know Ahinahina means silversword. That's a monstrous plant. Sometimes I dream about it at night."

"I've never seen a silversword," I said carefully. "It grows only in the crater, doesn't it—and I've never been up there. But I've seen pictures and I thought it was a beautiful plant. Especially when it's in bloom."

Noelle shivered. "All those little gray sabers of leaves—with tiny hairs all over them!" She shook her fingers, as though to free them of cobwebs.

"You're being silly," Marla told her. "They *are* beautiful." She went on to explain to me. "There used to be thousands of them growing wild up there—until feral goats nearly wiped them out. They grow in large rosette shapes for ten years or so, low to the ground. And then the plant shoots up a great stalk covered with purple flowers that can grow as tall as a man. It blooms once in its lifetime and then it dies."

Noelle flung down her napkin and jumped up from the table. "I don't want to listen!" she cried, and ran out of the room. For once something had come through to her strongly.

"I'll go after her," Marla said.

I got up too. "I'll go with you." She didn't want me, but she couldn't stop me, and I followed her out of the house in Noelle's wake. I wondered if Marla had upset her sister deliberately—and if so, why? She turned toward the rose garden, and I hurried beside her.

"Is it because of what happened in the crater that talk about silverswords upsets her?" I asked. "Your mother said she was sitting beside one of those plants tearing up its leaves when they found her."

Marla stopped with her hand on my arm. "Maybe you'd better let me handle this alone. You *can't* take her to Ahinahina. Just hearing the name sends her into a frenzy."

Perhaps that was what Marla had been trying to prove to me. She stood beside me on the path, looking plump and inscrutable—and determined.

"Please," I said. "I want her to come back to me, Marla. Is that so terrible?"

"Maybe it is." She hurried ahead of me, moving easily in flat-heeled shoes, her usual *muumuu* floating as she ran down steps into the tangle that had once been the rose garden.

I followed her to where Noelle sat once more on the bench of lava rock, turning a rose she'd plucked in her fingers. She looked perfectly calm and happy, and I realized that she had no recollection of what had just happened, or why she'd run out here. As quickly as that her agitation had vanished.

"Hello, Marla," she said, and looked at me. "Tell me who this is. Have I met you before?"

I wanted to reach across the chasm between us and snatch her back to reality. I wanted to tell her exactly who I was, but Marla's hand restrained me again. "It won't do any good, Caroline. She's already lost her way again."

Nevertheless, there was something she might understand and I moved from Marla's touch. "David is driving me over this morning, Noelle, and we'd like you to come with us. We're going to visit an interesting house, and you might enjoy the trip. It's not far away."

She smiled readily—that empty smile, with none of the gaiety I'd loved in my mother as a little girl.

"Of course," she said, "I'd love to go."

Marla sighed. "Okay—it's on your head, Caroline. At least David will know what to do if she gets upset. He's pretty good with her and she likes him. Anyway, she won't even know where she is unless you tell her."

It seemed to me that her words carried an undertone of malice, and I began to wonder about Marla's "kindness" toward her sister.

"I plan to tell her." I knew I sounded grim, but Marla was clearly part of the whole plan to keep Noelle exactly where she was.

On impulse I told her about David's analogy of the pressed Japanese flowers. "She's one of them, Marla. I want to see her open again—I have to try."

"There's something you aren't considering," she told me. Sometimes Marla could gaze off into space in a way that seemed to remove her from the scene around her—but not in the absent way Noelle took flight. There could be a sort of—mysticism?—about Marla, as though she could see beyond veils. "Those water flowers—I had them too as a little girl. Only mine were different. Mother got them from an elderly Japanese friend who made them himself. His flowers were especially beautiful—but sometimes they weren't flowers. They would open into snakes or toads, or wicked little Japanese foxes. Just the heads grinning up at you, instead of the flowers you expected. So be careful, Caroline. David's flower idea could bring you monsters. Let's go back to breakfast now."

I had thought too that the flowers, once opened, might not be beautiful, and David had said the same thing.

Marla took Noelle's arm to raise her from the bench, and guided her back to the house. I followed soberly, wondering if I might really be the insensitive blunderer my grandmother and aunt thought me. At least, there was one reassuring element. If I upset Noelle, she possessed her own escape mechanism that would return her to a world she seemed to prefer. But there was no one left but me to find, not just my mother, but a woman who was still young enough to have years of life ahead of her, and whose state cried out for rescue.

In any case, arguments for or against didn't really matter. I had to try.

6

Before we got into David's car, Joanna took me aside for a moment. "I don't like what you're doing, Caro. You see your own imaginary goal, though it's one that can't be achieved. Don't you suppose we've tried? Now you're ready to ignore all the possible disasters along the way."

When I didn't answer she went on. "At least be gentle with your mother. She's suffered enough."

"Of course I'll be gentle. Why wouldn't I be?" I knew I sounded impatient—perhaps because I couldn't entirely reassure myself, let alone my grandmother.

"She's much more easily disturbed than you realize. And you haven't seen what can happen. She goes to pieces in quite an alarming way. You might at least take Marla with you."

"No! I want to have a chance with her alone. That house must be filled with happy memories for her. Even I can remember happy times there."

"Were they happy, Caroline? Perhaps not always, so do be careful."

There was nothing more she could say, and she stood watching as we went out to David's car.

I'd put on a wraparound khaki skirt with a yellow flowered blouse, and as Noelle walked with me, happy enough now, and interested, she pleased me with a comment.

"That's a nice outfit you're wearing, Caroline. You're very pretty. I hope these jeans are all right—I thought we might be walking around a lot."

I thanked her and told her she looked fine. She had topped her jeans with a white shirt, tucked in to show the figure of a girl. Her short honey-blond hair was tied with a blue ribbon, though locks of it escaped across her cheeks. She'd tucked a yellow ginger blossom over one ear, and I could catch the familiar scent. She seemed so normal, and so much like the young mother I remembered. But that was one of the things that was wrong—that she should seem in some ways younger than her daughter.

Noelle got dreamily into the back seat, while I sat in front beside David. By this time I'd made the transition from old memories of our trip to the Needle and had returned to the present where he was merely a man I'd just met and knew very little about. Though I liked the look of him. If I were honest, I had to admit that.

He'd brought along his camera equipment and said that while he was taking pictures we could wander as we pleased. The art society members were out on a field trip today, so I could take Noelle around inside and watch to see whatever might spark her recognition.

It was less than a mile to Ahinahina, and we parked near a grove of monkeypod trees, their wonderfully symmetrical branches forming a feathery green canopy overhead. The long pods hung down like black exclamation marks amid the green. I'd always loved these trees when I was little. I could lie on the grass and look up at the pods and make up stories about them. Until insects, or pineapple bugs, began to bother me. I hadn't thought of pineapple bugs in years, but I knew what it was as one batted my face when I left the car.

I opened the back door and Noelle got out. Ahinahina had been created grandly in the Italianate style by its builder, and it was an enormous rectangle in shape, with a red tiled roof, white stucco walls, and arched doorways. The front door was unlocked and we stepped into an anteroom at the foot of a graceful, curving stairway that rose along the wall and was guarded by a wrought-iron rail.

I recognized the staircase at once—remembered my beautiful young mother drifting down it as though she floated. In my memory she was always laughing, and it seemed eerie to stand here and recall that light laughter that had sounded so joyously in this very place. Now the same woman stood beside me, dreamy and wistful, with a vacant smile, but no laughter to bubble over.

She drew away from me, as though something stirred in her, and walked to the foot of the stairs. There she stood looking up, and for a moment seemed puzzled, as though searching for something. Then she put her hand on the rail and started up.

David had come in behind us. "Better go with her, Caroline. I want to take some shots down here, and I'll come up later. Don't push her

—I expect they've warned you that her emotional balance is always precarious."

I nodded and started up after her. A stained-glass window shed jeweled spangles upon the stairs, and I stopped to look up at the marvelous bird of paradise in the glass. For me, it was a moment of recognition that held me enchanted. The bird was an old friend, about whom I'd made up fanciful stories.

Noelle too was staring at the bird, and I saw that her smile had become more real, more aware—though hers was a different enchantment from mine.

"Keith always calls that bird Turkey," she said. "He likes to give things silly names, and he was talking to it just this morning. He said, 'How would you like to have *your* feathers taken for the king's cape, Old Turkey?' "

The present tense she'd used told me her confused time sequence hadn't changed, but at least the house had made her recall something amusing from the past.

"I remember his saying that," I told her gently. "Do you remember what you said to him?"

"Of course. I told the bird up there that he didn't need to worry because only the underfeathers of the *iiwi* birds were used for those cloaks. Beautiful red feathers—used only for the *alii*. It took the royal feather pluckers years to collect enough for one cape."

"Wasn't there an *o'o* bird too—?"

"Yes!" Her eyes were bright with remembering. "The *o'o* bird had tufts of yellow feathers around its tail. When my mother told me about this I cried, until she explained that those birds weren't hurt. They just flew off to grow more feathers."

Now she was remembering back to her own childhood—farther than I wanted her to go. She seemed not to have noticed that I'd put myself in the picture.

She gestured toward the jeweled colored bird in the window. "Linny likes to make up stories about Old Turkey. She calls it a magic bird." For the first time since I'd returned, she laughed softly, echoing her own long-ago laughter, and went on up the stairs. She was simply taking this house for granted as part of her present world. There was no time warp here—time for her had simply stopped.

When we reached the second floor she stood still, looking down the long hall that fronted the house running almost its entire width. Doors opened on one side and big windows on the other. The spaces between the doors held tall cupboards and tiers of drawers, all painted white clear to the high white ceiling. There had been some changes here and they seemed to disorient my mother, so that she stood bewildered.

"It doesn't look right. Something's changed," she murmured.

I gestured toward the first corner room. "Let's explore this one, shall we?" It had been the bedroom she had shared with my father, and my nursery had been next door. How clearly it all came back to me—and so far, pleasantly.

She walked willingly enough into the corner room and stared about. It was unfurnished now, except for turntables in use by the sculptors who worked here. There were a few stools, and a long table covered with tools in disarray. On two or three stands clay models stood covered with damp cloth to keep them moist.

Noelle looked even more bewildered. "Where are we?" she asked.

"This is Ahinahina," I told her. "You used to live here a long time ago."

She dismissed my words. "No! Of course it's not Ahinahina! I picked out the furniture for our bedroom myself, and you can see that it isn't here."

"Isn't the chandelier the same?" I asked. "And look out the windows at the view—you can surely recognize that."

We walked to a corner window, where I'd been held up by my father so I could look out at the tremendous sweep of the mountain on one hand, and the distant sea on the other. In between, over lower treetops, the West Maui mountains stood up clearly far across the plain that had once been water, making this two islands. Haleakala's less craggy slopes rose nearer at hand, though it was still a long way up to the elusive summit.

I remembered. I could almost feel my father's arms holding me, loving and protecting. Such a safe place to be. My mother stood close and I put my arm about her, needing her in that moment of loss.

For Noelle, however, these views were familiar, so that she took them for granted as though they had no connection with this house.

"Did you ever go into the crater?" I asked softly.

"No—I never did." Her rejection was complete. "It's a terrible place. I never want to go up there. Not among all those silverswords!"

She ran away from me into the next room and stood looking around, growing more disturbed.

"This is Linny's room—it must be! But what has happened to it? Where are all her darling things? She loves this room—and it's empty now. Just a lot of easels and stools that don't belong here. And those paintings on the walls—I don't like them. I picked lovely Hawaiian scenes for her to look at. Something is terribly wrong—what is it? What have they done with my little girl?"

She'd begun to shiver, and this time I put both arms around her, trying not to shiver myself. I was taller now than she was, and stronger. She felt slight and frail in my arms, as though anything at all might break her. The scent of ginger blossoms was just as I remembered, but now she was the child and I the adult, holding and soothing her.

"It's all right," I said. "You'll find Linny. I promise you'll find her. Though she may be different by this time, you know."

She rested her cheek trustingly against mine for a moment, responding to loving touch as she always had. Then she pulled herself away. "Of course I'll find her! Perhaps she's in one of the other rooms. Let's go and look!"

Before I could stop her, she darted off, running down the long hall toward the far end of the house. I went after her more slowly, watching to see where she would go. Many of these rooms had remained empty when we'd lived here. Except for guest rooms, and rooms for the housekeeper and my Japanese nursemaid, my parents hadn't needed them. I remembered how the empty rooms had fascinated me, and how I'd loved to play in them, pretending I lived in a castle. There was one special room at the far end—a room with a balcony. . . .

This was the room Noelle had run toward, disappearing through the door. I followed and stood still to watch her. It was a corner room that opened upon the balcony I remembered.

"Linny?" Noelle called. "Linny dear, don't hide from me!"

"I don't think she's here right now," I told her gently.

Noelle paid no attention but ran onto the balcony to look down upon the wide rear lawn. I went to stand beside her. A small fountain in the garden near the end of the house was no longer in use, but there were still tennis courts beyond, though now they were overgrown with weeds. A strange feeling touched me—a strong anxiety that was close to panic. Something had happened down there in the yard—something I'd shut away all these years because I didn't want to remember.

My mother stood at the iron rail, her gaze fixed, as though she had once more lost herself in time. Because she too was remembering? "Tell me," I said. "Please tell me what happened down there?" She shook her head—not in denial but as if to clear away the mists.

"I can remember moonlight—after a warm day. I wore a white dress —an off-the-shoulder dress that floated when I walked. There was music . . ." Her words died away, her expression puzzled, searching.

"Yes—go on!"

"There was a party we gave down there one night, Keith and I. With Hawaiian music and singing."

Her voice faded out, because I too was remembering—moonlight. And Japanese lanterns hanging from the trees. The air was like velvet on my skin. My mother had told me I could watch from this balcony for a little while before I went to bed. That night my father had been more wonderful-looking than any other man, just as my mother was more beautiful than other women. He'd worn an embroidered shirt of pineapple cloth from the Philippines that hung outside his silky black trousers. I'd loved to see him in that shirt. I could pretend that he smelled of pineapples, just as my mother did of ginger blossoms.

Grandma Joanna was there too, and my Aunt Marla, both wearing fine *holokus* with little trains that swished as they walked. Chairs had been placed informally around on the grass, and some of my grandmother's Hawaiian friends had come to entertain with songs of their islands. I could *see* them down there—hear them! A man with an ukulele had sung a funny song in his own language, and then translated, so that everyone laughed.

But most of all I remembered a tall, beautiful woman in a *muumuu* printed with flame-colored flowers, and a wreath of scarlet blossoms around her dark, flowing hair. A lei of red and white hung about her neck, and she was even younger than my mother, and almost as beautiful.

The song she sang was of love that would never end, even when one of the lovers went far away across the sea. Her hands moved gracefully to the accompaniment of a steel guitar, and there was a drum picking up the rhythm in the background. When the woman finished her song the drum kept on throbbing—like a heartbeat. The beat of a heart that was breaking.

It was so sad that I had cried. I stood on my high balcony, looking down through the bars, since my head didn't top the rail, and tears ran down my face. I ached with the beauty and sadness of the song and the Hawaiian night. The drum stopped, and the woman laughed, bowing to applause. Then she took the circlet of scarlet flowers from her head and tossed it into the audience. My father caught it and he was laughing too.

That was when the night had turned suddenly ugly. My lovely gentle mother changed into someone I'd never seen before—someone who frightened me. I couldn't understand her wild words, but the sound of them was terrifying, and I saw my father fling his arms about her, not lovingly but to hold her back from whatever she meant to do. The rest of the party scattered, hurrying toward the ballroom. The musicians faded away with their instruments, leaving only the singer standing very proud and still—unfrightened, though my mother seemed to threaten her.

I had been so terrified by something I didn't understand that I'd started to scream. Three faces, raised in the moonlight, had stared up at me as my nursemaid came to quiet me and bring me inside. I clung to the bars for a moment longer and saw the singer disappear around the end of the house, while my father pulled my mother into one of the rooms below. As he drew her inside, I could hear his words—and now I remembered them, though I hadn't understood at the time.

"Hysterical!" he'd shouted at her. "Disgraceful! You're crazy—out of your head!"

My nursemaid took me to my room, but I lay wide awake in my bed, sobbing, until my father came to soothe and hold and reassure me. I'd loved him so much, and he had loved me more than I would ever be loved again. He told me that something had upset my mother, but she would feel better in the morning, and it was nothing I should worry about.

I went to sleep in his arms, and I couldn't remember very much else, except that I was told my mother had a sick headache and must stay in bed for a few days. I wasn't allowed to see her, and when she came out of her room something was different. Perhaps the seeds of change in her had started even then—because she really was fragile and couldn't handle reality.

All this had swept back to me in a flooding wave of memory, and when Noelle swayed against me now, I held her tenderly. She had remembered too—some of it at least.

"It's all right," I said. "All that was a long time ago. You mustn't grieve about it anymore."

She looked at me with tears filling her eyes. "He stopped loving me, you know—because of *her*. I can't remember her name anymore, but it wasn't her fault. She was very young. Younger than I was —and Keith was like that."

I didn't want to believe any of this—not my own memory, nor what she was saying, though she sounded perfectly sensible now, and she was using the past tense. All I could do was hold her close.

"It doesn't matter. It's all right now," I whispered.

With her own quiet dignity she stepped back from my arms, perhaps wondering why a stranger should try to comfort her so lovingly. "No," she said, "it *doesn't* matter. Keith is dead. He died a long time ago."

In this moment, when troubling memories had returned, she could face what was real, and I wondered if I dared take her a step farther toward recognizing me. But before I could speak, her expression changed to one of alarm—that wild, senseless alarm that could come upon her so easily.

"We've frightened Linny!" she cried. "I heard her screaming. I must find her—she needs me now."

What she heard was an echo ringing far back in the years, but I couldn't hold her, and again she ran away from me down the long hallway toward the stairs where we'd come up.

David had just reached the top, the camera he'd been using slung around his neck. As Noelle ran past, he caught her by the arm.

"We'll go with you," he said. "Slow down, Noelle."

She shook him off. "She's gone outside. I know where she'll be!"

David let her go, watching me as I came toward him. "You've been seeing ghosts too, haven't you?"

I couldn't tell him, and I only shook my head. We hurried down the winding stairway together, following my mother.

Noelle found her way to an arched doorway that led to the rear grounds. There'd been no rain lately in this up-country area, but though the grass was brown, trees shook their green branches in trade winds that were still blowing. Shallow steps led to a lower level, covered now by that wild growth which waited everywhere to take back its own territory from human encroachment.

"I must speak to the gardener," Noelle said, and avoided steps no longer used by running down a sloping bank. Far across the brown lawn on the right stretched the overgrown tennis courts, and the sight of these seemed to disturb my mother all the more. I could remember her playing on those courts and being very good at the game. Friends often came over to play with my parents, and sometimes Noelle had played against my grandmother, who always beat her. I was too small to hold a racket, but my mother had promised to teach me when I was older.

As she ran, a protruding root tripped her. She fell to her knees and

I reached her before David to kneel on dry grass, trying once more to quiet her.

"She's hiding from me!" Noelle cried. "Sometimes she can be such a naughty little girl. Linny, where are you? Don't frighten me like this!"

I couldn't bear what was happening, and I held her shoulders with firm hands and looked directly into those sea-gray eyes that broke my heart with their lack of comprehension.

"Listen to me," I said. "You *must* listen to me. A little while ago you remembered that Keith is dead—that he died a long time ago. Now you must try to remember more."

She grew quiet under my hands, as a child might when faced with adult authority.

"Let her be," David said, but it was too late for that.

"I brought you here this morning to help you to remember," I told her. "To *really* remember. Twenty-six years have gone by since you lived here with Keith and Linny. Everything has changed. When you find Linny again, she will be grown up—not a child anymore. I know it will hurt for you to understand this, but until you can accept what's real and face it, you can't return to your real life. You won't ever find Linny again the way you remember her, but it could be very satisfying for you both to find your grownup daughter."

For a moment she seemed to look deep into my eyes, questioning, and for a moment there was sensibility in her own. She put out a searching hand and touched my hair lightly. "It's very dark, almost like Keith's."

I held my breath, but she took her hand away at once, and I knew I'd lost her again.

"Why are we here?" she questioned. "What is this place?"

There was no use pushing her further now. I helped her to her feet and we started back across the lawn with David.

"I've finished my work, so let's take her home," he said to me. "I'm afraid this has been harder for you, Caro, than for Noelle. She has a safe place where she can hide from what's real. You haven't any such escape."

I fought back weakening tears. I wasn't ready to cry—not yet. If the dam I'd built against grief ever broke, I was afraid I'd go tossing downstream and out of control. Luckily, I could still hang on to my emotions.

David stopped to take one more outdoor shot as an afterthought, and Noelle watched him, her face bright and empty. She knew David and liked him. A few pineapple bugs zoomed in as we waited, and I batted them away—a familiar gesture.

When we returned to the car and I got into the back seat beside Noelle, I didn't put my arm about her this time, because she had gone far away. She didn't need or want my touch and I was a stranger again. Perhaps *I* was the foolish one—needing *her,* trying to recover what was lost to me in the past. The scent of ginger blossoms seemed heavy and cloying.

The moment we arrived at Manaolana, Marla came running to meet us, her anxiety clear as she pulled open the car door and helped Noelle out. When she'd touched her sister's face lightly with her fingers and peered into her eyes, she seemed reassured, finding no marks of change.

"She's perfectly all right," I told Marla, sounding more caustic than I intended.

My aunt stared at me. "But you aren't, are you?"

"She really came back for a few moments," I told her. "She remembered what was real. She *knows* that my father is dead."

Marla sighed. "That's nothing new—it never lasts. Why can't you be sensible and give up, Caroline?"

Noelle went with her sister toward the house, and I knew that for my mother nothing had happened. Why must I persist? What good would it possibly do to go on with this effort? Especially if remembering meant to her a returning realization of my father's affair with the singer?

David came around the car to where I stood staring at the house, not really seeing it, and he put a friendly arm around my shoulders. "Do you understand what's happening to you, Caroline? You've had to accept in a few hours' time everything the rest of them have grown accustomed to for years. That's rough and it's going to hurt a lot. Especially when you may be forced to give up in the end."

I almost wished he'd be angry with me for my foolish persistence, instead of sympathetic. Then I could have been angry with him, and that might have strengthened me. I didn't want to listen to the voice in my mind that whispered the same words: *Give up—run away!* This time I must stand my ground, no matter who opposed me. Not only for my mother's sake, but for my own as well. Everything in me told me that my instincts were right—and all the reasonable people around me were wrong.

Unexpectedly, David was smiling at me. "I remember that look—

stubborn. You used to be a great yeller, you know. Maybe it would help if you'd do some whooping right now."

"I wish I could. I've forgotten how."

"I know a good place to yell. I know just what you need. You need to have a look at something a lot older and bigger than you are. It improves perspective, and it's a treatment I've used a few times myself." The two women had reached the lanai and he called after them: "Wait a minute, Marla!" Marla stopped in the doorway, her arm about her sister. "Will you tell Joanna that Caro won't be with you for lunch? We're going to make a day of it. Up there." He nodded toward the mountain.

"Whatever you like," Marla said, and took Noelle inside.

"Get in the car," David told me. It was the same tone he'd used with me when we were children on the way to the Needle. But I was no longer six, and I *wanted* to be angry about something—anything at all, except more futile anger about my mother.

Before I could answer his peremptory words, however, Joanna hurried across the lawn. In spite of a knee that gave her trouble, she could move with a purposeful stride. She possessed none of the regal carriage of my Grandmother Elizabeth, but once more I sensed in her a power that was essential to her character. Joanna Docket was still in command.

David said, "Oh-oh, you're in for it now."

"You're going up to the crater?" Joanna asked as she reached us.

He nodded. "I told Caro she needed to have a look at something older and bigger than she is. She's had a hard morning."

"Maybe that's a good idea. But I wonder if you could wait until after lunch? That'll be in an hour or so. You're welcome to join us, David."

"Thanks," he said, "but why should we postpone?"

"Because I want to talk with Caroline *now*. Before she recovers from what she's just engineered." My grandmother read me all too clearly, penetrating past my guard. "Besides, isn't it better if she sees the crater in the late afternoon?"

"All right," David said, but he sounded doubtful. "I just had a feeling that she needed the antidote right away."

"Not Caroline!" She threw a straight look in my direction. "She's got a lot of me in her. But she asked for whatever happened this morning, so now she'll take the result. Life's full of consequences."

Head-on was the way Joanna had always dealt with life, though since I'd come here I'd begun to feel that she'd lost some of that old drive. But it was still there, and the years had only covered it thinly. Whether this reassured or threatened me, I wasn't yet sure.

"You'd better go with your grandmother," David told me. "I have an errand in Makawao—some pictures to deliver, and this film to develop. I'll be back for you around three or so."

I stayed beside the car, trying to make a last stand. "I wonder if anyone would mind asking me what I would like? You're both busy making plans over my head, but I haven't decided yet what I want to do."

David grinned at me, and for an instant I glimpsed the young boy's cockiness coming through this older version of the David I remembered. "Consider yourself asked. What would you like to do, Caroline?"

Having been consulted, I gave in with what dignity I could manage. "I'll talk with my grandmother and see you later."

"Fine." David got in the car and drove away. I walked into the house with Joanna, feeling that something was about to happen that I wasn't going to like.

Neither Marla nor Noelle was in sight, and Joanna seemed relieved. "Marla's probably gone upstairs to work on her new book. Since she sometimes dictates to a tape, Noelle likes to listen, and she'll be with her. What I want to talk to you about is private. Except for Tom O'Neill. I've asked him to join us. Let's go back to my office."

So she'd been that sure of imposing her will—inviting Tom even before she talked to me. Both my grandmothers were alike in their tendency to make assured plans and expect others to fall in with them.

Two rooms at the far side of the house from the kitchen and dining areas were Joanna's personal domain. The one at the back was a big, airy bedroom that I glimpsed as we passed the open door. The second room, at the front, held more bookcases, and featured a handsome koa-wood desk covered with papers and books. Obviously a working desk. Several handcrafted bamboo chairs with flowered cushions invited visitors. Straw-colored *lau hala* mats on the floor seemed immediately familiar—woven from the leaves of the *hala* tree, the pandanus, which had given island peoples a hundred uses. I'd loved to sit on those cool mats as a child, playing with my toys.

Joanna waited while I looked around, remembering much of what I saw. The tall pole in one corner was topped with a mass of red and yellow feathers—a *kahili*. In the old days a pair or more of such standards always accompanied the *alii*. When *kahili* bearers stood nearby, the populace knew that a member of the nobility was present. Now such *kahili* were museum pieces, though one saw imitations everywhere.

On one wall hung a stunning photographic poster in color of a silversword plant in bloom against the dark crater.

"That's David's work," Joanna said, watching me.

But now I was caught by a picture on another wall—one I remembered and had loved as a child—a painting of Iolani Palace in Honolulu. Grandma Joanna had told me stories about the days of the monarchy—sad, romantic stories that were real. The palace had been occupied for so short a time. Royalists and republicans had engaged in a bitter struggle, which ended with the last queen, Liliuokalani, being deposed in 1893 and imprisoned in a room of her own palace. By the time she was released, Hawaii was about to become an American territory and her reign had ended.

Studying the room had calmed me a little, and I was ready to listen to whatever my grandmother wanted to say.

Joanna switched on an overhead fan and motioned me to a chair. "You remember some of these things, don't you, Caro? You're on familiar ground, since you belonged to all this when you were little. No one wants to hurt or coerce you, but there are some things we need to talk about."

That meant my mother, and I braced myself.

"I suspect that what happened at Ahinahina this morning, whatever it was, hurt you more than it did Noelle. The sooner you realize that you can't bring her back to where she used to be, the easier it will be for you. Maybe it's just as well you gave this a try. You can go home more comfortably, once you've accepted what we've all known for so long. Perhaps the cruel thing was not that you've been allowed to think your mother was dead, but that when you learned she was alive I didn't tell you quickly enough how she had changed. I'm sorry, Caroline."

She seemed gentler now, kinder, and more like my Grandma Joanna. But I knew there was more to come, and I was silent, waiting.

She opened a bottom drawer in her desk and lifted out a long red box of Japanese lacquer with gold chrysanthemum emblems on the cover. She set it before her on the desk, but didn't open it right away.

"There's something more that you don't understand, or are refusing to recognize. Noelle must have seen whatever happened in the crater when she and Marla were hurt, and your father died. Something so shocked and frightened her that she had to hide it from herself. The mind can do that, as you know. It can shut out an event that's too terrible to be accepted. Do you really want to force her to remember? How is she to live if she does? She might even choose to kill herself."

I listened, appalled, yet clinging to some shred of hope I couldn't give up. "Isn't she dead already, the way she is now?"

"That's not the way to look at it. She's quite contented and we all love her and—"

"What have her doctors told you?" I broke in.

"She fell against a rock and bruised her head. There was only a slight concussion—no actual brain damage. She simply went away and never came back. Even though it may be psychological, there's still very little chance of recovery."

This was what I found impossible to accept. "Perhaps you've all tried too hard to protect her. This morning she told me she knew that my father was dead."

Clearly, my grandmother had been holding back a growing irritation with me, and I knew she was capable of angry explosions that could make even a ranch hand tremble. Though she had never been that angry with me. Now a flush had risen in her cheeks, and I began to fear just such an explosion.

She managed to control herself, however, and opened the long lacquer box. Something secret was about to be revealed, and I found myself tensing. I spoke in an effort to relax.

"Maybe you'd better close the door that leads out to the stairs," I said. "That is, if we're to be private."

"Why? There's no one up there. Marla's room is down the upstairs hall."

I could tell her without involving Marla. "Last night I stood at the top of those stairs and heard you and Tom talking. I didn't come there to listen, but when I heard my name I did."

My grandmother sat very still, one hand resting on whatever lay in the box. "I see." Her tone was ominously quiet—and that was more alarming than an explosion. "It hardly matters now, but I'm glad to know." She went to the door and her closing it was just short of a slam.

When she returned to her desk she lifted a tissue-wrapped object from the lacquer box and pulled off the paper. "Do you know what this is, Caro?"

I stared at the long wooden tool she held toward me. "Yes, you showed me that when I was little. I remember your telling me about how tapa cloth was made—that they used an instrument like that to beat the fiber of the paper mulberry into tapa."

"This is the same one. Take it in your hand, Caroline."

She'd always used my full name for solemn moments. I felt reluctant to touch the wooden object she held toward me—reluctant because of something that was in her mind, in the air.

I picked up the tool by its handle. The head was about fifteen inches long, with four flat sides. Those sides had been etched with small intricate marks that would later show up on the tapa as it was beaten with the heavy instruments. I'd read about the making of tapa cloth. These marks had been carved with shark's teeth, and the individual design would indicate the sign of the chief who owned the cloth.

"Turn it over," Joanna said.

I held the beater by its shorter handle, and at first when I turned it I saw nothing more than the marks etched into the wood. Then I noticed something else—a brownish stain darker than koa. A stain that spread over the sharp edge that divided two of the sides. I looked at Joanna, questioning.

"That's a bloodstain," she said. "The beater was found up there in the crater. We're not sure whose blood it is, since all of them were wounded. Marla dismounted, or fell off, and was kicked by her mare's hoof. Noelle was thrown against a rock. Keith was thrown too, and he received two severe wounds. Perhaps one came from this tapa beater, the other from the rock against which he fell. The police thought he must have struck one rock and bounced against another."

I set the tool down quickly. "Couldn't they have tested this for his blood?"

"They never saw it," Joanna said quietly.

"So what Grandmother Elizabeth told me is probably true! She said she suspected that my father was murdered."

Someone knocked at the closed door, and Joanna called to Tom to come in. He stood looking at my grandmother, questioning. His red hair was uncombed, his shirt stained with sweat, and there was a smell of horses about him.

"Lihilihi's fine," he said. "The foal came a little while ago, and she's a beauty." As he spoke his eyes found the tapa beater on the desk and he knew he wasn't here to talk about the foal.

"I'm glad," Joanna said. "I'll be out to see her later. Sit down a minute, Tom. I've shown Caro what turned up in the crater that day, and I'd like you to tell her about finding it."

He stared at her, still questioning, and for a moment I thought he would refuse. Then he brushed off his jeans and sat down in a bamboo chair facing me. "Do you think this is a good idea?"

"Where did you find it, Tom? And when?" she asked.

He still hesitated, as if choosing his words. "I went up there a day later. I found that thing behind a lava-rock bubble half covered with cinders. The stain on it looked like recent blood, so I brought it here to Joanna."

"Why not to the police?" I asked.

"That was up to your grandmother."

"There was no point in stirring anything up," Joanna said firmly. "Both my daughters were badly hurt, and Keith was dead. It was all over by the time Tom and I rode back from setting up camp to see what had delayed the others. Marla's injury wiped out her memory from the time when they rode into the crater. And Noelle had escaped safely into a place where she needn't face whatever happened."

"So a possible murder was concealed?" I asked.

Tom looked angry and Joanna made a despairing gesture.

"I suppose you could say that—*if* it was true. But what good would an investigation have done? No one who was up there knew the answer, and it would have been a terrible and senseless ordeal for us all. Are you willing now, Caroline, to force your mother into remembering some terrible experience—if it's even possible that she can? What good would it do anyone?"

I closed my eyes as though I could shut out the horror of the wooden instrument on her desk. "Perhaps she could remember *me*, without all the rest."

"If she remembers you," Tom spoke harshly, "then she's certain to remember the rest. You're smart enough to see what that could mean."

There were only two people who could have wielded the tapa beater—either Marla or Noelle herself. Suddenly I was afraid. Who had carried it up there in the first place? I'd held it in my hands, and the heavy tool could easily have been used as a weapon. Perhaps the frightened horses had done the rest. Yet someone could have struck my father with the intent to kill.

Joanna, watching me, nodded to Tom. "Thanks for coming. You've given Caroline something new to think about."

Tom threw me a last hostile look, saluted my grandmother with forefinger to temple, and went off.

Calmly, Joanna rewrapped the tapa beater and placed it in the red lacquer box. As evidence of a deed no one wanted to explain?

"It's nearly time for lunch," she said. "Shall we go in?"

As David had warned, Joanna had lived with this for years. It was easy for her to slip in and out of the past because she had more or less made her peace with it a long time ago. I hadn't. For me the events in the crater were as sharply disturbing as though they had just happened.

I followed Joanna down the hall, feeling more torn and uncertain than ever. Before we reached the dining room I stopped her.

"Just tell me this one thing—who would want my father dead?"

She answered me dryly. "Perhaps more than one person, Caroline. He wasn't the most admired man around here. I never wanted Noelle to marry him, but she had those stars in her eyes, and she was always more determined than she looked."

"Do you mind if I tell David about this?"

"I don't suppose it matters. David is discreet and he has a lot of good sense. If you won't listen to me, perhaps you'll listen to him."

I followed her into the dining room knowing that what she hoped was that David would advise me to let everything be—to let Noelle stay as she was.

I was just beginning to grasp the ramifications of what might happen if she ever came back to us completely. I could also see why they'd protected and even encouraged her amnesia—they were afraid to have her remember. So of course they would be antagonistic toward me.

And yet—my Grandma Joanna had invited me to come.

7

I remembered the dining room. It had seemed huge to me—very dignified and grand in its enormous reaches. Now it had shrunk, since I was older and taller, but it was still an impressive room.

A moss-green carpet bordered by dark wood stretched the length of the room. The long table, with its polished surface and woven place mats, could easily seat fourteen or more. A crystal bowl of roses graced the center of the table, flanked by candelabra, and their fragrance scented the room. A name returned to me out of a long time ago—*Lokelani*, Rose of Heaven. The Maui rose.

A great window of square panes occupied most of one wall and lighted the room, bringing in the outdoors and a view of trees and the rear lawn. On one wall hung a framed map of Maui, its browns showing the mountain heights, its blues the circling sea, with yellow shading into orange for the lower slopes. The human figure of the island was one I'd loved to study as a child, even though I hadn't fully understood what the map represented.

Marla and Noelle joined us, and since there were only four for lunch, the long table offered an expanse of empty space. Joanna said it made Susy Ohara happier if we dined here "properly," and kept out of her way in the kitchen. It was a simple enough meal—vegetable soup, a heavenly fresh salad, and Maui pineapple for dessert. I hardly knew what I was eating because I kept thinking about the things that had been said in my grandmother's office, and of the weight of that tapa beater in my hand.

For once, Noelle was talkative. The visit to Ahinahina had left her troubled.

"All the furniture was gone from Linny's room," she told her mother. "There were easels around and sculptors' stands. The pictures on the walls were different. What could have happened?"

Marla said, "Don't worry, dear. Everything will be all right." She spoke soothingly, but again I wondered how genuine her feeling was for her sister.

Joanna spoke to her daughter calmly. "I'm sure everything will be put back as it was, Noelle. The next time you go to that house it will all be as it should be." She glanced at me as she spoke, and I knew she meant that Noelle must never return to Ahinahina.

This continuation of the myth that no time had passed depressed me more than ever. Someone always closed the window that looked into those early years, leaving Noelle in her passive state. More than ever, I wanted to end this falsehood they all subscribed to—that everything was normal, and that Noelle was perfectly content. But at the moment I could only try to reach her before she slipped away again.

"We spent a lovely morning at Ahinahina, Noelle," I reminded her. "I loved what you told me about the stairway and the stained-glass bird in the window."

She looked straight at me, her uneasiness and uncertainty evident. Perhaps I was getting through just a little. But then Joanna distracted her by passing rolls down the table, and I had to restrain my quick feeling of anger. This game they played—how could I break through? I would certainly talk to David, and I didn't think he would be altogether unsympathetic.

When we'd finished lunch it was still too early for him to come for me, so I wandered outside into the sunny day. Mynah birds were chattering raucously in the camphor tree, and I wandered toward it idly. They flew off as I came near. These days the moment I was alone, my own unresolved problems engulfed me. My mother was only a part of my general unease, important as she was. Grief and loss were always waiting to snare me—as they did now.

How many times as a small girl had I walked this same lawn with my hand in my father's? It was he who had hung a swing for me from one of the great branches of the spreading tree. I'd loved to have him push me in my swing until I felt that I was flying high as the sky itself —high as the mountaintop. I'd been able to look into the upper boughs and I'd seen a bird's nest hiding there.

But now there were those who were trying to poison these memories—to spoil all that I'd believed my father had been; all that Grandmother Elizabeth had taught me to believe about him.

I sat on the ground and leaned my back against the tree trunk and thought of other things. Last night someone had hidden behind this tree, perhaps listening to David and me. Or watching the house? When we became aware of the presence, the person had gone crashing away through the brush, leaving the puzzle unsolved.

I rose and walked behind the tree, searching the ground for some evidence of whoever might have hidden here. Not until I discovered an overgrown path leading away into shrubbery and trees did an object on the ground catch my eye—something that looked like a doll lay half hidden under a hibiscus bush. I picked it up with a shock of recognition.

Though it was dressed like a doll, it wasn't one really, but a wooden copy of an ancient Hawaiian idol—an image of Pele, the goddess of volcanoes. The face was crudely carved and ugly in its anger—a dished-in face with a mouth that snarled and showed two rows of mother-of-pearl teeth. Not Pele in one of her better moods. I didn't know why this chunk of wood had held such fascination for me as a child. Perhaps its eerie quality appealed to me and matched the rather scary legends that I'd loved.

I remembered seeing it first in the living room at Manaolana. Grandma Joanna had let me play with it, since it wasn't a real artifact, but only a copy. The original, made of ohia wood, had been found in the crater of Haleakala, and she had bought this in a shop in Lahaina. She had let me take it from its shelf whenever I liked, and my small hands had further polished, rubbed, and probably dirtied its surface. After weeks of visits, my devotion was so plain that my grandmother gave me the figure.

I had taken it back to Ahinahina and showed it to my mother. She thought it ugly, but since I worried because Pele might be cold without any clothes, she said she would make something for her to wear. After all, when Pele appeared in one of her human guises, she wore clothes just like anyone else. What my mother sewed for her was a long cape, since the carved arms couldn't come out through sleeves. She made it of bits of red and yellow cloth, so that it looked like a pretend feather cape for the king—which was mixing things up a bit, but suited me fine. I made a tiny circlet of flowers for my violent lady's head, changing them often to keep them fresh.

Now my wooden friend still wore her cape, though it had faded and grown shabby. Again a circlet of flowers crowned her brow, though these had begun to yellow and wilt.

How long had she been lying here, lost in the shrubbery? Certainly not for days or weeks, since the flowers weren't entirely dead. Had it been Noelle who had lingered here last night, listening to David and me—then running away?

I hated to think of my mother clinging to the idol doll I'd so loved as a child, and perhaps playing with it herself in order to bring back her long-ago Linny. I wondered if she could even tell me whether she'd been out here last night if I asked. Anyway, I would try.

I carried the wooden figure into the house and wandered through the downstairs rooms, looking for Noelle. Marla had said her sister's room was near Joanna's, and when I found a closed door, I tapped on it. She called to me to come in. I opened the door and stood looking around in dismay. This was a child's room, not the room of a mother and wife. Noelle sat at a table painting in watercolors. She had made lovely pictures for me when I was little.

She looked over her shoulder, smiling, for once remembering my name. "Hello, Caroline. Come in."

I carried the wooden figure to her table and set it beside her. "I found this just now outside in the yard."

She dropped her paintbrush into a glass of water and touched the cape. "I thought I had Pele with me when I went out yesterday, but then I couldn't find her. Linny would never forgive me if I lost her. She likes this better than any of her real dolls."

"Then you were out near the camphor tree last night?" I asked. "Is that where you dropped it?"

She regarded me vaguely, losing touch with memory again. "I'm not sure. Anyway, it doesn't matter, so long as you found it. I'll take it to Linny now."

"No, please wait," I said. "First show me what you're painting."

It was pitifully easy to distract her. She pushed the paper toward me. "Don't pick it up. It's still wet and it might run."

The watercolor was dramatic in its bright colors, and quite beautiful. A red bird perched among green leaves, its long, curved beak reaching for nectar in pompons of red flowers. I recognized it as a painting similar to one she had made for me when I was little.

"That's an *iiwi* bird, isn't it?" I said. "And those must be *lehua* flowers."

She nodded, happy with my recognition. "Yes—it's one of the birds whose feathers were used for the kings' capes. The birds are still here in the wild uplands of Haleakala's slopes. And there are still forests of ohia trees with these red flowers."

"I remember," I said, pulling up a stool near her chair. "You painted a picture like this for me when I was very small. Come back to me—*know* me. Please try."

With a quick movement that smeared the painting, she pushed herself up from the table, her eyes wide and frightened. "I don't know who you are! I only paint my pictures for Linny. I don't know why you're here!"

I couldn't leave her in this agitated state, yet I didn't know how to reassure her. All I could do was go along with the myth in order to quiet her. Perhaps the others were right and this was all anyone could ever do.

"I'm visiting your mother," I told her gently. "You remember that, don't you? I came in just now to bring you the idol doll I found outside."

Her sudden movement startled me as she reached for the carved figure, ripped the cape from it, and snatched off the circlet of faded flowers.

"There!" she cried. "That's the way she really is. You're a *malihini*, so you don't know, but Pele is one of the dangerous gods. She can do a lot of harm if she chooses. I'm not supposed to let Linny play with her anymore. You had no business bringing her here. I won't let you hurt my little girl!"

Again she moved suddenly, angrily, picking up the carving as though it were a weapon she threatened me with. I moved toward the door in alarm, and she threw the wooden figure directly at me. I ducked just in time, and it sailed past my head and crashed into a framed picture on the wall, breaking the glass.

Joanna was in her office next door and she heard the crash and came running in. Noelle's face had flushed and she was trembling. Joanna held her tightly, calming and quieting. Her look accused me over her daughter's shoulder.

I was in a state of shock, totally unprepared for the violence of what had happened. It was as if the little *iiwi* bird she'd painted had attacked me.

Noelle stood stiffly, resisting Joanna's embrace, her look still wildly unfocused. Marla had heard too, and she seemed to realize what had happened as she came into the room.

"Let me," she said.

Joanna pushed Noelle toward Marla, who drew her toward the bed and coaxed her to lie down. Though her manner was quiet, it seemed to me that her hands were rough.

"We need to talk again, Caroline," my grandmother said grimly.

I followed her into her office, still deeply shaken. Joanna sat behind her desk, her anger with me turning to dejection, and I dropped into a chair feeling more than a little sick.

"I do understand what you're suffering," she said. "I only wish I could help you through this, but there's no easy way. You *must* let your mother alone. Most of the time she's gentle and perfectly amenable. But when she's upset she can become—dangerous. I can't bear to see her put into an institution—but that could happen if she ever injures someone seriously. Are you listening to me, Caroline?"

I was listening, but I was mute.

She went on. "This is why we're all very gentle with her. Why we keep up the pretenses you don't approve of. We try never to upset her. What's the use? She's out of our reach, and all you are doing is to make her regress. You lost your mother a long time ago, and the sooner you accept this, the better."

I didn't know whether I could ever accept. "Must I give up? Is that all I can do?"

"You'll have to. I blame your father most of all. There was always a delicate emotional balance in Noelle, and he was already driving her over the edge before they went up to the crater. When he died, she couldn't face the reality. We can't ask her to now. It's much too late."

Something in me still resisted the hopeless course they'd chosen. But I lacked the wisdom to deal with this, and apparently so far I'd only made things worse. The memory of that party in the garden at Ahinahina, when my mother had gone wild with anger, was still with me, and must be added to what had just happened.

"Listen to me," Joanna said. "Noelle was in a terribly emotional state those last few weeks. She was actually going to leave your father. She had told him that she would take you and come here to Manaolana, unless he was willing to change. She felt revengeful, and she told him straight out that while she'd leave him, she would never give him a divorce. She would fight him right down the line, and she would keep Linny."

This startled me. "But she loved him—"

"You were too young to understand, yet I always wondered if you didn't sense the emotions that were breaking around you during those last days with your parents. Your Grandmother Elizabeth didn't help any when she came for a visit, because she always took his side, no matter what. She never liked or approved of Noelle."

Joanna's words brought everything frighteningly close. "I knew there were—secrets. Something I *didn't* understand. So tell me now. Why was he changing toward my mother?"

"He was having an affair. Noelle found out about the woman and told him it had to stop. She could be fiercely determined under all her gentleness. And she had a temper when she got really upset. She may even have frightened him a little. But Keith never gave up anything he wanted, so they were heading toward serious trouble. I think it exploded that day in the crater."

"The tapa beater?" I asked softly. "Who do you think used it?"

She was silent for a moment, and I wondered if she were making up some story meant to satisfy me. "Perhaps it was Keith. What if he attacked Noelle, and then the horses got out of hand, so that he was thrown and killed?"

"Do you really believe that?"

"Does it matter? They both loved you. Neither one would give you up."

"Who was the woman?" I asked bluntly.

"Ask David. *If* you need to have an answer. I really don't know why you should, and I don't want to talk about it."

"I need to know because I don't believe everything that's said about my father. There's more to the truth than you're telling me."

She answered me sadly. "What does it really matter, Caro? Your father is dead, and your mother is as you see her. The only wise thing for you to do now is give them both up. Go back to San Francisco. Maui isn't your home any longer."

"No," I said. "I don't want to go yet."

"I was afraid that was how you'd feel. I used to be stubborn, but perhaps age helps soften that a little. You have no idea how often I've lain awake at night wishing myself futilely back to a time that's gone. The time when your mother and father were happy together, and you were such a delightful baby—a joy for all of us. Now I can only feel that you shouldn't have returned. I acted emotionally when I let you come. I suppose I was trying to recover something that couldn't be. You were better off before you knew what you know about your mother now."

I could only shake my head. "There's no place else I want to be. Maui has always pulled me back. Sooner or later I had to come."

"If it's any comfort to you, remember how Noelle still loves you. Perhaps she's the lucky one, because you're still in her life as you used to be, and she doesn't recognize the truth about Keith."

"That's to say that madness is an advantage!"

"Who knows? *You* don't enjoy accepting reality, do you? The reality that your mother has a terrible illness which doctors don't know how to cure. We can keep her happy most of the time. And when she becomes upset there are tranquilizers. She'll need them now, though we hate to resort to drugs. There are better ways to keep her calm. If you stay here for a little while longer, you must leave her alone."

"She knows my father is dead," I protested. "She told me so at Ahinahina this morning. She even knows that he died a long time ago. Just for a moment she was perfectly clear and sane. She was accepting his death."

Joanna only shook her head. "The lucid moments never last."

Marla came to the door and looked in on us. "She's quiet now. She'll go to sleep. David's waiting for you, Caroline. I told him you'd be right out."

I sat for a moment longer staring at my grandmother. She'd put her face in her hands in a gesture of resignation that was unfamiliar and despairing. I felt numb, empty of feeling, as I followed Marla down the hall.

"Never mind, Caroline," Marla said. "I know you didn't mean to upset your mother. You couldn't know that would happen." She held something out to me. "You remember that I asked if you'd return this to the crater? I've wrapped the lava rock in ti leaves, so I wouldn't have to touch it, and because that's the proper way to make an offering to Pele. It's right for *you* to take it. When you leave it up there say something appropriate—the right words will come if you'll let them."

It was hard to return to Marla's fantasy, but I took the rock in its wrapping of big green leaves. Holding it was still repugnant to me. This was the sort of superstition I wanted to resist.

Marla spoke earnestly. "Do you think there isn't good and evil out there, Caroline? Perhaps you can change what your father started. This could be the way to stop all the bad luck that's come to us."

The young part of me that still belonged to Maui and to all those Hawaiian legends couldn't reject her request as the older part of me wanted to.

"All right," I said. "I'll take it up there."

She came with me to the door and waited while I crossed the lawn to David's car in the side driveway. When I looked back she was gone. As I got into the car David saw my face.

"What's happened?"

"More than I can handle right now."

"All right—tell me when you feel like it. I can listen, at least. Maybe I can even understand."

His calm presence was reassuring. I didn't need that excitement that could sometimes rise in him. He noticed what I held in my hand. "Ti leaves? An offering to Pele?"

This, at least, I could answer. "Marla claims that my father offended Pele a long time ago by taking a rock from the crater. She says it must go back, and I'm the one to take it and make amends."

He didn't laugh, and I remembered the David of our climb to the Needle—the boy who believed in the old stories. "I know where you can leave it," he said, accepting the idea easily.

We drove to Makawao and took the road across to the Haleakala Highway. Above us, the crater rim rose free of clouds, though they had drifted in below to hide the switchbacks from view.

I was grateful not to talk. I had to become quiet inside myself first, so that my own inner trembling could stop. It was too easy to relive the moment in Noelle's room when my mother had hurled the wooden carving at me, no longer her gentle self, but someone frightening, unknown—and entirely out of control. There was horror here, and I dared not think about it.

At the lower levels cactus often grew beside the road, and there were trees with shaggy bark—eucalyptus, perhaps. Wild morning glory vines clung wherever they could find a hold, adding to the floral backdrop that was always Hawaii. Sometimes we bumped over cattle guards set into the pavement.

Fields of pineapple covered a section of hillside—green dots against the reddish earth, the symmetry of the fields following the contour of the land, forming a marvelously decorative pattern.

Houses were few as we climbed higher toward the summit. A sign warned: TURN ON HEADLIGHTS IN CLOUDS—so that cars coming down could see our lights. Though the white fluff was close overhead, the road was still visible.

At seven thousand feet we reached the lower Visitor's Center. We didn't go in, but David wanted me to see the pen of nene—the brown, speckled geese that were native to the crater and were almost extinct until recent efforts to save them were begun.

After nine thousand feet there was little growth on the mountain. Black rocks, sometimes jagged and broken, banked the road, and we'd climbed through an opening in the clouds and were on the high switchbacks, turning sharply up to each new level, always looking down upon the road below, where we'd been.

Now we could see Science City, with its observatory and experimental stations perched along the rim of the crater far above. White paint and metallic domes shone against the enormous blue of the sky.

Once a string of bike riders coasted past us, their clothes bright red and highly visible, all of them intent on the steep road down.

"Pigs and goats and the exotic plants were all brought in by early visitors, and they've damaged a lot of what was indigenous to Hawaii," he told me. "Native plants and birds didn't have the strength of the newcomers and they've been overpowered—some of them wiped out. The mongoose is an enemy stranger, for instance, and does a lot of damage. These rare geese are being bred up here now by the Park."

Our goal, David said was the highest overlook point, more than ten thousand feet up. We drove on to a still higher level, and when he'd parked the car we got out into the cold wind that always blew in these high, exposed places. In the winter there would be snow and ice up here, but those months still lay ahead. David zipped up his jacket and helped me with my short coat.

We walked to where the ground plunged steeply away, and I looked for the first time into the vast crater whose floor was three thousand feet below where we stood. At first it seemed like a barren moonscape, wild and black and desolate. But as my eyes became accustomed to the shock of a sight that was like nothing I'd ever seen before, I began to make out color in red cinder cones that rose from black shadow, and towered within the crater. Minerals that had been frozen into once molten rock sparkled with touches of green and yellow and gunmetal. Volcanic sands swirled down slopes in wide avenues to the crater floor, a lighter red than the dark rust and mauve of the cinder cones.

"You could fit all of Manhattan and some of Queens into this crater space," David said.

Two great gaps opened far across in the crater walls, and through these gaps clouds could pour in—sometimes from opposite directions, forming currents of air that warred with each other. The sun, dropping down the afternoon sky, lengthened smoky shadows in the tremendous bowl, and I began to feel tiny and unimportant, occupying as I did only a speck of time in the life of such tumultuous creation. Human awe mingled with a sense of something ancient and enormously powerful, so that my own problems seemed much less urgent. I could understand why Hawaiians regarded this as a holy place, formed by the gods as no human could ever build.

David had known this would happen to me. He had brought me here so that all that troubled me could recede for a little while in the face of something so immense and mysterious.

He drew my hand through the crook of his arm, as though humans needed to touch each other. It didn't seem strange to me to hold on to him tightly for a moment, just as I'd done as a small child. There was no mockery or censure in him now—this was my old friend who had brought me here. But I was no longer a small child. I was older, and lonely, and my response to his touch was far stronger than I'd expected—a sudden rush of warm feeling that startled me. I wasn't ready for this. Not yet.

I withdrew my hand from his arm and he led me to where a low-walled enclosure guarded silversword plants that had been set here to preserve and increase their number.

"The crater used to be full of silverswords," David said. "This species grows only in lava soil on this mountain. Unfortunately, wild goats and sheep and pigs as well as trampling cattle in the past, and vandalizing visitors, have made them almost extinct, like the geese. The Park Service is trying to save them with these plantings, as well as by controlling the animals who run wild so destructively. Of course, cattle no longer graze in the crater, and no one must pick the plants."

I had seen pictures, but never the real thing before. I looked down upon long rows of silver balls with curving saber leaves. The plants were a foot or so in diameter, with hundreds of pale gray-green leaves curving up from a central rosette.

"We're lucky," David said. "Look over there where three of them are blooming."

The blooming plants were astonishing. The silverswords had shot up central stalks covered with tiny purple flowers—stalks that made them as tall as a man. When the flowers faded after this once-in-ten-years blooming, the life of the plant ended. These three were fully in bloom, starred with purple—spectacular in their last glory.

I thought of Noelle sitting in the red sands of the crater, plucking futilely at silver leaves, and I asked a question. "David, where did it happen? The accident, I mean?"

"You can't see the place from here. It's an hour's ride or more into the crater by horseback. It occurred at a place where the trail runs along the shoulder of a steep cinder hill. A misstep could send horses and riders plunging, and that's what happened. There's been more than one accident out there. Park rangers patrol the area on horse-back and on foot, but they can't be everywhere."

"Still—three horses falling?" I said. "All at once?"

He looked at me and then quickly away. "I flew in by helicopter one time and saw the spot where it happened. If one horse fright-ened another, they could all go down."

"I'd like to believe it was only an accident. But I don't think I do. I've a lot to tell you, David."

"I'll listen, whenever you want to talk. Let's get out of the wind. There aren't many visitors right now, so if we climb up to the obser-vation room we can talk quietly."

I stood for a moment longer looking down into the oval disk of the crater. There were a great many cinder cone hills of various sizes down there—some black, some garnet red, with valleys of shadow folding in among them. It all seemed bare and stark and desolate—yet I could see cliffs far across where patches of green showed life. That was where rain must fall, where the forests began.

I was aware of a silence so immense, so untouched, that the laugh-ter of a child somewhere behind me had no effect on the vast still-ness, any more than a single treble note struck on a piano would have broken the silence. Only drums would stir those sleeping echoes, I thought, and I wanted to hear no drums on Haleakala.

David touched my arm, bringing me back, and I turned away from so disturbing a mystery, and went with him.

8

The highest building crowned a hill that was part of the crater's rim, and we climbed steep steps, my breath coming short in rarefied air. The circular observation room, with its surrounding glass panes, offered far views in all directions. Other islands of the Maui County cluster floated on blue seas, with West Maui resembling the separate island it had once been. Lanai and Molokai lay beyond, and Kahoolawe, the island the Navy had used for practice bombing. Even Oahu was visible on the horizon until clouds began to billow in. In the other direction, the Big Island of Hawaii could be seen, its active volcanoes quiet for the moment.

Up here we were on the same level as Science City, which rose outside the Park limits and wasn't open to visitors. However, it was the dormant volcano itself that held my attention with its enchanted moonscape.

"It is a place for the gods," I said.

"There used to be *heiaus* down there—outdoor altars," David told me. "The stones of one were found in a cinder-cone crater by two young girls earlier in this century. Stones that are in the Bishop Museum now. In the days of the chiefs, when people moved about on foot, the way through the crater was a shortcut to Hana and other villages on the water. One legend has it that Egyptians found their way here in ancient times, and their word for altar, *heikal,* is strangely like *heiau.*"

I turned my back on a bleak immensity that was more than I could absorb. Now that I'd gained enough distance from my own problems, I could talk about them quietly.

"I'd like to tell you," I said.

David led me to a bench away from the few visitors who stood at the windows. As I began to talk, it all came back to me vividly—yet I could deal with it more quietly now as I described the scene in my grandmother's office, when she had showed me the tapa beater with its ominous stain, and what Tom O'Neill had said about finding it. Then I went on to the moment when I'd come upon the carved Pele figure and had taken it to Noelle's room.

"I don't know exactly how it happened, but my mother became so excited that she threw that heavy piece of wood at me. It was terrible to see her lose control like that."

"I know," David said. "I saw it happen once myself. That's why they try to keep her happy and calm."

"Joanna told me that before the ride into the crater that time, Noelle was getting ready to leave my father and take me away from him. My grandmother blames him for whatever happened. She said he might have tried to kill my mother that day. But I can't accept that, David. I really do remember how much he loved her."

"We'll probably never know for sure. Must you know?"

The spell of the crater was wearing off and I was beginning to get stirred up all over again. "It's too easy to make him a scapegoat, since he can't speak for himself. But if that's what they're doing, why are they doing it? Who is protecting whom?"

"It doesn't matter anymore. You don't have to listen."

"I keep telling myself that. Telling myself that only *now* matters, and I must think only of Noelle. Perhaps my grandmother and Marla are right and the only sensible thing to do is to leave her alone. She was like a wild creature when she threw that carving at me. There's one thing more, David—Joanna said you might know who my father was having an affair with. But you were only a young boy, so how would you know?"

He stirred uneasily beside me. I sensed that this was something he didn't want to talk about, and I let it go.

"You're probably right," I said. "Even if you do know, and would tell me, how could it matter now?"

"You may meet her one of these days," David said. "She's a fine person, so perhaps it's better if you aren't prejudiced ahead of time."

"The thing that bothers me is that while it was all so long ago, and shouldn't matter, they are all behaving as though it does—Marla, Tom, Joanna."

"Let them live in the past—you don't have to."

"My father would never have tried to harm my mother!" I had come full circle again.

"Let it go. You can't know what to do until you find your own peaceful place. That's why I brought you up here—I'd like you to find it. If the gods are willing."

I didn't know what he meant, but I went with him more hopefully as we returned to the car.

"You still have that rock to dispose of," he said, as I picked it up from the seat beside me. "We'll drive to the next level below, and walk down a trail for a little way. Then you can find a place to leave it. It would never do just to toss it into the crater."

When we'd parked near the next overlook building, we walked to the beginning of the Sliding Sands Trail. From above I had seen the narrow threads of trails winding into the depths, but I found this wide enough to walk on, though gravelly in places.

"Of course, no vehicles are allowed in the crater," David said. "Its wildness is carefully preserved. There are only three rather primitive cabins, plus one ranger cabin out there in what we call the backcountry, so supplies are brought in by mule. Visitors either hike in with backpacks or ride horses or mules. Bikes are illegal inside the crater. We won't go far—you can see what's already happening."

As David pointed, I looked toward a far gap and saw the clouds boiling through. Even as we watched, they tumbled down the *palis* —those Hawaiian cliffs—and began to fill up a portion of the crater. Far down on the trail a hiker with a red backpack was visible.

I held up the rock in its ti leaf wrapping. "Where shall I leave it?"

"It doesn't matter. Anywhere beside the trail. It's an old custom Marla's picked up. If you leave something for Pele, you'll be brought out safely."

He was only half joking, and one couldn't stand in this place without being aware of much more than our earthbound eyes could see. I followed the trail a short distance, and then knelt to place the rock in the cinder dust. Marla had told me to say a few words, and I spoke in a whisper, lest I awake echoes in the tremendous silence below. A silence that seemed all the more hushed because of clouds floating down into the crater, filling its basin with smothering fog.

The words came easily. "I'm sorry for what my father did. I return what belongs to this place." I placed the rock in its green wrapping beside the trail and went back to David.

"Come on," he said, "we'll be lost in fog any minute. But perhaps it won't spill over the top, and you'll be lucky."

He took my hand and pulled me along, and I sensed again that excitement that could stir him. It didn't disturb me now, as I understood it better. David had managed to keep some of the young boy's wonder that I'd sensed in him long ago. Perhaps that was why he could savor so keenly whatever he did. My own spirits lifted in response to the exhilaration that charged him now.

We climbed to where we could stand below the overlook building, but away from its shadow. The sun of late afternoon was at our backs, not yet ready to set.

"You have to stand alone," David said. "You must find it for yourself —if it happens."

He walked away, and I stood on the edge of the crater looking out over the great sea of clouds that had filled it. Only the outer ridges of rock showed above a whiteness so thick that it seemed to have substance of its own. As I watched, the clouds piled up until the far rim vanished, and now I saw what lay against the mounded whiteness.

A great luminous circle of light shone against the clouds, and in the center of the rainbow circle I could see the shadow of a human figure. It took me a moment to realize that it was *my* shadow, ringed by that miraculous rainbow. I moved my arm, and the distant shadow moved with me.

From a little way off, David spoke softly. "Hawaiians say it's our own spirit we see reflected upon the clouds. You're very lucky—it doesn't always happen. But I thought you might be—I thought you might be given a sign."

Whatever he said I could believe. I could believe that somehow, in some inspired way, that was the reflection of my own spirit—soul— shining out there in that circle of light. No one could behold such a vision without being touched and changed. While I had come to Maui for some small human purposes of my own, now something more was being given to me. Something far larger—a destiny? At this moment the word didn't seem too large for me to accept. I was here because—something—was meant to be. I didn't need to understand. In a little while I would go back into my own small human perspective, but I wouldn't forget what had touched me here.

The air had grown colder as the sun dropped, and I could feel the chill as I returned to where David waited for me. It felt good to be out of the wind and inside his car. He seemed to understand that I needed a few moments to return from wherever I'd been, and he didn't start the motor right away.

"What did I see?" I asked him.

"The explanation is prosaic enough. They call it the Brocken Specter because it was first described by someone who saw it a long time ago in the Harz Mountains of East Germany—on the Brocken Mountain. But you can forget all that. Here it belongs only to Haleakala, as the silversword does. Hawaiians have a wonderful word—*mana*. You say it with the accent on the second syllable, and it's a wonderful word that means many things. Power—spiritual power—energy, the life force. There is certainly *mana* when your spirit shadow is cast out on the crater in its rainbow light. Remember that, Caro—use it. Don't let the everyday world wipe it out for you."

"Thank you, David," I said softly. "I'll try to hold on to what I felt."

He nodded and reached into a pocket of his jacket. "I have something for you—something I've kept for a good many years. Once I promised you this, but I never gave it to you because things happened so fast and you flew away from Maui before I had a chance."

He'd drawn out something folded in tissue paper, and I took it from him. Inside the paper lay a string of wooden beads. I held them up in wonder, remembering the time when I'd climbed to the Needle with David above a sea of candlenut trees.

"A lei of kukui nuts!" I cried. "How could you have remembered?"

"Koma's mother made this for me to give you. These are brown, and harder to find than the black. I asked her to do this right after our trip up the valley. She was one of your Grandma Joanna's protégées, and quite young at the time. Joanna helped Ailina to get started singing at the big hotels. Of course, that was before she married, before Koma was born. When you left for San Francisco, I put the beads away, thinking that someday my little friend would return. So there you are, Caro."

I put the lei of smooth brown beads over my head. They felt warm, as though they would always hold the sunshine of my island. I leaned over and kissed David on the cheek, as I'd sometimes done when I was little. He laughed, pleased, and kissed me back—only suddenly it was different. For just a moment we looked at each other with unexpected recognition—with a new awareness that I wasn't ready for. Neither was he, for he moved away from me and started the car. The naturalness of my little girl's gesture was lost, and I wished I'd been less impulsive.

Before we could turn out of the parking lot, a man in the gray shirt and olive-green pants of a park ranger looked in at David's window.

"Hello, Koma," David said. "You remember Caroline—you met her last night."

Koma's smile was impersonal, and I sensed the same reserve in him that I'd felt before. Because I was a *haole-malihini?* White and a stranger?

"That was a good meeting last night," David said. "I'm glad you spoke out as you did."

"I had to. If we're going to save what's left of Hawaii we have to let people on the mainland know that it *needs* saving. And that it's worth the trouble." He looked at me. "My mother wants to meet you, though I don't know why. She's working as a volunteer at Baldwin Home in Lahaina. Maybe you'll be going there."

It wasn't a question, and he told us "aloha" before I had time to respond.

"That young man doesn't like me," I said. "Why should his mother want to meet me?"

"She probably remembers you when you were small and she was often at your grandmother's. She made those kukui beads for you with love—in spite of everything."

That sounded enigmatic. But I was beginning to put things together. She was a singer and my grandmother's protégée. I remembered the beautiful young Hawaiian woman who had sung that night at Ahinahina. I remembered my mother's anger.

"David, is *she* the one? I mean the one my father . . . ? Koma must have heard the stories, and that's why he doesn't like me. Though it's hardly fair. David, I don't want to meet her."

"A little while ago you were curious. I didn't mean to open this up, but now that you've guessed, I think perhaps you really should meet her. I don't know how she'll feel toward you, but now that you've put the rock back, you can help to mend something else—if only in a small way."

"From so long ago? When I had nothing to do with whatever happened?"

"You were Keith's child. There are wounds that take a long time to heal."

Yes, I thought. I carried such wounds, and so did David in the death of his wife.

"Who did she marry?"

"A young lawyer who came here from Manila—Carlos Olivero. It must have been a happy marriage, and perhaps it made up for what went before. They just had the one son—Koma. Carlos died about ten years ago."

"If she knew him, she'd remember my father."

David spoke almost absently. "It doesn't matter. You've seen what was in the clouds for you—so what will happen will happen."

"No freedom of choice? I don't believe that!"

"Oh, you'll have all the choices there are. It will be interesting to see what road you take."

Sometimes he made me feel uncertain. I hadn't accomplished the transition into the full spirit of Maui yet. That still seemed a little mystical and out of my reach. Yet I had stood on the rim of the crater and I had seen a vision. So what was happening to me?

"I hope I can choose wisely," I said, but he didn't answer.

He started the car down the mountain along the switchbacks, and clouds blew past our headlights like wisps of smoke until we came into the clear below and David turned off the lights.

When I looked up toward the summit I saw that clouds now lay across the top in straight lines that dipped in the middle as though they were being sucked into the crater's mouth. The sky toward the west was turning pale lavender, with streaks of golden light that painted the high-piled clouds. Hints of rose had begun to show, touching the dark shapes of the West Maui Mountains where they stood up in silhouette against the sunset.

As the car turned back and forth down the mountain, my spirits began to lift again, and I knew that nothing would ever be the same for me. Perhaps I would even welcome the chance to meet Ailina, if it ever arose, because I might learn from her. About my father, if she would talk about him. Surely about my mother. I needed to know about them as human beings, not just as the mother and father of a small child.

"I'm glad you took me up there," I said to David. "I'm glad I was lucky."

He must have heard the new lift in my voice. "What's up there always helps. Perspective! Let's stop for an early dinner before we return to Manaolana. Maybe there's some more talking to be done."

I was willing. For the first time, everything seemed to be coming together for me. Something had focused, and I must hold on to that for a little while at least. Even the need to help my mother seemed more tuned in—as though a direction had been given me, even though I still wasn't sure what it was.

"It's better to be whole and well," I said, half to myself. "Noelle can deal with what is real if she can just come back to life. I don't think she's as fragile as they all believe. Anyway, I have to try."

David touched my hand lightly. It was a gesture of affection, of

approval, and the sudden rush of warmth I felt again disturbed me.
Slow down, I warned myself. This, at least, was a choice I could make.
Of course there was affection between David and me. Its roots lay far
back in the years, when a boy of twelve had been kind to a little girl
who was like a younger sister and who adored him. The relationship
was far more uncertain now, and filled with possible pitfalls. I'd
rushed all too easily into Scott's arms, and I mustn't repeat that
pattern. I wasn't free of Scott yet, as I knew all too well in the night's
dark hours. And David wasn't free of his wife. Rebounds were dangerous, and not what either of us would want.

Our trip down the mountain seemed shorter than the way up.
Before Pukalani, where the road to Makawao turned off, we followed
a side road David knew. Along the way, a strange, slithery little
animal darted in front of us.

"That was a mongoose," David said. "There aren't any snakes in
Hawaii for them to kill. They were brought in originally to get rid of
rats and mice. But they also kill poultry and wild birds that live on the
ground. They rob nests of eggs and baby birds, and there are no
predators to take care of them. That's the trouble when you monkey
with nature. The mongoose doesn't know that he's not allowed on
United States soil."

David pulled into a parking space beside a restaurant built where
the hillside dropped away to a deep valley. Inside, encircling windows offered a distant view. We were early and found a pleasant
corner table where we could look out upon a giant avocado tree, its
reaching branches heavy with green fruit. On the other side lay a
shadowy valley plunging down the mountain.

The sky had begun to darken and lights were coming on in the
direction of the airport, so that the curving road that led along the
Hana coast became a line of sequins—lights that vanished into the
rain forests that grew almost to the water.

Before we ordered, David went to phone Manaolana to let Joanna
know we wouldn't be there for dinner. When he returned and we'd
ordered the fish catch of the day—*aku*—I asked about David's parents.

"My father's still a doctor in Hana—semi-retired. He was born on
Maui, though he went to medical school in the States. My mother's
history is more unusual. Her great-great-grandfather was captain of a
ship that sailed out of New Bedford for the Pacific islands. He met her
great-great-grandmother in the port town of Lahaina in West Maui.
She was full-blooded Hawaiian royalty—descended from the chiefs—

or at least that's the legend. He married her and took her home to New England, where her life must have seemed strange and probably wasn't very happy. My mother is the first descendant of her line to return to Maui. She met my father here—and stayed. The same story in reverse. Except that she loves it here. She was a teacher until she retired. Now she's especially interested in Hawaiian history and the restoration and preservation of all that's historic. It can be so easily lost to the bulldozers. She's in Honolulu now, talking to a few legislators about protecting our lands. My mother's a persuasive lady."

"I'd like to meet her sometime. What fun to have Hawaiian *alii* on your family tree."

"The blood's pretty thin by now, but I'm proud of it anyway. I like to brag to Koma and other Hawaiian friends. Maybe it even gives me a bit of an *in*."

"What about your father?" I asked.

"He's the contrast to my mother—quiet, not so electric. He has a great sense of humor, and great compassion for those who need him. I think he's gained a lot of wisdom over the years. Sometimes I even listen to him."

"You're lucky to still have your parents," I said.

"I know. Caro, they'd like to see you, since they know Joanna well, and they remember when you were born. Could you drive to Hana with me sometime soon?"

"I'd enjoy that. Besides, the only way I can get to know my own parents the way they were is to meet people who knew them."

"Kate—my wife—would have liked you. And I think she'd have approved your wanting to help Noelle. She was a good therapist, and it upset her that Joanna would never let her try to help your mother."

"That seems strange."

He hesitated. "I suppose it always comes back to the same thing you've mentioned—that all of them, Joanna, Marla, Tom, feel that Noelle's memories might be too awful for her to live with if she recovered fully."

"I'm tired of hearing that! I can't believe that it's better for her to stay the way she is."

The kindling I recognized stirred in him again. I suspected that he could be a passionate advocate when both his mind and his emotions were involved.

"Good!" he approved. "I think you've changed since you went up the mountain, Caro."

"If I have, it happened when I saw the rainbow circle in the clouds —holding *me* in its center."

"I know—it shows. You've—come together somehow. I can feel it. If there's any way I can help, Caro—"

It was good to have him on my side. Especially since no one else seemed to be. "Thanks. I may need that. Did your wife think it was possible for my mother to be brought back?"

"Kate didn't know that. She managed to talk with Noelle a few times, and she wanted to try. I think she might have helped—she was brilliant in her profession. She could have made a name for herself on the mainland, but she wanted to work here because of the mingling of races. So many tensions have built up over the years. We never seem to learn how to trust one another. When Captain Cook sailed in, the world came with him."

"His murder must have set off chain reactions. Is it really known how it happened?"

"Murder is the wrong word. A lesser chief stole a longboat from Cook, and when Cook came ashore to recover it, there was fighting and Cook was killed. But it was the *kahuna*, the priests, who killed him, not the common people to whom he'd earlier become a god."

"I've read some of this, but it's never been clear to me. Cook accepted the role of a god, didn't he?"

"That was part of his arrogance. The islanders had been promised that their god, Lono, who had gone away, would return. Lono ruled thunder and storm, and brought needed rain for agriculture. So when Cook and his men appeared in the beginning with their firearms, all the omens foretold by the *kahuna* seemed right, and the people believed that Cook was the god returning to his islands as he'd promised. Cook took advantage, knowingly, of that little mistake."

"Part of his legacy was all the diseases the islands had never known, wasn't it?"

"Yes, though he made some attempt at first to keep his men from mingling with the people—something that didn't work. Anyway, the omens changed after a few years, and then the *kahuna* claimed he wasn't the god Lono after all. Many Hawaiians were killed in the fight over the boat, as well as Cook. Later the English went ashore and burned and killed. They put two heads on posts and took them as trophies. So who was the savage? Of course I'm simplifying. It's a complicated story, and has been written about pretty accurately."

The waitress came with our dinner, and as she served us I thought about David's wife, wanting to know more, yet not quite daring to ask. There were times when he seemed to move into some remote place that allowed no one to step past his reserve. I suspected that the pain of his loss was still private, and he would share it with no one.

"Tell me about your son," I said.

"Peter's a good kid. You'll meet him if you come to Hana. He makes friends instantly. Sometimes it seems as though it's an advantage *not* to have a white skin here on Maui, but Peter has friends in every group. He's a mixer, and maybe he'll do some good when he grows up. He already cares about the islands, about Maui. But of course you can get island rivalries along with everything else. I wonder if humans can ever learn to get along with one another."

After that we talked about impersonal matters, and stayed away from either of our marriages. David told me a little about his photographic work and the series of books he was doing on the islands. Koma Olivero had agreed to do the text for the book on Maui. He was especially interested in the chapter on Kahoolawe—the bombed island—and David hoped they could set a few records straight.

"Koma's talented with music too, like his mother. She doesn't sing professionally anymore, but they have a small group that does benefits for various causes, or private parties. They do the old songs, not the Hollywood variety of Hawaiian music. He's written one song himself that I especially like—'Song of the Volcano.' "

David asked about my work then—what did I want to do? The old question I could never answer.

I shook my head. "I've never really found out. Right now my focus has to be my mother. After that, I don't know."

"Things can open up," David said. "Sometimes the path appears and all that's doubtful falls into place."

"What if there was a way to take her up to the crater?" I wondered. "Not just to the rim, but down in among all those cinder cones, where it happened. I wonder if that would be dangerous for her."

"Kate used to say that with mental illness there's never only one way. You may have something there."

I kindled to his eagerness. David had stayed involved. He was more alive than any other man I'd known. Except perhaps my father?

"I know how it might be managed," he went on. "But you'll need to approach it slowly. In a few days, if you'll drive with me to Hana, we could try a dress rehearsal before you attempt the real thing."

"What do you mean?"

"I think I'd better not tell you right now. If you don't know, you won't let anything slip that might cause them to stop you. Give me a little time. I don't want you to be disappointed if I can't work it out."

I was willing to leave it at that. We had talked our way through nearly an hour and a half, and when we finished our coffee it was time to start back. I'd had a lovely, stirring experience, thanks to David, and I felt reluctant to return to all the tensions of Manaolana.

On the main road cars were still coming down the mountain from the crater, so it was a slow trip. When we arrived, we found the grounds, as well as the house itself, ablaze with light. Several ranch hands were taking orders from Joanna, who stood on the lanai, obviously in command. She watched our approach and waved the men away—a sturdy, solidly placed figure.

"Pilikia," David said, and I remembered the Hawaiian word for trouble. That was also the name given the mare who had thrown Marla in the crater.

Marla came running toward us, past her mother. "Noelle's missing! We found out only an hour or so ago that she was gone. Tom's out driving side roads looking for her. Of course you didn't see her on the main road, did you?"

"We stopped for dinner, so we could have missed her. Everything seemed to be all right here when I phoned."

"We hadn't found out then. We don't know how long she's been gone. When Tom was somewhere else, Noelle went out to the stable, saddled Ginger, and simply rode off. We've been searching the areas nearby, but goodness knows what direction she may have taken."

"Has she ever done this before?" I asked.

Joanna answered me. "Not for a long while. She's been perfectly quiet and contented for months." I could hear angry accusation rising in my grandmother's voice.

Marla put it into words. *"You* stirred her up today, Caroline. She hasn't behaved so badly in years. You aren't good for her!"

I let that pass. "You've searched her room, I suppose?"

"Of course." Marla was impatient. "She's not there."

"That's not what I mean. Do you mind if I look?"

Some apprehensive urge that I had to obey was prompting me, and I didn't wait for consent. They came with me to the room that was furnished as if for a child, and I stood for a moment looking around.

Several pretty watercolors—painted for the child who didn't exist —lay on the table. Other sheets lay face down and the wooden carving of Pele, now without her cape, had been used as a paperweight. The surge of anxiety increased in me, and I turned the three sheets face up. Marla gasped, while Joanna stood frozen in the doorway, and David put a supporting arm around her.

All three were crayon drawings of the crater of Haleakala. Noelle, who had told me that she'd never been there and that it was a terrible place, had drawn her terror in wild colors from accurate memory. One was a view from the top, showing red cinder cones, with streakings of ocher and black and buff that swirled into a wind pattern down a slope. The second drawing was an impression from within the crater, with crude figures of riders falling from rearing horses. Both came very close to the truth that was hidden deep inside Noelle's brain.

"She's doing her own therapy," I said, and turned to the third sheet.

This was imaginary—a depiction of sheer terror. Pele herself had returned to set the dead volcano on fire with streaks of crimson shooting skyward, sending rocks and lava into the air so that one could sense the explosive force that shook the mountain.

All were rough, crudely drawn—but somehow powerful. "She's gone to the top now, hasn't she?" I said to Joanna.

All the strength went out of my grandmother. She stumbled toward a chair and dropped into it. Marla, however, came to life.

"We'll go after her. If she's on the Olinda Road—which she likes to ride—we can overtake her by car. If she's cut up through pasture lands only riders can catch her."

"I'll drive," David said. "Come along!"

"I'm going with you," I told them, and moved toward the door.

Joanna roused herself to spring from her chair and grasp my arm. "They don't want you, Caroline. You only mean trouble for Noelle."

We faced each other, and I knew that for once I was stronger than my grandmother. I spoke gently as I moved from her grasp.

"She's my mother. I have to go. Don't worry—we'll find her."

She gave in and let me go.

David had started the car, and Marla was already in the front seat when I reached them. I got in beside her, and as we drove off I looked back to see Joanna standing on the lanai, her short gray hair ruffled in the wind.

She wouldn't forgive me easily for this confrontation, but all I wanted now was to find Noelle.

9

Only occasional local traffic followed the Olinda Road. No one in the car spoke at first, but I could sense Marla's seething anxiety—probably mixed with anger toward me and fear for her sister. She was forced to accept my presence in the car, but she did it in a silence that was almost vibrant.

"Look!" David said. "There ahead!"

Our headlights picked out the hindquarters of the climbing mare. Noelle had put on jeans and a sweater, and tied a scarf around her head against the wind. She sat the saddle with ease, the reins held comfortably in her left hand, the other hand resting on her right thigh. She didn't look around as we passed her, but reined in when David drew to the side of the road just ahead.

We all got out, and Marla ran back to take Ginger's bridle, while David held up his arms. "We've come to take you home, Noelle."

She sat quite still, looking down at him. "I *must* go up to the crater, David. It's Keith. He's been hurt up there and he needs me."

"That's all been taken care of," David told her gently. "Let me help you down."

In the lights from a passing car I saw her eyes for a moment, wide and frightened. Then she swung her leg over and dropped into David's arms.

"I'll take her now," Marla said. "We're going home, darling. There's nothing to worry about. You *know* you want to go home. Can you ride Ginger back, David, and I'll drive?"

"Sure." David swung himself into the saddle, while I followed Marla as she led Noelle to the car and helped her into the front seat.

When I got in beside my mother, I could feel her trembling, and I put my arm about her. She leaned into it trustingly.

"It will be all right," I said. "We'll be home soon."

"How did you know where I was going?" Noelle's voice shook, but her words were sensible.

I answered her quickly, before Marla could put her off. "We saw the crayon drawings you did of the crater. So we knew you had that in mind. You were remembering, weren't you?"

"Yes. I was remembering."

Marla had turned the car around. "Well, don't try to remember! Don't think about the crater at all." She spoke roughly.

"But I can't help thinking about it," Noelle protested. "Sometimes it just comes into my head and won't go away. Today when that happened, I tried to put the pictures in my head onto paper."

"That was a good idea," I told her, forestalling Marla again. "Though I didn't understand the one where Haleakala seemed to be erupting. It's been dormant for a long time, hasn't it? I don't think there's any activity up there."

"It was *like* an eruption when everything happened that day." She spoke fearfully. "It was like my whole life erupting."

"Can you tell me about it?" I asked.

Marla made an angry sound of objection, but Noelle went on.

"I don't remember exactly. Sometimes pictures come into my head, but they slip away so easily. Look—there's David on the road. Be careful, Marla."

Marla drove past horse and rider with a beep of the horn, and then snapped at me. "Can't you leave her alone, Caroline?"

But I couldn't do that—not when my mother had begun to open up a little.

"This morning at Ahinahina," I reminded her, "you told me you knew that Keith was dead—a long time ago."

"That's enough!" Marla cried. "Don't try to remember, darling. You know it makes your head hurt."

Noelle began to cry softly like a bewildered child, and all I could offer was the pressure of my arm about her. There was nothing further to say now, but there would be a time when I could get her away from Marla. I had the strong feeling that my mother was almost ready to open the past and face all the things she had shut away.

There was one more question I could ask her now, however, before she slipped away altogether.

"Noelle," I said, "do you have any idea how the tapa beater got from your mother's office up to the crater? You remember the beater, don't you?"

Apparently this was a dangerous question. Marla lost her temper and told me to shut up. Noelle seemed to crumple against me and grow even more fragile. When she spoke I knew she'd retreated from reality.

"Where are we? Why isn't Linny with us?"

By the time we reached the house, Noelle was clinging to her sister, who knew the right words of reassurance. False reassurance, I was beginning to feel.

Joanna rushed out to meet us, and as soon as I was out of the front seat she reached for Noelle. I watched unhappily as she held and soothed her daughter, who still needed her. She and Marla both helped their charge into the house, and I suspected there would now be more tranquilizers, more shutting away of the past that seemed to frighten them all.

I stayed outside in the cool evening. Sounds drifted toward me from the stable of horses stamping, making their own snorting noises before settling down for the night. Since I hadn't been out to the stables, I decided to explore. There was moonlight and outdoor light besides. I walked around the house, following the direction of the sounds. David would bring Ginger back here, and I wanted to thank him for dinner and the whole afternoon. In spite of what had happened to Noelle, I had the feeling that I would never be quite the same again.

The stables weren't as large as they'd been when I was a little girl, and only the nearest building was in use. A few ranch hands and stable boys were employed now, and Tom supervised the operation.

I found Tom outside, rubbing down his own horse. "Did you find her?" he asked as I came up beside him.

"Yes. She was riding toward the crater."

"Crazy," he said. "She really is crazy." He sounded both angry and sad, and I knew he must be remembering Noelle as she used to be—before she'd married my father.

"I don't think she's crazy," I told him. "She's confused and she's shutting out something she's afraid to remember. But sometimes she comes very close to facing whatever it is she's hiding from. Don't you think it might be better if she faced it?"

He patted the flank of the chestnut gelding and led the horse into the stable. I followed as Tom put the animal into its stall and watched as he hung up the tack and went outside, never answering me.

"Do you mind if I wait here until David brings Ginger back?" I asked.

"Suit yourself."

I sat down on a bench outdoors. The stable smells were laced with the scent of night-blooming jasmine—a familiar mix that reminded me of when I was a little girl and had loved to visit my grandmother's stables.

Tom stood a little way off, lighting his pipe. "You wouldn't talk all that wishful stuff about her not being crazy if you'd heard her yesterday when she came out here to see me. She was off on one of her hunting-for-Linny spells, and she brought along that ugly wooden idol you used to play with when you were small. She was talking to it as though she expected it to tell her where you were."

"Maybe she was asking Pele to help," I said. "What happened then?"

"The usual thing. She forgot what she was doing and went off somewhere, leaving the carving behind."

"Oh?" I said, pricking to attention. "Where is it now?"

"I meant to take it back to the house, but I must have left it somewhere."

So he was the one. I didn't feel much surprise. "I found it this afternoon, Tom—out behind the big camphor tree. You must have dropped it there when you ran through the bushes last night. Did you hear anything especially interesting from David and me?"

He came straight to me, his pipe clenched between his teeth, and for just a moment I thought he was going to shake me. But though he put his hands on my shoulders, he only held them firmly.

"Go home," he said around the pipe stem. "Go home before something happens to you. This isn't a good place for you to be."

I sat very still under his hands, and after a moment he released me and stepped back. I got up quickly and would have returned to the house, but David came riding in on Ginger just then, and I waited for him in relief. Tom had frightened me a little.

"I'll take care of her," Tom said as David dismounted.

"Thanks, Tom. Good night." David held out a hand to me, and we started toward the house together. "How is Noelle?"

"They're wrapping her in cotton wool again," I said, "and everyone's angry with me, including Tom."

"Tom?"

"Yes. He's the one who was listening near the tree last night. He's made his dislike for me clear ever since I came."

"Maybe they're all beginning to open up, Caro. All those pressed-in flower petals are stirring. If you stay with it, everything may come into the open."

"I'm not sure that's a safe course," I told him. "Marla thinks they could turn into dragons and serpents, instead of flowers. Sometimes I think that I don't even want to find out."

"You know better than that," he said. "No matter what comes, it's better to know. Maybe better for them all. Just give it a little time. You've stirred them all up enough for now."

"I don't have much time. Any minute Joanna's going to pack me off home. Only San Francisco isn't my home anymore."

"You grew up there. Isn't there any pull left?"

"For the city, perhaps. San Francisco's a great town."

"But not for the people?"

"After I married, I lost touch with old friends." I didn't want to explain that Scott had liked only *his* friends.

We were nearing the house, and David said, "There's no need for me to come inside. I'll call you soon and see how things are going. We'll plan to drive to Hana when my mother comes home from Honolulu."

"Thank you for dinner," I said formally. For a little while up there on the rim of the crater, we'd seemed very close, more than old friends. I touched the kukui beads. "And thank you for these."

"Sure," he said, and went off to his car.

I waited on the lawn as he turned toward the road, feeling unsettled, unsure. As I approached the lanai, I looked back for a moment at the camphor tree, where David and I had stood talking last night. What sense of guilt had sent Tom rushing off, not wanting to be found eavesdropping? So much so that he'd been angry when I brought the matter up.

At least I knew now who had listened, though not *why*.

No one was around in the living room, but I could hear voices in the direction of Noelle's room. I went upstairs and sat on the window seat in my room for a while, trying to sort out my day. One thing I knew. When I had seen that strange spirit shadow cast into a rainbow circle on far clouds, everything had seemed to come into focus. As though I had come to Maui for some special purpose from which I must not be deflected. The word "destiny" had come into my mind, and I found it a heartening word because in a way it seemed to settle everything. Yet it didn't altogether please me because I couldn't rely on being "led." I had to take action about all those things myself, and

I still didn't know what practical steps might help my mother. Or me. All I had was a distant goal—as distant as that shadow on the clouds.

I didn't want to think of what David might come to mean to me. In that direction might lie quicksand, and I needed no more pain. The thought of Scott could become too quickly urgent, and I wanted none of him—ever again. Yet he still intruded between me and any other man. David mustn't be used as a protection from my memories of Scott.

I touched the kukui beads again, feeling for an instant the joy I'd felt when he'd given them to me. Then I took them off and dropped them into a drawer. They belonged to my childhood and I couldn't recover that.

Something had quieted in me momentarily, and I fell asleep easily enough. I didn't open my eyes until the dark hours of early morning. Some sound had awakened me, and I lay still, breathing the scent of ginger that had come into my room.

The moon had long set, but a silvery shaft of starlight came through the window and I caught the shimmer of a woman's white garment and the glint of a white flower tucked into her hair. She stood near enough to my bed so that I caught the light sound of her breathing.

There was no telling whether Noelle meant me harm or just wanted to talk to me. I tensed, ready to spring up if she made any threatening move in my direction. Though it wasn't so much the fear of any harm she might do me that made me afraid, but the feeling that she was being pushed too far over the edge of sanity into a place from which she might never return.

I lay quiet and waited.

Her white garment murmured softly as she moved closer to my bed, and I had to make an effort not to roll away out of reach. First I must know what she intended.

Starlight showed some dark object in her hands, and she moved suddenly, swiftly, to place it on the pillow beside my head. Then she turned toward the door. But now she didn't move lightly—as though she no longer cared whether I heard her. A board creaked under her foot, and she stood still for a moment—perhaps waiting to see if I'd wakened.

I moved my hand to touch the object on my pillow, and my fingers found the dished-in, angry face of the Pele carving. There could be more than one kind of harm intended. She moved again toward the door, but this time I moved too. I flung back the bedcovers and sprang up to run across the floor and catch her by the arm. The scent of ginger was strong and sweet.

"Wait, Noelle," I whispered. "Stay and talk to me. Tell me why you brought me the Pele figure."

Her laughter was wry—and it was not Noelle's. She turned around and in the light from the window I saw that the woman I'd captured was Marla.

"Okay," she said, "we'll talk. Turn on the light, Caroline."

Angry with her trickery, I switched on a lamp with a sharp click. The night air from the mountain was cool, and I picked up my robe and slipped into it.

"What are you trying to do?" I demanded.

Her plump figure was well covered by the long white gown, and she looked calm and amused as she went to close the casement against the early-morning breeze. She was pleased with herself, and I grew all the more irritated.

"When did you wake up?" she asked me. "When did you know I was here?"

"When I smelled the flower you're wearing."

She touched the ginger blossom. "That was a nice touch, don't you think—just in case you woke up before I could place Pele beside you. Hand me that blanket, Caroline. It's cold."

I picked up a blanket from the foot of the bed and flung it at her. "Stop stalling, Marla."

She wrapped the blanket around her shoulders and dropped into a chair, while I got back into bed, the carving still in one hand.

"I was trying to scare you," she said. "What else? Of course, I keep forgetting that you're not the little kid I remember."

"I don't think you forget that at all. You enjoy mischief-making. But if this silly trick was intended to make me pack up and run back to San Francisco, it isn't going to work."

"I can see that. I suppose I make up too many scenarios inside my own head, and then I'm surprised when someone real walks in and spoils the script for me. I just thought a little scare might help you to decide. It would be a sensible decision, Caroline."

"I have decided. I'll stay as long as Joanna will let me."

"You've changed since you went up to the crater. I could feel it when we were driving down in the car, after we found Noelle. What happened up there, Caroline?"

That was nothing I would talk to her about. "You might as well accept the fact that I mean to stay a while longer."

"A week," she said. "We'll give you a week more on Maui."

"Isn't that up to my grandmother?"

"Oh, we'll make it an entertaining week—there's so much you haven't seen yet. We'll keep you so busy you won't have time for all this pointless worry about Noelle. She's perfectly happy when you leave her alone."

"I'm not sure a vacuum is a happy place to be. And I don't want to be entertained."

"But of course you must be! Hawaiians are noted for their hospitality. I already have a plan in mind—a special performance to be put on in your honor."

"Stop it, Marla," I said. "Just tell me one thing—who carried that tapa beater up to the crater when my father died?"

Her light, rather jolly manner evaporated, though she tried again to put me off. "You mentioned that to Noelle tonight, but I don't know what you're talking about."

"I'm sure you do. Joanna showed me that tool and said Tom found it up there after the accident. Is that my father's blood on the wood?"

Marla came to stand beside my bed, her eyes very bright in lamplight. "You wouldn't want to know about that," she told me, and ran out of the room, leaving the door open behind her.

I got up to close it, feeling as though some new weight pressed heavily upon me. Marla stood in the doorway across the hall, her smile malicious. She was being mysterious again, and I might have closed my door without speaking but she stopped me.

"Wait, Caroline—I forgot to tell you. We're driving to Lahaina today. We'll have an early lunch and leave right afterwards. It's a trip you'll enjoy. So get some sleep. Good night, Caroline dear."

She disappeared into her room, giving me no chance to answer. I went back to bed again, but not to sleep for a long while. Birds outside the window were announcing dawn when I finally drifted off. My dreams were threatening, but when I awoke around eight, I couldn't remember them, and didn't want to. Only the ominous mood they left behind remained. The vision in the crater was fading, and the day ahead promised nothing but more smoke screens and distractions thrown across my path. A determination to help my mother meant very little until I could find something definite to hold on to. It was impossible to fight with mists that always moved out of my grasp.

Tom, as usual, had breakfasted early, and I was glad not to see him when I went downstairs. My grandmother looked gray and depressed, and anything but pleased to see me. Marla was late too this morning, and she sat eating French toast with pineapple preserve. Beneath her straight, dark bangs her eyes were watchful, even a little cautious—as though, perhaps, she wasn't as sure of me as she pretended.

"Noelle has a headache," she said. "She was ill most of the night. So are you pleased with yourself, Caroline?"

I didn't mean to take guilt onto myself. None of them was entirely innocent when it came to upsetting Noelle. Otherwise, she would never have headed for the crater as she'd done. I dropped bread into the toaster and poured myself a cup of coffee.

Marla, however, meant to leave nothing alone. "Early this morning Caroline had a spectral visitor," she announced to Joanna. "Maybe she'd like to give you an account."

I wouldn't allow Marla that satisfaction and I said nothing. Joanna had breakfasted, but she brought more coffee to the table and sat down beside me without comment.

Marla was not to be put off. "I'll tell you, if Caroline won't. I put on a white *muumuu*, stuck a ginger blossom in my hair, and carried that wooden carving of Pele into Caroline's room. I left it on her pillow meaning to make her think Noelle had been there. But she woke up and caught me."

Joanna swallowed black coffee and looked at neither of us.

Perhaps our combined silence was making Marla uncomfortable. "I just wanted to give Caroline a good scare. To make her leave sooner than she plans. You'd approve of that, wouldn't you, Mother?"

Joanna sighed. "Sometimes Marla enjoys tricks for the sake of tricks, Caroline. She probably wanted you to catch her. It would be more dramatic that way."

"I can never fool my mother," Marla admitted cheerfully.

There seemed to be only one person toward whom she was genuinely sympathetic—Noelle. Yet her concern for her sister seemed intended only to hold the status quo.

"We're going to Lahaina today, Mother—Caroline and I," she went on. "I plan to see Ailina Olivero and ask her to put on a little show for Caroline while she's here."

Joanna came to life. "No! That wouldn't be wise. Especially if Ailina came here."

"Oh, we can pack Noelle off for the evening, so there'd be no strain for her. Though by this time she may not even remember who Ailina is. I want to do this, Mother."

"And you'll do as you please, of course." Joanna gave up, as she would never have done in the past. It was as though nothing was worth fighting for anymore.

I didn't like the idea of Marla's plan, and I didn't want to meet the woman who had betrayed my mother. "I agree with my grandmother, Marla," I told her. "I don't want to see her."

Marla reminded me of a Buddha figure sitting there—calm and plump, her faint cryptic smile hiding secrets. Whether her secrets were real or imaginary, I could never tell, but I suspected that Marla amused herself by stirring up the very serpents she'd warned me about.

"We'll leave right after lunch," she said, ignoring my plea.

In the end, it was easier to give in as Joanna had done. And once I'd decided to go through with this meeting, a certain curiosity began to stir in me. Ailina had told her son that she wanted to meet me, and I still wondered why. How well had she known Noelle? There could even be something she might explain about the past. Perhaps I'd better take the opportunity Marla had offered, even though the meeting would probably not be pleasant.

"All right," I agreed.

Marla's smile was sly. She'd never had the least doubt that I would do as she wished.

She went outside before I finished breakfast, and when I left the table I hurried down the hall to Noelle's room. The door stood ajar, and I tapped lightly on the panel.

"Come in . . ." It was no more than a whisper.

From an open window the sunny blue morning poured into the room and the air was soft and fragrant. Noelle lay in bed, a breakfast tray untouched on the table beside her.

"Good morning," I said. "May I help you with your breakfast?"

"I'm not hungry." Her voice was still faint. "My head hurts. Marla says it always hurts after I do something foolish. Last night I rode out on Ginger, didn't I?"

"Don't you remember?"

She shook her head and turned her cheek against the pillow, closing her eyes. I sat on the bed beside her and took one of her limp hands in mine. Her skin was smooth and tanned, soft and well cared for. But hands show age before anything else, and this wasn't the hand of a young wife in her twenties. Blue veins lay close to the surface and the tendon ridges were marked. I traced the length of her fingers, wishing I could offer her comfort. But not only comfort—escape from the prison that held her.

Suddenly she opened her eyes and looked at me out of gray depths that seemed limitless. Startled, I let her hand go.

"You remind me of someone," she said. "I keep thinking about that and wondering who it is. But I don't believe we've ever met before you came here—have we?"

I hated this question that I didn't dare answer. I couldn't try again until she was ready for the truth that I longed to give her. I stood up and moved around the room. The pretty watercolors, painted for Linny, still lay on her worktable. But someone had removed the angry volcano pictures.

A framed photograph stood on a shelf, and I picked it up. The enlarged snapshot was of a man, a woman, and a child: Keith, Noelle, and Linny.

My father had been as good-looking as Grandmother Elizabeth always claimed, but this was a more recent picture of him than all those boyhood photos she kept on display. This was how I remembered him—vigorous-looking, strong, charming, as though for Keith Kirby enchanting adventures always lay ahead. Yet here his smile seemed to question and perhaps challenge whoever held the camera. He stood a little apart from my mother, with the small child I'd been in between. A solemn child that day. I had clung to both their hands, as though I wanted desperately to hold them together. My mother hadn't smiled. Indeed, she looked angry as she faced the camera. The body language of the two adults seemed to indicate that only the child connected them.

I carried the framed picture to Noelle's bed. "Do you remember who took this?" I asked.

She looked at the glossy enlargement and then away. "I only kept it because I don't have many pictures of Linny. I used to have, but they've all disappeared. I hated Keith that day, though I can't remember now what made me so furious with him. It's funny the way I remember some things and not others. Marla thinks I shouldn't try to remember. But sometimes I *want* to—and when it won't come, my head starts to hurt."

"Last night you were trying to remember, weren't you? When you rode off on Ginger?"

Her shrug seemed to dismiss last night. "I'm not supposed to think about that. This picture was taken a long time ago. I know Keith is dead. Though I can't remember what happened, and no one will tell me."

"So this picture of Linny is also old. She would be grown up by now, wouldn't she?"

"I suppose so." Noelle brushed a hand across her forehead in confusion. "If that's true then I've missed all those years of watching her grow—years that are lost somewhere, so I can't bring them back."

"Linny has missed knowing her mother too," I said.

"Don't be silly!" That was Marla's sharp voice from the doorway. "Linny's gone outside to play, Noelle, and you'll see her in a little while. So do get up now and eat your breakfast. I'm sure your head's better by this time, and I'll make you fresh toast and bring some hot coffee."

Noelle looked uncertainly from her sister to me, puzzled again. Nevertheless, she sat up in bed obediently, ready to get dressed.

I bent to kiss her on the cheek, and she accepted my caress in the same puzzled way, lost once more, as she so often seemed to be when Marla was present. There would be no further chance for me to be alone with her now, and I left her to Marla and went out to the lanai.

Joanna had started off toward the stables.

"May I come with you?" I called.

She nodded indifferently. "If you like. I'm just taking a walk."

"Escaping?" I asked, falling in beside her as she turned toward the road that led past the nearest stable and up toward the paddock.

"I only wish I could, Caro. But nothing is ever going to be any different from the way it is now. That's what you must accept for the time that you're here."

"I don't want to accept it! *You* used to stand up to things when I was little. I remember how strong you were, and how I always counted on you."

She walked on, her eyes fixed straight ahead. "Marla's changed a lot from when she was young. She used to be terribly jealous of Noelle. She felt that her sister had everything she lacked—beauty, popularity, then a husband and a daughter. I'm afraid some of her resentment was my fault. Marla wasn't always a lovable child, but she was sturdy and strong, where Noelle needed much more care and attention. I suppose I showed more affection for Noelle than I was able to show Marla."

"So now perhaps Marla's getting even?"

Joanna looked startled. "How can you say that? She's changed to a much more loving sister, and she looks after Noelle with great care, and tries to spare her any hurt or unhappiness. I appreciate what she's doing, and I try to make up for my not caring enough in the past."

Somehow, I wasn't convinced, and I wondered if my grandmother was simply fooling herself. More and more it seemed to me that Marla's treatment of my mother showed a hint of the malicious, perhaps even the cruel. But this wasn't what Joanna wanted to believe.

We'd climbed to where paddock fences began, and we both sat down on a big outcropping of rock to watch the horses. Lihilihi was there with her new foal, and I watched the gangly little thing with pleasure.

The sun had risen above the mountain, and the wide top of Haleakala stood clear high above us. Nearby, hibiscus and oleander bushes were bright with shades of red. I wanted to let all purpose, all struggle flow out of me and accept the tranquility of the morning. But I hadn't yet earned the reward of peace, and wasn't sure I ever would.

"Tell me about Koma's mother," I said. "I'm going to Lahaina with Marla this afternoon, and she said we'd see her there. You don't want this to happen, do you?"

"I don't want her to come here. You can do as you please. I don't suppose it matters—nothing matters anymore."

"That's not the way you used to be," I protested again. "It's not really the way you are now. I've seen you take hold. If you took a stronger stand with Noelle, maybe she could be helped."

Joanna only shook her head. "The grandmother you remember disappeared a long time ago. I'm too old for this sort of battle now."

"You've given up to Marla! But I'm not sure that's the wise thing to do."

"I'm not sure of anything anymore. Be quiet now, Caroline. Look at the horses. Let everything else go."

I tried to obey, but there was a tightness in me that wouldn't unwind. She sensed it and after a while she relented and began to talk quietly about Koma's mother.

"I think you'll like Ailina. Everyone always has."

"Including my father?"

At least I'd sparked some interest in her. "Who told you that?"

"Yesterday, when we went to Ahinahina, I remembered something that happened one evening when I was small. Ailina and some other people were singing in the garden and playing Hawaiian music. My mother became terribly angry and made a scene. Small as I was, I knew the beautiful Hawaiian lady had caused the trouble. I've talked about her since with David. If I'm to meet her today, I ought to know just what I'm getting into."

"Look, Caroline, your father was the way he was. I couldn't condone, and I didn't like him for what he was doing to Noelle. I sometimes had the feeling that he was trying to get even with *his* mother. Perhaps that was his main drive. Not that it excuses him. If we don't take responsibility for our own actions, we can't ever be whole human beings. In fact, I wonder how many of us achieve that anyway. Events get in the way. It wasn't only Noelle your father injured; it was Marla too. She was idiotic enough to fall in love with him."

"Marla! *She* was in love with my father?"

"It doesn't matter anymore, so you might as well know. She used to have a gift for deceiving herself and thinking whatever she chose about any situation. She even believed for a little while that Keith would divorce Noelle and marry her. Which, of course, was nonsense. Even if he couldn't be faithful, Noelle was the one he came back to. At least until Ailina came into the picture. I don't think Ailina even liked him in the beginning, but she was very young, and your father was a charmer. As long as your mother could laugh and take what he did lightly, things went fine on the surface. It was when Noelle stopped laughing that it all turned sour."

"Weren't there other men for Marla after my father died?"

"Not really. Oh, she was pretty enough in those days, and she never wanted for a man. But your mother isn't the only one whose emotions were frozen into the past. I suppose your coming here has stirred everything up again for Marla."

"She seemed fond of me when I was little."

"You weren't any threat to her then. Now you are—because of Noelle. She's become more of a mother to Noelle than I've ever been."

"Why is she taking me to meet Ailina? Why couldn't her plans be managed by telephone?"

"Who knows what script she's following in her head? Marla's always been too imaginative. You might as well go along and play it by ear."

That was all I could do. Though perhaps there would be something more, if Ailina were willing to talk about my father.

"Anyway, Caroline, you'll be going home soon, and then you can put this behind you and start living a life of your own."

There was no use arguing with her about that.

She went on, changing the subject. "David phoned this morning. He wanted to know how Noelle was and he asked about you. You weren't up yet, so I didn't have much to tell him. He wants you to go to Hana with him day after tomorrow—Friday."

In spite of all my warnings to myself, the thought of a whole day spent with David lifted my spirits. I needed something to look forward to.

Joanna went to the fence and called to Lihilihi. The mare came readily to nibble the carrot held out to her, and her lively child came with her on legs still not quite certain.

"When you found Noelle last night," Joanna said over her shoulder, "did she say anything about why she was riding up the mountain?"

"She said Keith was hurt and she had to go up there to help him. I talked to her a little while ago and she seemed to be mixed up in time again. But somehow, I think she *wants* to remember."

Joanna surprised me with a sudden outburst. "Sometimes I want her to! Almost anything would be better than the way things are now."

"Then you're on my side," I said eagerly. "You'll help me?"

Her brief show of emotion died away at once, and she spoke listlessly. "Caro, honey, it isn't possible. Marla and Tom are both against what I might have done—perhaps should have done—long ago. They're sure this would destroy Noelle, and I can't fight them. I never could."

If my grandmother felt like this, she was a captive in her own house. If she could just be roused to stand against those two, perhaps I'd have a chance with Noelle.

"I can understand about Marla," I said. "But why Tom?"

"I suppose he still remembers his old feeling for her."

"I wonder. He tolerates her, but he also seems impatient with her at times."

She turned her back on the nuzzling mare, and leaned against the fence, facing me. "How can you possibly be sure that Noelle would be any better off if she remembers? What if Marla and Tom are right? Noelle must have seen everything that happened. Her mind has had the wisdom to put the truth—whatever it is—away from her. This is something we can live with. The other way—Noelle might be taken from us because of her spells of violence. If she ever injures anyone, we could lose her. How can I make you see this, Caroline?"

The awful thing was that my grandmother might be right. "I wish I could find a way to be convinced of something. Of anything."

"Listen to me!" Joanna's lethargy lifted again. "What if Marla believes that Noelle herself wielded the tapa beater—that she was so angry with Keith that she attacked him? What if she should remember that *she* caused her husband's death? Your father's death?"

Everything in me rejected this. "Do you believe that?"

She shrugged, giving up again—the old seesaw. I was sharply aware of her own attitude of self-defeat, and I gave up too for the moment.

"I'd better go back to the house and change my clothes if we're to drive to Lahaina," I told her. "Marla said we'd have lunch early before we leave."

"Have a good trip," Joanna said absently.

When I paused partway down the path and looked back, she stood at the paddock rail staring up at the mountain. As though *it* held all the answers.

In the house I went upstairs and changed into my favorite cool dress of hyacinth blue. Sandals with low heels would help for walking. At the last minute I put on David's kukui lei that I'd rejected last night. My thoughts seemed as muddled and disoriented as Noelle's.

There was one question no one had answered—which one of the riders had carried the tapa beater to the crater? I would find out from Marla today. Somehow I would persuade her to tell me before this coming trip was over.

10

Once we were down the mountain, the highway across the isthmus into West Maui was a fine road, wide and fast. Now there were sugarcane fields wherever space offered. We passed signs that read: SMOKE AHEAD, since in Hawaii cane was burned before it was harvested, to concentrate the sugar. Once we passed a fiery field where the burning seemed out of control, but men were working around it to contain the flames.

As we followed the road around their base, the massive West Maui mountains cut steeply down on our right, slashed by deep ravines. Since their rise was close and more precipitous, they seemed higher than Haleakala, though their height was only half as great. In some places the road had been sliced through black lava rock that crowded us toward the sea. On our left were beaches—sometimes smooth sand, sometimes stretches of rock or pebbles. White-crested rollers surged in to be challenged by tiny figures on surfboards, balancing skillfully in their ride toward shore, or else tumbling into roaring foam, bodies and boards tossed together wildly.

In several places little parks had been created between road and beach, furnished with picnic tables and shade trees—protected spaces for all to enjoy sand and water. Places where the condominiums and hotels could never encroach.

This morning both sky and ocean wore their pure Hawaiian blue, while far-out puffs of white cloud traveled swiftly before the wind. Sunlight glittered on every swell, turning water to a shade of emerald as it neared the shore. In some places the water came nearly to the road, and during a storm this highway must become impassable. There weren't too many roads to offer choices on Maui.

I still held back from asking my question, because once it was asked the atmosphere between Marla and me would change. For the moment, she was trying to keep everything friendly, though I felt sure she hadn't relented in the least about hurrying me home to San Francisco.

"Tell me about David's wife," I said. "He talked about her a little yesterday."

"I never liked her much," Marla said frankly. "I think she looked at all of us at Manaolana as interesting neurotic specimens. Especially Noelle, of course. Luckily, my mother would never let her treat Noelle."

"Why luckily?"

"Because I think Kate's probing would have made everything worse. Oh, she was plenty smart and successful in her work. She knew a great deal—but she didn't know *us.*"

"How did she die?"

"A drowning accident. Currents can be tricky off Maui, and she wasn't Hawaiian born. Of course her death hit David pretty hard. And Peter too—their little boy. David's just beginning to come out of it, though I doubt if he'll ever find another woman who can measure up to Kate in his eyes. So be careful, Caroline."

There was the malice again. Marla always saw too much.

We didn't speak again until she nudged me. "Look at the monkeypods!"

We were passing a grove of wind-twisted trees, their flat tops offering a canopy of shade.

"Henry Perrine Baldwin planted a number of monkeypods on Maui, including those. As well as poinciana regia and other trees. He wanted to leave a legacy of beauty for future generations to enjoy. Baldwin, of course, is one of the old missionary names on Maui, and there are still descendants of the family living here."

"Were they among the first missionaries to come?"

"Dwight Baldwin was. Since he was a good doctor, as well as a missionary, he devoted himself to the care of bodies as well as souls. You'll see the house where he lived, since Ailina Olivero is working there as a volunteer. It was a big family and Baldwin descendants became the planters and businessmen who changed the island's entire fortunes."

"Those early landowners must have had it made, with all the help available for their sugarcane and pineapples."

"Those first white landowners got the land easily because the Hawaiians couldn't conceive of land ownership. The land had always belonged to the gods. Most native Hawaiians had the good sense to prefer fishing to working in fields and canneries. Besides, the planters found they could get cheaper labor by bringing in workers from outside. The Chinese came first, and then the Japanese, who've settled on all the islands. There were Scotsmen, too, who migrated to the islands, as well as Norwegians, Germans, and Portuguese. The Filipino wave came last. Now Samoans come from American Samoa. There are Tongans too—mostly illegal, like the Mexicans in California. The language problem has been really something, but that's why we're such a wonderful, rich world mixture."

As we rode along beside the water, the fascination of waves rolling in below the road held me. In the land direction clouds flowed through gaps above steep slopes that were sometimes green and planted, sometimes bare. We followed through a tunnel cut in the rock, and for a few moments daylight dimmed. Then we were around the curve and approaching the town. The island of Lanai floated across the water.

"Lahaina's a mixture of the old plus a lot of tourist honky-tonk," Marla warned. "There was a day when it was the whaling capital of the world, but thank goodness we're leaving the whales alone now. Even more important to history, it was the first capital of Hawaii, when Kamehameha the Great united the islands. Of course, it's been more than a hundred years since the monarchy moved the capital to Honolulu."

These were Marla's islands, and her voice warmed as she talked about them. They were my islands too, but I was still a stranger, and while I listened with interest, there were more personal things I wanted to ask about.

"Marla, do you know who took that picture of my father and mother and me that I saw in Noelle's room this morning?"

"Of course I know—I took it," she said.

I thought of the challenging smile my father wore in the snapshot, and Noelle's angry expression. Even I, clinging to their hands, had looked sober.

"What did you do to make them both so mad at you?" I persisted.

She wasn't playing Buddha now, and she spoke caustically. "How should I remember? I was always ruffling somebody in those days. I guess I was born a rebel."

Her denial came so quickly that I suspected she remembered

something very well. Something disturbing that must have happened that day.

She changed the subject quickly. "What did you do with the rock I gave you to return to the crater?"

"David took me down the beginning of a trail and I left it there."

"What did you say?"

"I don't remember exactly, but I think I spoke the right words. I didn't feel like being anything but respectful."

For once Marla gave me a smile of approval. "Thanks, Caro. Now perhaps everything will be better."

I asked a direct question. "What is it you're afraid of?"

"I don't think you really want to know." She gave me the same answer she had before, when I'd asked who had carried the tapa beater up to the crater. Since we were back to the same response, I pushed my real question.

"Don't put me off, Marla. Who carried that museum piece up the mountain? And why?"

"It was there for anyone to pick up who walked into my mother's office."

"That's not what I asked."

"So she huffed and she puffed and she blew the house down! Is that what you really want, Caroline?"

"What if it has to come down before it can be built up again?"

She didn't answer. We were coming into Lahaina now, and small modern houses climbed the slopes between cane fields—some of them probably company houses built for workers.

Along the waterfront, older structures had been restored—through the efforts of the Lahaina Restoration Foundation and Maui Historical Society, Marla said. Much of the original flavor of this little seaport town had been preserved. No one could build anything new that was out of character, or destroy what was old.

Every possible type of shop crowded elbow to elbow along Front Street, and tourists in sun hats, bright skirts, and shorts thronged the sidewalks. Shops offered everything from seashells and black coral to oriental antiques and fine ivory and jade. Art galleries and restaurants mingled with historic buildings—all a hodgepodge that one didn't find to this extent in other parts of Maui.

The street was narrow and traffic moved slowly bumper to bumper. Marla watched for a parking place, and she was lucky. "This is Baldwin House," she said as she pulled in to the curb. "Let's go find Ailina."

I put my hand on her arm before she could get out. "Please answer my question first. I want to know about the tapa beater."

She drew away from my touch. "You're a lot more than meddlesome and inquisitive. You can't let anything alone, even though the status quo has been possible to live with for all these years. All right, then—I'll tell you. Your mother is the one who carried that horrible thing up to the crater in her saddlebag. Now are you satisfied? It couldn't have been for a harmless purpose, could it? She was in a rage that day."

After what Joanna had told me, this was what I'd been afraid to hear. Yet I still had to push it further. "What really happened, Marla?"

She threw up her hands, and then slammed them down on the wheel. "Sometimes I wish I knew, and sometimes I'm glad I don't. I can't even remember getting to the top. When I woke up in the hospital a piece of my life was gone. Just as so much of Noelle's is gone. But I was luckier, because I lost only a short space of memory. Believe me, I've read a lot about amnesia since then, and it can come in all sorts of forms. It's not something medical people can always pin down and explain. Or cure. Mine happened because of a blow to my head when poor old Pilikia kicked me. Tom had to shoot her, you know, but I was out of it by that time."

She started to leave the car, and then turned back to me. "Can't we just let Noelle alone?"

What had seemed so right to me when I'd stood on the rim of the crater, filled with courage and a feeling that I could rise above anything I'd ever been, no longer seemed clear and certain, and I couldn't answer her.

"Let's go in," Marla said. Out of the car's air conditioning, the afternoon was warm and sunny—warmer than up on Haleakala's slopes. The name Lahaina meant "cruel sun," but this was October and not the hot time of year.

Marla led the way along a walk to where the Baldwin Home (as a sign called it) sat well back from the street among tropical trees and shrubbery. Two long porches—lanais—fronted the structure above and below, and the house stood with its whitewashed walls facing the street, simple, square-built, and dignified. Its front posts were painted green, as were the window blinds. A house well suited to the climate.

"It's been restored to the way it was in the 1850s," Marla said. "It was built earlier, but in that year an extra room and a second story

were added because Dr. Baldwin's family had grown, and he entertained visitors from all over the world. Though the Baldwins weren't
the first missionaries who came here. An earlier minister, the Rever-
end Richards, even left the ministry to take political office under
Kamehameha the Third, and he really furthered education in an
enlightened and forethinking way. Baldwin came a bit later. He
made an impact both as a minister and as a doctor. In 1851 he
probably saved most of the population of Maui, Molokai, and Lanai
from a smallpox epidemic. Medicine and the teachings of the Bible!
You know what the Hawaiians called the Bible? 'God in a little black
box.' "

Marla was talking to distract me, and I knew she didn't want me to
think any more about the tapa beater.

We climbed brick steps to the lower level, where a woman in a gray
muumuu sat at a small table, providing brochures and information to
visitors. Marla asked for Ailina and we were told she was inside.

For a moment I felt uncertain about meeting this woman, but no
one was in sight as we walked into a cool, airy room, from which
other rooms opened on either hand along the width of the house.
More windows overlooked a back garden, so air could blow through.
The walls were painted white, and grass matting covered the floors.

In the adjoining dining room a table had been set with blue willow-
ware, and a high plate rack near the ceiling held decorative china. All
the furniture was beautifully made and simple—in character for this
missionary family.

As I stood looking around, Ailina came in from another room, and I
stiffened. I wasn't ready to be open-minded about this woman whom
my father had loved.

"Hello, Ailina," Marla said. "This is Caroline Kirby—Ailina
Olivero."

While many Hawaiians were small in stature, this woman was tall
—in fact, majestic in her build. Beneath a blue, flower-printed
muumuu her body formed rounded contours, and her shoulders
were wide, her carriage splendid—a beautiful woman with a face
that had kept its softness of rounded cheek and chin. But there was
warmth here too, and no animosity toward me. Her large brown eyes
were long-lashed, and her hair, drawn into a mound high at the back
of her head, was a glossy black. The creamy brown of her skin appeared flawless, and the movements of her hands had a dancer's
grace as she came toward me holding them out in greeting. She was
glad to see me, and I began to relax in spite of myself.

"Keith's daughter," she said. "Welcome to Maui. I remember you
—a pretty little thing who resembled your mother, except for your
coloring. Now you look much more like your father."

Here was an unexpected openness. No one had been willing to talk
about my father, but perhaps this woman would.

"Can we go somewhere to sit down and talk?" Marla asked.

"Why not the Banyan Tree?" Ailina suggested. "Lahaina's favorite
meeting place. I've arranged to take some time off, so we can go now,
if you like."

We walked the short distance to the park. The red-roofed structure
of the old Pioneer Inn offered a shaded walk, and beyond the building lay the harbor. Down a side street we could see masts and moored
boats.

We crossed to the banyan tree that W. O. Smith, a sheriff of Lahaina
had planted. I'd expected a large tree, but this tree was a forest in
itself. From a single banyan, brought originally from India to be
planted here, branches had extended and dropped down aerial roots
that grew into thick trunks, which in turn threw out still more trunklike roots, until a third of an acre was occupied by what looked like a
grove, but was really only one tree. Stone walks wound beneath
large-leafed foliage, and benches offered places where one could
rest. The Indian banyan, unlike the Chinese variety, never dropped
unpleasant purple fruit as did those in Florida.

We stopped for a moment to watch a white man who was weaving
beautiful green hats from *lau hala* leaves. Maui was a wonderful
place for artists of one kind or another who liked to be independent
and work on their own. The green color would turn to straw, but the
hats and the small birds that ornamented them would still be handsome and well crafted.

Before we sat down, a road sign caught my eye and I wandered
over to look at it. The legend read:

LARGEST
BANYAN TREE
1873

Above it a dark-skinned Kamehameha I was shown with folded
arms, his red-and-yellow cape flowing from his shoulders, his helmet
curving forward in its distinctive manner. The sign was appropriate
and striking, as it was used for notable places.

Marla stopped beside me. "You'll see that helmet curve picked up
everywhere. Watch for the roof of Pizza Hut here in Lahaina!"

When I sat down on a bench, the two women took a place on either side of me, and now Marla wasted no time.

"I have a favor to ask of you, Ailina. While Caroline is here, she really ought to see some real Hawaiian dancing, and hear some of the old authentic songs. Do you think your group could come to Manaolana in a few days and put on a performance? Say on Saturday? We'd ask some neighbors in so that you'd have an audience."

Ailina turned to me questioningly—a silent question that I didn't understand.

"I would enjoy it," I said, reversing my earlier rejection of the idea. I knew now that I wanted to see this woman again—I needed to talk with her. Whether I would like her or not was another matter.

"All right," she agreed. "I'll phone the others and we'll set this up. I'll let you know. I have to go to Honolulu tomorrow, but I'll be home by late afternoon, and we don't usually need much notice."

It had all been arranged so quickly, and since I knew that Ailina would leave us soon and we'd be on our way back up-country before I could propose the plan that was growing in my mind, I had to speak out while I had the chance.

"Is there any way I could talk with you, Ailina? I mean for more than a few minutes? You knew my father and mother when I was little, and there's so much I want to ask about."

"*We* can tell you whatever you want to know," Marla put in quickly.

"But you don't tell me. You put me off and stop my questions."

Ailina studied me with eyes that seemed to hold warm memories and no resentment. "Of course we can talk. In fact, I know exactly what we can do—if you're willing. Perhaps you can stay with me in my apartment tonight. You could even come with me to Honolulu tomorrow, if you like, and we'd have a real chance to get acquainted."

I couldn't help responding to her warmth, in spite of Marla's obvious doubts. "I'd like that," I told her. A respite from Manaolana might be just what I needed.

"Then it's settled," Ailina said, and there was a certain calm authority in her manner that allowed for no disagreement.

Marla was anything but pleased with this sudden turn, but there was nothing she could do about it. "All right—if this is what you want to do, Caroline. Shall I come back for you tomorrow?"

"I need to make a trip up-country," Ailina told her, "so I'll drive Caroline back tomorrow afternoon."

After a bit more discussion concerning the Saturday entertainment, we all walked back to Baldwin Home, and Marla got into her car. We stood on the lanai and watched her drive away.

Ailina's voice carried the soft voweled sound of the islands, just as her son's did at times—when he wasn't angry about something. Now, however, a sadness crept in as she remembered.

"I'll never forget when we were all young together and I often visited your grandmother's ranch. My family lived in the Kula area, though they're all gone now. We went to school together—Noelle, Marla, and I, though we were in different grades."

"I hope you'll tell me about that time," I said. "There's so much I know nothing about."

She gave me another of her direct looks. "I understand what you want to know. We'll go to dinner when I leave here, and we'll talk all you like. Now I must get back to work. I can leave in an hour or so, and if you'd like to wander around this house for a while, you may enjoy it."

A new group of visitors had strolled up the walk and were mounting the steps. Ailina turned to greet them, and I went again into the pleasant, well-shaded rooms. In an end bedroom I sat down by a window to wait. Over the double bed hung mosquito netting mounted on a hoop that hung from a hook in the ceiling. At one side an opening in the net would allow one to get into bed and close the netting. Window screens had come much later. Under the bed was the authentic white chamber pot.

It was strange to sit in rooms that were empty except for occasional visitors who strolled through, and think of the families who had lived here. This would have been a house filled with children's voices, with laughter and undoubtedly with tears—all gone now, yet somehow lingering with a gentle, intangible echo that I could almost sense.

My mind wouldn't stay with the Baldwins, however. The darker thoughts of my mother that both Marla and Joanna had planted were growing tendrils that curled about my will to act. I could remember Noelle's sudden furies when I was a child—taken for granted, because she was the mother I knew. There was also the spell of rage I'd seen when she hurled the Pele carving at me. What had she intended when she'd placed the tapa beater in her saddlebag? There could have been no possible reason to take it with her that day unless she meant to use it as a weapon. Against my father?

So where did this leave me in what was to be my purpose here? What if my grandmother and aunt were both right in believing it was better for Noelle to stay as she was, simple and childlike—and safe. Could I talk to Ailina about any of this? I wasn't entirely sure of her yet, or even of my own feeling toward her.

I sat for another hour or so, watching family groups wander through. Two or three women even paused to talk to me, asking questions I couldn't answer.

When the house closed for the day, I went with Ailina to where she had left her small Japanese car. We drove out of Lahaina onto a wide highway that led north around the curve of West Maui. The islands of Lanai and then Molokai were in view across the water now. If the road had circled on, we could have returned to Wailuku and East Maui by a northern route. The well-paved road didn't go through, however, and there were still Hawaiian villages in the farther section, where people preferred to stay isolated and undisturbed by the tourists crowding the Gold Coast.

Too often, visitors who came to Maui saw nothing but luxury hotels, condominiums, tennis courts, golf courses, and beaches. The main attractions that had caused developers to open this long stretch of coastline to Kaanapali and beyond were, of course, the six lovely bays of the area. Good restaurants abounded, most of them with views of beach and ocean, some lighted outdoors at night by Hawaiian torches —all the panoply of "romance" that belonged to the islands. Yet there was so much more to Maui than this.

By now the sun had dropped low in the sky, and here in West Maui the sunset would be especially beautiful when the sky was right.

"Look ahead—*mauka,*" Ailina said.

I remembered the word for "toward the mountains." *Makai* meant "toward the sea"—the two directions most often used on Maui.

Following the direction she'd indicated, I saw a long hill rising steeply from the highway, topped with a double row of Norfolk Island pines.

"That's Pineapple Hill," Ailina said. "Those pines mark the road along its crest. Papillon runs its helicopter trips from up there. Sometime you must take the flight around the island, and especially into the crater."

"David Reed drove me up to the summit," I said. "I even saw my shadow on the clouds."

"How did you feel about that?"

"Awed. Uplifted. For a little while all my indecisions began to clear. But now they're coming back." It was surprising how easily I could talk to this woman whom I'd expected to resent.

"You'll find your way. Seeing the Brocken Specter is a good omen. In a little while we'll talk. We're going to the Kapalua Bay for dinner because it's one of the most beautiful hotels on the island, and you should see it. It's older than some of the glitzy ones, and it has the sort of dignity that often gets lost in all the eagerness to please tourists with the ultraspectacular. Your grandmother likes to go there when she comes to Lahaina."

Ailina had phoned ahead for reservations, and we left her car with parking attendants and entered an enchanting lobby. Straight ahead, a three-story-high open space cut through to the ocean—a space filled with hanging vines and greenery, through which birds flew as if they were outdoors. By this time they were twittering their night songs.

We walked out upon a wide lanai on this upper level where we could sit in the open and watch the sun go down above Kapalua Bay. The name meant "arms embracing the sea," Ailina said. Always, the Hawaiian language was filled with words of emotion—words that built charming pictures.

Ailina ordered drinks, and my margarita came with a tiny orchid floating on its surface.

I watched the sky, absorbed in the spectacle. Clouds mounded above the horizon, reflecting color that changed even as we watched. A splendid palette of gold and coral and aquamarine was splashed lavishly against the encroachment of a darkening sky. The scene was beautiful and romantic, and as sentimental as Hawaii was supposed to be. It needed only the presence of someone to hold my hand and share the magic.

Ailina watched me instead of the sky. "I used to come here with Carlos sometimes. It gets to you, doesn't it?"

I nodded, watching the sun. Its brilliance had faded so that I could look at the glowing yellow eye as it sank into the sea. Just as it disappeared, I caught the rare green flash that could occur at sunset. For an instant the sun itself turned green as it vanished.

"We were lucky to see that," Ailina said. "It doesn't always happen. Shall we go downstairs for dinner now?"

I turned my back on the beauty of a sky turned to flame—a beauty that made me feel lonely—and followed her. The dining room, set on the lowest level of the great open space, was dusky now, with candles on the tables and muted lights shining among the palm trees and hanging vines that formed part of the room. A tiled floor and wicker and bamboo tables and chairs added to the cool, tropical effect.

Sliding glass doors stood open to the night air. Doors that could be closed when storms swept in from the sea.

When we'd ordered, Ailina looked at me across the table, and I knew the time had come. She was waiting for my first question, and I began hesitantly.

"Tell me about my father."

"Do you want happy memories, or do you want the truth?" she asked.

I liked her directness, which was very different from the evasions that surrounded me at Manaolana.

"I'm beginning to glimpse some of what may be the truth," I told her. "Until now I've had only a little girl's memories from a time when I adored my father. Plus, of course, all the superimposed inventions my Grandmother Elizabeth provided—and believed herself. That's all I have. Did you ever meet Elizabeth Kirby?"

"Just once," Ailina said. "I could see the probable source of what Keith became when he grew up. Though maybe we offer too many excuses these days. Somewhere we all have to take the blame for what we do. Though it was a long while before I could accept this myself."

She was silent, remembering, and I waited quietly until she went on.

"Not that there was anything really wicked about your father. Keith just needed more admiration, love, sympathy, approval—a constant nurturing—that no one woman could provide. He enjoyed playing a dashing adventurous character that was only partly a fiction he made up about himself. By the time I knew him, it had become so real that I think he'd lost sight of anything that lay underneath. Forever Don Juan—or Errol Flynn! Both pretty immature roles, I'm afraid. Of course I was pretty immature then myself."

She spoke without rancor, simply standing back with an objectivity she had learned over the years. Nevertheless, a glimpse of the old pain came through. My father seemed to have hurt everyone.

I told her about the scene in the garden at Ahinahina as I remembered it. "Were you the woman who sang to my parents' guests that night?"

"Yes." There was regret in the single word. "I didn't intend what happened. I was terribly in love—with your father. Though at least I was realistic enough to know that he would never leave your mother for me. Or for any other woman. Though toward the end he was angry with her, and even talking about divorce. I wonder if your mother ever understood that *she* was his safe haven. Perhaps she was too angry herself to recognize that. The old Hawaiians had a saying, 'Anger is the thing that gives no life.' "

"But what woman wants to be just a safe haven?" I objected. "Were there many other loves for him?"

"I suppose not, really. I was nursing a very young broken heart, and it seemed that way to me."

I felt achingly sorry for my mother. When I'd grown up I too had run after the will-o'-the-wisp of a charming man who had thought for a time that he was in love with me.

"Why won't anyone at Manaolana talk to me about my parents as they were in those days?" I asked.

"It's a sore subject, and they probably don't want to hurt you. Or hurt themselves by dredging everything up."

"Joanna said Marla was in love with him too."

"I'm afraid she was."

"But there's more to their remembering, or not being able to remember, isn't there? Marla believes that Noelle wanted to kill my father that day when they rode up the mountain. Perhaps Joanna believes this too, and it's why they all want Noelle to stay as she is."

Ailina accepted this quietly. "I've often wondered what really happened. In a way, it's convenient that no one could tell the story afterward. Just the same, Caroline, I think you should accept the fact you don't really know the truth. I wonder if anyone does, or ever will."

"Perhaps my mother knows, if she ever dares to face it. But then what would happen?"

It wasn't a question anyone could answer, and Ailina didn't try. I'd stirred up unhappy thoughts, and sometimes she seemed to go far away, so there were long silences.

"Is it possible for you to leave everything as it is?" she asked after one of those trips away into her own thoughts.

"That's what they all want me to do. They're trying to protect Noelle from whatever happened up there in the crater."

"Perhaps they're trying to protect you as well."

"I don't want that! Maybe they think that if I'm frightened into believing that my mother killed my father I'll stop asking questions."

"*Will* you stop?"

"Do you think I should? No—never mind. I'm the one who has to decide. As I told you, when David took me up to the crater yesterday I saw my shadow on the clouds in that rainbow circle of light, and I felt strong and determined and sure. Then I came back to being helpless and confused. Just the same, I still think the direction I took up on the mountain is the right one."

Ailina nodded gravely. "Sometimes we have to believe in the course that's been revealed to us. I saw that vision once myself when I was young and frightened—because I'd fallen in love with a man I couldn't have. What I saw made me strong enough to give him up."

She'd had more strength than I did, even when she was young, and I said so.

"But *you* are strong," she told me. "I can see it. You're not always sure, but you can carry through on what you decide to do."

"I hope you're right. It hasn't seemed that way. It's been more like a restless search. I suppose the first thing I must do is give up all those old memories of my father, since none of them was real."

"No!" Ailina reached her hand across the table and covered my own firmly, briefly. "He was also all the things you remember. Perhaps he loved you most of all. So keep that."

I was grateful, but not entirely comforted. "Sometimes I feel as though my mother is being used as a scapegoat at Manaolana."

"That might be true. But if she doesn't realize it, does it matter?"

"It matters to me."

"That's something you have to deal with in your own way. But just for now, Caroline, can we put all those things aside and think about you in another way. What do you want for yourself?"

"I don't know. I've never really found out. Ailina, how did you get over your feeling for my father?"

"I was lucky. I met Carlos Olivero at the right moment. He had just come here from Manila, and he was already a successful lawyer. I expect the contrast—with Keith, I mean—of his being solid and dependable counted with me. Though he could be an exciting man too. The thing that mattered most was that he didn't want anyone else. We were married nearly twenty-five years. When he died six years ago I thought my life was over. Of course it wasn't. I have plenty to do. Since I don't have to worry about money, I can take all the volunteer work I want. Koma has helped me enormously and we both care about our islands."

"David introduced me to your son."

"Yes, I heard. Koma carries around a lot of passion and sometimes he doesn't use it wisely. He's bitter about what he feels the *haoles* have done and he doesn't want their greedy encroachment to continue on Maui. I agree with his principle but not always with his methods. For a long time here our very history was put down, and even our language was forbidden to be taught in some schools. All that's changed now, so that there's a renaissance for what's old. We're learning to be proud of our unique history and we want to keep it alive. But no one can go on forever being unforgiving because of the past, no matter what the injustices were. We do need to remember, but not to be so bitter about what can't be helped. Those who did all the wicked things we resent are dead, and none of that can be changed. If we hadn't been annexed by America, some other nation would have gobbled us up. Those were the days of colonization, you know. Japan, perhaps, would have taken us over. Or Russia.

"However, Koma doesn't want to look at any side except the narrow one he focuses on. I'm afraid he enjoys his anger. He hates not being a pure-blooded Hawaiian, and blames me for that—though I'm not pure-blooded either. Very few really native Hawaiians are left."

She had talked for a long while, and I'd listened, absorbed, sensing wisdom and compassion that she must have come by through all those difficult years.

When we finished our coffee and were on our way again, back to Lahaina, she spoke about our trip to Honolulu tomorrow. She had already made a reservation for both of us on the small island-hopping plane.

"We're going to Iolani Palace, since I have an errand there. After Carlos died I lived in Honolulu for a while, and I was able to help a bit in the restoration of the palace. So I'm permitted to take a visitor through now and then. You're Hawaiian-born, Caroline, and you need to experience what is your history too. David Reed's mother is in Honolulu now on a visit, and I phoned her this afternoon and asked her to meet us at the palace. She knew all those people at Manaolana and Ahinahina when you were little. Way back in time there was a royal lady on Helena Reed's family tree, and she's been able to trace the line back, even though that particular princess lies buried in New England."

"I'll be eager to meet her. Thank you."

"She told me that David is driving you to Hana soon, but she liked the idea of seeing you alone ahead of time."

I wondered why, and felt a little uneasy again.

First, however, before tomorrow arrived, there was to be an entirely different and much more unsettling meeting ahead of me. Something for which I was totally unprepared.

11

The generous home that Carlos and Ailina had built years before was tucked into a fold of the mountain near Lahaina. Trees sheltered it on three sides, leaving the front open for the tremendous view.

She took me to her upstairs sitting room that opened onto a wide lanai, where we sat down in bamboo chairs to enjoy the dramatic sweep of light along the Kaanapali coast. The islands of Molokai and Lanai floated as dark patches on a moonlit sea, and the land's edge, with its winding indentations of bays, made a long, sparkling line against the water beyond.

For a little while I could feel relaxed and almost content—able to put troublesome thoughts away. I was grateful to Ailina for making this possible. Then the fragile moments of peace were shattered when Koma's voice reached us from the terrace garden below. Koma never seemed to bring serenity with him.

"Do you mind if I come up?" he called.

Ailina told him to come and then glanced at me apologetically. "This may not be pleasant. My son is a fervent young man, and I'm afraid he resents your coming to Maui."

"Because I'm my father's daughter? But that's hardly fair."

"Since when does 'fair' have much to do with anything?"

We returned to Ailina's pleasant sitting room, aglow now in lamplight with warm sun colors and cool greens. A splendid framed photograph of the crater of Haleakala occupied a central wall. David's work, Ailina said.

When Koma came in he greeted me with no enthusiasm, and his mother caught his look at once.

"Relax," she told her son. "Caroline has a Hawaiian heart that she's just beginning to learn about."

Koma sat down, and I could sense his restlessness. He would look right in a *malo*, I thought—the loincloth from early years. Maybe with a spear in his hand.

"We need your help," he said directly to his mother.

"Another demonstration against the bombing of Kahoolawe?"

"Right. And your name counts. You're not a crazy fanatic like me, and people listen."

"I suppose demonstrations help bleed off some of the rage," Ailina said, "though I'm not sure how much attention the Navy pays to them."

He almost smiled. "We won't ask you to get arrested." He looked at me. "David's coming with us. We can count on his support. At least we could until lately. Do you realize how many people you've managed to upset since you came here, Caroline Kirby?"

"I'm only trying to help my mother, who doesn't even recognize me," I told him.

"You've upset Joanna. And she's had enough to bear. She'd lend us some help on the Kahoolawe effort, but she's not feeling well, and Marla says that's your doing."

Ailina shook her head at her son. "Let Caroline alone. You have to do your thing, and she must do hers. Tomorrow I'm taking her to Honolulu—Iolani Palace. A good place to recover some of what's old and must not be lost."

Mention of the palace seemed to add to Koma's unhappiness, and he got up. "I just wanted to make sure you'd speak for us," he said to his mother.

"All right. You'll give me the details when everything's set?"

"Sure. Probably in a couple of weeks. I'll see you."

For just a moment he stared at me—a mocking look that I didn't understand. Then he went off, taking with him some of the heat that his presence had brought into the room. When he'd gone, Ailina, clearly upset, couldn't indulge in ordinary conversation anymore. She showed me to my room and brought me pajamas and a few other items.

"I still have a little work to do tonight—paperwork," she told me. "Do you mind?"

When she went off to her own room, I stepped out on the lanai again, to sit in darkness, enjoying jeweled lights that followed the coastline. I wasn't at all sleepy, and I needed to let everything grow quiet inside me.

I hadn't been there five minutes, however, before a whisper came up to me from the terrace below. "Come down here, Caroline. We need to talk. Don't tell my mother I'm still here."

That sounded ominous. I didn't want to talk with Koma, but there seemed nothing else to do. Stairs led down from the lanai, and I went to the lower level, where a flowering hedge offered privacy.

"I hoped you'd come outside again," he said. "Visitors usually do—for the view. I've decided that there's something you'd better know, though my mother would probably kill me for telling you this."

He began to prowl the terrace, his restlessness worn like a garment. Perhaps it kept others from coming close, since he was always moving away.

"What do you want to tell me?" I asked.

He stopped in deep shadow, close to the house, so I couldn't see his face. "It's time you knew that you and I have the same father, Caroline Kirby."

I could only stare in his direction, trying to find him in the dim light. He laughed softly.

"That takes the wind out of your sails, doesn't it? I know a lot about your dashing father, though I never knew him personally, since he died before I was born. Thank God!"

"Did Ailina tell you this?" I managed.

"She knows that I know, though she didn't tell me. She wanted me to be Carlos's son. As I wanted to be. And still feel that I am. It was Marla who told me a few years ago when she was angry with me about something. So I talked to Joanna—who knew everything, since my mother went to her when she knew she was pregnant."

I hadn't grasped this fully yet—there were too many ramifications. I didn't even know why he was telling me.

"Did Carlos know?" I asked.

"Yes. My mother told me about that when I asked her. She was honest with him from the first—before they married. He loved her and he wanted me born as his son. Now it doesn't matter—not a whole lot. He will always be my real father. I never liked what I heard about Keith Kirby, even before Marla told me the truth."

"Why are you telling me this now?"

"Maybe because I think you bring *pilikia* wherever you go. Trouble. Bad luck. To David, especially. But to Joanna too, and probably to your mother. There's a lot of your father in you, and I think you ought to know what he was like. Then maybe you can just cut off and go home."

"If you're so great on fairness and justice, then you shouldn't be deciding about me. You don't know anything about me—any more than I do about you. All we know is that we don't like each other."

He stepped out into the terrace light and I could see his grin. "Agreed!"

"I've already learned about my father and Ailina. It doesn't matter, and your existence doesn't change anything for me. It's my mother I want to help."

"A lost cause. Go home!"

"You forget—I'm Joanna's granddaughter. That gives me a stubborn streak. You're making it stronger."

It was then that something so incongruous struck me that I began to laugh. Koma came at once to stand before me.

"What's so funny?"

I was closer now to crying, and I told him, "I was thinking about how interesting it would be if my Grandmother Elizabeth in San Francisco could meet her grandson."

"I can imagine. What's she like?"

"She's elegant and very proper. Narrow in her views. Intolerant of anyone outside her own circle. She doesn't like Hawaii or Hawaiians."

"Maybe I'd be good for her."

I stood up to go inside. "Maybe you like *pilikia* yourself. Maybe that's really why you told me. You like to upset people."

"And you are upset, aren't you, Caroline? To have me for a brother!"

"I'd have picked someone I might like better."

His smile flashed in the darkness. "So long, *haole* sister," he said, and slipped away into the night.

I went inside and returned to my room. My thoughts wouldn't be quiet now. All my life I had loved and admired my father as the hero Grandmother Elizabeth had created for me—and as I remembered. Ailina had said I must hold on to the memory of his affection for me. But I could only feel more sorry than ever for my mother because of what she'd had to endure at his hands. Probably she'd never known about Ailina's pregnancy—at least she'd been spared that.

It was not a good night for sleeping, and I spent it with a good deal of tossing. I was glad when daylight came and I could get up early for our trip to Honolulu.

After breakfast we drove the short distance to the airport at Kaana-pali and boarded a small plane for Oahu. Ailina arranged for me to sit beside the pilot, where I would have the best all-around view. I was glad for the complete distraction of this trip, which would leave me no time to think about anything back on Maui.

I watched the red earth of the airstrip slip away beneath one wing as we headed out over a sea that looked navy blue this morning. We island-hopped, flying almost level with the steep cliffs of Molokai, in one place looking up a green valley slashed between precipitous sides.

Oahu was only twenty-four miles and after the short flight we came in behind Honolulu through the gap at the top of Nuuanu Valley. There great cliffs plunged down the mountain in the historic *Pali*—where Oahu warriors leapt to their death far below, rather than be captured by Kamehameha's men. We could look into the small crater of Punchbowl, now a military cemetery occupied by rows of white crosses in a place where there had once been human sacrifice. Bloody history came down from the ancient past to the present—because men had always played war games. Only in our present, desperate times did it appear that ordinary people everywhere were beginning to cry, "Enough! Give us peace!"

The modern city of Honolulu, with its tall buildings crowding seaward, lay spread below us. Diamond Head rose at the city's far limits, thrusting into sea and sky just as I'd seen it in a hundred pictures. Surf rolled in along the strip of white sand that was Waikiki, where giant hotels welcomed tourists, dwarfing the Royal Hawaiian and the Moana—once *the* big hotels on the beach.

Our plane turned toward the opposite distances of the city and came down on a portion of airport set aside for smaller craft.

The palace was in the center of town, and the long taxi ride gave us time to talk. Because we were going back into history, Ailina spoke about the way the monarchy had ended, and especially about the last queen. Liliuokalani's tragic story would always haunt the palace where she'd reigned for so short a time before Americans took her kingdom away.

"The Iolani's a beautiful building," Ailina said. "There are always those in any city who want to tear down what's old and build something new and commercial. I'm glad Hawaii has chosen to spend the money and time to restore the palace. It's a symbol of a day we mustn't forget. We need pride in what we were, in ourselves, so we can hold up our heads in the present. I want to remember—not to judge—but to appreciate."

"Tell me about Queen Liliuokalani," I said.

"When her brother, King Kalakaua, died, she inherited the throne and a weakened kingdom. But there were white men in Hawaii who wanted to see the island annexed by the United States—even though President Cleveland wasn't in favor of this. Power was seized illegally by a powerful few, and Cleveland's hands were tied unless he wanted to order troops in to shoot other Americans. Those who coveted power brought in a warship and trained its guns on the city. The queen, rather than see the blood of her people flowing in the streets of Honolulu, abdicated. She was imprisoned in house arrest for nine months in the palace on a trumped-up charge of treason to a government that had imposed itself on Hawaii. The real reason was that those who'd seized power were afraid that the people would rally to her aid—as they might very well have done, if she'd been free."

These were things I hadn't known fully about my islands, and I listened, absorbed. The palace would mean more to me now.

Ailina went on. "The queen was very much loved by Hawaiians, and in those days she hated Americans—with good reason. There was a young princess, her niece, who was being educated in England, and who was next in line for a throne she never occupied. There are those who say that Kaiulani's young death was because of a broken heart.

"The annexation came about a few years later, when President McKinley was in office, and it happened peacefully except for one aborted attempt at rebellion. But there are those who will always feel that America stole the islands from their rightful rulers and people. My son is one of those who resurrect old angers and hold on to hatred and resentment."

I thought of how much Koma must hate the half of him that was white, because of my father. *Our* father.

"Let's not forget," Ailina said, "but let's not go on eating our hearts out because of the past. Just so the old mistakes aren't made all over again. We're trying to live together as Americans, but we don't forget the past, and we *are* Hawaiian Islanders—all of us."

When we left the taxi near the palace grounds, we walked toward the front of the great square building that stood upon its ten acres of land in the center of Honolulu's business district. The park around was filled with trees and plantings and pleasant walks.

"Iolani means 'royal hawk,' " Ailina said. "The last king, Kalakaua, built it to take the place of a smaller, termite-ridden building that was torn down. He'd traveled abroad, and he admired European culture. He wanted this to be a splendid palace where distinguished visitors could be entertained, and celebrations held. Though I guess it wasn't all that comfortable to live in. The monarchy occupied Iolani for only thirteen years. The last day the Hawaiian flag flew alone over the building was on August 12, 1898. Then it became the capitol of the Territory and no longer a royal palace. It was the state capitol until 1969. Over there is the big new capitol building, and as soon as the legislators moved out, restoration on the palace was begun. Now it's been brought back as far as possible to its original state."

The stone building—a hundred and forty feet by one hundred, Ailina said—was surrounded on two levels by long verandas—Hawaiian lanais. Slim pillars with metal railings and arches ran all the way around, ending on either side of the front tower. Smaller towers rose on each corner, and wide metal steps led up to enormous doors into the central hall. At the top of the front tower the flagstaff flew both the American and the Hawaiian flag—that flag with eight stripes, representing the principal islands, plus the admired Union Jack that had been placed in one corner.

"Before we go in," Ailina said, "I want to show you something. The first Kamehameha's statue stands elsewhere and of course he never saw this palace. But Liliuokalani's brief reign, as well as her imprisonment, was inside those walls. Here she is."

We had stopped before the proud figure of a woman portrayed in bronze. She stood on a circular base, not set too high above her people. She wore the traditional *holoku*—that long, flowing garment with a yoke at the neck, and a small train behind. Her hair was drawn into a mound on top of her head, and there was strength and nobility in the clearly modeled face. Queen Liliuokalani had been a writer and a musician, and one of her songs would always be sung in Hawaii —"Aloha Oe."

Lettering around the base was in Hawaiian, and Ailina translated: "It says: *The spirit of Liliuokalani.*"

For me, the most touching thing about the statue was that someone had placed a red ribbon in her open hand.

"For a while our history was forgotten, put aside," Ailina went on. "Even our language was almost lost. Of course, this isn't true anymore, and there is a wave of nostalgia for the past, and a pride, a need to know about ourselves and our history, before that's lost too. We remember now what was done to the queen, and to us. Though I don't want to remember with anger—these are different times, and we are different people."

Ailina too had a proud bearing. For all her gentleness with me, an air of authority and pride was part of her very carriage.

"Over there," she said, "just across from the palace grounds, is Washington Place, which was Liliuokalani's residence before she became queen. She died in this century—in 1913."

Near the steps of the palace a sheltered spot offered a place for visitors on tour to wait. It was empty now, and we went to sit down on a bench for a few moments before going in.

"David's mother will be waiting for us, so we'll go inside in a moment. I just want to tell you a little about Helena Reed. For about five years David's father and mother lived in the Kula area, where the hospital is. His father was a very good doctor, and Helena taught school. They became close friends with Joanna and often visited Manaolana. Helena and Noelle became close, so she knew your mother very well. She remembers you when you were little, and she was living in the area at the time when your Grandmother Elizabeth came to visit Ahinahina. She wants to talk to you alone for a little while, so we've arranged this visit. I have my own errand, so you can be by yourselves."

The uneasiness that I'd put aside edged back. But I shouldn't be apprehensive about David's mother—she might be one of those I could talk to. I suppose I was beginning to fear learning even more about my parents.

"Let's go now," Ailina said, and we walked toward the steps leading up to the lower front lanai. There we sat down for a moment in order to draw cloth slippers over our shoes. Ailina was recognized and we were permitted to pass.

The beautiful floors—once carelessly scarred when the palace served as the capitol building, and was used by the military command after Pearl Harbor—had been completely refinished and they gleamed like glass, reflecting our images in glowing, polished wood. We stepped into a great hall that took up most of the central area, and ran straight through, dividing the rooms on either hand. The ceiling was high and distant, and down the big room were niches where valuable vases and statuary had once been displayed—mostly empty now, since only a few such treasures had been recovered.

"The Throne Room first," Ailina said. "For me, it's not just a room."

Everywhere koa wood glowed warm and reddish—all handsomely restored. Ailina led the way into a long space that occupied most of the side of the building. The splendid pink-and-green carpet, with its motif of ti leaves, had been woven in Boston to copy the original carpet that had worn out long ago. Ailina was full of knowledge of this place, and she spoke of it all with pride. In the center of the room stood a circular velvet seat, again a copy of the original seat designed for this room. Lights burned in many-globed chandeliers, their sparkle caught in hanging crystals.

But the focus of the room, inevitably, was the dais at the far end, two steps up, and carpeted like the rest. Above it hung the royal canopy, crowned with gilt, though the platform itself stood empty.

"There should be thrones," I said. "There should be *kahili* standards on each side."

"That's one of the things that upsets those who've concerned themselves with the restoration. The thrones that belong here are in the Bishop Museum, and the museum won't give them up to the palace—where many of us think they belong. So the platform stands empty until the dispute is resolved. There are those who feel we should just have copies made, and no one would know the difference. But others feel that the real thrones belong here."

Ailina heard emotion in her own voice and smiled at me. "You can tell where I stand—I get carried away. In the face of all the other problems that face Hawaii, I suppose it isn't sensible to be upset about a pair of old thrones from a kingdom that no longer exists."

"Maybe it's possible to care about both the old and the new."

"That's what I believe, Caroline. Of course, the Bishop is one of the great museums of the world. You must come back when you can spend all day there. So much of Hawaii's treasure has been carried off to other countries, but they have fine collections of feathered capes, and so many other things. Of course, the jeweled crowns are there, and that is a safer place for them to be seen. Do you see the small door at the back of the platform? That's where royalty could retire to put on robes for any ceremony."

She moved toward the platform and turned around, her movements graceful as she extended her arms. She was a stunning woman, and I thought she couldn't have been any more beautiful when she was young. I could imagine the attraction she had held for my father. But she'd had so much more to grow into than he could have appreciated. Strange that I was finally seeing him more clearly, and with less pain.

Ailina's arms seemed to encompass all the space around us. The room was hushed, with the sounds of Honolulu shut away behind lanai doors. She began to speak softly, painting word pictures for me.

"King Kalakaua and Queen Kapiolani held their coronation in a pavilion outside the palace, so it could be witnessed by everyone. It must have been a glittering affair. Then, not so many years later, when the king died, his body lay here in state, and mourners thronged through this same room where royal receptions had been held."

"But the last queen never had a coronation, did she?" I said. "Or poor young Princess Kaiulani."

"The princess was American under the law by the time she died in her early twenties of pneumonia. They say that on the night she died in the home her American father had built for her in Waikiki—where a hotel now stands—the peacocks in her garden screamed so loudly they could be heard a long distance away in the city. There might have been a reason for their screaming—some people said—because of all the unusual lights in the middle of the night, and the comings and goings that disturbed the peacocks. But Hawaiians, who understand such matters, know that the peacocks were grieving for the princess who had loved them. There's another nice touch to that story. The Chinese jasmine that grew in her gardens was the princess's favorite flower, so it was given the 'pikake'—a corruption of the word 'peacock,' to honor her.

"And you're right—there were no more coronations here. What was held in this room was Liliuokalani's trial. Unjust and bent toward only one outcome—her imprisonment for what they called treasonable acts. Acts people believe she had no part in. Besides—treason to whom? How could there be treason to the United States, which didn't own the islands, when the real treason was toward the queen, and committed by a handful of white men?"

"I've never understood exactly how the takeover happened."

"It was done by fiat, by seizure, by saying, 'Let it be done.' A law was passed ignoring the will of the people. A law that allowed only the big landowners to vote. That meant the *haole*. Liliuokalani had been appointed by her brother as his heir to the throne. But now a republic was created by eight hundred votes, and the rest of Hawaii was never heard. By trying and imprisoning the queen, they could remove her as a symbol for whom the people might have been willing to shed their blood. By the time she was freed and went to Washington to plead her country's cause, it was too late, and no one listened. At least, after the annexation took place, the vote was returned to the people, where it's been ever since."

Ailina moved away from where the thrones should have been, and I went with her.

"There were happier times before all this happened." Again, her arms embraced the room with their graceful gesture. "This was a room made for balls, and the Royal Hawaiian band played for dancing and parties. King Kalakaua's own song that he wrote with his bandmaster, Henri Berger, was played as the anthem of the islands— 'Hawaii Ponoi.' "

The room was peopled for me now because of her words, and the hushed sound of her voice. It wasn't hard to imagine two thrones on the platform, with ten-foot *kahili*, their tops of royal yellow feathers moving gently as they were held high on either side of the king and queen. I could hear the whisper of music in my mind, and catch the gleam of jewels women wore to grace their romantic, last-century gowns. Guests from all over the world would have attended. A world long gone—no longer real—yet it had *happened.* Stirring events had taken place in this room of vanished thrones, and I wanted to count myself one of those Hawaiian Americans who must remember.

Perhaps Ailina, watching me, understood a little of what she'd made me feel, for she smiled at me warmly as we moved toward a doorway.

"Not all the *haole* of that day were for annexation," she told me. "In fact, many worked against it for more noble reasons than those who overthrew the kingdom might have had. That's enough for now. I'm glad you can feel it, Caroline. Sometimes feeling is a lot more important than facts. But now we must go and find Helena—I know where she'll be, but I'll show you one more room before we go upstairs."

The long dining room across the hall had been used for state occasions, and was furnished almost as it had once been, the table set with silver and even the original china in place. Again, there was a beautiful carpet in a pattern of small flowers, as though the room were a meadow—woven, of course, to duplicate the carpet that had once graced this room.

"One of the worst things that happened as far as the palace was concerned," Ailina said, "was that when the rooms went into use as offices, an auction was held—callously, with no awareness of what was being done. Too often when we're living history, we have no sense about the future or of what ought to be preserved. All the palace furnishings, all its fabulous treasures, were sold at auction and scattered across the oceans. When restoration began, appeals were sent out for whatever could be located to be returned to Iolani. A great many people discovered articles in their possession that had come from the palace—many on the mainland. So most of what is shown in these rooms has been returned and was here in King Kalakaua's time. In rooms where the furnishings are sparse, the recovery hasn't been complete. Now there are Acquisition Funds, and an Acquisition Committee."

We moved out into the great hall again, and Ailina went on.

"It's taken a great deal of money to do all this. Of course, there are always those who believe it could be better spent. But I don't agree, and I'm glad our legislature could understand. We need to feed our minds and spirit as well as our bodies. It's necessary to know where we came from as well as where we're going. Hawaiians have needed that sense of self-worth they used to have. That's important for all of us who belong here, no matter what color our skins."

The koa-wood staircase was more than twenty wide steps up to a landing, where the stairs divided into separate flights mounting to the floor above.

"You can touch the banister," Ailina said, smiling. "The docents who take the tours through always warn each group that nothing is to be touched, no furniture is for sitting. The one thing in the palace you can place your hand on is the banister of this staircase."

The wood felt smooth as silk to my touch as we climbed to the hall above, where the royal suites and guest rooms had been located. Ailina led the way toward a corner room at the far end of the hall, and I caught glimpses of other rooms as we went past. Most were furnished, but this room stood completely empty. No one was here, no picture hung on the walls, no single piece of furniture stood anywhere.

"This room will never be furnished," Ailina said. "It's a room that's haunted by sadness. This is where Queen Liliuokalani spent her nine months of imprisonment. She wasn't even allowed to ride out in her carriage because it was safer for those who'd plotted against her to keep her out of sight. For exercise she was only allowed to walk on the lanai outside her room. Yet she kept her dignity through the whole ordeal, and they say she never broke under battering at her trial. What she cared most about were the people of her islands."

Even now, I thought, the cruel injustice of what had happened was remembered, and was part of what made Koma angry. It seemed fitting to keep this room empty—a stark reminder.

"Weighing on the other side," Ailina said, "there's something the queen dowager, Liliuokalani's mother, said, and her words have stayed with me ever since I read them. I think I can quote them exactly: '. . . destiny does not respect mere justice. Events march. The world changes. For myself, I can only pray that God will bring Hawaii a good future. I do not think I ought to tell Him how.' So perhaps out of all that was cruel and unfair and stupid, even back to the days of the chiefs—some good has evolved for Hawaii, even though we still have to fight against outside forces for what we want to keep. Iolani Palace stands as an important symbol of a great many things that have meaning for Hawaii."

A woman was walking on the lanai outside the empty room, and she must have heard us, for she breezed through the door with her hands held out to Ailina, and for the first time I faced David's remarkable mother.

12

Helena Reed must have looked at least ten years younger than her age. She wore a silk blouse of dusty rose, with a belted white skirt, and except for a wedding ring of twisted gold, her only jewelry was the small pearls in her ears. She was tall, with elegant legs and long slim feet in white sandals. Her short hair, still brown, had been carefully cut to give a casual, easy-to-keep air, and she wore rosy lipstick with a touch of blush on her cheekbones. In contrast to Joanna, she was a woman who cared about how she looked. Moving with scarcely suppressed energy, she came into the room to take Ailina's hands and kiss her cheek. Then she turned to me, again with both hands extended.

"So this is the Caro I remember so well—grown up. Welcome home!"

I liked her at once. There was a warmth in this woman that would be extended to others.

"You were my mother's friend, weren't you?" I said, and gave my hands into her strong clasp.

"I hope I still am." Her dark eyes held a directness that was rather like David's. "We must talk about that today. David's told me how troubled you are."

Ailina said, "There's no place to sit down in the palace, so why not go outside to the banyan tree? I'll find you there in a little while." She took an envelope of snapshots from her purse. "These pictures were sent to me from New York. A friend discovered some things in a shop there that may belong in the king's bedroom. There's a photograph there that shows the room as it used to be, and I want to make some comparisons before I turn this over to the committee."

"Fine, we'll meet you outside," Helena said, and we walked down the stairs and went outdoors.

The banyan tree was old, and had dropped a great many trunklike roots, but it had yet to catch up with the size of the tree in Lahaina. A yellow poinciana bloomed generously on the palace grounds, and there were monkeypods and a kapok tree, among others. A few visitors moved about, while office workers used the park as a shortcut, or a place to sit in the open air. Honolulu traffic bustled all around us, but its tall buildings were held away by the acres of the park, and this was a quiet, peaceful place.

"I'm glad you're coming to visit us in Hana," Helena said when we'd settled on a bench in the shade.

"I'm looking forward to it," I said. In spite of the friendliness of her greeting, there seemed something solemn in the air between us.

"I'm glad we could arrange to meet before you came out. How is your grandmother?"

"I'm not sure," I admitted. "She seemed better when I first came than she does now. Perhaps I've upset her. She was glad to see me at first, but now she only seems to want me gone."

Helena nodded soberly. "They're all afraid at Manaolana—haunted. This started right after your father's death. Perhaps even before. It's lessened over the years, but I suppose your coming has opened all the old wounds again."

"I don't think they want my mother to recover."

"I know how you must feel. I was in and out of Manaolana around that time. I'd come the day before to meet your Grandmother Elizabeth. Keith was very proud of his mother, and he wanted me to persuade Noelle to be kind to her and not upset her while she was here. He believed that I had some influence with Noelle, since we'd been friends for most of our married lives. That's why he invited me to stay at Ahinahina for a few days."

"So you were there at the time of the—accident?"

"Yes. Afterwards, I stayed on with Elizabeth for a few days to do what I could. Your mother hadn't been all that nice to her—I suppose Elizabeth was so openly on Keith's side, and things were going wrong."

"I can't remember my mother being anything but kind. Except for angry spells once in a while. Elizabeth may have asked for it."

"You must remember Noelle that way, of course. And she was kind to everyone most of the time. But your father was driving her up the wall."

"Because of Ailina? I know about that. Even Ailina has told me a little."

"Ailina was young and a very beautiful girl. And your father could put out a lot of charm when he chose. I expect he bowled her over. One night he brought her in to sing for his guests, and—"

"Yes—I've remembered that night, and how upset my mother was."

"The trip up the mountain was just a few days later. I was there and Noelle was in as excited a state as I've ever seen her. I was doing my best to distract and quiet her. Marla, who can sometimes be insensitive, and was pretty young herself, chose that time to come over and try her new camera."

"So that's when she made that picture? I've seen it in Noelle's room. I wonder if Marla put it there?"

"It's possible. But it's your Grandmother Elizabeth I want to talk about. How was your life in San Francisco?"

I was quiet for a moment, aware of the park, of Honolulu's voice around us, but Helena was waiting for my answer, and I didn't think her interest was idle.

"I only learned recently that Grandmother Joanna and my mother were still alive. Whatever letters came for me, and whatever letters I wrote, were all held back. I can never forgive Grandmother Elizabeth for that. As soon as I learned the truth I phoned Joanna that I was coming to Maui."

"Yes. David told me how you found your mother in the garden. But you're young enough to heal, Caroline. I don't think Joanna ever will."

"All my memories are of a woman strong enough to take anything. But she's changed and I'm sorry for that."

"Noelle is a tragedy she's had to live with every day. At least, with Elizabeth, what happened was over and done with. And she had you to help her recover."

I couldn't answer that—it was so far from the truth.

Helena went on quietly. "I admired Elizabeth Kirby in a great many ways. Though I only knew her slightly."

"Then you couldn't have known her at all! I'll be happy if I never see her again." I heard the bitterness in my voice, but I couldn't hold back my feelings any longer.

"Then I'm sorry for her," Helena said. "She must not have a great deal left in her life."

"She has her hotel—that's all she really cares about."

"I can understand how it must have been for you. You were such a loving little girl, and you'd always been approached with love. Elizabeth comes of different stock. I'm not sure she knows how to show affection, yet perhaps she feels just as deeply as Joanna does."

"She wouldn't let my father go! She kept a sort of shrine to his memory with pictures and clippings and trophies he'd won. None of it had anything to do with his adult life. She shut that out as though it never existed. She shut out my mother. Only I was there every day to remind her."

"I see. It's true that I hadn't understood any of this. But I do know that Elizabeth was in a state of anxiety during those last days at Ahinahina before the accident. Your mother couldn't have enjoyed having her there, ready to champion Keith at every turn, ready to blame her daughter-in-law for whatever was wrong. Your father's angers went a lot deeper, where your mother's were like summer storms. She was threatening to leave him, yet she said she'd never give him a divorce. If Elizabeth and I hadn't been there, I'm not sure what he might have done. I think your father could never take opposition of any kind."

There were conflicting stories here—he'd wanted a divorce, he hadn't wanted a divorce. But did it matter which was true?

"I don't know if he'd have married Ailina," I said. "I really do remember how much he seemed to love my mother."

"They wouldn't have wanted you to sense what was happening. They both loved and protected you. I've always thought that if your mother had been able to take his affair with Ailina more calmly, and had just waited, it would have died out."

Had my father known that Ailina was carrying his child? Would that have been thrown in my mother's face? But that was a question I couldn't speak aloud.

"The trip to the crater should never have been made at that time," Helena said. "It was arranged so that Elizabeth could ride up the mountain with them. We all love to show off that stupendous crater. Your grandmother had done some riding as a girl, and Joanna had been getting her up on a horse again, so she was actually enjoying it."

I couldn't remember any of this, and probably hadn't been interested.

"They invited me to go along," Helena continued, "but I didn't feel like making the trek under the circumstances. There was too much unpleasantness in the air, and I felt apprehensive. Even Elizabeth began to see how explosive the situation was between her son and Noelle, and she tried to call off the trip the night before. Your father insisted on going, even though he was furious with Noelle. Of course, that was what Elizabeth was afraid of. By that time, Noelle was frightened too—she knew how violent Keith could be. But Marla assured her that she'd be there and everything would be fine. So Noelle agreed to go."

"But Grandmother Elizabeth didn't make the trip after all?"

"No. She claimed a migraine the next day and stayed behind. Afterwards, she blamed herself. She felt that if she'd been there she might have prevented what happened."

"I suppose you know that Marla had a thing about my father too?"

Helena sighed. "When Marla was young she had the sort of ego that could make her believe in fantasy."

"She still believes. She told me it was Noelle who carried the tapa beater up to the crater."

"Tapa beater?"

But of course Helena wouldn't know about that. "Never mind," I said. "I'm glad you came over to the palace and I could meet you. But I'm still wondering why you wanted to see me and open all this up."

She answered quickly. "David thinks you'll never be in one piece yourself until you find out all that happened on the mountain. He wanted me to tell you whatever I could remember."

"I only want to know because of my mother. The rest doesn't matter to me. Joanna and Marla, and even Tom, who seems to have been in love with Noelle before she married my father, all think she's happier left alone."

"David's wife didn't believe that."

"Oh? But I understand that Joanna wouldn't let Kate Reed examine Noelle."

"She couldn't officially, but she was able to talk with Noelle a few times—or tried to. She told me once that if your mother could ever be brought to where she would face what had happened, there might be a chance. But she felt that Noelle was basically fragile and Kate wasn't sure what the result would be."

"David seems to have some plan in mind. He spoke about a 'dress rehearsal' when I come to Hana."

"Yes—he's told me. It worries me a little. Tell me something—do you think Noelle's happy the way she is? Are they right to leave her alone?"

"I don't think so. She flew into a rage with me a day or so ago. And she tried to run away and ride up the mountain by herself. That doesn't sound very happy to me."

"I'm only guessing, but Noelle used to be my friend. I know her pretty well. Sometimes recently I've felt that something she's hidden behind all the protective layers is trying to get out. Maybe it needs to get out before she can be well."

"Thank you," I said. "That's what I believe too."

"I've heard Kate talk about this type of amnesia—the hysteric kind that's more psychological than physical. It seems to come in all possible variations. Sometimes Noelle seems perfectly rational and even recognizes the present time. But such moments never last. It's as though she doesn't dare allow them to last—because there's a part of her that is terrified."

"I'm glad we've talked," I said. "Your knowing Noelle as a friend helps."

Ailina was coming toward us from the direction of the palace, and she looked elated. "I think my friend in New York is on to something, and we'll recover some more bits and pieces for the palace. Are you ready for lunch? There's time before we catch our plane back to Maui. You'll join us, Helena?"

We walked through Honolulu's busy downtown traffic, and among its tall buildings—all nonexistent when the palace was built. Jake's was a busy and popular restaurant, but we found a table downstairs where we could be served promptly. Ailina and David's mother talked about mutual interests, and they seemed to realize that I'd gone far away in my thoughts, so they left me alone.

Afterwards, out in bright sunshine again, Helena came with us to a taxi stand. "I'll see you in Hana," she said, and took my hand. "Aloha, Caroline." As always, the word carried warm affection, and I found I could say it easily in return.

When we drove off, I looked back and saw Helena standing at the curb in her dusty rose and white, her chin tilted in her special, vital way. I wondered how close she had been to David's wife.

We talked only a little on the way to the plane, and kept to safe subjects.

"If I'm here long enough," I told Ailina, "I'd like to take lessons in Hawaiian. It's a beautiful language."

Ailina smiled. "I had that idea once myself. It didn't work out."

"*You?*"

"For a time the language was almost forgotten, and now there are arguments about it. For a while everyone wanted to be Western. We use a great many Hawaiian words casually, but we don't put sentences together and *speak* it very much. So I went to a class for a few weeks. For me, it was hopeless. The experts themselves can't agree on pronunciation or spelling or meanings. Hawaiian is coming back a little now, but it's changed, and we can't recover all we've lost. There's a sort of pidgin in use, but that's a private language, and if outsiders try to use it they're resented. Of course, Carlos and I always spoke English, though he knew Spanish as well, from the Philippines. I remember once when I wanted to know how to say 'I love you' to him in Hawaiian, I asked a few people. They laughed at me and told me they said it in English. The closest I could come was *anoi*—for beloved."

"At least," I said, "there's an effort to preserve history now. Today I could glimpse what's being done. You're a part of that—you and Helena and so many others." I touched the kukui lei around my neck. "David says you made these for him to give me when I was little."

She looked pleased. "Yes—I'm glad to see you're wearing them. That was a long time ago."

Too much that was good in my life seemed to belong to a long time ago. But Noelle was *now*, and so was I, though I mustn't use Noelle to escape thinking about me.

We spent a good many hours together that day, Ailina and I, and by the time we'd made the plane trip back to Kaanapali, and driven across to East Maui and up the mountain, I felt that we'd become friends. I didn't want to think about Koma at all, or about how he tied Ailina and me together in a strange way. I couldn't tell her what her son had revealed.

When we reached Manaolana it was past dinnertime and Ailina wouldn't come in. "You'll have a lot to sort out now, Caroline. But I think you can handle it."

No one came to greet me and the house seemed very still. I wasn't hungry, so I went straight upstairs. Now the thought of Koma that I'd been holding away thrust itself into my mind, demanding attention. The relationship was hard for me to absorb. It would have been different if I'd liked him. But we had nothing in common, and he liked me no better than I liked him. Perhaps that was why he'd told me—to see me squirm, and to further hurt my image of my father.

The blood tie really didn't matter—didn't mean anything. When I walked into my room I felt utterly weary and unable to take anything more. But there was something new to deal with immediately.

At first glance it appeared that someone had scattered flowers across the bedspread. But as I looked more closely I saw that these weren't the petals of real flowers, but something far more ominous. What lay there was the ruin of the splendid silversword poster I'd seen in my grandmother's office. It had been cut into pieces there on my bed, so that the whole formed a sort of jigsaw puzzle. The silvery green leaves of the base were bunched near the foot, the black of the crater behind them. The great stalk with its little purple flowers grew upward toward the pillows. At the top lay jagged bits that had formed the sunset sky, with a single bright star shining all by itself. The whole poster was there in rough form.

I thought of Noelle sitting in the volcanic sand of the crater, plucking at the leaves of a silversword—lost in meaningless occupation, while her husband lay dead, her sister unconscious, her own mind rejecting what was too awful to face.

Someone moved in the doorway behind me, and I whirled around.

"Sorry," Marla said. "I didn't mean to startle you. How was your trip to Honolulu?"

"Look," I said, gesturing toward the bed. "Who did this?"

She came into the room, her look suddenly guarded, and picked up a bit of paper that showed several purple blooms. "Interesting. Even imaginative—if it was meant to scare you. I expect it's a warning, Caroline."

"Stop it!" I told her. "Did you do this?"

She dropped the bit of paper. "I wish I had thought of it. But I don't really believe I did. Not unless I've had another lapse."

This was mockery, but I pounced on her. "What do you mean? Have you had other lapses?"

"How would I know? But I don't really think so."

"Noelle?" I asked.

"It seems likely. She can be very creative at times, and I think she doesn't like you. If you stay here, you can probably look for more tricks and tormenting. Perhaps something inside her knows that she's better off as she is. Maybe she's sane enough to grasp for safety."

I began to gather up the scraps of paper as Marla watched me.

"What are you going to do?" she asked.

I didn't answer, but went on collecting them into a stack on the bed. When I looked around again, Marla had gone. I dropped the pieces into a plastic bag and went downstairs.

Lights burned in the living room, but no one was there. The scent of night flowers drifted through from the lanai. I walked down the long hall to Noelle's room and found the door ajar. She sat in a chair near a lamp, and when I stood still in the doorway, I realized that she was reading aloud—from a child's book.

She heard me as I stepped into the room and looked up, smiling. "Hello? I'm practicing reading this story aloud. Then when I read it to Linny, I can do it really well. She loves the dramatic parts, and I like to act them out."

Familiar sadness rose in me, but I thrust the feeling away, and went to Noelle's bed, where I scattered the silversword poster like confetti across her spread. The pieces fell carelessly, forming no pattern.

Noelle put her book aside and came to look. "How pretty! They might make a picture if they were put together. Is this a new sort of puzzle?"

"It used to be the silversword poster that hung in your mother's office." I spoke quietly, watching her. "Someone cut it into all these pieces and arranged them on the bed in my room."

She turned away at once. "I hate silverswords. I always think of death when I see silverswords—though I'm not sure why."

"You don't remember that trip all of you made to the crater so many years ago? You don't remember sitting there plucking at a silversword plant after your husband died and your sister was hurt?"

She shook her head vaguely and returned to her chair. "Don't be silly! Keith will be home any minute now. Linny's gone out with him, and I'll read to her when she comes in. Please take that horrid stuff off my bed."

Lamplight touched her fair hair and the soft curve of her cheek. She looked heartbreakingly young as she watched me, wide-eyed and innocent—a loving young mother and wife, incapable of any crime.

I went quickly to kneel before her and took both her hands in mine. I held her gaze, compelling her to look into my eyes.

"It's time for you to come back," I said softly. "You've been away for much too long, and I don't think you are really happy where you're hiding. That trip to the crater was twenty-six years ago. Twenty-six years! Keith died when he was thrown from his horse, and Marla was kicked by her mare and badly hurt. You were there too. Your mother and Tom found you and brought you to the hospital in Kula. You really can remember this if you try. It's all there in your brain, and before you can be well again you have to coax it out."

She pulled her hands away from mine. "What have you done with Linny?"

"Listen to me!" I caught her fluttering hands and held them

tightly. "*I* am your Linny. I was that little girl you loved so much, and you are the mother I loved and still do. Come back to me—please come back. We need each other."

There seemed to be some cognizance in her eyes—a hint of frightened recognition. Then she rejected the danger. "Stop making things up. I'm going to tell my mother about your lies. Whoever you are, she won't let you stay here anymore."

"That's right," Joanna said as she came into the room. "Caroline is going away very soon. I want to talk to you, Caroline."

Noelle smiled at her mother, looked blankly at me, and picked up the book she was going to read to Linny. Once more defeated, I gave up. As I followed Joanna toward the door, something on Noelle's worktable caught my eye—a pair of shears. I picked them up and saw the scrap of purple caught between the open blades.

"Wait a minute," I said to Joanna, and showed her the scissors. "Those pieces of colored paper on Noelle's bed used to be your silversword poster. Someone cut it up with *these* scissors and left it on my bed. Nicely arranged to show the picture."

Joanna looked at the scraps scattered on Noelle's bed, and marched out of the room. "Come with me right now," she commanded.

In her office she glanced at the empty wall space where the poster had hung, and then picked up a folder on her desk.

"These are your plane tickets home, Caroline. They are for Monday. There's nothing to keep you here. You may stay for your trip to Hana and for Ailina's entertainment the following night. That's all Maui has left to offer you. Go home to the grandmother who raised you, Caroline. You and I are two different people now, and we can't ever find each other again. Noelle is contented and safe—and she's better off left that way."

It was the old song that one of them was always singing.

"But she's *not* contented!" I cried. "A lot of the time she's frightened and trying to run away from herself."

"You don't know anything about it!" Joanna pushed her hand through her short gray hair, scowling at me. "Take these tickets, Caroline. On Monday you'll be on that plane. I want you away from here before something much more unfortunate happens."

I took the folder of tickets from her. "I don't know whether I can use them or not," I said, and walked out of the room. Before I went upstairs I stopped at the hall telephone to call David. There was no answer. I would try again tomorrow—it was getting late now. If he had any plan regarding Noelle, it had better be moved up and hur-

ried along. In spite of my brave words, I might have to board that
plane on Monday.

I stayed in my room for most of the evening, going downstairs once
for a sandwich. Early the next morning I phoned David again, and
this time he answered.

13

It was midmorning and I was walking along the road to Ahinahina, where I was to meet David. When I'd phoned, he'd said he had to go over there to get another shot or two, and if I could wait for him there we could talk away from Manaolana.

Again the morning was beautiful and the trade winds had died away, so the air was quiet. I walked along absently, my mind filled with the things I wanted to tell David. Everything except what I'd learned about Koma. That was better forgotten.

Since I was walking on the left verge of the road toward traffic coming up, I didn't turn when I heard a car behind me. I had no warning until it speeded up suddenly and swerved across the road toward me. I barely had time to leap out of the way, and I fell onto my knees in a tangle of spiky weeds and rough stones in the ditch. Frightened, I looked after the car as it crossed to its own side of the road and drove on down the mountain. I recognized the tan jeep from Manaolana, though I couldn't see who was driving as it speeded off.

I got to my feet unsteadily and took stock of the damage. One stocking was torn, and my knee bruised and bleeding. The driver must have known that I'd jump out of the way—so he probably hadn't meant to strike me, but just to give me a good fright. I was thinking "he," but it might have been a woman. Most likely Marla.

There could only be one reason. Someone was sure that I was getting too close to what had happened in the crater and was warning me. Threatening me. To make sure I would be on that plane? There was no use trying to guess which one of them had driven the jeep. They could all drive it—probably even Noelle.

I returned to the road, limping as I tried to hurry. All I wanted now was to get away from traffic.

At Ahinahina I went around to the wide back lawn, where David had said he'd meet me. There I found a water faucet and with tissue from my handbag I dabbed dirt from my raw knee. Further repair would have to wait until I got home.

I was just finishing when David came toward me from the house. He looked wonderful, with the sun on his hair, and a wide smile that told me he was glad to see me, no matter what the reasons that had brought me here. When he saw my knee, he looked concerned, and for just a moment I wished I could have been six years old, so he could comfort me.

"The jeep from Manaolana tried to run me down," I told him grimly. "I don't know who was driving."

"That knee looks nasty. Shall I take you home?"

"Let's talk first," I said.

"All right. Let's go to the far end of the house." David took my arm. "You're sure it was your grandmother's jeep?"

"I'm sure. I rode up in it when I arrived."

Today there was activity all through the art center, and I could hear voices echoing through windows above us.

"Tell me all of it," David said as we sat down.

I went back to the trip with Marla and Baldwin House, where I'd met Ailina.

"I liked her," I told him, "and I enjoyed staying overnight in her apartment." I didn't mention Koma, but skipped ahead to Honolulu and Iolani Palace. I told him about standing in the room where the last queen had been held as a prisoner, when Helena Reed had come to join us.

"Your mother's a remarkable lady. She was very good for me. We sat outdoors for a while and she talked to me about my mother and father, and of what had happened just before they rode up to the crater."

"My mother's good at pulling things together," David said. "She liked you—she's told me that on the phone. But she's also concerned for you, quite aside from your mother."

"Right now there's nothing for me that's aside from my mother. First I must help her—then I can look out for me. Noelle *isn't* happy. I think her sudden angers grow out of her frightening confusion."

I told him about finding the cut-up poster on my bed—and about those moments with Noelle and Marla.

"Joanna has bought me plane tickets for San Francisco, and she wants me to leave on Monday. So there are only a few days left for me to reach her—if I ever can. When I try to be direct and tell her the truth, she simply slips away from me."

"I don't know . . . After this jeep incident, perhaps it's safer for you to go. Things seem to be getting pretty mean—even dangerous."

"I suppose I'll have to go. But, David, you were thinking of some plan—something we might try with Noelle. What did you mean?"

"I wanted to try out what I had in mind—to see what you thought. It might be drastic. But now we'd better make it the real thing on the first try."

"What are you talking about?"

"A trip into the crater. I have a good friend in Hana who owns a helicopter and still does occasional trips. When I talked about a rehearsal, I just meant that we could fly in and see if we could locate the place where the accident happened. But now we'd better take your mother in on the first try, if we can. That's what I had in mind."

This was startling and a little frightening, but at least it was direct action.

"Do you think you could bring Noelle with you when we drive to Hana tomorrow?" David asked.

"I'll manage it somehow," I promised. "Marla and Joanna never let my mother out of their sight for long, and they don't trust me at all. So it may be hard to do."

"Let's go back to Manaolana so you can take care of that knee. Maybe I'd better talk to Joanna and see if I can sell her the idea of taking Noelle to Hana."

"Thank you, David. You've done so much for me since I've come here. More than anyone else."

He was watching me, his eyes kind. "It's what I want to do."

I wanted more than that. But I didn't trust my own feelings.

He helped me up from the bench, and I limped my way to his car and got in.

"I won't say anything about my near-miss with the jeep," I told him as we drove back to my grandmother's. "There's so little to go on, and I don't want to make everything worse. I'll just say I slipped and fell into the ditch."

When we reached the house, Joanna was out in the stable with Tom, and David went to talk to her. I stayed outdoors to wait. Leaning against the big camphor tree, I listened to a cardinal singing to itself in the high branches. Once more I thought of my first night at

Manaolana, when David and I had stood near this tree talking, and Tom had been there, listening. What *had* we talked about that could have mattered to Tom? I'd told David what I remembered as a child at the time of my father's death. I'd talked about my mother and father. And David had told me about the bombed island of Kahoolawe. But there seemed nothing here that would cause Tom to run off so we wouldn't know he'd been listening.

Except—one more thing returned to me sharply. I *had* told David that my Grandmother Elizabeth believed my father had been murdered. Of course he would have told Joanna and Marla what he'd heard, and perhaps had set them on guard. In that case, he might very well not want us to guess what he'd heard. So was he making his own plans to force my leaving? The attack by the jeep seemed to point first of all to Tom.

My knee was stinging and I wished David would come back. I tried to listen to the bright little bird on the branch above me, tried to close my mind to everything else.

A few moments later I heard voices and saw David and Joanna coming toward me. They seemed to be talking pleasantly enough, and David smiled as they reached me.

"Your grandmother thinks it will be a good idea for Noelle to come with us to Hana tomorrow. Noelle likes my parents and she'll enjoy the trip."

"And you'll have a last day with her," Joanna added. "I hope you'll use it wisely. Now then, Caro—you've had a fall. Let me see that knee."

"Take care of her," David said. "I'll be here at eight in the morning, Caroline. We'll need to make an early start."

Joanna looked at my knee and took charge. "Come inside. This won't be the first time I've patched your skinned knees."

I went with her meekly, and sat in a chair in her rather austere bedroom. Joanna was never much for personal frippery. She hurried into the bathroom for bandages and a small bottle or two. As she cleaned and patched up my scraped knee, some of her recent stiffness toward me fell away, and she seemed more like the grandmother I remembered. I was once more a child to her, and she was fixing a hurt.

When she was satisfied with her bandaging, she said, "Let's sit outside on the lanai for a little while—it's such a beautiful day."

For once I felt relaxed and at ease with her, and a sore knee was a small price to pay for this brief closeness. We sat together on the bamboo couch, with its bright green-and-orange cushions, and it seemed a natural gesture when she took my hand into her own.

"I'm sorry, Caro, about the way things have gone. I should never have let you come in the first place. I was giving in to my own need to see you again. This time we'll write to each other. Please? There's so much I want to know that we haven't had time to talk about. Your marriage, for one thing. What went wrong, Caro?"

This was hard to tell her about, but perhaps I needed to. "I mixed Scott up with all the love I still felt for my father. That wasn't fair to Scott, any more than it was to me. All I remembered, all I felt, was that I wanted someone who would love me as much as my father had. And in some ways Scott seemed like him."

It was good to talk to her, good to open up and free myself of the festering.

"Your father loved you," Joanna said. "And it's true that no other man will ever care as much in the same way. But of course you don't want that, do you?"

"There's still a pull that I'm not rid of yet."

"You'll recover. You're on the way. Just be careful about your trip tomorrow. Let it be a happy day with Noelle. I'm glad you've had some time with Ailina. I admire her, and the way she came out of that unhappy time with her head high."

I didn't want to touch the matter of Koma. Not in this peaceful moment when we could be close. Then my grandmother herself spoiled what I was feeling.

"I know what Marla told you about how that tapa beater was taken up to the crater—that Noelle herself carried it up there. But that isn't entirely true."

At once I was back in the midst of confusion.

"Marla would like you to believe in Noelle's guilt when it came to your father's death. It would be much easier for everyone, wouldn't it, if she was the one to blame? But it wasn't Noelle who put the tapa beater into her saddlebag. I did that myself. Keith was in a rage, and he frightened me. I didn't want to see a gun carried up there—much too risky. That thing was lying on my desk and was the only defensive weapon I could pick up in a hurry. By that time I knew the trip was a bad idea—too many volatile emotions around. But Keith wouldn't call it off. He claimed that he wanted his mother to see the crater, since she'd probably never come to Maui again. She disliked Hawaii thoroughly."

"I was surprised that she'd even consider the trip," I said.

"She didn't for long, and she tried to persuade Keith not to go. By that time, I think she was afraid of his real intentions. But even when she backed out that morning, he insisted upon going. Of course Noelle did as he wanted. She had her moments of rebellion, and she could fly into summer storms, but she went on that fatal trip as though there were no other choice. Hawaiians say, 'There's no stopping when the Hoolua wind opens up.' That's the strong north wind that nothing can stop. Events were marching that day, and it was all inevitable. Of course Marla was off in her own fantasy, and she would do anything to be with Keith, even though it was only Ailina who interested him by that time."

Joanna seemed lost in some distant space of her own.

"You *do* know what happened," I said flatly.

After a moment she roused herself. "Yes. Afterwards, Tom and I misled everyone about the fact that we'd gone ahead to make camp. It's true that we did. But I was worried, and I rode back alone to meet them. So I saw it all, Caroline."

She seemed to shrink into herself and grow older before my eyes.

"Poor, poor Noelle," she murmured.

I took hold of her arm—hard. "Tell me the truth. Was my father murdered?"

Even now, when she'd said so much, she didn't answer directly. "They never knew which of two wounds Keith died from. Either might have been fatal. They decided that his head must have struck one rock as he fell, and then bounced against another. Since the cause of the accident seemed clear enough—frightened horses—there was no point in deciding. So there was no further investigation."

"What frightened the horses?"

"No one really knew. The weapon wasn't to be found because I picked it up and hurled it far away behind some rocks. Where Tom searched, because I sent him there the next day."

Even now, when she'd come so close to revelation, I knew she didn't mean to tell me who had wielded that murderous weapon.

"Why have you told me this?" I asked.

She flung out her hands. "Because you'll be with Noelle all day tomorrow, and if you understand you will leave her alone."

"Who struck him?" I had to be relentless.

"Caro, please don't go on with this."

"Do you know who killed him?" I demanded.

She seemed to crumple into herself. "Even though I was there, I don't really know. No one knows. Just go home and forget about all of us at Manaolana, Caro. Our guilt and unhappiness isn't yours."

"I don't know how to do that," I said miserably. "Anyway, it's my unhappiness too. I'm involved through all of you—because my father died, and because Noelle is the way she is."

Joanna recovered herself and stood up. "All I ask is that you do Noelle no harm on this trip to Hana. Whatever it is, let her keep what she knows."

Harm wasn't what I wanted for Noelle. But it seemed that the most terrible harm had already been done. I stood up beside Joanna and asked one more direct question.

"Why did Marla lie to me about Noelle putting the tapa beater in her bag?"

"To protect me, of course. She knew I put it there. Poor Marla. She's always wanted to please me, and she used to be so jealous and envious of Noelle."

"Because of my father? But she managed to have an affair with him, didn't she?"

"It wasn't much of an affair. And none of that matters now. When it comes to the tapa beater, I suppose she thought that blaming her sister wouldn't make any difference. But that's enough—let's stop this and go inside."

I didn't move. "Marla spends so much time with her sister. She seems to be kind and considerate toward her."

"Why not? Noelle is like a child, and there's none of the old rivalry left. Perhaps Marla even feels some guilt herself—that she has something to make up to her sister."

I doubted that, trusting Marla's "consideration" less than ever. I looked around uneasily, wondering where she was, and if she could be hovering somewhere within earshot.

Joanna caught my look. "Don't worry. Marla's taken Noelle to the library in Makawao in the jeep."

I was silent. If it had been Marla at the wheel, rather than Tom, then everything fell into a pattern.

My grandmother saw my troubled look. "I'm glad, for your sake, Caro, that you're going to Hana tomorrow. It's better to get away from here. Though it may be difficult to keep Marla from going with you, since you're taking Noelle."

"She mustn't come," I said quickly.

"I know she shouldn't, but I'm not sure we can stop her."

In the living room, Joanna bent to make certain the bandage on my knee was in place.

"How did this really happen, Caroline? What made you fall into that ditch?"

I couldn't tell her. There was enough for her to worry about. On impulse I put my arms around her, and suddenly we were holding each other and crying a little when Marla walked in, followed by Noelle, whose arms were full of books. Her eyes looked bright and watchful.

"A touching scene!" she said.

My mother carried her books—picture books!—to a chair and dropped into it, quickly absorbed.

Joanna said brusquely, "I've some work to do with Tom," and strode out of the house. When Marla went upstairs I followed her, limping a bit. She seemed not to notice, and I stood in the doorway to her room when she went inside.

"Well, come on in," she said reluctantly.

I'd never been in her room before, and I looked around with interest. This long corner room was larger than mine. A big window opened toward the mountain, and side windows overlooked the row of eucalyptus trees that hid the stables. A desk stood at an angle to one window, with an empty sheet of yellow paper rolled into the typewriter, and a tape recorder near at hand.

The room seemed to swallow me into riotous color. Blue-greens and copper tones, mixed with busy flower designs, were everywhere, from bed to sofa. The white walls were covered with Maui scenes, framed and unframed. Marla too apparently collected artifacts from the islands—clay and wood figures, pottery, tools and weapons—a muddled array. I wondered how anyone could live with such a stir of objects and colors.

Marla sat down at her desk, and waved me toward the sofa. "You haven't told me about your time with Ailina or your trip to Honolulu, Caroline. How did it go?"

"I enjoyed all of it. David's mother came to meet us at Iolani Palace, and I liked her very much." I was talking to mark time, waiting for an opening when I could take her by surprise.

She watched me with bright interest, and I suspected that she was playing some new secret game. "It's strange to think that a long time ago Ailina and I were rivals for your father's rather easy affections. Of course we were both pretty stupid to fall for a man like Keith. Can you imagine, Caroline, that there was a time when I thought Keith would divorce Noelle and marry me! Idiotic, of course."

I didn't believe that she regarded any of her own actions as idiotic, or that she ever forgot or forgave.

"Didn't it trouble you that my father was married to your sister?" I asked.

"Noelle? How could *she* ever hold a man like Keith? He needed someone alive and exciting—someone he could match wits with!"

"Like Ailina?" I said.

She began to fiddle with her typewriter, rolling the paper back and forth. It wasn't in her to receive a thrust without making a return lunge.

"Of course, I've always wondered about Koma," she mused. "I've always suspected that he wasn't Carlos Olivero's son. Isn't that an interesting thought, Caroline? How would you feel about having Koma for a half brother?"

Since I knew that *she* had been the one to tell Koma the truth, there was no point in continuing any of this. I no longer wanted to surprise her.

"I don't suppose Koma or I would care, one way or another," I said. "We don't much like each other."

I started toward the door, and she spoke again, lightly. "Have you had a fall, Caroline?"

That brought me around to stare at her.

"The grass stain on your skirt," she pointed out. "And those red streaks that look like Maui earth."

How did she dare to do this? I was the one to be taken by surprise, but at least she'd given me an opening.

"Yes," I said, "I had a fall." I pulled up my skirt to show the bandage. "A jeep came very close to me on the road this morning. So close that I had to jump into a ditch to save myself."

Her bright, intense look grew even sharper. "You'd better take care, Caroline. Don't become accident prone."

"Joanna said you were out in the Manaolana jeep, driving to Makawao."

"That's right—I was."

I decided on a direct attack. "It was you, wasn't it? You tried to run me down."

"If I'd tried, I'd have succeeded. I missed you, didn't I?"

"And the silversword poster? That was your doing too. You cut that up and then blamed Noelle!"

My accusation didn't upset her in the least. "Why not? You've spelled trouble for all of us ever since you came. I'm just sorry that nothing I've tried so far has worked to drive you away. But don't worry—I'll think of something better."

Chilled by her tone, as well as her words, I wondered if Marla was not far more unbalanced than Noelle.

When I didn't answer, she went on.

"Oh, I meant to tell you—when I returned the jeep to Tom just now, he said Noelle was going with you to Hana tomorrow. Of course I will come too. She mustn't go without me. I can sit with her in the back seat and keep her happy on the long drive."

"That's not a good idea," I told her quickly. "I don't think you want her to be happy. What *do* you want, Marla?"

Her look darkened. "Would you really like to know?"

"I think I do know. You want to keep my mother exactly as she is. But why?"

This time I'd gone too far, and now her antagonism was free of restraint and in the open. There was even a sort of madness stirring in this room with its clashing colors and quarreling designs. Marla took a step toward me and I fled back across the hall to my room.

There I dropped into a chair, upset, and not a little frightened. The glimpse I'd had of Marla's consuming jealousy of her sister was devastatingly clear. No matter what Joanna thought, it still existed. Marla's own clever brain and real talent had never balanced the scale against all she coveted in Noelle. I had the depressing feeling that if I tried to talk to Joanna about any of this, she would laugh at me. Over the years Marla had convinced her mother of something that wasn't true.

Nevertheless, Marla must *not* come with us tomorrow. If she were there, everything I hoped for with Noelle would be defeated. But how she was to be stopped I didn't know.

14

We were all waiting on the lanai for David early the next morning. Noelle and I wore jeans and shirts, and had put on low-heeled shoes, since there might be a lot of walking on this trip. I had seen to it that we brought sweaters as well. The added touch of the kukui lei was for luck. We might need a lot of it today. My knee felt a little sore but I could ignore it.

Marla had announced several times that she was coming with us. At breakfast Joanna told her bluntly that she didn't want her to go, and that I should have this last opportunity to be alone with Noelle. Marla said nothing in answer, and I knew she'd do as she pleased.

When David's car drove in and I saw him walking toward us across the grass, I knew how much I'd been looking forward to this day. It might be the last time I'd have with him, so sadness was mixed with pleasure. Since I couldn't stop my growing feeling for David, I would give in to it for today, and just enjoy being with him.

When he reached the lanai, Marla spoke quickly, announcing her plans. "I'm coming too, David. Noelle needs me."

"That's not a good idea, Marla," he told her quietly.

Her smile was sly. "If I'm there to watch out for her, you can spend more time with Caroline."

He ignored that. "It's still not a good idea. By Monday you'll have your sister to yourself. So don't begrudge this one day she can spend with her daughter—and Caroline with her mother."

Joanna glanced uneasily at Noelle, who sat a little way off on the lanai, rummaging through her big shoulder bag. The words "daughter" and "mother" slipped past her as they always seemed to when used in connection with me. Her mind simply discarded what she was afraid to hear.

"Let's get started, Caroline," David said. "I don't know when we'll get back, Joanna."

"Make it a good trip," Joanna told us, sounding uneasy.

When we started toward the car, Marla came after us. I wouldn't have been surprised if she'd simply climbed into the back seat and defied anyone to put her out. David looked grim by this time, and she might be tangling with more than she'd bargained for.

Unexpectedly, it was Tom O'Neill who stopped her. I hadn't noticed him near the far corner of the house, but apparently he'd recognized what was happening.

"Marla!" His sharp tone allowed for no argument. "You're going to help me with the horses today. My stable boy's off. Remember?"

"I've changed my mind," she told him. "Not today, Tom."

"Today," he said. Just that one word, but this time she heard the command in his voice, and crumpled surprisingly. Her expression of amused malice vanished and instead she looked wary. Of Tom? What was going on here?

As we started off, I turned to wave to Joanna, and saw that Marla was walking toward Tom, her usual cocky assurance gone. She had given in completely, and this was something I wanted to know more about.

"What happened?" I asked David. "How did Tom manage to get Marla to do what he wants?"

"I don't know. Sometimes I've wondered about that on other occasions."

Noelle, sitting between us, the oversized bag on her knees, unexpectedly answered my question. "Marla's afraid of him. She doesn't want him to get mad at her."

"Why is that?" I asked carefully.

But she only went off at a tangent. "I'm glad she didn't come with us. Sometimes you'd think Marla was older than I am—she gets so bossy. Now we'll have a lovely time. I haven't seen your parents for months, David."

She sounded perfectly lucid, so perhaps this would be a good trip for her. David glanced across at me and nodded. "I thought you and Caroline would enjoy this, Noelle."

"Oh, we will!" she cried, and I sensed a new excitement in her. Because she was escaping from her keepers at Manaolana? "This is like old times, David. Do you remember when we drove to Wailuku and you left me at the library and took Linny up to see the Needle? Afterwards I joined you for a picnic at the Japanese Gardens. Linny talked about that trip for days."

I put my arm around her. "Do you realize how long ago that was—how many years?"

She laughed. "Not years. Just a few months, I'm sure."

"But you said 'old times' just now—remember?" I *had* to push this whenever I could and try to break through.

"Now you're mixing me up, Caroline." She pushed away from me petulantly.

Too much of the time she behaved and sounded like a child herself. Yet somehow during the coming hours I must try to help her to grow up to the present. No matter what the risk, this was a chance I had to take and I couldn't turn away now. The thought of the crater was always there in my mind. The moment when we really took her back to the past would be the moment that might help her to remember—or else break her completely. In the meantime, all I could do was to pick up every opportunity to push a few small realities.

For a time we stayed away from troublesome topics. I found myself looking at David often as he drove, liking so many small things about him. The way his hair dipped over his forehead, the set of his jaw when he firmed it. He wasn't a man to antagonize, I thought—but he was a man for a woman to feel safe with. That was a very dated notion, except that one couldn't be quickly rid of something in a woman that still wanted to lean on the protector of old, while nevertheless being independent. A nice trick, if it could be managed.

Once, when he felt me watching him, he sent me a quick warm look that made me feel suddenly like a young girl on her first date. Young enough to wonder about all the mysteries that still lay ahead; young enough to plan and hope—and fall in love.

Go away, Scott, I thought—and strangely enough, the memory of him seemed to be fading, so that only anger remained. Before I could be free, I had to rid myself of that too. I remembered what Ailina had said: *Anger is the thing that gives no life.*

We drove down the mountain and through Paia, a little town beloved these days by artists. There were small shops along the way, and houses set back from the road amid flower gardens. The coast road to Hana led east from Paia.

I knew the distance wasn't great in miles, but only maniacs traveled the Hana road in a hurry. The climbing snake turns to the crater were simple compared with this road which snapped in and out at such sharp angles that we often traveled in opposite directions within the same few minutes. We could see where we were going ahead, and look back to where we had been—always across indentations of water. The scene changed so constantly that I hardly dared to blink lest I miss some of the enchantment.

Jungle descended these eastern slopes of Haleakala, since the mountain was central to all of East Maui, its wild state practically impenetrable in some places. Often we looked out upon vast spreads of green that were the massed tops of trees, rippling gently in the wind. Hues and textures changed constantly. Sometimes a hill ahead looked like brocaded green satin, and one hardly saw the ruffling that changed the pattern until the car drew close. Darker greens were splashed at times with scarlet flowers that startled with their intense contrast. I knew there were orchids out there, perhaps the lovely bird-of-paradise and the ubiquitous wild ginger. Of course there were all shades of hibiscus, the state flower of Hawaii. However, the red flashes came too swiftly and were too distant to identify.

Always the sea curled in far below the road, and glimpses of rocky cliffs were frequent. Sometimes jungle-clad precipices dropped away to an ocean that cut mercilessly into these shores. With the sun not yet overhead, shadows helped to sculpt the rain forests and the great banks of ferns that overhung the road. This was the more tropical part of Maui, where rain fell most often. Occasionally the jungled slopes moved back and we passed banana groves, bamboo forests, and always a variety of palm trees. Sometimes taro patches appeared —tiny farms cut out of the jungle.

Now and then a road sign in the shape of a taro leaf pointed us on our way. We saw only a few clusters of houses near the road, and other humans appeared only when they passed us in a car. David drove at a steady, comfortable pace.

Black lava rocks broke the surf as it hurled itself upon the land, sending spray high in white showers that fell back into the water. Sometimes we caught the dazzle of a mountain stream hurling itself down a cliff to join the fierce seas below, leaving only a thread of silver to interrupt the green.

After a time, however, beauty itself could become a surfeit. The whipping road, the smothering avalanche of greens, the endless sea breaking over rock and beach—all became a monotony I could no longer absorb and give my full attention to.

Beside me, Noelle was growing restless. She opened the shoulder bag on her knees and began to search inside it. What she drew out shocked me. She had brought along the ugly Pele carving that I had played with as a child. It was no longer dressed as a doll and the drooping breasts and protruding belly were on display. The crude copy of the original carving, with its dished-in profile and glaring mother-of-pearl eyes, made me thoroughly uncomfortable. There seemed menace in the figure now, and I wondered how I could have been so attached to it as a child.

"Why did you bring that along?" I asked.

She held it lovingly, touching the smooth wood with something like affection. "I brought it for Linny. Marla said she has probably gone ahead to Hana and is with your parents now, David."

I would have liked to shake Marla. However, Noelle never seemed to realize that with all her hunting and hoping, she never really found Linny, and she always forgot her search before she had to face the truth she hid from herself.

David glanced at the figure. "You may have a use for Pele later on, Noelle, so perhaps it's a good thing you brought it along. My father and mother are looking forward to seeing you, so we're going to drop you off at the house. Then Caroline and I are going to drive on along the road to a special place I want her to see. Mother will hold lunch for us until we get back. Afterwards, we'll take you on a helicopter ride. Perhaps to visit Pele herself."

"I'd like that," she said, not really understanding, and stroked the carving on her lap.

We hadn't much farther to go to reach "heavenly Hana," as the tourist brochures advertised it. David said there had been no road for cars through here until 1927. The little fishing village had eventually evolved into a thriving sugar town, and all the hills around were once covered with plantations. This had lasted until the end of World War II, when the demand for sugar fell, and Hana was too remote for hauling. Then one man's creative foresight saved the area from disaster.

"There's a huge cross of lava rock that's been erected to Paul Fagan's memory," David said. "He realized that the fields which had been planted for sugar that was no longer in great demand could be turned into grazing for cattle. So Hana Ranch was born and the *paniolos* moved in."

David had stopped the car in a place where we could look out over the town and Hana Bay.

"It must have been pretty exciting—the way they shipped cattle to market. They drove the herds down the road through town to the wharf, and everybody got out of the way. Some of the animals would run right into the sea and start swimming, so the cowboys had to learn water herding. On swimming horses, they drove the Herefords out to the ships, where cranes and slings got them on board amid a lot of noisy bawling."

"Didn't Captain Cook sail into this little bay on his voyages?" I said.

"Yes, it's been written about. But that bay isn't always as calm as it looks today. The Hana coast is exposed to storms that can blow in and pound the land. Then all the beautiful waterfalls turn into torrents and there can be flooding from both sea and mountain. An undersea earthquake off Kodiak Island, three thousand miles away, sent a tidal wave to hurl some pretty bad destruction on this coast. That's the tsunami that can strike all of the islands, so that we've had our share of death and devastation from the sea. The dark underside of paradise."

Now the bay looked beautiful and blue and peaceful, with a rim of white sand around the water.

"They have canoe races out there," Noelle said suddenly. "Keith and I came here to watch them one time. I wanted to bring Linny, but she was too little."

"Tell me about that time," I urged.

She had put the carving back in her bag and only shook her head as she lost the thread of memory.

"They still hold races," David said, "but these days the racing canoes are built of fiberglass. Not as romantic as hollowed trees, but more practical. Do you see that dark hill out there that puts an arm around the far end of the bay to the right? It's a cinder cone, really, under all those ironwood trees—one of the volcanic vents from Haleakala. Once that cone was used as a fortress, since it could be defended. Fierce battles were fought there between Maui and the island of Hawaii. Let's go on into town now."

Hana was a town of pretty little houses and abundant flowers. We took the higher road into the small business section, and parked near the Hasegawa General Store, about which a famous song had been written. This was one of the "sights" of Hana, and we went into the well-ordered chaos of the store. Harry Hasegawa sat behind his desk near the door, where he could summon help for anyone who needed it. Prominently on display were shirts that bore the legend: I SURVIVED THE HANA ROAD, and visitors were buying happily.

We drove on to the Reeds' home, a low brown house built with natural woods, with an overhang that shielded windows from the sun, and a generous screened lanai across the front. It was set well back from the street in a typical Hawaiian garden. No English formality here—one stuck things in the ground and stepped back to let them grow in any way they chose, resulting in a riot of color and fragrance.

"Peter's in school now," David said as we left the car. "I hope you'll meet him later."

Helena and Larry Reed came out to meet us, and Helena gave each of us in turn a warm hug of greeting. The pale green *muumuu* she wore became her and she looked as well groomed and elegant as when she'd dressed more formally in Honolulu. Her straight carriage gave her something of the same presence that Ailina seemed to have, and I felt again the energy she seemed to exude. An energy that was part of her ability to savor whatever experiences came her way. Her embrace for me was genuine and warm.

Dr. Reed was as tall as David, with a tanned face and brown eyes that held laugh creases at the corners. His handclasp welcomed me, and both of them gave a special loving greeting to Noelle. She seemed at home with them at once, and didn't mind when David said he and I had better get started for Kipahulu.

"Don't hurry," Helena said. "I've planned a cold lunch and we'll have it whenever you get back."

"Have you heard from Frank?" David asked.

"Yes, he phoned a little while ago. Everything's set." She glanced at Noelle, who was paying no attention. "You're to call him when you're ready to meet him. He's kept the afternoon free. He remembers"— again the glance for Noelle—"everything very well."

"Fine. We'll see you later," David said, and we returned to the car.

"Frank is the man who'll take us to the crater?" I asked.

"Yes, Frank Wilkie. In his younger days he flew a number of trips for the Park Rescue service. He was the one who brought Noelle and the others out of the crater that day."

The road beyond Hana hadn't been repaved recently. It was narrow and bone-jarring. Not quite the whiplash road we'd just followed, but bad enough, even though it had been cut inland away from the sea.

"There's been a battle going on," David said, "between those who want the road paved and those who want to keep it as it is in the hope that tourists won't want to make this pilgrimage. Of course they do anyway."

"Where are we going?" I asked.

"Wait and see. I don't want you to see this place as a curious tourist. I want you to *feel* it. There's a lot about Hawaii that's mystical, and this is one of those places with special vibrations."

When we reached the Seven Sacred Pools, we found a parked bus, its passengers swarming on every side with their cameras. We crossed a bridge where there was a lovely view of the waterfalls, but we didn't stop. A side road farther on, with no particular marking, led us toward the water. From this a dirt road turned off and we drove to where we could park near a small green-and-white Hawaiian church. On a tongue of land that reached into the ocean lay a small cemetery with old stones set in the ground. A grove of trees offered a hushed retreat, and we stepped with care between the graves. Only the wind that blew across this headland, and the sound of the sea washing its shore, stirred the quiet.

When we reached the grave David was seeking, he stopped. "Hawaiians say this place has *mana*, like the crater. The word's meanings are mystical. Sometimes it stands for prestige and authority. It can also mean worship and spiritual power, and this is what I sense when I come here. What do you feel, Caroline? Before you look at the stone, what do you feel?"

I stood very still and allowed the quiet of this shaded grove to flow through me. *Mana* was not something you put into words—here it was a spiritual presence that somehow filled the air.

The grave was a flat, rectangular space, filled with the traditional smooth stones used to cover Hawaiian graves—hundreds and hundreds of stones. Larger stones rimmed the whole and supported the small ones within. In their center lay a slab of granite with carved lettering kept clear by the wind. I bent to read the simple markings.

CHARLES A. LINDBERGH

BORN MICHIGAN 1902   DIED MAUI 1974

Following was a line from Psalm 139 that Lindbergh himself had chosen: . . . *if I take the wings of the morning and dwell in the uttermost parts of the sea . . .*

I could sense the spirit of this place—the mysterious *mana* that graced and protected a spot which would face ocean and sky far longer than the man had lived.

David spoke softly beside me. "It's a moving story. Lindbergh knew he was close to death, and he had himself flown back from a mainland hospital to his home here in Kipahulu—where he could plan for his dying as he had planned the way he lived. In the week left to him he had time to be with his family as he wished. He chose to be buried in a plain eucalyptus coffin, refusing any hero's funeral. There is room here for his wife when her time comes—so their spirits can soar together as they did in life."

David was making it vivid and real—what had all been remote before.

"Some of what happened after his death is disturbing," he went on. "This place became a shrine almost at once. Which would have been fine, if it had been treated with reverence and respect. During the first year a few hundred came, and then the number doubled, tripled —until now there are busloads every day, besides those who brave the road in their own cars. Every stone that covered the grave disappeared in the first year—carried away as souvenirs by the insensitive. Lindbergh knew about 'hero hunters' and the Vermont granite slab was chosen well—large enough and strong enough to defeat desecrators."

A ginger lei rested on the stones before the plaque, and I wished I had something to leave. In the pocket of my jeans was a narrow yellow ribbon I'd brought to tie back my hair. I weighted it down with a stone, and left it to show bright and brave amidst the gray stones. My own small tribute to a man who had never wanted tributes, but whose spirit could still be felt in this quiet grove.

We walked around the far edge of the cemetery and came upon a row of small graves where pets had been buried. The headstones were marked with words like "Loved by . . ." with the young owner's name following.

No one was inside the small church, and we sat down for a few moments to let the silence fill us, and to speak our own quiet words in our minds. I felt very close to David and grateful to him for giving me this experience which couldn't be put into ordinary words.

Before we left, David showed me a sign with words Mrs. Lindbergh had written.

> May we remind you that this church is a place of worship and the graveyard is consecrated ground. You are welcome to enter the church in a spirit of reverence and to walk quietly in the surrounding paths. We ask you not to step on the graves or disturb the stones or flowers out of respect for the dead and consideration for the feelings of their relatives.

Outside we wandered for a little while longer, listening to the sea and the wind.

"Hawaiians have always understood about heart and spirit," David said. "I hope the young ones never lose that. It's good that the language is coming back because it's a language of emotion. I hope we modern Hawaiians never forget all that exists in the air and space around us."

"Thank you for bringing me here," I said. *"Mahalo"*—a warmer word.

He put his arm about me for a moment. A *close* moment in more than the physical nearness. Then he said, "We'd better get back. Now we come to Noelle."

I found that I could think of my mother more quietly, and with less pulling and tearing inside me. Just as something had touched me when I stood on the rim of Haleakala's crater, I had been touched here in this place as well. With David's help, I would be able to deal with whatever was to come.

15

We were on our way, with Noelle in the seat between us, and she was looking forward happily to an adventure she hadn't as yet understood.

Lunch had been a pleasant time, and we'd enjoyed Helena's chicken salad, hot bran muffins, and iced papaya. I'd never seen Noelle so animated. Helena and Larry Reed had known how to make her welcome and set her at ease. When I saw her like this, I wondered how healthy Manaolana could ever be for my mother, with its atmosphere of hidden guilt, and that cotton-wool protection always intended to keep her as she was.

On the way to the small flying field outside of Hana, David told me more about Frank Wilkie, and the mission he'd flown to bring out my father's body and Joanna's two injured daughters.

Noelle was searching her big bag again, paying no attention. His words might just as well have been in a foreign language, the way she shut them out. When she found what she was looking for, she brought it out triumphantly—a man's gold ring, set with a stone of apple-green jade.

"There!" she cried. "I knew I had my good-luck ring with me."

I'd recognized the ring instantly.

It was too big for her slim fingers, and as she started to slip it over her right thumb, I held out my hand. "May I see it, please?"

She gave it to me readily, and as I balanced it on my palm the old feeling of sadness and loss filled me again. How many times my father had let me play with this ring when I was little—though only when I stayed close to him so I wouldn't lose it.

Carved cunningly into the hard jade was the tiny face of a Chinese demon—a face that had always fascinated me. Suggested eyebrows slanted down, scowling, the eyes were crossed, the nostrils merely suggested, and the wide mouth had been carved into a ferocious grimace. My father had purchased the ring in a shop in Hong Kong, and he'd liked to wear it on the little finger of his right hand.

"Tell me about this," I said to Noelle as I returned it to her.

As she slipped the ring absently over her thumb, some disturbing memory touched her. "Keith was wearing this when—when something awful happened." She brushed a hand across her eyes, puzzling. "Afterwards my mother took it off his finger and gave it to me. She thought I should keep it—not Keith's mother. I never liked Keith's mother, and she didn't like me. So this ring has always been with me, and sometimes I take it out and wear it for—for luck."

I touched the ring lightly. "What luck, Noelle? What is it you want most?"

For once she didn't mention Linny, or tell me that Keith would be back any minute. Instead, she wondered aloud. "Sometimes I—I really don't know who I am. Or what has happened to me. Sometimes, more than anything else, I want to find *me.*"

"I can tell you some of those things you want to remember," I said softly.

But she was already shaking her head. "No! People are always *telling* me things. I don't know what I can believe. I have to feel it inside myself."

Perhaps Noelle was wiser than any of those around her.

"We'll try to help you to do that today," I said, and glanced at David, who nodded gravely.

"That's right, Noelle. That's exactly what we want to accomplish."

She began to slip away once more, and I called her back. "Tell me about the ring. How can such an ugly little face bring you luck?"

She answered easily. "That's because Orientals use horrid faces to frighten away demons. But this little face wasn't as strong as Pele. She can be vengeful and destructive, you know. Though I think she tried to help me. I really saw her that day."

"Where did you see her?" I asked, holding my breath.

"Up there." She looked out the car window toward the mountain floating high above us on a bank of clouds that cut off the lower slopes. "I was lying where I'd fallen when my horse went down. Pele came and picked me up and set me down beside a silversword plant. She told me the plant would help me to escape from everything wicked and unhappy. I wasn't sure I wanted that . . . but I suppose it's what happened. I can still remember the smell of those leaves as I plucked them. Not very pleasant—a little like an aster."

She raised her fingers to her nose and sniffed them. "It's gone now. But I still can't remember."

"What did she look like, Noelle? Pele, I mean."

"She was beautiful—a young maiden. That's one of her guises, when she comes back to visit her old home on Haleakala. But when I stared at her too long, she disappeared into the mist and floated away. That's all I can recall."

"I understand," I said. "Perhaps we can help to find *you* today. At least we can try."

"Oh, look!" She waved a hand. "There are planes out there, and a helicopter!"

I'd lost her again, but the mists had parted a little, and I had the new reassurance of what *she* wanted in her more thoughtful moments.

When David parked his car near the field, he didn't get out right away. Instead, he spoke quietly to Noelle.

"What we're going to do—where we're going to take you—may be upsetting, Noelle. It may hurt. Someone you loved has died. Another person you loved has gone away and grown up, and returned. Years have passed, and I hope you can be brave enough to face these things that are real, Noelle. Things that you've perhaps been concealing from yourself."

She seemed suddenly on the verge of tears. "I don't know what you mean."

"Never mind," I said quickly. "We're going up in that helicopter now. Have you ever flown in one before, Noelle?"

"I don't think so." She twisted the jade demon ring on her thumb.

As we walked toward the planes, Frank Wilkie came out of a small building. He was a stocky man with wide shoulders, thinning gray hair, and a rugged look about him. His manner was one of easy assurance laced with humor—a manner often found in flyers. As he came toward us he looked first at Noelle.

"Hello," he said, holding out his hand to her. "I don't suppose you remember me, since you were in pretty bad shape the last time I saw you, but I remember you very well."

Though she gave him her hand, his words clearly meant nothing to her, and she was looking past him toward a small plane that was taking off.

David introduced me, and Frank said, "Everything's set."

We walked to where the helicopter waited and climbed aboard. The few seats were separated by an aisle, and David took the front seat beside Frank, while I sat behind him, across from Noelle. She seemed pleased and interested in this new experience. What might lie ahead was already gone from her mind, in spite of our attempted warnings.

We took off in the smooth, slightly tippy lift of such craft, and flew for a short distance along the coastline. The noise level was high, and there could be no talking unless we shouted. On sightseeing flights, passengers were given earphones into which the pilot would speak. But today we had a grimmer purpose than sightseeing.

The curling white road between jungle and sea was the one that we'd followed toward Hana only a little while before. When we turned inland over miles of rain forest, we seemed to skim the tops of the trees. Once we hovered low enough to be opposite a waterfall that plunged down a cliff in a column of moving silver to lose itself beneath the green canopy of the trees. Sometimes as we circled we saw sugarcane, and green patches of pineapple fields, separated geometrically with strips of red earth in a pattern an artist might have conceived. We were climbing now, and the trees had thinned to growth that wasn't as tall as lower down, and the light green of kukui gave a mottled effect as we rose still higher toward a slit in the crater walls.

The clouds had let us through, and while I realized that the gap was probably miles across, it looked frighteningly narrow compared with the steep walls on either side. It must have taken a tremendous blast to blow such a hole, hurling chunks of granite far off into the sea.

I looked across at Noelle, to find her happily absorbed in what lay outside her window. No threatening hint of what was to come had penetrated as yet.

Through a window ahead, as we rose, I could see the live volcanoes on the Big Island—Mauna Kea and Mauna Loa, a hundred miles away, peaceful now against a serene sky.

We flew between the cliffs and were suddenly above a bare and desolate moon world, inside the crater. Shadows of high clouds made patches of light and dark below us, emphasizing contrast. It was a world of subdued colors—mauve and garnet and ocher in grotesquely twisted masses of rock that had once been tossed into the air to fall back upon this weird landscape. This was very different from standing on the rim looking down.

Frank Wilkie had found his landing place, and we dropped toward the floor of the crater, three thousand feet down, so that the green world beyond vanished. Red sands spread in a curved wind pattern beneath the plane, and volcanic mounds rose all about us in irregular shapes, cast up by explosive forces ages ago. The shades of red were like dark fire etched into rock, and a great deal of the carving had been caused by erosion over the centuries.

Noelle touched my arm and I turned to her quickly. She looked disoriented now, and anxious, so I held her hand tightly across the narrow aisle.

We were dropping down to land, and for a moment I glimpsed distant buildings along the rim, and Science City's silver domes. Then they disappeared, hidden by immense cinder cones all around us.

We settled gently, the wind of our blades whipping red dust into the air while our noise desecrated the silence. Gradually the blades stopped turning and the awesome echoes died. I got out into an enormous emptiness and a silence that pressed down upon me, vast and unfamiliar. Only a tiny moving spot on a distant trail could be seen as a ranger on horseback. Nothing else stirred except a sudden gust of dervish wind that whirled sand into the air, so that we closed our eyes and turned our backs.

I watched Noelle carefully, waiting for the recognition that must come. But though a little uncertain, she still seemed interested in this new adventure.

After the sunshine of Hana, the air was sharply cold, and a sweater was hardly enough to provide warmth. In the face of this unearthly world, we spoke softly and moved on quiet feet. *These* echoes were something we didn't want to rouse. All about us the colors seemed to grow more visible and intense, and more unlike the colors of the earth I knew.

I remembered my first impression of black desolation, which hadn't been true at all. As the eye became accustomed, one saw the strange, unearthly beauty of this place. The greens of high, distant cliffs contrasted with hills of gray boulders, while nearer cones were streaked with an intensity of reddish color. Among the lava peaks that surrounded me, I could glimpse quiet pockets of white cloud here and there. Not far away, on our own level, grew an entire field of silverswords, low on the ground, not blooming now, and among them several nene geese browsed.

Noelle shivered and I put my arm around her. It wasn't the mountain chill that made her tremble, but something she must be feeling as she looked around. She began to turn the demon ring on her thumb, as if she called upon it to ward off evil that might touch her in this place.

Our feet slipped on volcanic sand as Frank led the way. Parts of the crater floor were strewn with rocks of all sizes—some broken from larger masses, some volcanic "bombs" that had been shot from the depths of the earth. There were "bubbles" too—round, hollow mounds, some small, some with openings large enough for a man to crawl inside.

We climbed laboriously to the trail near which Frank had landed, and where we could step onto firmer ground.

"We'll walk around the shoulder of that next cinder cone," Frank said, and started off ahead of us. This cone was black, which seemed ominous in this place of ancient fire.

I held Noelle's hand as she came after me—our long-ago roles reversed, since I was watching out for her.

David came close behind us. I knew that he had never lost his capacity for full involvement in whatever cause he gave himself to. Noelle had become such a cause and he was both anxious and eager for the outcome.

We walked around the steep slope of the cone, following the trail, and came again into a mottled landscape—Pele's own playground.

"Do you remember this place, Noelle?" Frank asked gently. "This is where the accident happened. This is where your horses went down and you all fell. I found you clear down there when I came to bring you out."

Noelle stared at him, frightened now, and I knew that in a moment the screen would come down and she'd escape into her own safe world where nothing could touch her.

"Don't run away!" I cried. "I'm your daughter. I am Caroline, and I want to help you go back through what happened so that you can return to what's real. Please try. *Try* to remember what happened and tell me."

My words about being her daughter slipped past unrecognized, her guard against such knowledge still secure. Nevertheless, my appeal seemed to have reached her. She covered her face with both hands and words began to come—so softly at first that I could hardly hear. Then she grew more vocal, as though she lived again a scene long past.

"I know he wanted to kill me. We were all mounted, and he rode his horse straight at me. He meant to—oh, I don't know what he meant! But that's when I remembered the tapa beater. Mother hadn't wanted me to go on the trip, and she'd put it in my saddlebag, where I could reach it quickly. It was all she could think of that might protect me. I didn't believe until that moment that he meant to hurt me. But when I saw his face, saw him coming—I *knew*. I snatched that thing out and . . ." She dropped her hands, staring toward where the frightened horses must have slid in panic down the lava chips.

"Then what happened?" I urged. "You needn't blame yourself—just go on remembering."

"So many awful things were happening. I was terribly angry. I can remember how heavy the tapa beater was in my hand. Then a horse was screaming, rearing—and we were all jumbled together right here in this narrow spot. I think Keith went down first. He fell off his horse when I struck him. Marla was down too, trying to stop Pilikia from bolting. I couldn't hold my horse and she fell right down there!" Noelle pointed. "I was thrown off into the sand. They told me afterwards that Marla's Pilikia broke her leg and Tom had to shoot her."

"What happened after you fell?" I asked softly.

Noelle was quiet. The vagueness was coming over her again—the settling mists. "It's hard to remember . . . I think that's when the maiden came. She was so beautiful and kind. She carried me to where a silversword grew and told me I needn't remember anything that would trouble me ever again. The silversword would help me and take all the pain away. I can remember how silent everything was when all the noise stopped. I remember my mother bending over Marla after her horse kicked her. And Tom . . . I don't know when he came. I began to do as the maiden told me and I broke off bits of the silversword leaves. They're downy like a moth's wings—did you know that?"

"Go on," I said.

"There isn't any more. I just went back to the time when all of us were happy. I had my little girl and Keith loved me—and I was never so angry that I wanted to kill him."

Frank had moved a little way off as Noelle talked, to give us privacy. She spoke half to herself, half to me, though with no recognition of who I was. David came to touch her shoulder gently, so that she looked at him.

"Did you really strike Keith, Noelle? Is this what you need to face and accept?"

"I—I don't know. I don't remember." Suddenly she pointed down the slope. "Look! There are silverswords down there. Let me go down—I must go down!"

David held her gently, firmly, until she gave up the struggle and swung her bag off her shoulder to open it. She took out the carved image of Pele and held it out in front of her.

"I brought this for you," she told the mountain. "So please let me go." For an instant she held it out in both hands like an offering, and then let the figure drop so that it rolled and bounced down the cinders, to land among the silverswords.

For a moment she stood watching it. Then she began to cry and this time it was David who held her gently, and whom she seemed to recognize. I wondered if her own action had released her from the spell she'd been under for so long.

"We'd better take her back to the helicopter," David said. "We mustn't push her any further."

Frank led the way back. He couldn't have understood all that had happened, but he had stepped back discreetly—a kind and considerate man.

I let David take Noelle back along the trail and stayed where I was for a moment. Somehow, Noelle must have sensed all along where we were going, and so had brought the ring for protection, and the Pele figure as an offering to appease the lady of the volcano.

The others had moved out of sight around a curve in the trail, and I was aware of the immense and terrible silence around me. It was as though a strange, primitive sense of danger touched me, and I ran to catch up with the others. This was a place of death and disaster—a haunted place—and I wanted no more of it.

We descended to where the machine waited, incongruous and out of context here. Noelle had grown wilder in her weeping, and David and Frank had difficulty in helping her aboard. As I waited, I could hear the bleating of feral goats on some distant *pali,* followed by the sound of a shot—a sound that ricocheted and echoed endlessly.

"Hunters," Frank said. "Goats destroy everything they can eat, so the Park allows hunters to come in and cut down their population."

Noelle was in her seat and Frank motioned me to get aboard. For a moment longer I stood looking around this place I might never see again, but which was likely to haunt my dreams forever. Some small wild plant bloomed near my feet, and I saw with wonder that a butterfly hovered over it. A butterfly on the moon! Even volcanic cinders could breed plant life, and the crater wasn't so empty of growth as it seemed at first.

"We'd better hurry," Frank said, and I looked up to see that clouds were streaming through one of the gaps. "They can fill up the crater fast, and we don't want to be caught down here."

The wind pushing clouds through, was like pouring cream into a bowl, even though the sky above us was clear and blue. I hurried to climb the steps and fasten myself into my seat, while the machine shattered the silence with its own indifference. Noelle was crying harder than ever, and my concern for her grew. I couldn't be sure yet what her tears meant.

Frank took us back to Hana by a shorter route, and when we'd landed, David thanked him, and we led Noelle to the waiting car. She had never stopped crying, though she wasn't sobbing wildly now, and she didn't reject my arm about her.

When we reached the house, Helena came out on the lanai and took charge of Noelle, who had turned into a frightened child. She took her out to the kitchen to fix her a dish of ice cream and soothe her tears.

"Are you all right, Caroline?" David asked. His eager excitement had fallen away, and I knew he was as unsure of the outcome with Noelle as I was.

"I don't know what will happen now," I said, "but I think we had to do this."

"She can't be much worse off than she was. At least she's come closer to the truth."

"Closer to realizing that she may have killed my father?"

"We don't know that. She may have been angry enough to try, but somehow I don't think she was ever strong enough to have struck that blow—even if she believes she did." He looked past me down the walk. "Here's Peter—I'm glad he's home in time for you to meet him."

The boy came up the walk, dropped his books, and ran to hug his father. David swung him up and then put him on his feet to face me.

"This is Caroline Kirby, Peter. She's Noelle's daughter, and Joanna's granddaughter. Caroline, this is my son Peter."

He took the hand I held out, his brown eyes like his father's, his ready smile his own.

"Yes—hello. Grampa said you were coming. Is Noelle here now?"

"She's in the kitchen with your grandmother," David said. "I think there's ice cream if you want to join them. I'll come along in a minute."

I started to follow, but David stopped me. "Wait. Give Noelle a little time to recover. She and Peter are friends, and maybe he'll help more than anyone else right now. Besides, my father has something he wants to show you."

Dr. Reed had come out on the lanai. "Yes, I do have something I want you to see, Caroline. Will you come into my office for a minute?"

Dr. Reed was as big a man as his son, and as rugged-looking. The rim of hair around his tanned head made a fringe of dark silver. His eyes, too, were direct in the way they regarded me, and I had the feeling that he would listen to his patients with empathy.

He led the way to a small cluttered room at the back of the house. Since he was no longer in full practice, he'd given up his larger offices. The room's windows looked out upon banana plants and a papaya grove. The clutter inside looked fascinating. Books were set sideways on top of other books, paintings and photographs crowded one wall, and various bits of pottery were set about. Not particularly old, so perhaps they were gifts from his patients.

The desk was an old-fashioned rolltop that he said had come by ship a long time ago from Yankee New England. The top was pulled back now to show a small portable typewriter, and piles of paper. David had said he was setting down his memories of his days in Hana as a doctor.

He indicated a big leather armchair beside his desk for me, and sat down in a swivel chair that tilted when he leaned back. From a shelf behind the desk he took a framed enlargement and held it out to me. It must have been taken shortly before I left Maui, and the little girl in the picture held on to a young David's hand, looking not at the camera, but up at her friend.

I had to blink to keep back sudden tears as I turned the picture. "That was a wonderful time."

David's father agreed wryly. "I'm sure it was. Times often seem pretty wonderful when we look back. It's a funny thing about you and your mother. Noelle has spent all these years trying to run away from the past, while, according to what David says, you're trying to run back. Maybe you're both wrong."

"Maybe neither of us can help that," I said.

"Joanna phoned me when she knew you were coming here, and she's very concerned about you."

"Yes. She's concerned enough to send me home. She's bought plane tickets for me to use on Monday. Which doesn't give me enough time with Noelle."

"Perhaps she's thinking about your happiness. Perhaps she's even protecting you."

"From the truth of whatever happened up on the mountain? But I can't run away from that."

He was watching me keenly. "Then don't. I'm just repeating what I sensed in Joanna, but I'm not sure she's right. You could find yourself a room in Makawao or thereabouts, rent a car, stay on. I doubt if Joanna will keep you from seeing Noelle if you confront her with your presence."

"I wonder if I could—" I said doubtfully.

"Why not? How does Marla feel about you?"

"She's become my mother's keeper and she doesn't want me around to interfere."

"And Tom O'Neill—how do you get along with him?"

"I don't. From the first he hasn't wanted me here. But he's not important. He does what my grandmother says."

"Don't underestimate Tom," Dr. Reed said quietly.

I remembered the way Tom had kept Marla home when we'd left Manaolana this morning, and I told Dr. Reed about that, puzzling aloud.

"What if he's begun to think that you might be good for Noelle after all?"

"He makes me uncomfortable. I can't imagine him coming over to my side. Do you know anything about him—where he came from?"

"It's no great secret. Tom killed a man a long time ago. He got off on self-defense. Your grandmother rescued him when he was in pretty bad shape, and he's devoted to her. Of course, he always knew that Noelle wasn't for him. But who knows what fantasies a solitary man like Tom can turn around in his head?"

I didn't really want to talk about Tom, though these facts didn't surprise me. "It's my mother I worry about—the way she's trapped."

"Maybe you have to learn how to give her up."

I started to object, and he went on quickly.

"I don't mean entirely. Stay and help if you can. But it's time for you to put your own life first, don't you think?"

That was what Helena Reed had suggested in Honolulu. So they had discussed me.

"You might even find it interesting to face up to *your* present," he added.

"Noelle *is* my present," I protested. But was she? For all my involvement, was I using Noelle to escape figuring out my own life?

He reached for another picture on a ledge behind him and held it out. "This is Kate—David's wife."

For an instant I didn't want to look at the photograph. But of course I took it from him. Kate's was an arresting face, with individuality and strength. She would have known how to handle her life—a difficult ghost to compete with.

"She belongs to another time," Dr. Reed said quietly. "We all have to let her go. Just as you may have to let other lives you've lived go. In these past days you've been good for David. I appreciate that. Helena and I are grateful."

He stood up, and I rose with him. "Thank you," I said. "You've given me a lot to think about. I'm grateful too."

When we reached the kitchen, Noelle was finishing her ice cream happily, while Peter talked with enthusiasm about his last whale sighting. He was a bright, attractive boy, and as friendly as David had said. Noelle seemed to know a good deal about whales and was responding. The crater appeared to have been forgotten.

I was pleased when Peter included me in the discussion and I could tell him about a time when I'd seen whales off the Big Sur coast of California. Everything was happening on the surface—and that was best for all of us right now.

David was sitting with his mother at the far end of the table, and he'd risen when his father and I came in. "We'd better start back—it's a long drive. Noelle's feeling better now."

I'd have liked to get better acquainted with David's son, but that would have to wait. If I listened to Dr. Reed, it was possible that I wouldn't be leaving right away after all. The idea had quickened a new excitement in me that wasn't altogether concerned with my mother.

Noelle was tired, so when we went out to the car, we let her lie down in the back seat. For most of the trip we were quiet. David gave his attention to driving, and I had a lot to think about.

What would happen to Noelle now, or what direction she might take, I couldn't begin to guess. I didn't know whether we'd done her good or harm. But one thing I was sure of. The moment I got back to Manaolana I would return the plane tickets to my grandmother.

Of course, I should have known that the unexpected was usually what happened, and that it would delay any plan about the tickets.

When we reached the house, David came inside with Noelle and me. In the living room Joanna sat talking with two visitors. My

Grandmother Elizabeth Kirby and my former husband, Scott Sherman, were with her, drinking tea and waiting for my return.

I was shocked speechless, but Noelle was not. She came to life
excitedly, and her behavior startled us all.

16

Noelle went directly to Grandmother Elizabeth. "I know what you want!" she cried. "But you can't make me. I won't go up to the crater. Let Keith go with anybody he pleases—but not with me!"

For once, Elizabeth Kirby looked completely stunned. I glanced at Scott, who had risen when we came in. His slight smile removed him from the scene, kept him safely separate and uninvolved.

"Hello, Caroline," he said.

Marla, who had just appeared in the hall doorway, set down the plate of cakes she carried, and hurried to put an arm about Noelle. As if Joanna willed what was happening to go away, she closed her eyes, and I understood what my grandmother must be feeling.

Wild accusations continued to pour out of Noelle as she pushed Marla away. Whatever we might have accomplished with her today had been wiped out at the sight of her mother-in-law.

David stood back, looking concerned, and I went to him quickly. "It will be all right. We'll handle it somehow. Thank you for all you've done for us today."

There was nothing he could do here, and he understood. "Phone me tonight. I'll be home all evening." I nodded and he went out.

Noelle was out of hand now, in spite of Marla's effort to restrain her. "You want me to go up there with Keith and never come back! You know what might happen up there, don't you? You want to take Linny and Keith away from Maui. But I won't help you—you can't make me go on that ride to the crater today!"

Marla swung Noelle around so that her sister was forced to look at her. "Listen to me! Of course you needn't go. I won't let anyone

make you. You never need to go up to the crater again, if you don't
want to. I promise."

Before her sister's assurances Noelle's rage melted away. She
looked around the room until she found me, bewildered now, questioning.

"But we did go again, didn't we?" I said. "We were there this
afternoon—in the helicopter, and you remembered what happened."

Marla gasped and threw me an angry look, but Noelle went on,
speaking directly to Elizabeth now.

"Yes—I have remembered. Keith wanted me to fall. He tried to
frighten my horse so she'd stumble in that dangerous place. Only *I*
was the one who made Keith fall." She broke off, turning to me again.
"But that couldn't have happened today. We did go up there this
afternoon, didn't we? And I began to remember."

"That's right," I told her gently. "You remember a lot of what
happened. You saw the silverswords and everything began to come
back to you. But all this was a long time ago. The next step you need
to make is into *now*. It's a big step, but you're on the way to making
it."

Marla wouldn't stand for that. She took possession of her sister in
her own way. "You don't have to think about any of this, Noelle
darling. You know it hurts your head. You've had a long trip, and
you're tired. Besides, Linny has been asking for you, so let's go look
for her."

Marla had won again, and I felt angry and helpless. Noelle fell
docilely under her sister's spell, and went out of the room as though
the rest of us had ceased to exist.

Elizabeth had recovered from her first shock. "She's quite mad,
isn't she?" she asked Joanna, and then turned her attention to me.
"Well, Caroline, you might at least greet me."

I had time now to consider Elizabeth and Scott, and I realized that
I felt nothing toward either of them except indignation.

I kissed Elizabeth's cheek dutifully, and she seemed satisfied that
the amenities had been served. I was far more concerned about
Joanna, who seemed to have crumpled into her chair, but first I had
to answer Elizabeth.

"My mother isn't in the least mad," I said. "She's confused about
time, and she's cut something off in the past that she can't bear to
remember. It's surfacing now, and I think you can see what it must
have been. So perhaps, since you've come to Maui, this is the time for

you to help. To start with, you can tell us what Noelle was talking about. What happened that day before they set off for the crater? You've always hidden something, haven't you?"

Scott sat down beside Elizabeth and put an arm around her stiff shoulders. "You don't have to take any of this, Grandmother."

Grandmother! He'd never called her that when we were married. I paid no attention but went on with my direct appeal: "Tell us what happened!"

Elizabeth didn't exactly wilt. If anything, she sat more poker-stiff than before, but her face seemed to fall into new lines, and her lips trembled before she tightened them.

"There's nothing to tell. Noelle's charges haven't much to do with the truth. I suppose I shouldn't have urged her to go on that trip when she didn't want to. But Keith had his heart set on it, and I didn't want him to go off alone with Marla. She was an impossible young woman in those days. And much prettier than she is now. Of course, there was that Hawaiian girl too, but she wasn't deceitful like Marla. Your father couldn't help the appeal he had for women, but I never dreamed what would happen. My son was killed—your father, Caroline—and you can hardly take Noelle's word for anything. If you went up to that dreadful place today, I hope you cried for your father, Caroline."

I answered her as quietly as I could. "I can only cry for the father I remember, and he wasn't real. I can't cry for the man who injured so many people."

Scott said, "Stop it, Caroline! We didn't come here to stir up a past nobody can affect. We wanted to see how you were getting along. We want to take you home with us, darling."

The endearment set my teeth on edge. I remembered all the "dears" and "darlings" which, with Scott, were always a prelude to something cruel he meant to say. He was smiling at me with total confidence, as though there were no question that I'd come to my senses and would now be ready to return to San Francisco, and to him. I could see his arrogant good looks clearly now, and I saw something in his smile that I'd never recognized before. It had always seemed to express the very essence of his charm and what seemed to be his caring. It also displayed his excellent teeth, and I realized suddenly that what it really expressed was an absorption in himself. More than anything else, Scott Sherman admired being admired.

Suddenly I realized that neither of these two people had the power to affect my life in any way that I didn't wish.

"I'm sorry this has been upsetting for you," I said. "But of course I'm not going home with you. I'm staying right here with Grandma Joanna."

I went to sit on the arm of Joanna's chair and rested my hand on her shoulder, whether she wanted me here or not. She seemed to grow a little taller in her chair, and she reached up to cover my hand with her own strong one, once more in control.

"I'm sorry too, Elizabeth," Joanna said. "I never expected anything like this to happen. Caroline, please pass those cakes to our guests."

This sociability startled me, until I caught the gleam in Joanna's eyes. She'd always been a battler in the past, and now that she'd recovered from her first shock, she meant to enjoy a bit of dueling with Elizabeth Kirby.

Elizabeth, however, forestalled any cake passing and stood up. "Marla has shown me my room, and I'd like to go up to it now. Of course we won't impose on you for longer than tonight, Joanna. Tomorrow we will talk, Caroline. When you're not so upset." She had recovered fully, but Joanna had no intention of letting her off.

"Oh, you can't possibly leave until Sunday, Elizabeth," she told her. "We've planned a lovely entertainment here tomorrow night in Caroline's honor, and you must both stay. It will be old-style Hawaiian—not fire juggling and grass skirts."

"Of course we'll stay," Scott agreed cheerfully. "Grandmother will feel better in the morning, when she's rested. Besides, I want to have some time with Caroline myself."

He escorted Elizabeth from the room, without waiting for my response. He was simply not capable of understanding other people's feelings and wishes. He never would understand, because he didn't care. He knew how to put on a flattering performance that would please Elizabeth, but he didn't even understand her.

So where had *I* been during those years with him? Years of putting my head in the sand!

When they'd gone I spoke firmly to Joanna. "I *am* going to stay, you know. You can just turn back those tickets."

"Caro honey," she said, "nothing would make me happier."

There was no way, however, to escape Scott when he returned to the room.

"Come for a walk, Caroline," he said. "I want to enjoy a Maui evening outdoors. It was cold in San Francisco when we left."

Now was as good a time as any to have this out with him. When we left the house, I turned deliberately toward the stables. Tom would be there, and he wouldn't be any more welcoming toward Scott than he'd been to me—and that was exactly right for the moment.

Scott slipped his arm companionably through mine. The sun was low in the sky, and birds were singing their settling-down-for-the-night songs. Flower scents seemed to have intensified, and gold was tinting the blue. Up on the mountain clouds hid the crater, and it seemed hard to believe that I'd been up there in that red cinder world only a few hours ago.

"I've missed you, Caroline," Scott said tenderly. "You'll never know how much. I know you have a lot to forgive, but perhaps by now your perspective is better. Can I hope for that?"

"My perspective is certainly better. But whether you'll like it or not, I don't know."

"Oh, come on! You can't tell me you've forgotten everything we had together in the beginning, darling."

"What came later wiped that out. I'm not going back, Scott."

He stopped me on the path and swung me about to face him. "You don't mean that. You don't mean that you're willing to give up everything Elizabeth has planned for you?"

"She can't plan my life anymore! She knows that!"

"But I don't think you understand. She means to change her will if you don't come home. If you stay in Maui there won't be anything left for you."

"There's nothing she owns that I want. I don't want her hotel, or anything else she might leave me. When I think of that shrine she kept in my father's memory, I feel ill."

"But if this isn't left to you, she'll allow the hotel to be sold. She'll leave everything to her pet charities. And she has a lot to leave, Caroline."

I began to catch a glimpse of light. "You mean if we remarried—which is what she wants—then . . ."

"That's not what I'm talking about, darling. I want you back even if there isn't a penny involved."

"I don't think you really need to worry, Scott. Grandmother Elizabeth has always rewarded the faithful."

"You've become so hard, Caroline. You're not the same girl I knew in San Francisco."

I walked more quickly, wanting to reach the stable. "That's true.

And I don't ever want to be that woman again. This is what you need to understand."

In a moment he would lose his pose of affectionate patience with me, and there was no point in allowing that. He didn't matter to me anymore, and the full realization left me giddy with relief. He and my grandmother had brought me a gift they'd never intended.

"Come along," I said cheerfully. "There's someone I want you to meet—another old retainer."

I could sense his anger rising, but that didn't matter either. He had lost the power to hurt me, though I hadn't been absolutely sure of that until this moment.

Lights burned in the tack room and office adjoining the stalls, and the door was open. Tom stood by a window looking morosely up at the mountain bathed in golden light. Noelle sat perched on a corner of his desk eating an apple, and she smiled as we came in. The familiar stable smells, the sound of horses—tails swishing flies, a hoof stamping, a snorting neigh—all this carried me back to the times when my mother had brought me here as a little girl. Another lifetime ago, but I could remember.

"I've run away from Marla," Noelle said happily. "Tom lets me come here whenever I need to escape. Who is this, Caroline?" She waved her apple at Scott.

He answered her stiffly. "I'm Scott Sherman. I'm your daughter's husband."

"Former husband," I corrected.

For an instant Noelle's look wavered uncertainly, and then she turned to me. "Is this man saying that *you* are my daughter?"

"I've been trying to make you understand that," I said. "It's time you accepted me."

Tom looked around and I saw something in his face, in the set of his shoulders, that I'd missed before. When he spoke to Noelle his tone was gentle, yet somehow hopeless.

"Maybe it *is* time, Noelle. Maybe you'd better listen. What happened was all a long time ago. You needn't be afraid anymore."

I watched Noelle, and I could tell by her vague look that our words had done no good. But at least Tom seemed to have given up his opposition. Perhaps this was why he had kept Marla from going with us this morning; perhaps he was willing now to let whatever happened take its course.

"Thanks, Tom," I said.

He shrugged and turned back to the window.

I tried again with Noelle. "You went with David and me up to the crater today, and you started to remember everything. You must go on remembering until it all comes clear."

"I don't know if I want that," Noelle said. "There's something that may hurt me—I can't let it come close!"

Tom had heard enough, and he walked toward the stable door. Scott, completely at sea, stepped out of the way to let him pass.

I had a sudden idea and called after him. "Wait, Tom. I've been wanting to go for a ride. The sun hasn't set yet, and I won't stay out long. Could you saddle a horse for me? I'm sure Noelle can show Scott the way back to the house. I need to get away for a little while."

"I can see why you would," Tom said dryly. "Wait outside and I'll bring out a horse."

"Have a good ride, Caroline," Noelle said. "But don't go up to the crater." Then she held out the bowl of apples to Scott. "Have one, and then I'll take you back to the house."

He said, "No, thanks," and followed her out the door without another look for me. There'd been a time when shutting me out would have mattered. It didn't anymore, and I hoped he would begin to write me off.

I didn't wait outside, but went into the long stable. The stalls were partly empty, since some of the horses were off on a sunset crater trip.

"I haven't ridden much lately," I told him, "so give me a mare who's fairly docile."

"What I ought to do," he said, "is give you the meanest horse we've got and let you break your damn neck."

I spoke before he went into a stall. "I know you don't like me, and that doesn't matter. Though I don't understand why."

"Then you're not very bright. Everything was quiet here, and life wasn't so bad for any of us. I was afraid you might start stirring things up because of your mother—and that's just what you've done. Why should I like you?"

"Just the same, you stopped Marla from coming with us today— and that was a break. Why did you help us with Marla?"

He was stroking the mare, throwing a saddle over her back and fastening the girth. When he spoke again, the spurt of anger had gone out of him.

"Maybe I can see by now that it's no use. Maybe you're the storm that's brought the tidal wave, and there isn't any way to stop what you've started. Not even *you* can stop it."

"So you've decided to give up?"

"I've decided to help you—no matter what. It's the best way to get it over with. Though you won't thank me when it's done. What happened today?"

"Frank Wilkie flew us into the crater, and we walked with Noelle to where it happened."

"I thought David might pull something like that. I guess it's time. Though I don't know what this will do to Joanna. Maybe all any of us can do now is head for high ground. Must be I'm getting old—I don't care anymore. When Noelle winds up in an institution someplace, I hope you'll be satisfied."

He led the mare out of the stall and patted her flank.

"This is Pom-Pom. She has a good disposition, though she'll nip if you annoy her. Feed her a carrot and get acquainted."

I held out a carrot and the mare nibbled. "Don't you want to know what happened to Noelle up in the crater?"

"I don't suppose anything really happened or Manaolana would be in an uproar by now."

He was right—nothing much had happened, and Noelle was just as she'd been.

We went outside and Tom helped me to mount. My bandaged knee hadn't bothered me on the trip, but it was beginning to hurt—something I could still ignore.

"Do you know where David Reed's cabin is on the road to Olinda?" I asked Tom.

"Sure. Just keep going uphill. You'll see it before the road ends. It's small and not very fancy. There's a big monkeypod out in front."

I turned Pom-Pom toward the drive and Tom gave her flank a slap that caused her to break into a trot.

In spite of everything, my spirits lifted. I was free of Scott forever, and that was a wonderful feeling. It was no concern of mine if Grandmother Elizabeth was still trying to put him in my father's place. I didn't care. I would stay on in Maui, look for a job. Perhaps find a place of my own, as David's father had suggested. Begin a whole new life. *My* life. I would still do whatever I could for Noelle, and I didn't believe in all that tidal-wave stuff Tom had talked about.

It was lovely riding this road with the sun of late afternoon behind me, and the feeling of my "special island" around me. I could hardly wait to see David.

I recognized the cabin with the monkeypod tree in front, and rode across a patch of grass. Two cars were parked on the drive, and I remembered tardily that Koma Olivero lived here too. He was the last person I wanted to see right now, but that couldn't be helped. Maybe Koma would have to get used to having me around.

Pom-Pom announced our presence with a snort, and David came out on the small lanai.

"Hi," I said. "Will you invite me in?"

He helped me down from the saddle, and for a moment I stood close to him—reluctant to move because this was where I wanted to stand. But Koma too had come outside and was regarding me sardonically.

"We have a visitor," David told him, letting me go.

"Then bring her in and we'll put her to work," Koma said.

This was the first time that I'd seen him since I'd learned about our relationship, yet everything was as it had been before. Whatever existed between us was prickly with disliking.

I followed them into a roomy kitchen where a big round table held stacks of envelopes and xeroxed sheets. Koma pulled out a chair for me and waved toward the stacks. "Those are notices of our next area meeting of the Protect Kahoolawe Ohana. You can help."

David said, "Hold on, Koma. Caroline's just had a pretty upsetting experience, and maybe she'd like to talk about it."

"So she can go ahead and talk." Koma shoved a pile of envelopes and paper toward me. "Fold and stuff!"

"I can talk later," I told David. "I'd like to help, if you'll tell me what you're doing. What's the Protect Kahoolawe Ohana?"

"*Ohana* means family—a related group," David said as he joined Koma at the table. "It's been going for a number of years, and of course the original idea was to stop the bombing of Kahoolawe. Though it's now becoming a symbol to rally under for other Hawaiian causes as well. That's the way I think it ought to go."

"You can seal and stamp too, if you want." Koma pushed a dish with a sponge toward me. "I don't suppose that a *malihini* like you even knows that in 1981 the whole island of Kahoolawe was named in the National Register of Historic Places—to be protected and preserved. In the past the Navy has invited other nations to come in with ships and planes and fire away. Practice for when they want to bomb real targets. Now New Zealand, France, Japan, and Australia have promised not to bomb the island."

David's own fervor came through when he took up the story. "A lot has been accomplished. Resolutions have been passed in both houses of our state legislature to stop the bombing. Kahoolawe's one of the eight major islands in the Hawaiian chain—it should be reclaimed."

"Has the bombing wrecked all of it?" I asked.

"The target area's been limited to one side of the island," David admitted. "But practicing gunners and bombers haven't always been accurate. There are whale sightings constantly here, and whales have sensitive hearing that can be injured. I've gone over there with Navy guides and there were still unexploded shells and duds. Some are outside the target area, so you don't go wandering around, even now. There's pressure on the Navy to clean it all up, and the situation isn't as bad as it was a few years ago."

Koma pushed another stack of envelopes toward me. "*We* are part of the pressure that changes things. Sometimes bureaucrats forget about us—the people. Anyway, weaponry today is so far advanced that we don't need to kill off an island with bombing. The Ohana can move on to other matters."

"To be fair," David said, "earlier damage was done to the island by Hawaii's rulers when the monarchy shipped goats over there. Wild goats have multiplied and they've eaten the vegetation down to its roots, so there's nothing to hold the topsoil, and nothing can live. Even in the days of sailing ships, people used to report red clouds of dust rising from Kahoolawe because its earth was blowing away. The Navy and State Forestry have planted tamarisk trees to hold the soil, since that's the one tree goats won't eat. This is helping to stop the erosion."

"Can it ever be reclaimed and settled?" I asked.

"Someday it will be." Koma sounded positive—as he was about everything. "Ranching was done over there before World War II."

David went on. "Of course there are those who claim the island's not worth saving because there's no water and no one could live there. But people in other parts of the world have lived on islands where there was only rain water, and water brought in by ships. Look at the Virgin Islands, and Key West before it was piped in."

"If the people don't have the last word, what can you do?" I asked.

Koma lost none of his fervor. "This is still a democracy, and when enough voices are raised, governments listen. First there's one voice —one lone voice shouting. Then another joins in—which makes two. That's the beginning of addition—and multiplication. There's been a strong *ikaika* going on here—a force and energy working for us, maybe even guiding us—something powerful that rises out of Maui earth. It's our job to get more people to join the Ohana for the good of Hawaii."

David picked up Koma's words. "Not everybody agrees with all we've done, but we have an obligation to tell the story of Hawaii's need over and over, until more *kamaaina*, whatever their skin color, become involved. There's strong feeling rising these days out of our land. *Aloha aina* means 'love the land,' and that's our cry. If we take care of the land, it will take care of us, and that's true everywhere."

Scorn came into Koma's voice. "Over on the mainland Hawaii just means a place to swim and sit in the sun and listen to steel guitars. But *aloha aina* applies everywhere—to humans and animals and fish in the sea. If we don't begin to love the land—the earth, the water—all of them!—we lose them all."

I could sense the ardor in him now that would carry everything before it—not to destroy, but to build.

"Koma's right," David said. "The Navy's done a survey, so that five hundred historic sites on the island have been recorded. It should be a national treasure, yet the paths of shells have gone right over one of the richest petroglyph fields in Hawaii."

"What can *I* do?" I asked, caught up in the fervor I could feel in this cabin. "I need a job."

Both men stared at me. "Here?" Koma asked. "But you're going back to San Francisco."

"That's been changed. I've told Joanna that I'm staying, and she's agreed. I think she really wanted me to stay all along. It's mainly Marla who'd like me gone. Koma, my mother is beginning to remember. I don't know if her mind will ever be right again, but she's coming closer to the present all the time."

His antagonism toward me had softened a little. "Hey," he said, "that's good!"

"You're coming tomorrow night with your mother, aren't you?" I asked. When he nodded, I went on. "I wonder if you could consult with Ailina about a song or two you might include? Sometimes music can bring back memories more than almost anything else. Ailina may know some song that my mother liked. Something that could be a bridge to the present."

"Sure," Koma said. "I'll tell her. Come to think of it, there's a song I wrote that Noelle always listens to intently. So maybe I'll include that one too."

"You'll have more people in your audience now," David told him. "Caroline's other grandmother and her former husband are here."

Koma looked startled. "Oh?"

I didn't trust the sudden gleam in his eyes. This "other grand-mother" would interest him.

"Whatever you're thinking, forget it," I said. "Let her alone. What happened wasn't her fault." For once, I was taking Elizabeth's side, but only because I didn't like Koma's sense of the dramatic and what he might do under such circumstances.

He laughed at my caution. "Maybe this affair that my mother's roped me into will be interesting after all. And maybe it's time to tell David, Caroline. What do you think?"

All his mockery was back, and I didn't answer.

He went on flippantly. "There's something I never got around to telling you, David. Caroline's my half sister. How about that?"

David wasn't thrown by the news. He grinned at us both. "Re-markable! My best friend and my best girl!" He saw my face, and went on quickly, "Don't you remember, Caro, when you were six years old and I told you you were my best girl?"

"I remember," I said, and touched the kukui lei.

David turned quickly to Koma. "Look, friend, I don't know what you're cooking up for tomorrow night, but take it easy. No use hurt-ing a lot of people because of something that happened a long time ago. Including your own mother."

"Don't worry," Koma said—and I worried. "I'll try to behave—so long as nobody pushes me. Or condescends. Sometimes people from the mainland bring their own hang-ups over here and start throwing them around. Maybe it's time to tell my own girl about this. Though right now she doesn't think much of *haoles,* so it may be a shock. I'll have to overcome that—I have to work on it in myself, my mother says. You'll meet her tomorrow night, Caroline. Elika's hula is *omaikai loa.* That means outstanding, in case you don't remember. Now what about this ex-husband—what's he doing here?"

Koma made me thoroughly uncomfortable, and meant to. "I didn't invite him, and he's going to stay an ex-husband. I expect my grand-mother persuaded him to come with her." I glanced toward a win-dow and got up, eager to escape an atmosphere that had become much too charged—because of Koma. "I'll have to go. It's nearly sunset, and I don't want to ride back in the dark. But I'll help with any odd jobs you may have for me on this Kahoolawe project."

"No pay—strictly volunteer," Koma said. "Aloha."

David came outside with me and gave me a foot up into the saddle.

"I'm glad Scott's going to stay an ex," he said. "You've had a pull toward San Francisco ever since you came—I could feel your uncertainty. Are you sure now?"

"I'm sure. I've been confused and uncertain about a lot of things. I hope I can find my direction now."

"That's good. Tomorrow night will be over soon, so don't let Koma worry you. I'll talk to him."

"It's not just Koma I'm worried about. Or anyway, he's the least of it. I don't know what may be boiling under the surface in my mother after what we started today. Marla's still trying to push her back into her Linny state. And I'm not sure anymore what Grandma Joanna wants. I have the feeling that in some way she's been trapped all these years—caught in something she couldn't escape."

"We'll see it through," David said. "Hurry home now."

I turned Pom-Pom toward the road. There was a lot more I wanted to open up with David, but Koma's presence had changed that. There would be another time.

A sunset of amethyst and crimson had slashed the sky, and I rode into flaming color feeling strangely calm. If happiness could ever be calm! David had said *we* would see it through, and for this bright moment that was enough.

17

I let Pom-Pom amble along toward home. She was ready to go faster than I wanted, but I held her back. What waited for me at Manaolana wouldn't be pleasant, and I could do nothing more than mark time until tomorrow night was over. The whole idea of this "entertainment" left me increasingly uneasy.

Hedges and trees made the road dusky as the sun dropped out of sight and the quick twilight of the tropics began. Now my uneasiness connected itself with the night around me, and the sense of the mountain at my back. There were no cars, and houses were set well off the road in this stretch, so Pom-Pom and I were alone. At least being in a saddle gave me a little more control, and the ability to get quickly away if it was necessary. But that was foolish—away from what?

When a shadow moved on ahead by the side of the road, I checked the mare. Even on a horse I didn't want to meet someone inimical to me here in the vanishing light. The shadow stood still as well— perhaps only waiting for me to pass.

"Who's there?" I called.

The figure stepped out on the road. "Caroline? Is that you?"

It was Grandmother Elizabeth. Relieved, I got out of the saddle to drop down beside her. "Is anything wrong?"

"Nearly everything. Walk back with me, Caroline."

I led Pom-Pom as we walked toward Manaolana.

"I needed to talk with you alone," she said, and was silent.

I could never remember Elizabeth hesitating about anything she wanted to say, but she seemed uncertain now. I waited, and after we'd gone a short distance she went on.

"As soon as Scott and I were on the plane, I began to wonder if I was doing the right thing in coming here. I felt I had to see you and make sure how *you* felt. But there are too many memories of Keith here. Perhaps it was the only thing to do, but I came for the wrong reason."

"You mean to bring me home?"

"Yes. I can see now that you belong here. Perhaps you never really belonged in San Francisco, though I tried to fit you into a pattern that I thought was sound. I failed. Nevertheless, I've missed you, Caroline."

I'd never expected her to admit such a thing—or even to feel it—but before I could say anything she went on.

"Oh, don't think I'm going sentimental at my age. I'm not Joanna, who's always ready to drip with emotion. I've just wanted to do the right thing for you, Caroline."

The "right thing," I was afraid, would always be her thing. "Joanna has deep feelings and she expresses them—or used to. But she's far from sentimental." I realized that Grandmother Elizabeth would regard love as cheap sentiment. Though who had loved my father more? "I suppose you had to do what you thought was right," I added, keeping my tone even.

"What else can any of us do? When we're wrong we only find out when it's too late. Not that I believe I was wrong. No matter what you think now, you couldn't have grown up happily in Maui. Nothing would have been as it was before. There's too much wrong in Joanna's house. It's still wrong. I don't mean just because of your poor mother. They're all still haunted by Keith's murder. Perhaps that's the real reason why I came. Because I wanted to settle that question once and for all."

She stumbled over a stone in the grass, and Pom-Pom shied toward the road. I quieted the mare and took my grandmother's arm, aware of how thin she was, so that I felt the sharp bone of her elbow in my hand.

As quietly as I could, I told her more about what little I had learned today. Noelle had blurted out some of it. "This afternoon a friend of David's flew Noelle and David and me into the crater. Frank Wilkie is the man who brought them out of the crater after what happened. Noelle walked with us to the place where the horses fell. For a few minutes she really began to remember. She remembered that my father was angry and tried to attack her. He tried to ride her down, and she thought he was going to force her over the cliff."

"No!" She was fully Elizabeth Kirby again. "I don't believe that for a moment!"

Again I answered quietly, "I wonder if we can ever dare to say, 'I don't believe.' That closes all the doors and nothing new ever comes through a closed door." Or a closed mind, I might have added. "So we go on believing what we choose, and maybe we never catch a glimmer of what might be learned if only we'd leave everything open."

She looked at me quickly in the dimming light. "You've changed, Caroline."

"Not enough," I said. "I'm still trying."

What I was trying to do at the moment was to hold to my surface calm, and suppress the bitterness against my grandmother that wanted to rise again. I didn't succeed entirely.

"You've always believed what you wanted to believe about my father," I told her. "And you've tried to make me feel exactly the way you did."

She drew away from me and started ahead, but I held her back. My own anger was suddenly in the open, and perhaps it had to be released.

"For once you're going to listen to me!" I cried. "Whenever trickles of the truth about my father have tried to come through—as must have happened at times—you just slammed the door again. You wanted me to *worship* my father. You tried to see another Keith in Scott so you could imprint my father's pattern all over again. But Scott can't be Keith. Not that hero on a pedestal. Or even the man who lived for his own pleasure. He's too weak for that. You've always had to be stronger than anyone else, no matter how much damage you did!"

We were on the private road to Manaolana now, and she stopped to face me—not giving in for a second. But these things had been suppressed for too long, and I had to spill them all out.

"You've never listened to me before, but you have to listen now. You chose to think my father was murdered, and you blamed others for his death. But you've never blamed *him*. Not even though he may have asked for what happened."

"I don't blame him now!" she cried. She stumbled again in her smart shoes, and I caught her arm.

We could see the lights of the house shining through the trees. For a moment, feeling drained, I wanted more than anything to get on Pom-Pom and ride away—escape, as my mother had tried to do. But there was still one thing more I had to say to Grandmother Elizabeth.

"The time has come for you to blame him—to start seeing him the way he must have been. I've learned all sorts of things about him since I came here. And from different people. I think he must have always been a taker. Perhaps you taught him that. He manipulated women and used them—including you. But you would never see that. All you gave me were the myths you built up around him—and fooled yourself with."

"Keith died—he was murdered!" She sounded defensive now, fighting for everything she'd believed. At least she had believed these things on the surface. Perhaps somewhere deep inside her some ugly truths were trying to get out. I felt a sudden misgiving about what I had done, and I tried to speak more quietly.

"Please listen to me, Grandmother Elizabeth. What we need to accept now is that none of this matters. What happened doesn't matter by this time. He's gone and all that was a long time ago. We have to work out our lives as they are now. I've thought that it might help Noelle to recover if only she would remember what happened. But perhaps that was wrong too. I'm not sure anymore that I want her to go back to what happened."

"Because she killed my son?"

"I don't know. I don't think anyone really knows, even though they've been protecting her. All I want now is for her to realize that time has passed, so she can accept me as her daughter. Let her keep her blank spaces about all the rest."

Elizabeth answered me sharply. "You're as wrongheaded as ever! It certainly matters if my son was murdered and someone has gone unpunished. It matters to all of them at Manaolana because they're frightened about something."

She hadn't changed. She would never see anything except her own course.

"Tell me one thing," I said. "What did Noelle mean when she said she wouldn't go to the crater, and you couldn't force her to go?"

"But that wasn't true! She's distorted everything in her poor, crazy mind. By that time I was trying to persuade them all to call off the trip. Keith wouldn't hear of that. He told me that everything would be all right—that he had a plan. He told me—" She broke off suddenly.

I caught her up at once. "What plan?"

She went on as though she hadn't heard me. "I *did* ride after them. But I didn't make it to the top. I can't tell you any more."

Or else she wouldn't tell me. We'd reached the camphor tree, and there was nothing to do but give up for now.

"Go ahead to the house," I said. "I'll take Pom-Pom around to the stable."

She walked away from me, her back stiff and her head high. I watched her go with a grudging sense of admiration. Perhaps she bluffed as much as anyone else—maybe even more, since she didn't dare allow anyone to guess her vulnerability. I felt an unexpected pity—which was the last thing Elizabeth Kirby would want.

Tom was waiting for me, and he took charge of Pom-Pom. "Did you find David's cabin all right?" he asked.

"Yes. I had no trouble." I followed him down the wide aisle between stalls and watched as he began rubbing Pom-Pom down. I stroked her nose and fed her the reward of an apple, postponing my return to the house.

"The old woman's going to blow everything sky high, isn't she?" Tom said.

"What do you mean?"

"I remember her. I'll bet you don't even know that she rode after them up Haleakala that day?"

So he'd known about that. "Do you think she made it to the top?"

"I didn't say that. She was too soft from city living. But one of the horses had been out, and I found it tethered to a tree here when I came back. Nobody else said they'd had it out. I saw her the next day and asked her straight out if she'd ridden up there. She looked like she wanted to spit in my eye and she walked off without answering."

It was possible that even Elizabeth could have had misgivings and tried to stop what she'd indirectly started. But I couldn't deal with anything more right now, and I started for the door.

"Take the flashlight," Tom said. "And you'd better hurry. I think a squall is blowing up."

There'd been no rain since I'd come here, but where the air had been calm a little while before, now the tree branches were thrashing, and the luminous night sky had clouded over. Wind tugged at me as I hurried along the path to the house, grateful for the flashlight's beam.

Inside, good dinner smells came from the kitchen, and when I looked into the dining room I found Grandmother Elizabeth, who would never have done such a thing at home, dutifully helping to set the table. She looked perfectly calm and in control, and I trusted her less than ever. Vulnerable she might be—but who knew why?

As I went down the hall to Noelle's room, I could hear sheets of rain slashing against the house, while wind gusts made the windows rattle. I found my mother standing before glass doors in her room, looking out at the lighted area around the house.

She smiled as I came to stand beside her. "Lono's beating his thunder drums tonight. Do you hear them? There—that was a lightning spear. He's the god of thunder, and of growing things too. He brings the rain that we need so badly."

Her mood seemed calm, undisturbed, in spite of what she'd been through earlier that day. Perhaps the gift of being able to put away memory as she would a cape was good for her.

"I'm painting a new picture," she said. "I've been working hard on it, though it's not nearly done. Just the idea is there. Would you like to see it?"

I walked over to the easel and found that this painting was no childish concept. The canvas was fairly large, and she'd used acrylics, though not bright colors. The strange scene had been painted entirely in earth tones, from wheat to beige to deep tan. A wide window occupied most of the picture, and the observer stood outside looking into a room. I knew it was outside because a few straw-colored vines with dead brown leaves clinging to them wove beneath the window and along what was the wooden siding of a house. Nothing else of the building had been shown. The interior of the room into which one looked was as drably colored as the rest, and barely sketched in. The one thing clear was another window across the room, again shown with a vine and dead leaves. This slightly smaller window looked through to another window, which looked into another—and on and on into infinity. There was something eerie about the painting, and terribly unsettling.

"What does it mean?" I asked.

She shook her head, and jumped as a thunderclap sounded outside. "I'm not sure. It was what I had to paint. I suppose there are rooms after rooms after rooms—but I only cared about the windows. Because you can look through windows."

"What do you see when you look through these?"

"That's the trouble—I don't know. They get smaller and smaller, and there's nothing at the end—just tinier windows forever. Too tiny to paint."

She turned from the easel and dropped into a chair. Rain beat against glass, and a branch somewhere scraped across the roof. Outside, the evening was filled with sound, and sometimes lightning slashed the garden, followed by Lono's thunder drums.

Noelle looked at me solemnly, not childlike now—more like the woman she needed to become. "Perhaps I was painting my memory. Perhaps that's what it's like when I try to go back in time. It all becomes tiny and disappears. I don't know how to reach through all those windows."

I sat beside her, and she let me take her hand. "Perhaps you don't need to see through to the end. Just close all the windows and let what lies beyond go. It doesn't matter if there are things you can't remember. It doesn't *really* matter, so long as you can cross the years to the present."

"I wonder if I can do that," she said wistfully.

"Perhaps you can. You know now that Keith died a long time ago. How he died isn't important anymore. Just accept that years have passed and you're older now. The Linny you remember is gone, back there in the years, but she's not lost, because she still lives inside me. I used to be Linny, and I can remember how it was. I can remember the lovely times we spent together, and how much I loved my young mother. I'm grown up now, but I'm still your daughter. We can love each other in a different, new way. We can become friends."

Her eyes never left my face, but there was a difference in her expression—as though she grew older as I watched—still beautiful, but a woman in her early fifties—which she really was. She took both my hands in her own and held them tightly, looking deep into my eyes, searching.

Then her gaze shifted toward the door. "Hello, Marla. Come in—I want you to meet my daughter."

Marla came in slowly, her face as dark as the storm outside. "My God!" she said, and stared at Noelle.

"It's all right," her sister assured her. "Caroline—who is really Linny grown up—has been helping me to come through the years. There's so much that's missing, but she thinks it doesn't matter anymore."

"Of course it doesn't matter," I said. "It's the good things that you'll want to remember."

Marla had been struck speechless for once. She saw the painting on the easel and went over to it. "What's this?"

"It's not a picture for Linny," Noelle said quickly. "It's for me. Though I don't think I'll bother to finish it, now that I needn't look back through all those windows."

I heard the sound of Marla's breath as she released it. This change in her sister wasn't something she would welcome.

My concern about what might happen tomorrow night increased. My mother's new, precarious hold on reality could be so easily destroyed, yet any suggestion of this to Marla would bring denial, because this was what she wanted.

Marla took a step closer to the painting, studying it. For some reason it seemed to fascinate her, and she spoke as if to herself.

"I wonder what it would be like to go back and back and back through all those windows—clear to the way it was before. Perhaps that was the really happy time, Noelle."

When she turned from the painting, she looked a little dazed, and I wondered if she was thinking of those missing moments from her own life that lay far back in the years.

But except for her effect on Noelle, it wasn't Marla who concerned me most now, and I began to make a plan of my own. Somehow, Noelle must be spared the emotional danger that might be present for her tomorrow night. Marla herself had planned the evening, and everyone had fallen in innocently with all she'd suggested. Joanna had protested at first, and then given in. Now I must convince my grandmother that Noelle shouldn't be allowed to become a victim of Marla's manipulation. The moment I could see Joanna alone, I would talk to her, convince her.

Marla put an arm around her sister. "Come along now, dear. We're ready for dinner."

As always, her manner was the one she used in addressing the young, confused person she saw in her sister.

Noelle answered her with a new dignity that gave me a little hope. "All right, we'll come in for dinner, and I want to sit next to Caroline tonight. We need to get acquainted all over again."

She walked ahead of us toward the dining room, and Marla spoke in a whisper to me. "It won't last. She'll start looking for Linny any minute now."

"Not if I can help it," I said, and Marla gave me a black look as we followed Noelle to the dining room.

Joanna glanced at us casually as we came in, and then looked more closely at Noelle.

"Come and sit down," she said.

I sat beside my mother on one side of the long table, with Marla at the opposite end from Joanna, and Elizabeth and Scott across from us. Of us all, I think Scott was the most uncomfortable. He had no idea of what the undercurrents at Manaolana meant, but he was indignant with me, and ready to show his displeasure. He still hadn't understood that I no longer cared. By now Grandmother Elizabeth had retreated into her own reserve that enabled her to dismiss what she didn't understand. She paid no attention to the talk around her, barely answered when anyone spoke to her, and seemed not to notice the change in Noelle. I wondered what she was planning now.

On and off, as we ate, Joanna studied my mother intently, still puzzled and questioning. She knew her daughter as she'd been when time had stopped for her, but this new Noelle was a stranger. It occurred to me that no one in this house had ever seen the mature Noelle. Later I would try to explain the unexplainable to Joanna, and persuade her to help, but for now she would have to find her own way.

It was a strange, uneasy meal. I was still afraid that Noelle might slip away again at any moment, as Marla had promised she would.

When lightning struck brilliantly nearby and a clap of thunder shook the house at almost the same moment, Noelle jumped and began to tremble. I remembered that she had been afraid of storms when I was little, and I put my hand on her arm.

Manaolana's lights dimmed and went out.

"A power line's down," Marla said. "I'll get more candles."

Those on the table flickered in disturbed air, and the room beyond was shadowy except when lightning brought everything to life for a moment. It was a livid illumination—not like any other.

When extra candles had been placed around the room, we went on with our meal. Joanna attempted to keep a desultory conversation going, and sometimes she spoke directly to Noelle. My mother said little, though she didn't seem frightened anymore. She must feel rather like a stranger at this table, since she'd stepped into a new space where everything was unfamiliar. There was no telling what might be happening in her mind now, though I hoped that she would be able to talk to me and tell me before long.

Once during the meal, she brought tears to my eyes. I'd been aware that she watched me now and then—perhaps seeking Linny in the woman I'd become? Whatever conclusion she'd reached, she suddenly rested her hand over my own on the table, and I knew this was a loving gesture from mother to daughter. As unexpectedly as this, I seemed to have recovered, if only for the moment, the mother I'd come to Maui to find.

Marla, cynically watchful, said, "How touching!" If I had regained a mother, she had lost a dependent child, and she didn't like it at all. Marla was still to be reckoned with.

The storm had lessened a little when we heard voices at the front door, and Tom O'Neill burst into the dining room, wearing a dripping slicker over shirt and jeans.

"Is your phone working?" he asked Joanna. "David's been hurt. Koma brought him down to my place, but I guess a pole must be down somewhere, because I can't get through. We've carried him into the living room. I'd better go for a doctor right away."

Joanna took charge, first trying the nearest phone and finding it dead. "Yes—go get the doctor," she told Tom.

I rushed into the living room, where David lay stretched on a sofa. A streak of blood had trickled down his cheek, and in the wavering candlelight he looked deathly pale. Koma wiped off the blood with a piece of gauze Joanna brought, and then slapped him smartly on each cheek, trying to bring him to. There was nothing I could do except kneel beside the sofa and take one of David's cold hands into mine.

"Tell us what happened," Joanna said to Koma.

He looked up from his ministrations. "This *pupuli*—this crazy guy —went out to take pictures of the storm. He thought it was far enough away and he has a new camera. Photographers get carried away—anything for a good shot! I got in my car and went after him. He was out of his car and ready for the next flash of lightning against the mountain. But the storm shifted. There was a big clap of thunder and lightning struck a tree not far from where Dave was standing. The shock knocked him cockeyed. I dragged him to my car and came down here to Tom to get help." He slapped David's face again. "Hey, man, come out of it! You're okay—come on!"

David obliged by blinking his eyes, and my heart began to beat again. He pulled his hand from mine and shoved Koma away. "Stop that, you crazy *kanaka!* I'm all right. What happened?"

"You almost got struck by lightning," I told him. "You're the crazy one!"

David winced as he turned his head and stared at me. "What're you crying for?"

"Is that so strange?"

He sat up and put an arm around me. "I'll be around for a while— don't worry."

Joanna said, "Lie down, David. Tom's gone for Dr. Murdock."

David paid no attention, but when he tried to stand up his rubbery

legs betrayed him, and he sat down again. "Okay, I'll wait till Doc
Murdock comes. But there's nothing wrong with me."

"Only your wits," I said. He was going to be a difficult man to live
with but never dull. For once I had no doubt about what I wanted
from life.

For the first time I became aware of the others standing around in
the dim room. Grandmother Elizabeth sat in an armchair, with Scott
standing beside her. She watched with a realization about David in
her look, and no forgiveness for me. She was still a woman with only
one concern—my father, her son.

Marla had fallen into her accustomed role, trying to reassure
Noelle, whose attention was on me, and I hoped my mother was still
holding on to reality.

"Susy's making fresh coffee," Joanna said. "Koma, you're as cold
and wet as David. Will you start a fire, Scott, please?"

Scott seemed eager to do something useful. Perhaps even he had
recognized in those moments how I felt about David. So the storm
had accomplished something.

Elizabeth nodded toward Koma. "You might introduce me to this
young man, Joanna."

For the first time I thought of the dynamics that existed in this
situation. I'm sure Joanna thought of them too, but she made the
introduction casually.

"Elizabeth, this is Koma Olivero. Koma, this is Caro's San Francisco
grandmother who's here to visit for a few days—Mrs. Kirby. And this
is Scott Sherman, who has come with her."

Koma took Scott's offered hand, and then turned his full attention
to Grandmother Elizabeth. Almost anything could happen now.

"Oh, sure," he said. "I heard you were here." He spoke carelessly,
but he was still giving her that baleful stare. "I'm Ailina's son," he
added. "Maybe you remember Ailina?"

This was skating dangerously close to explosives, and I was relieved
when Joanna put a stop to it before Koma carried everything too far.
She didn't give Elizabeth time to admit that she remembered Ailina.

"Koma, will you see if you can hurry up that coffee? Tell Susy the
instant will do, and she can hold the brewed for later."

Koma gave her a mocking look that told her he knew exactly what
she was up to, but he went off meekly enough to the kitchen. However, it wasn't Koma's way to leave things alone, so there might still
be confrontation ahead.

David had begun to shiver and I picked up a knitted throw to put

over him. When Koma brought the coffee I held the cup so David
could sip the hot liquid.

Dr. Murdock arrived shortly and patched up the cut on David's
forehead. Mostly David was suffering from shock, he said, but he'd be
fine. He was a lucky man to have come through a close call like that.
He'd better keep quiet for a day or so.

Koma's concern was for David now. "I'll get him back to the cabin.
Do you think you can walk, David?"

This time David's legs behaved a little better, and with Koma to
lean on he started for the door. I wanted to go with them, I wanted to
do all those instinctive nurturing things that I'd never known were in
me before. But David gave me a look of affection, of promise. I was
almost glad Lono had intervened.

Koma had one last word—for Joanna. "We'll all be here tomorrow
night. Count on it."

Somehow, I didn't like the emphatic sound of that, and I felt a little
sorry for Elizabeth. Joanna caught my eye and nodded slightly. She
was the one who might be able to keep Koma in hand.

Elizabeth watched them go. "What a strange young man. I don't
think he likes me."

"Maybe he doesn't like *haoles* from the mainland, Mrs. Kirby,"
Marla said.

I would be glad when tomorrow night was over, and Grandmother
Elizabeth was on the way home with Scott.

Noelle slipped away from her sister and came close to me. "Show
me your room, Caroline. I don't think I've been in it since you came."

So she was still in the present—or at least I hoped so. I went
upstairs with my mother, eager for any moments when she wanted to
be with me. We carried candles, and when we reached my room,
Noelle looked around, remembering.

"You used to stay here when you visited Manaolana, didn't you,
Caroline? My mother always said you loved this room."

"It's wonderful to be here again," I said, watching her. She was
beginning to move back and forth quite easily between the young
Linny and me, and that was reassuring.

She sat on the window seat and looked out into a wet world that
shone in lights that had come on around the house. I touched a switch
and blew out the candles.

"When you were a little girl"—she spoke dreamily—"David was
the one you loved most, next to your family. I was watching you

downstairs, and I think you still love him, don't you, Carolinny? Do you mind if I call you that?"

I sat beside her on the window cushions. "I'd like that. But not Linny anymore. Yes, I love David very much."

"Then it will be all right," she said calmly, and I felt strangely comforted. It was as though she had come back to me possessed of more sensitivity than I could ever have hoped for. Yet I knew there was still a delicate balance that nothing must disturb until she was really safe. It was Marla I didn't trust.

When I left my mother I went downstairs to find Joanna alone in her study. She looked up from a letter she was writing, read my face, and put down her pen.

"We have to get Noelle away from here before tomorrow night," I told her. "I think Marla's up to something."

"I'm sure she is. The change in your mother at dinner seems encouraging, but I'm not sure it can survive the emotion of listening to Ailina sing. Yet this is what Marla wants."

"But that's wicked, unfeeling!"

"Marla's afraid of change."

"Why? Why can't she accept Noelle as she ought to be?"

Joanna turned away from my look. "There are other reasons mixed up in the way she feels. It's not in her to accept. Poor Marla. Poor all of us!"

"What are you talking about?"

"Only that Marla will rationalize everything she does in her own way, and no one can ever convince her that she's mistaken."

"How can we stop her?"

My grandmother pushed a hand absently through her short hair and the gesture was one of defeat. "I've never found a way to do that."

"You're giving up!" I cried. "And you never used to. Help me to rescue Noelle from what might happen tomorrow night."

For a moment I thought she would oppose me, and then she nodded. "You're right, Caro. Perhaps there's a way—something that might work. Run along now while I make a phone call. It's better if you don't know anything until it's too late for Marla to interfere."

I leaned over to kiss her cheek and she patted me as she used to do when I was small. It was a good moment in this strange day.

When I went to bed that night I felt more hopeful—not only for Noelle, but because my feelings for David were out in the open.

On the mountain Lono rolled distant thunder like a warning—a warning I didn't mean to heed. It was up to me to make happiness happen, and I wouldn't let anything defeat me.

So much for Lono's drums!

18

Nothing disturbing happened in the early part of the next day. Noelle made a lei for me to wear that evening, and I watched her pluck the outer petals from tiny vanda orchids, leaving only the brightly colored centers to be threaded. She worked with skill and delicacy, arranging the flowers so they faced in opposite directions, making the lei round and full.

When it was finished she slipped it over my head and kissed me on each cheek in the customary way. It was a moment that brought us very close. Afterward she sprinkled the flowers lightly and put the lei in the refrigerator to keep for tonight. It mustn't be bagged, she warned, or watered too much, or the orchids would turn white.

Everything was geared toward preparation for the evening. Guests had been invited, the lanai cleared for use as a stage, and folding chairs brought in to set up around the lawn. Not that there would be any large audience—just a few neighbors and relatives.

When I had a moment I phoned David and was pleased when he answered, sounding more like himself.

"I'm doing fine," he said. "Doc thinks I'd better be quiet today, but I'll look in on the party tonight for a little while at least. I want to see you, Caroline."

"I want to see you too," I told him.

Just a few words on the telephone—and I knew everything was right between us.

That afternoon I spent a few hours with Grandmother Elizabeth and found her apprehensive, as though she too dreaded the evening ahead. For her, the memories of my father would be of the wrong sort. Scott was merely marking time, anxious to be aboard that plane tomorrow.

Late in the day, Joanna took me aside to reassure me about Noelle. "Everything has worked out well. A cousin who lives nearby is coming to take your mother to stay with her tonight. Marla won't know where she is until it's too late. So this is one strain we can avoid for Noelle."

Now I could relax a little.

We had a light early supper, and afterwards Noelle simply disappeared. Marla was busy with preparations and seemed not to notice.

When we'd eaten, Joanna climbed the stairs to my room in spite of her knee, and placed a dress box on my bed. "This is for you to wear tonight, Caro honey."

I unwrapped the box and lifted out a pale lavender *muumuu*, its yoke embroidered in white eyelet. The vanda lei would look beautiful against it—a slightly darker lavender. I was pleased and touched, but before I could thank her, Joanna went on.

"Everything's arranged. Noelle has gone with Cousin Melly."

"How did she take leaving?"

"She's easily distracted, you know, and she loves Melly's dogs. I'm sure she'll be all right."

The old Noelle might be, but if there was really a change in my mother, would being spirited away upset her? Anyway, it would be worse to have her here. This was what I had wanted.

"Don't count on too much," Joanna warned. "You'll only break your heart and do no good."

There was no answer to that. I *had* to believe in something that no one else easily accepted.

When Joanna left, I dressed in her beautiful gift, and when I put on the vanda lei the combination was perfect.

After yesterday's rain, this had been a lovely Maui day, filled with sunshine and light breezes. By evening a full moon had risen to add its gentle radiance to the Japanese lanterns that Tom and some of the other men had hung around the lawn. The lanterns reminded me of that other time when I'd watched as a child from a balcony at Ahinahina—an occasion I didn't want to recall. Haleakala hid her head beneath clouds, and I tried to forget what else lay hidden up there.

Women in light dresses, a few in elegant *muumuu*, began to arrive. They wore shoulder shawls and scarves against the cool, while the men were dressed in informal jackets or sweaters over well-cut slacks. It was definitely a *haole* gathering.

Ailina appeared with her troupe, a steel guitar over her shoulder. Koma carried another guitar, and an ukulele tucked under one arm. Eliki, Koma's girl, who would do most of the rhythmic dancing, wore a long wraparound skirt sprinkled with colorful blossoms, her shoulders bare above a matching bandeau, and several white leis about her neck.

The last member of the group was a young Hawaiian man with a knee drum of the sort that had been used historically only in the Hawaiian chain, out of all the Polynesian islands—as Joanna explained to me. A coconut was cut in half at the widest part, the meat scooped out, and sharkskin stretched tautly over the opening. The drum was tied above the young man's knee, and he played it with a braided fiber switch that produced its own special tone.

Now the guests were taking their places around the lawn, and Joanna saw to it that Grandmother Elizabeth and Scott were seated near the front. I slipped away to the back where I could get a wider view of what was happening on the lanai stage. David arrived at the last minute and came to sit beside me. To my relief he looked fully recovered from his experience in the storm. There was time for only a quick, reassuring squeeze of my hand, but that was enough for now.

Ailina began by explaining that these were songs she and her friends had grown up with—songs not always written down, though there was an effort being made to preserve them. They were songs of mountain and beach, of waves and sky—and always of love.

Koma had a good voice, and at one point he accompanied himself with the ukulele and sang a funny song about a young Hawaiian boy courting his sweetheart. He translated for us ahead of time so we could follow the story as he strutted and sang. I could glimpse the eager young man who had caught a fine fish to give his girl—only to learn that fish wasn't what she wanted.

Eliki's dancing was beautiful. The gentle swaying of hips, the fluid motion of graceful, storytelling hands, was what such movements must always have been, though not the more exaggerated hula that tourists expected.

Leis of gardenias and carnations mingled their scent with night-blooming blossoms in the garden around us. Koma had dressed in light trousers and a white shirt open at the throat, and he'd hung a lei of sweet-scented green *maile* vine around his neck—a lei that was always left open at the bottom.

Underlying the strings of the steel guitars a note of melancholy sounded. These guitars weren't electrified, and there were no microphones, so the music was softer and more natural than I'd heard at the hotels. Yet it could be spirited and lively too. As I listened with David beside me, sharing this, the minor chords seemed beautiful in their sadness, because joy would come later, as the music seemed to promise.

I noticed that Tom and some of his men stood over in the direction of the stables, watching. Joanna had invited them all to come, but they'd remained in their own little groups, apart from the guests.

Applause during the intervals was warm, so that affection and appreciation flowed between performers and audience. As the evening went on, however, I began to experience a sense of something being not quite right. When I looked around intently, I saw the reason for my uneasiness.

Over near the deep shadow of the camphor tree a white dress glimmered. Noelle sat with her back against the tree, white ginger blossoms in her hair and a ginger lei around her neck.

"I must go," I told David. He saw her too and nodded. "She isn't supposed to be here," I whispered. "Joanna sent her away."

The performers were taking a break and guests had stirred to talk among themselves. Before I could escape, Marla dropped into the chair next to me, her expression triumphant.

"I brought Noelle back," she told me. "My sister belongs here tonight."

"Why?" I demanded. "Why must you submit her to this?"

"Don't you see? It's a test. If she can get through Ailina's singing, then she really has improved. Did you and my mother think you could put something over on me?"

What I saw was Marla's cruel determination to keep Noelle as she had been for all these years.

"You're afraid to let her remember!" I challenged. I knew how disturbingly true this was.

"You're so foolish," Marla said, as she had said to me before. "You don't understand how dangerous it would be for Noelle to remember. But I do."

I stood up, but when Marla would have come with me, David reached across to stop her, his hand strong on her arm, so that she sat down, angry but helpless.

I ran across the lawn as Ailina struck a chord on her guitar and the knee drum rustled.

Noelle smiled at me calmly as I reached her and dropped down on the grass at her side.

"I didn't want to miss this," she said, "even though Mother doesn't want me here. So I phoned Marla and asked her to come and get me."

So that was how it had happened. Not by Marla's choice but by Noelle's own decision. She sounded perfectly normal, undisturbed, and I began to hope that everything would be all right.

Her next words reassured me further. "Ailina's older than I remember, but she's even more beautiful. I think she must be a fine woman."

"She is," I said in relief. Marla's test would have an outcome she didn't expect. I slipped an arm through my mother's as we listened together.

Before each number Ailina told a story about the song they were going to present, and now she was talking about one that her son had composed and written the words for.

Koma put aside ukulele and took up his own steel guitar. I watched him, wondering how I really felt, knowing that my emotions toward him were partly resentment against my father, partly antagonism toward Koma himself. And perhaps also curiously because this young Hawaiian was my half brother.

"I've called this 'Song of the Volcano,'" he said, and struck his opening chords. Then he began to sing in his strong, melodic voice, the words clear and the tune stirring.

> *Kahuna* drums are beating
> Where the fires roared;
> The sun's first rays are striking
> Where cinder cones were formed.
> Maui men, awaken! Maui women, come!
> The mountain sleeps, your island lives,
> And new days must begin.

Koma's own strong feeling for his island came through as he sang. There were more verses, and always the refrain that called the people of Maui—*all* the people—to save and protect the land. My resentment and antagonism faded. Koma and I weren't likely to become friends, but I could understand a little better now what drove him.

The applause was warm when Koma sat down and Noelle clapped along with me. Once more Ailina came to the edge of the lanai to speak to the audience.

"We have a request tonight—for a special song. A tune that also belongs to our island, though it was written in the thirties by a *malihini*, it's one that Noelle Kirby used to like. I understand she isn't here tonight, but this is for her anyway."

So Koma had delivered my message, and I wondered if Ailina, with her special sensitivity, knew very well that Noelle was here; had perhaps glimpsed her white dress in the shadows near the tree.

The song was "Sweet Leilani," and Ailina sang it tenderly, with Koma accompanying her on his guitar, and Eliki swaying gently, allowing her hands to ripple. When the second chorus came, all the audience began to sing with her.

I was watching Noelle and now I sensed her growing tension. "I used to have a record of that song," she whispered to me. "I used to play it over and over. Until I finally smashed it. Ailina used to sing it in those days, and that spoiled it for me. She shouldn't have sung it here tonight."

"Perhaps she doesn't know what it means for you," I said. "Perhaps she only remembers that you used to like it."

Noelle rose from the grass. "I can't listen anymore. Too much is coming back." She held her head between her hands, crushing the ginger blossoms in her hair so that their perfume rose too sweetly. "My head feels stuffed with things I don't want to remember. I'll go to my room now. My mother mustn't see me."

"I'll come with you," I said.

We wove our way behind hedges and through the garden to the back of the house and entered a rear door. In Noelle's room, she turned on a lamp and closed the blinds.

"I'm tired," she said. "Please don't tell anyone I've come back. When Marla smuggled me out, I left Cousin Melly a note. But she goes to sleep early, so she won't miss me until morning. By then it won't matter. I need to be quiet now, Caroline—I need to think."

There was nothing I could do but leave her. "I'll go back now before someone misses me. Is there anything I can bring you?"

She stood before the strange painting of the endless windows, all done in their neutral beige tones. "Isn't it strange? I didn't paint windows looking *out*—only windows that looked in and back. Into what, Caroline? Back to what?"

"It doesn't matter," I said. "I expect you got rid of certain feelings by painting it."

She smiled at me—a smile tinged with sadness. For all those lost years?

"I suppose it really doesn't matter anymore," she said. "It's enough that I've found you again. You *are* my daughter. I keep telling myself that—though so much is missing."

When she held out her hand I went to her quickly, and this time she put her arms around me and held me tightly—almost fiercely, as though I might be taken from her again. The crushed scent of ginger blossoms was more like a miasma now, and almost sickening. Too much that was disturbing seemed to be rising in her.

"Perhaps I'd better not leave right away. I'll stay until you're asleep."

She pushed me away. "No, that won't do. Someone is always coddling me, protecting me. I have to find my way alone. I know that now." When I still hesitated, she smiled again. "I'll be all right, Carolinny."

Tears were wet on my cheeks when I went back to the gathering. There was too much sadness in this reunion with my mother, and I knew it couldn't be any other way.

I reached the lawn in time to hear Ailina bring the evening to an end with Queen Liliuokalani's loveliest and most sorrowful of all farewells—"Aloha Oe." A song she had composed when she was a princess. The guests were singing too, and I stood near the big tree and joined them. Ailina sang all the verses clear to the last moving phrase of the chorus, "Until we meet again"—the sadness of parting and the promise of return, all in these few simple words.

David must have left, but I knew I'd see him soon. Marla was inside, helping to carry out refreshments, and the larger group was breaking up into small ones. Only Koma noticed me out near the trees, and he came toward me across the grass.

"It was beautiful," I told him. "Thank you—*mahalo*. Your volcano song is wonderful. Have you had it published?"

He shrugged. There seemed a new uncertainty in him. "Ailina wanted to do this for you. She thinks a lot of you, Caroline, even though you're *his* daughter."

"As you're his son."

Again he shrugged that off. "Everyone likes you." He sounded puzzled, and I laughed.

"Some people don't like me at all."

He gave me his sudden, flashing smile that always carried an edge of mockery. "Maybe I'll get used to you—if you stuff enough envelopes. Hey—you've been crying."

"Doesn't everyone always cry over 'Aloha Oe'?"

"Sure. But not as much as they used to. Only people who have strong feelings about Hawaii. Most of your years weren't spent here."

"That doesn't make me alien. Maybe I've always belonged." Food had appeared on small tables on the lanai, and guests gathered around. Koma waved his hand. "I'm hungry," he said, and went off with his graceful lope—natural perhaps because his people had run on beaches for ages back? A whimsical thought, but the stereotype suited him.

I went to Ailina, to tell her how much I loved the music and her singing.

"That pleases me," she said. "Koma has told me that you know about him. I wish you had more time to get used to us."

"I have all the time there is now," I said, and she understood.

"I'm glad if you've decided to stay. But now, Caroline, look over there. Someone needs you."

I followed the direction of her gaze and saw Grandmother Elizabeth sitting a little apart, not belonging to any of this. Scott stood nearby, looking bored. Neither of them really knew how to let in new experiences that might open windows. For the first time I felt sorry for her in a new way, and I suppose I surprised her when I put an arm about her and kissed her cheek.

"I know this visit has been disappointing for you, Grandmother Elizabeth," I said. "But tomorrow you'll fly home. The Prince Albert can't get along without you."

She nodded stiffly. "I hope you know what you're doing."

"I'll bring your first great-grandchild home to see you," I said recklessly.

That startled her. Then a gleam I recognized came into her eyes— a planning look. But I wasn't afraid of her plotting anymore. If there were ever great-grandchildren in the future, they would never be possessed by her. I would see to that.

Scott still held himself apart, pretending not to listen, his expression blank until she turned to him. "I'm tired. I never like to eat this late in the evening, and I don't know all these people." Nor did she want to—that was the trouble.

Under the spell of "aloha" I could make a last gesture with Scott, and I held out my hand.

"I'm sorry, Scott. You'll find a mainland girl who'll make up for me. But I'm glad you came—it's cleared the air a little."

He shook my hand indifferently, and I wondered if the air around Scott would ever be clear.

When they'd gone in I stayed to meet several distant relatives, some of whom might be future friends. When I'd helped Joanna and Marla and Susy Ohara to clear up after the guests were gone, I said good night and went down the hall to Noelle's room. I opened her door softly to look inside. Pale light from glass doors showed her asleep—childlike, with a hand beneath her cheek. Her quiet breathing reassured me and I was about to close the door when I glimpsed Marla in a chair beyond the bed, lost in shadows. I beckoned to her, and she came into the hall. I pulled Noelle's door shut firmly.

"Leave her alone," I said. "She isn't going to have the relapse you wanted."

There must have been something in my voice that warned her, for she gave me a startled look and went away.

I climbed the stairs to my room, glad that the evening was safely past, and that nothing disastrous had happened. When I got into bed full weariness took over, and I went to sleep at once.

Somewhere in my dreams the scent of ginger blossoms intruded, as it had done once before in the night, and I woke up in sudden alarm. Noelle sat on my bed. She'd turned on a light, and I saw that she wore jeans and a sweater and had tied a scarf around her head.

"Wake up, Carolinny," she said. "There's something we must do. Dress warmly and put on walking shoes. Don't make any noise—I don't want a hue and cry."

I sat up sleepily and looked at my watch. It was ten past four and would be daylight before long. "I'm tired," I protested. "I don't want to go anywhere. Can't it wait till later?"

"There's something I must do—whether you come with me or not. If you won't come, I'll go alone. But I'd rather have you along."

She sounded perfectly sensible, but now for the first time I saw what she held tucked under one arm—the tapa beater. That brought me fully awake.

"Tell me what you're planning," I said.

"No more talk. Come or stay—take your choice."

The only other choice was to rouse the house, and that would bring Marla into this—which might be the worst thing I could do. Noelle seemed to be in the present and not at all confused, but the tapa beater frightened me. I got up and dressed as quickly as I could.

We crept softly down the stairs, remembering the steps that creaked. Noelle had discarded the lei and the flower in her hair, but the scent of ginger still clung to her, and though it was the comforting scent of my childhood, it didn't comfort me now.

We went out the front door and it locked automatically behind us, so that I wondered how we were to get back in when this expedition was over. I didn't become really alarmed, however, until I saw the jeep parked near the driveway. Noelle ran toward it and opened the driver's door.

"Don't worry—I can drive it," she assured me. "Just get in."

Whether this was madness or sanity, I couldn't tell, but she sounded as though she knew what she was doing. I got in and she started the motor and we drove out on the road to Makawao. From that sleeping town, we crossed to the Haleakala Highway. We weren't talking now, and Noelle was intent on her driving. I held my breath to see which way she would turn. If we turned *makai*—toward the sea—I could start breathing again. But I knew very well that this wouldn't be her direction. She turned the jeep up the mountain toward the crater, and I settled back for the long drive ahead.

Though the tapa beater lay inert on the seat between us, it seemed to have a life of its own for me, as though some terrible memory had been ingrained in the wood. We weren't just going up the mountain —we were going back into the past. Because that was where Noelle had left her life a long time ago.

The crater lay hidden high above us, Haleakala's head standing free of clouds against a luminous, near-dawn sky. I thought of Koma's song.

> *Kahuna* drums are beating
> Where the fires roared . . .

I wanted to hear no drums at dawn on Haleakala—either real or imagined.

19

Cars were already on their way up the mountain to catch the sunrise, so we wouldn't be alone up there, and that, at least, was reassuring. If something happened that I couldn't handle, there would be other people around.

Noelle managed the long loopings of the road with surprising skill, as though there'd been no hiatus in her driving. Our headlight beams shone clear of mist on the road ahead.

Although Noelle couldn't have been up here in all the years since the accident, she knew exactly where she was going. When she was young, she'd have gone camping in the crater, as Maui young people did, and all this was part of her, in her blood and instinct.

Once when I stared at her intently, trying to read whatever her face might tell me, she sensed my look and smiled. "I'm all right, Carolinny. Really I am—don't worry."

She found her way to the lookout buildings she wanted, and parked the jeep. When we got out it was cold and windy—bone-chilling. I looked longingly at lighted windows above, where visitors were gathering in warmth to view the sunrise. Noelle, however, walked to where a trail led away into the crater. Since day was about to break, the darkness had lifted, with promise of the sun to come.

Within the great bowl, however, clouds were piled like white foam from cliff to cliff, though the sky above was clear. I hung back, and she gestured with the tapa beater. "Come along—this is the trail I want."

"We can't go down in that! We'd fall over the first cliff. We could never find our way."

She didn't seem to hear me, and I sensed that something in her had moved beyond reason, so that she was driven by a single purpose that nothing could deflect.

I looked around for a park ranger—for anyone who might stop us, but no one seemed interested, and no authority was near. Noelle moved with such certainty that if I didn't follow, she would take the trail down without me, and be lost at once in thick mist.

"Wait!" I cried. "Wait for the sun—look!"

That held her for a moment in wonder. No redness stained the sky for this dawn—it was pure gold beyond the far *palis* of the crater. The Midas light spilled over the distant rim and touched the cotton fluff below, turning it to gold as well, so that now it seemed that the sun itself was held in the bowl of the crater.

As we stood looking down, a helicopter broke the silence noisily, bringing visitors to view the sunrise. It flew above molten gold, its tiny shadow following beneath.

Noelle had no time now for the sun. "Come!" she said again.

I still held back. "If you mean to go back to where it happened, it would take hours on foot. It's too far, and much too cold down there at dawn."

She threw off my arm and started along the trail. And then the strange transformation that could happen so quickly in the crater began. A dawn wind whipped through one of the gaps, shredding the puffs of cloud so that they rose and flowed out an opposite gap, to be dispersed in a windy sky. It happened as we watched, and in a few minutes the crater below was clear and filled with the light of a rising sun. Only wisps clung here and there in protected crevices.

Noelle hurried now, her footing sure, and I went after her. A red cone loomed below us, its head nearly as high as the trail. The sun touched it to a fiery hue, bright and blinding.

"I know a shortcut," Noelle called to me over her shoulder. "Dig in your heels and let the cinders carry you down."

She was already on her way, with sand thrown up behind her in two waves. I could only copy her. We went down through gray ash that whispered around our feet and left trails of yellow behind us marking our descent. Cold wind whipped us as we plunged down in an avalanche of cinder sand.

At the bottom I sat down to empty my shoes, and Noelle did the same, for what little good it would do us. Walking was difficult with no trail to support us, and I knew we were probably doing something crazy and dangerous. People who wandered off the trails could be quickly lost in this vast crater. Already we were deep in the heart of a dead world, and out of sight of the rim and the observer buildings. This seemed a world far more empty than when we'd come into it by helicopter. Only Noelle and I existed—two tiny humans about to be swallowed into Pele's mountain. Gusts of wind roared around us, rousing the echoes and pushing us back.

Now there was an expanse of rough breccia to stumble across. I'd read about these beds of small, irregular volcanic rocks caused by explosion, buried by mud slides, and then exposed by the erosion of centuries. They kept emerging, even on the trails, and it was a relief to reach more finely ground sand.

Sometimes the wind hurled biting cinders into our faces, so that we had to turn our backs. Noelle, for all her determination, was tiring. When I put my arm around her I could feel her shivering excitement. For a moment she clung to me, less confident of her course.

"We need to find shelter until the sun warms the mountain," I told her. "Aren't there cabins down here?"

"Not near here." Her teeth chattered as she spoke. Dawn shadows were long and black around us—cold shadows still hiding from the sun.

Noelle shifted the tapa beater from hand to hand as her fingers stiffened with cold.

"Why have you brought that?" I asked when we stopped again for breath.

She held up the wooden object as though surprised to find herself carrying it. "I'm not sure. I just knew it had to come with me." Once more she pointed with it. "There's a lava bubble over there. Maybe it's big enough for us to crawl into out of the wind. We could rest a little while and then go on."

On to what—to where? But I knew the answer very well. Nothing would stop her now in this journey back through the years.

We reached the rough dome of lava and Noelle found an entrance to the hollow of the bubble, and we crawled inside out of the biting wind. There wasn't much room, but the rocky dome arched over us and the cold air inside was still. We held each other for warmth, and in a little while our shivering stopped. I hoped we could stay until the sun rose high enough for the crater to warm a little.

Then, as suddenly as the wind had risen, its fierce howling abated, and the roaring that filled the crater stopped. The new silence seemed to beat against the opening to our cave, and I was half afraid I might hear drums in the stillness—the *kahuna* drums of Koma's song that had once sounded in this haunted place.

I don't know how long we sheltered before we heard the noisy sound of a helicopter, not flying over high above but circling into the crater—as if searching for something in this bowl of golden dawn. Suddenly I *knew*. I crawled out into the open and stood up, with Noelle right behind me.

The helicopter circled not far away, and I waved my arms frantically. Beside me, Noelle stood staring upward, and I knew she didn't want this rescue—if that was what it was.

Someone in the helicopter saw us, and it came hovering down, to light a little way off from where we stood, sending up gusts of stinging sand. As the blades chattered to a stop, steps were lowered, and David came down, helping Joanna after him. I was relieved to see that Marla wasn't aboard. The pilot, Frank Wilkie, stayed in his seat while David followed Joanna as she came toward us. She looked more frightened than I'd ever seen her, and the moment she reached us she put her arms around her daughter.

"Are you all right, Noelle? You gave us a terrible fright! Melly got up in the night for milk and found your note in the kitchen. So she phoned me. I called David, and he asked Frank to bring us here." She turned to me in reproach. "Why didn't you stop her, Caroline?"

"No one could stop me," Noelle said. "I had to come back to find the place. That's what I must still do."

"No!" Joanna cried. "It's a long way from here that it happened. We'll take you home now, dear."

Noelle seemed not to hear her. "Look!" she cried, waving the tapa beater. "Over there—the silverswords."

I saw them then—a number of silvery-green mounds, not yet in bloom. Noelle pushed aside her mother's hand, and I went with her toward the plants. I knew what she wanted, but perhaps there was another way.

"You don't have to go back to where it happened!" I cried. "You can remember right here. Hold that tapa beater with both hands and let it tell you. Tell yourself!"

Joanna heard, but she made no further effort to stop whatever was about to happen.

Noelle reached the first of the silverswords and dropped to her knees before it. She reached out to touch the leaves and then looked at me as I came to kneel beside her. Something in her eyes seemed to come into sharp new focus, but whatever it was brought her no joy, no relief. Tearing sobs seemed to dredge up all the grief she had run from over the years. A grief none of us could deal with. I dared not offer the comfort of my arm around her. Joanna came to sink down on the sand on the other side of her daughter. She didn't touch her now, but spoke to her gently, softly.

"It's all right, darling. You can tell us what you remember. It doesn't matter anymore."

Noelle's sobs died away, and she began to speak quietly. "Marla wanted me to believe I killed Keith. She told me so over and over. She said if I tried to bring everything back, that's what I would remember. So I shut it all away."

Joanna shook her head in despair. "That was wicked! Marla knew very well what happened."

"She hated me," Noelle said, perfectly calm now—accepting. "Marla would have liked to be me—the way everything was *before*. But you're right, Mother, and it doesn't matter now, because I do remember—and I didn't kill him. Do you want me to go on?"

Joanna nodded mutely.

"All right. Keith wanted me to fall that day. I think he wanted me to die. I loved him and he tried to kill me. I'd told him I would never give him a divorce. I said I'd never let him marry Ailina or anyone else. All because I was jealous and angry."

Again she looked searchingly at her mother.

"You know what happened. Must I go on?"

"It's time, darling," Joanna assured her. "And this is the place. You needn't hold anything back."

Noelle stared at the tapa beater in her hands. "We were quarreling up there where the trail winds along. Marla was with us and she saw what happened. When Keith rode toward me I knew I was in danger, and I had *this* in my hand. Remember, Mother—you put the tapa beater in my saddlebag. I tried to strike Keith with it to save myself. But I wasn't strong enough. You were the one who saved me."

Joanna closed her eyes and Noelle went on.

"You'd ridden back to us and you saw what he was trying to do. You snatched this thing out of my hand and you struck him with it. So *he* fell. But then all the horses except yours spooked. I can't remember the rest because I was thrown too, and when I came around I was someplace else in my head. I couldn't bear it that my husband had tried to kill me, and that I'd wanted to kill him. I *wanted* to kill him! And I couldn't face that, Mother. So I ran away to where nothing could hurt me anymore. I tried to keep everything the way it was— before."

Joanna held her tightly. "No one blames you. At first I wanted to go to the police and tell them everything. But you were off in your own world, so I waited. If there was a trial and I was convicted, who would take care of you? I believed that Marla wouldn't. From the time when she was little she was jealous of you, yet she would never let anyone love her. God knows, I tried. If I wasn't there you would have been put into an institution, where you might never get well. I didn't care what happened to me, but I had to protect you, darling. If you can understand—"

Noelle rose from her knees and pulled Joanna up with her. With a strong gesture she threw the tapa beater far away. It fell into loose sand, and I watched it disappear of its own weight.

Then she put her arms about her mother and they held each other for a long, loving moment. When Noelle held out her hand to me, I couldn't speak—I just hugged them both, and perhaps all three of us began to mend.

David stood back a little, waiting, and Noelle smiled as we reached him.

"Thank you for calling Frank," she said, "and for bringing my mother here. I think everything will work out now—except for Marla."

Joanna said, "She knew we were coming after you. She was up and awake, but she wouldn't come with us. She said it was all over and she must go back through the windows. I don't know what she was talking about. She did change, you know, after you were hurt, and she took care of you and loved you."

I knew better. Marla had managed first of all to fool her mother—at the same time that she was doing everything she could to keep Noelle from recovering.

Joanna and Noelle climbed into the helicopter, while David waited for me. "Are you all right, Caro? You scared Joanna badly."

"I had no other choice. I had to come with her."

"Yes—you were the one she needed. I had a feeling you'd manage, but Joanna had a bad time when she knew Noelle was gone."

"I don't think I've grasped everything yet," I told him.

One of the awful things I still had to face and accept was that my father—that hero Grandmother Elizabeth had wanted me to love— had tried to kill my mother. Though all this happened so long ago, for me the revelations were *now*.

"What do you think they'll do?" I asked.

"Joanna can handle it, and I hope Noelle can too. About Marla, I'm not sure. Shall we get aboard, Caro—we'll talk more later."

Whirling blades carried us out of the crater, and I looked down into that landscape that would haunt me forever.

The flight down the mountain took only moments. Frank landed us on the wide lawn at Manaolana, accepted our thanks, and took off again. Tom came running from the stables, his main concern for Joanna.

"It's all right, Tom," she assured him. "Noelle has remembered everything. So now I'll do what I should have done all those years ago."

Tom spoke impatiently. "Come off it, Joanna. We don't need any more martyrs. Why should you take the blame for what was Keith's fault? You couldn't do anything else but save Noelle. Besides, it was probably the fall that really killed Keith. Nobody knows for sure, not even you."

"I'll think about it," Joanna said. "Where is Marla?"

"That's what I want to talk to you about. You know how crazy-envious Marla's always been of Noelle. She's pretended she wanted to protect you—so she didn't want Noelle to remember. But what she was really bent on—and I've tried to tell you this a couple of times—was to keep Noelle a victim. Now she knows that if Noelle's recovered, everything she's done to her sister will come out. And I guess from what she's been babbling about, there's plenty. So after you went up the mountain she fell apart—really cracked up. She started heaping blame on everyone else for all she's done. So I got hold of Doc Murdock and he came over and gave her a shot of something. She's resting now."

Joanna started toward the house. "I'll go see her right away."

"Better not." There was something in Tom's voice that stopped her. "What you could do," he went on more quietly, "is send her away someplace for a while. You've got to let yourself off the hook, Joanna. You and Noelle need some quiet time together. So how about that cousin of yours over on Kauai—the one who runs a small nursing home for special patients? You could send her there to get some help."

For just an instant Joanna's step faltered, and Tom steadied her. "You've had enough!" he told her brusquely.

She sounded almost meek as she answered him, and I could see her deepening relief. "Thank you, Tom." He gave her a small salute of respect and affection, and went back to his horses. Noelle put an arm about her mother as they went toward the house, and Joanna straightened, taking hold again.

It was still early morning, and as David and I followed, I saw Koma in his ranger uniform leaning against a post of the lanai. His expression was one of wicked amusement that meant he was up to something.

After the crater, this scene seemed from another world—not altogether real—and I remembered that Grandmother Elizabeth and Scott were flying home today.

Elizabeth Kirby sat with her back as stiff as ever, and her lips pressed together. Their suitcases had been brought down, and Scott stood with a foot on one of them, smoking a cigarette, clearly eager to get away, and probably unaware of the dynamics between Koma and Grandmother Elizabeth.

Joanna spoke to her as she went past with Noelle. "Don't worry, Elizabeth. I'll see that you catch your plane. We'll have breakfast first."

I stopped beside David as we reached the lanai. He too was aware of whatever was in progress.

Apparently Koma had tossed out some cryptic remark that hadn't gone past Elizabeth. She looked very handsome and dignified in her gray San Francisco suit and brimmed hat, and she wasn't in the least pleased with Koma as she spoke to him.

"You might as well know," she said, "that I had a talk with your mother last night. She felt that peace needed to be made between us, and I don't blame her anymore for anything that happened. When we talked, I asked about a few things—including a date. The date of your birth."

Koma stopped looking like a boy about to throw a firecracker, and turned into a serious young man. "So?" he said, for once uncertain.

"So!" she echoed. "You understand me perfectly well. This is nothing that pleases either of us, but neither can we do anything about it. I admire your mother and I don't admire my son as much as I used to. You have a good deal of his charm and his impudence, young man, but I think you're not very much like him."

Koma nodded, uncertain now of this woman who was his grandmother. "I hope you're right," he said, and stepped down from the lanai. "Maybe we won't meet again, Mrs. Kirby. But anyway—aloha."

Grandmother Elizabeth nodded gravely, recognizing that the word was a salute, however grudgingly given.

Koma stopped beside David and me, and his smile carried the natural warmth of our islands, without mockery.

"I quote from my mother, who is full of Hawaiian proverbs," he said. " 'The hidden answer to the riddle is seen.' "

"Thank you again for last night," I told him. "And especially for your song."

"Sure." He flicked his fingers at us. "So long, Dave. See you later. Just let me know, Caroline, when you're ready to start licking more stamps."

When he'd gone, Scott said, "What was that all about?"

"I don't think you'd understand," Elizabeth told him, and looked at me. "But I believe you do, Caroline."

I felt unexpected affection for this other grandmother, and a new respect. She had lost a great deal, and like Joanna, she had made mistakes. Also like Joanna, she would handle whatever needed to be handled.

David drew me away from the house. "I can't stay for breakfast, but I'd like to talk with you for a minute."

We began to walk idly along the tangled path that led to the rose garden.

"In a little while you're going to start worrying," David said.

"That's probably true. What do you think Joanna will do?"

"She'll follow her conscience, now that she's free of what she believed was the need to protect your mother. But it won't matter, one way or another. I agree with Tom. Not even Joanna can prove that she killed your father. There's no real case against her, and not even a weapon. Noelle took care of that by throwing away the tapa beater."

And Marla, in her own way, had taken care of herself.

"I suppose all that is true."

"Tom has a lot of good sense and he'll look out for both of them. So that leaves you and me."

We'd reached the steps that led down to the rose garden, and he drew me toward the bench where I'd first seen my mother.

"It might be a good idea," he said as we sat down, "to leave Noelle and Joanna alone for a while. So how about you coming to Hana for a visit? My parents would enjoy having you, and I'd like you to know my son."

"I'd love that," I said quickly, and leaned into the arm David put around me. Now I could stop all my restless searching.

"I'm glad you grew up and came back to me, Caroline," he said. "We have plans to make when you come to Hana."

Yes—plans!

"David, I know now that I've never wanted to be anywhere else."

He kissed me and held me close—a lovely moment in that wild garden, where I'd known such grief only a little while ago. David and Maui—they were what I'd wanted all along.

We walked together to his car, and I watched him drive away. There was time ahead now—for both of us.

For a moment I stood looking up at the mountain. Haleakala's long broken rim stood above the clouds, hiding all that strange world that lay within. I thought of the silverswords I'd seen up there struggling to exist, shining in barren lava soil—a symbol, perhaps, of all our struggles. And I thought of the moment when I'd seen my spirit shadow cast into a rainbow of light, like a portent I might someday fulfill.

As I started toward the house there was a new lift in my step. I had the strong feeling that now Manaolana would live up to its melodic Hawaiian name that promised hope.

AFTERWORD

My affection for Hawaii began during my earliest years. My father had lived in the Islands during the time when the last queen's tragic story was unfolding. Liliuokalani's musical name was a familiar one in our home—then in Yokohama—though I was too young to understand what had happened during the annexation of Hawaii by the United States. My father loved the people, the land, the music of the Islands, and I grew up with his stories as part of my own emotional heritage.

My first stopover in Honolulu was in 1918, when my mother brought me home to America after my father's death in China. The First World War had just ended, and I didn't see the Islands again until after the Second World War. Each time stories stirred in my mind, and I knew I wanted to write about Hawaii "some day." When the time finally came, I decided to focus upon Maui, and now I could stay a little longer and begin to absorb something of these islands as they are today. *Silversword* is the result.

One point should be made. Nowadays, descent into the crater is restricted by the Park, and helicopters are not allowed to land, except by permit for rescue missions.

For readers who might wish to know more about our fiftieth state, there are several books I would like to recommend. *Born in Paradise* by Armine von Tempski gives a splendid picture of long ago Maui and is still to be found in some library collections. *The Brook* by Barbara Lyons is a charming account of the author's childhood on Maui (published by Topgallant Press in Honolulu).

Mary Kawena Pukui's volume of Hawaiian proverbs gave me some colorful quotations, and the *Pocket Dictionary* she compiled with Samuel H. Elbert and Esther T. Mookini was always beside me as I wrote.

Then there is the moving and beautifully written *Kaiulani, Crown Princess of Hawaii* by Nancy Webb and Jean Francis Webb—a book that helped me to better understand the time of the monarchy, so that when I visited Iolani Palace in Honolulu, I knew something of what had happened there.

A splendid pictorial source is the handsome volume, *Maui No Ka Oi*, text and photographs by Robert Wenkam. And I am indebted to Lucretia Pladera's charming account of *The Palace*, with illustrations by Richard Gallagher.

So many people were generous in sharing their experiences with me and providing information and advice. I am grateful to Inez Ashdown, who told me I must write with a "Hawaiian heart"; to Jessie Bosworth of the Maui Historical Society; and to Joyce Van Zwalenburg, director of the Maui Public Library. I want to thank Barbara Lyons for her warm hospitality, and for letting me "borrow" her lovely home for my story (though I've changed it a bit to suit a work of fiction).

When I left Maui after my visit, I know that I parted with a piece of my heart. So *mahalo*, Maui, and aloha.

Phyllis A. Whitney